**Michelle Smart**'s love affair with books started when she was a baby and would cuddle them in her cot. A voracious reader of all genres, she found her love of romance established when she stumbled across her first Mills & Boon book at the age of twelve. She's been reading them—and writing them—ever since. Michelle lives in Northamptonshire, England, with her husband and two young Smarties.

**Melanie Milburne** read her first Mills & Boon novel at the age of seventeen, in between studying for her final exams. After completing a master's degree in education she decided to write a novel, and thus her career as a romance author was born. Melanie is an ambassador for the Australian Childhood Foundation and a keen dog-lover and trainer. She enjoys long walks in the Tasmanian bush. In 2015 Melanie won the Holt Medallion, a prestigious award honouring outstanding literary talent.

**Also by Michelle Smart**

*Her Sicilian Baby Revelation*

**Passion in Paradise collection**

*A Passionate Reunion in Fiji*
*His Greek Wedding Night Debt*

**The Delgado Inheritance miniseries**

*The Billionaire's Cinderella Contract*

**The Sicilian Marriage Pact collection**

*A Baby to Bind His Innocent*

**Also by Melanie Milburne**

*Penniless Virgin to Sicilian's Bride*
*Cinderella's Scandalous Secret*
*Billionaire's Wife on Paper*
*The Return of Her Billionaire Husband*

**Once Upon a Temptation collection**

*His Innocent's Passionate Awakening*

**Wanted: A Billionaire miniseries**

*One Night on the Virgin's Terms*

# THE COST OF CLAIMING HIS HEIR

MICHELLE SMART

# BREAKING THE PLAYBOY'S RULES

MELANIE MILBURNE

MILLS & BOON

First Published in Great Britain 2020
by Mills & Boon, an imprint of HarperCollins*Publishers*
1 London Bridge Street, London, SE1 9GF



ISBN: 978-0-263-28225-2

MIX
Paper from
responsible sources
FSC® C007454

This book is produced from independently certified FSC™ paper
to ensure responsible forest management.
For more information visit www.harpercollins.co.uk/green.

Printed and bound in Spain
by CPI, Barcelona

# THE COST OF CLAIMING HIS HEIR

MICHELLE SMART

# CHAPTER ONE

THE ROAR FROM the watching crowd was deafening. Becky Aldridge, wiping tables in a deserted hospitality marquee, guessed Emiliano Delgado, owner and player of the Delgado team, had scored. Whenever the Delgado team had played during the past three weeks of the cup competition the spectating crowd had tripled. Becky had started work there knowing nothing of the polo world. She still knew nothing of the game, but of its star player she'd learned a lot. Mostly that everyone fancied him.

Carrying the last of the dirty glasses to the bar, she realised she had company: two dogs happily scooping up chips and other goodies carelessly dropped on the grass.

'Jenna?' she called out, and was not in the least surprised to receive no reply. Jenna, who was supposed to be manning the bar with Becky, had done another disappearing act, no doubt to watch the ongoing semi-final. Jenna was a major Emiliano Delgado groupie and the font of all Becky's knowledge of the half-Spanish, half-Argentinian billionaire hunk.

After checking that none of the handful of people mooching about outside the marquee were the owners of the dogs, Becky approached the pair armed with tiny chunks of hotdog sausages to tempt them. It worked. The dogs acted as if they were old friends, tails wagging and happily eating off her hand. Supplying them with a bowl of water, she took a seat at one of the outside tables and dialled the number that was on both their collars. It went straight to a generic voicemail.

'Hi, my name's Becky, and you can stop panicking because I've got your dogs with me. I work in the hospitality marquee opposite the fairground. It's the marquee with the pink roof, so you should find me easily enough, but if you get lost just call me back. I'll look after them until you get here. Okay then, bye.'

Throughout her rambling message, the two dogs sat and watched her. They really were gorgeous things. The bigger one was a golden retriever with dopey eyes, the smaller one a beautiful mongrel.

'Don't worry,' she told them as she stroked their heads, 'I'm sure your mummy or daddy will be here for you soon.'

A thirsty passer-by entered the tent. Becky's worries about what to do with the dogs were quickly dispelled when they followed her to the bar. Indeed, so obedient were they that when she commanded them to stay in a hidden corner of the bar area they curled up together and kept a watchful eye on her.

Half an hour passed. Jenna returned mere seconds ahead of the next influx of customers. The match had finished, with the Delgado team winning the semi-final six-five, and the boisterous crowd was keen to celebrate. So busy did the hospitality tent get that Becky could only give the dogs the odd pat on the head here and there and sneak the odd bit of hotdog to them.

'What the hell are they doing here?'

In the midst of pouring five pints of lager for a rowdy group of young men and trying to tune out that they were all ogling her breasts, Becky hadn't noticed the manager's return. Mark was looking at the dogs as if they were the carriers of disease.

'They appeared during the last match,' she explained over the noise. 'I've left a message with their owner.'

'They can't stay here.'

'Why not? We don't prepare food in here.'

'This isn't ruddy doggy day-care. Get rid of them.'

Placing the third pint glass in front of the customer, she immediately started pouring another. 'They've lost their owner.'

'I don't care. Get rid of them.'

'Let me finish doing this round and then I'll take them outside and wait for the owner.'

'No, you'll get rid of the flea-ridden mutts and get back to work.'

'Have a heart,' she beseeched, knowing as she spoke that she was wasting breath. Mark had proved in her short time there that he didn't have a heart. 'I'm sure…'

He grabbed her arm tightly and snarled into her ear, '*I'm* sure that if you want to keep your job you'll do as you're…'

A low growl cut Mark off mid-flow. The smaller of the dogs had joined them and was sitting on its haunches beside Becky, staring at the manager with its teeth bared.

Whether he did it reflexively or deliberately Becky could never be certain, but Mark's reaction to the small dog growling at him was to kick it. The dog yelped. Becky's reaction to this cruelty was instinctive and immediate; she threw the full pint she'd just finished pouring straight into her boss's face.

The marquee fell into silence.

His face like an overripe beetroot, Mark wiped the lager off his face with his hands. '*Bitch.*'

Outraged at Mark's despicable actions, Becky scooped

the whimpering hound into her arms. 'You kicked a defenceless dog, you monster.'

'You're fired.'

'I don't care. You're despicable and I'm going to report you.'

Through all the flurry of drama, Becky had failed to notice the reason for the crowd's fall into silence, and that was the tall, lean figure dressed in the Delgado team green and white striped polo shirt, streaked with mud, who'd made his way to the front of the bar and was staring at Mark with unmistakable loathing. 'You kicked my dog?'

Mark, recognising him, paled. 'It was more of a tap,' he mumbled.

Becky, too distressed and angry to care that the great Emiliano Delgado had appeared or that Jenna was having palpitations beside her, kept careful hold of the dog while she wiped a tear away. 'He *did*,' she said. 'He was shouting at me, and this gorgeous boy—' she kissed the top of the dog's head '—was trying to protect me, and Mark kicked him.'

There was a moment of stillness as Emiliano looked from Becky and the dog to the now cowering Mark. And then he pounced. With an agility that belied his size, Emiliano vaulted over the bar, grabbed Mark by the scruff of the neck and proceeded to drag him out of the marquee.

As the golden retriever decided to follow his master, Becky hurried after him with the mongrel still in her arms, and got the retriever to heel.

In the open air, Emiliano threw Mark to the ground. 'I should kick *you*,' he raged as he loomed over him, 'see how you like being kicked, but you're not worth it. Now I suggest you leave before I change my mind. You can consider yourself fired.'

'You can't…' But, with one look at Emiliano's face, Mark quickly stopped his protest to cover his own face.

Emiliano laughed menacingly. 'If I say you're fired, you're fired.' Then, turning to the breathless, heavily made-up woman in hot pants and a vest who'd just run up to join him, he said, 'And you're fired too. I pay you to look after Rufus and Barney for me. They escaped on your watch.'

The woman's face paled as quickly as Mark's had done. 'It was an accident,' she pleaded.

'An accident because you were too busy trying to get into Juan's jodhpurs to pay attention to them. Anything could have happened. Get out of my sight.'

And then he turned to Becky, who'd watched the exchange with fascination.

The retriever nuzzled against her leg. The mongrel licked her face. She wondered if they were sympathising for the tongue-lashing she was about to receive for not taking better care of them—after all, she really shouldn't have kept them behind the bar so in a way was partly responsible for Mark's gross overreaction.

Clear brown eyes scrutinised her for what felt like for ever before a smile broke out on his face…

Her heart slammed. What a smile that was. It lit the whole of his face and, with that smile, Becky understood why Jenna and the thousands of other groupies were so infatuated with him.

'What are you doing the rest of the day?' he asked, stepping over to her and holding his arms out for his dog.

'Working…' Between them they got the dog from her arms into his, a feat not made easy as Emiliano was a good foot taller than her dinky size. She caught a wave of faded cologne mingled with fresh sweat and found her nostrils twitching for another sniff. 'Well, I was supposed to be working. I'm not sure if you firing Mark means I'm still fired or not.'

'I'll give you five hundred pounds if you'll look after the boys for me.'

'You what?'

He gave a lopsided grin. 'I've a final to play in three hours and I've just fired my dog-sitter.'

*Two months later*

Emiliano read the looping handwritten letter for a third time before scrunching it into his pocket and storming out of his English home. A phone call to the woman who'd just ruined his day went unanswered. Scowling at the heavy clouds overhead marring what should be a quintessential summer's day, he wasted thirty minutes searching for her, checking his world-class stables and the paddocks first.

As if he didn't have enough to contend with, what with the weekend at his Machiavellian mother's villa in Monte Cleure coming up and having to share air with his half-brother. He hadn't seen Damián since their father's funeral nearly six months ago. If he had his way, he'd never have to share air with him again, but this time tomorrow he'd be stuck in his rotten company.

When his phone rang he snatched it out of his pocket and scowled again to see his vet's name pop up on the screen rather than Becky's. Not even the excellent news that Matilde, a superlative mare he'd had to retire from racing, was pregnant, could bring a smile to his face.

A figure walking over his pastureland in the distance caught his attention. Two smaller four-legged creatures bounding around it confirmed the figure to be Becky, and he marched briskly towards her.

His boys spotted him first and ran over for some fuss.

'What is the meaning of this?' he demanded when he reached her, waving the letter in her face.

She rolled her eyes and reached down to scoop up the dogs' ball with the launcher in her hand. 'My official resignation.'

'I do not accept it.'

She whipped the launcher through the air, sending the ball flying and the boys tearing off after it. Then she looked at Emiliano and shrugged. 'I'm leaving whether you accept it or not.'

'How can you do this to the boys? They adore you.'

'And I adore them, but when I took this job I told you it would only be temporary.'

'How am I supposed to find someone else at such short notice?'

She folded her arms across her considerable chest and gave him the look of patience mixed with exasperation he'd become so used to. 'Four weeks is hardly short notice, not when I told you two months ago I'd only be able to do the job for three months. I wrote the letter as a courtesy and a reminder for you to pull your finger out and find someone else. You've plenty of time to find a replacement.'

'I don't want a replacement.' In the two months she'd been their live-in sitter he hadn't had a moment's worry about his boys' care. 'I'll double your salary.'

Rufus had dropped the ball at her feet. She scooped it up and launched it again then flashed the smile that always made Emiliano's chest lighten and his loins throb.

At first glance, Becky was ordinary-looking. The day he'd met her she'd been wearing a uniform of black shirt and formless trousers, her ordinary long dark hair tied back, ordinary face free from make-up. Had his boys not found sanctuary and protection with her when they'd run away from Greta, their previous dog-sitter, he would never have looked twice at her. He'd already offered her the job as Greta's replacement when she'd smiled. And *pow*!

She dazzled. She was *beautiful*. Drop-dead gorgeous. Large green eyes, a snub nose and lips so wide and plump his mouth had yearned to feel if they were as soft as they looked. Days later, he'd seen her 'ordinary' hair loose and realised there was nothing ordinary about that either. A gleaming dark chestnut, it fell in thick waves halfway down her back. Added to the package was a friendly if occasionally fierce nature, a quick wit and a love of dogs that matched his own. If Becky Aldridge wasn't in his employ and therefore forbidden fruit he'd have bedded her in a heartbeat.

But she was in his employ and, if he had his way, would remain so.

'You're more than welcome to double it, starting now,' she said lightly, 'but I'm still leaving. I start my new job in six weeks.'

'Six weeks?' His outrage was immediate. 'Then why leave me in four?'

'Because I have things I need to sort before I start.'

Like a place to live. Becky had viewed rental properties online close to the laboratory she was soon to be working at and had set the ball rolling on one of them, but she still needed to buy furniture and get settled before she started the job.

'Tell them you've changed your mind.'

She smiled sympathetically. Poor Emiliano. Born into unimaginable wealth, he'd spent his life believing whatever he wanted he could have. Reality could be twisted to suit his needs. When she'd agreed to take the job he'd obviously decided to ignore the temporary bit and assumed he could charm her into staying.

'No.' She hadn't spent years working her brain to mush to throw it all away.

Before he could explode at her flat refusal, his phone rang. He glared as if it had personally offended him before answering.

While he chattered away in his native Argentine-Spanish, her resignation letter slipped from his hand. Clear brown eyes met hers and, with a malicious grin, he squished it with his boot.

She rolled her eyes. Having a four-month window before starting her research role at the end of September, Becky had sought a temporary job that kept her busy without being mentally taxing. Her brain needed a break. The hospitality role at the polo venue had fulfilled both criteria but she'd taken no joy from it, so when Emiliano had offered her the job as his live-in dog-sitter she'd jumped at the opportunity, accepting it on the strict understanding that it would only be until mid-September.

Becky had been raised with dogs and loved them. They were loyal in a way people never were and minding Emiliano's wonderful hounds certainly beat dealing with drunk humans. They were affectionate too, always wanting to cuddle up to her, something that never failed to make her heart swell. Working for Emiliano and living on his busy estate filled with no-nonsense horsey people had been a joy. He was the easiest person she'd ever worked for. In fairness, her job could hardly be called work, more paid fun, but as she'd learned during their first meeting, for all his good humour, you crossed him at your peril. Only a week ago, he'd unceremoniously fired one of his grooms for not meeting the high standard of care he required for his horses. He was equally ferocious on the polo field.

She'd finally got to grips with the game and even started enjoying it. By always wearing her shades, no one could see her eyes following Emiliano's every move. It was never deliberate. There was something about the way he charged around the field on a horse—she would never understand why they insisted on calling them ponies—that captured her attention. Truth was, he captured her attention whatever he was doing. Truth was, even if she hadn't intended the job to be temporary from the start, she would still be resigning.

Long, lean and broad-shouldered, Emiliano's long face could have been crafted by Michelangelo. Wide, clear brown eyes, high cheekbones and a wide firm mouth counteracted a too-long nose. Topping it all was dark brown hair cut short at the sides and long at the top, which he rarely managed to tame. Becky quite understood why he set so many fully-grown women's pulses racing and it was becoming increasingly hard to keep her own pulse controlled around him or the jealousy that coiled inside her at the groupies who fawned over him wherever he went. A natural flirt, Emiliano had the ability to make any woman feel he only had eyes for her. Becky had to constantly remind herself that when he fixed those come-to-bed eyes on her and bestowed her with his lazy lopsided grin it wasn't anything special. Her reaction to it was nothing special either, as all the fawning groupies would testify.

It was the dreams that disturbed her most. Dreams from which she would wake flushed and throbbing. Meeting his eyes after one of those dreams was excruciating. Hiding her internal reaction to him was becoming harder by the day. The sooner she left the better. The sooner she started her new job and put her mind back to good use, the sooner she'd stop thinking of him and her life could return to normal.

His mood was much brighter when he ended the call.

'The Picasso they said was not for sale? It's mine,' he told her triumphantly.

'Congratulations.' As well as being one of the world's most successful horse breeders and a top polo player, Emiliano had a penchant for art and had opened galleries free to the general public in London, New York, Madrid and Buenos Aires filled with the exquisite work he'd acquired. 'If you open a gallery in Oxford you can display it there and I can visit when I have time off.'

'Oxford?'

'Didn't you read my résumé?' When he'd offered her the job, he'd told her to email her résumé to his PA for the staff files. She'd assumed basic curiosity about the woman he was entrusting his precious dogs to would compel him to read it.

He folded his arms across his chest and, face smug, said, 'I didn't need to. I'm an excellent judge of character.'

With another exaggerated roll of her eyes she shook her head and patted her thighs for the dogs' attention. The first drop of rain had landed on her nose and she wanted to get them inside before the heavens opened. 'You've got four weeks. I suggest you get recruiting.'

'I don't need to recruit,' he called as she strode away. 'You're staying.'

She turned back to face him and walked backwards. 'You're delusional.'

'Don't you know I always get what I want, *bomboncita*?'

'Then consider my leaving a much-needed favour to your ego.' Giving him one last cheeky wave, she turned back around and, dogs running alongside her, jogged back to the pretty cottage he'd given her as a perk of the job.

# CHAPTER TWO

TRAVELLING BY PRIVATE jet was, Becky decided the next day, something everyone should experience once in their lives. Travelling by private jet with a grumpy billionaire, however, was something everyone should avoid. Not even Rufus and Barney had been able to put a smile on Emiliano's face.

She didn't have the faintest idea why a visit to his mother's villa should suck away his normal languid good humour and she didn't want to know. It was hard enough dealing with her physical response to him without adding personal issues to the mix, so she stuck her earphones in and closed her eyes. Even while she pretended to sleep for the duration of the flight she felt the tension emanating from him. When they landed and he stomped down the metal steps from his plane as if trying to smash through them, she bit her tongue to stop the questions clamouring on it forming. His bad moods, infrequent though they were, rarely lasted this long.

Swept from the airport by a gleaming black limousine, she had to peer through the tinted windows to see anything of Monte Cleure, a tiny principality wedged between France and Spain. From what she could see, it gleamed as brightly as the car.

It seemed as if no time had passed before they entered a

rambling estate with breathtaking gardens. Becky peered again through the window, awestruck by the sprawling villa with its pale yellow walls and terracotta roof gleaming under cerulean skies rising before them like a squared-off horseshoe.

'We'll drop you and the boys at your lodging first,' Emiliano informed her. His jaw had set so tight she was surprised he could get any words out.

The driver came to a stop outside a one-storey lodge set in a thicket of woodland. One of a dozen identical staff lodges, it was painted the same colours as the main villa.

'Pretty,' she observed, only realising she'd spoken aloud when Emiliano's jaw loosened a touch.

'You should be comfortable here. Anything you're not happy with, let me know and I'll get it sorted.'

She ruffled Rufus's head and smiled. 'I'm sure we'll be fine.'

'You have the run of the estate to walk them.' As Emiliano's mother refused to allow his dogs in the villa, they would stay with Becky for the weekend. She didn't doubt Emiliano would drop in to visit them and whisk them away at every opportunity. 'Carry your passport with you—there's an army of security guards patrolling the land.'

'Are they armed?'

'*Si.*'

The driver opened her door. 'I'll try not to get shot then,' she quipped.

She caught a glimpse of white teeth before she swung her legs out of the car. The dogs jumped out after her and waited as she said goodbye to their master.

Emiliano saluted. '*Chau, bomboncita.*'

'*Hasta luego,*' she replied. See you later. Usually when she said one of the Argentine-Spanish terms she'd picked up from him he grinned. This time his smile was more of a grimace.

She watched him be driven away, wondering again why a visit to his mother should put him in such a bad temper.

Emiliano greeted the merry widow, his mother Celeste, with the air-kisses they'd used since he was a boy.

'No lady-friend with you?' she asked, tucking her arm into his elbow as they strolled the villa's grounds.

For some reason his mind immediately flew to his English dog-sitter. 'Not this time.'

'That's not like you, *mijito*. I always look forward to seeing which ravishing creature you'll have on your arm for my party. My guests do too.'

Celeste's annual summer party. The reason he was there.

'I've been too busy to date,' he lied. Truth was, he hadn't been on a date in two months. The women who swarmed around him like wasps around an open jam jar had lost their appeal. He had no idea why.

'Thinking ahead to when you take over the Delgado Group?'

'Pointless considering Father's will might still turn up.' Eduardo, his adoptive father, had died nearly six months ago. The day of his funeral, Emiliano's half-brother Damián had discovered the will missing from their father's safe. Emiliano didn't need to communicate verbally with him to know Damián thought him responsible for it, and for the missing document that had signed the Delgado Group into Damián's sole control. If they weren't found within the next three weeks then, under Monte Cleure's archaic law, the eldest son inherited everything. Which meant Emiliano would inherit the multibillion-dollar finance business Damián had been promised and, if Emiliano was feeling charitable, had earned the right to inherit.

'It might,' she conceded. 'But if it doesn't your father's empire falls to you.'

He tightened his lips to stop them saying, *He wasn't my father.* His real father had been an Argentine polo player who'd died when Emiliano had been ten weeks old. A year later, Celeste had married Eduardo, who'd adopted her baby son and given him his name but never his love or approval. Emiliano's only usefulness had been as proof of Celeste's fertility. Eduardo had needed an heir for the business. He'd found that in Damián.

The irony that the unwanted non-blood spawn might inherit Eduardo's entire estate was almost funny. The months Emiliano had spent working for the Delgado Group a decade ago had ended in disaster and acrimony. Having zero interest in finance, he'd only taken the job for Celeste. It had been the last thing he'd ever done or would ever do for her. As a child he'd worshipped the ground she walked on. And then he'd woken up to who she was. A narcissistic bitch.

But she was still his mother, his flesh and blood. She was a hard woman to feel any kind of affection for but he supposed he felt something akin to love for her.

'I don't want it,' he said.

'Then what will you do? Give it to Damián?' she added with a tinkle of laughter.

Emiliano smiled grimly. Where his relationship with Celeste was complicated, his relationship with Damián was simple—they loathed each other. They might not have exchanged a word in a decade but they had to suffer each other's company twice a year. It had always given him perverse pleasure to bring a scantily dressed woman with him to the annual summer party. Seeing Damián's serious face pucker with disapproval was a never ceasing joy. Damián, like his father, had always thought the worst of Emiliano. Proving them right was something that never grew old.

'I don't know what I'll do.' Burn it to the ground? That was one possibility.

'I appreciate your life is full with the running of your stables…' she made it sound as if he had a couple of small paddocks he kept his horses in rather than world-class stables strategically located around the world in which he bred and trained horses for racing, polo and dressage competitions '…and the polo team and that you would be reluctant to step back from it. I have invaluable experience with all aspects of the Delgado Group. If you feel running it would be too much for you, I am willing to step in and run it. On your behalf, of course.'

'Of course.' He hid a knowing smile. He'd been waiting for this conversation. Celeste was power-hungry in all aspects of life. It wouldn't surprise him in the least if it came out that she'd been the one to steal Eduardo's will and business document. If they were found, any influence Celeste had on the business would be gone. Damián would want to keep control for himself. 'But this is a conversation for another time. When's Damián due?'

'His jet's just landed, so not long. He's brought a lady friend.'

'So you said. Must be serious.' Damián hadn't introduced a woman to the family in, oh, it must be fifteen years. He was probably scared Celeste would frighten them off.

Celeste arched her brows. 'Be nice to her.'

He grunted. His beef was with his brother and no one else. 'I'm going to freshen up. I'll see you at lunch.'

'We'll eat outside. You are *not* to bring those mutts.'

He answered with a grin and strolled back into the villa

he'd spent much of his childhood in. His mother's insistence that he not bring his dogs to lunch was too great a challenge to resist.

Emiliano straightened his bow tie with a grimace. He loathed wearing suits of any kind but DJs were the worst. Usually he enjoyed Celeste's summer parties. The guest list was always inspired, hundreds of the rich, famous and eccentric letting their hair down and behaving disgracefully, staggering to their waiting cars and helicopters clutching their lavish goody bags.

However, there had been little enjoyment to be found so far that weekend, and he didn't see why the party should be any different. On the surface, things were exactly as they always were when the family came together: Celeste acting the role of High Priestess, Damián brooding, Emiliano finding amusement in his discomfort, the two brothers ignoring each other in a deliberate manner and making no effort to hide their mutual loathing. But the tension that was always there when they came together felt different this time. Suspicion and distrust underlined every movement and left him with an acrid taste on his tongue.

On impulse, he pulled his phone out and called Becky. She answered after three rings.

'Where are you?' he asked.

'Walking the boys and trying not to get shot by your mum's security guards.'

He grinned. He could always trust Becky to put a smile on his face. 'Will you be back soon?'

'I doubt it. We're about two miles away in the forest. Why? Is everything okay?'

No, everything was not okay. There was a feeling of dread in his stomach much like he'd experienced as a child in the days before his school reports had been sent out.

'*Si*. Just thought I'd visit the boys before I start behaving disgracefully and shaming my family.'

Her laughter echoed like music in his ears. 'I imagine we'll be back in half an hour.'

'Don't worry about it. I'll see you...them...in the morning. Have a nice evening.'

'And you. Enjoy the party.'

'I'll try.'

He put his phone in his pocket and drank a measure of the Scotch he'd poured himself. As he sloshed it round his mouth, he imagined Becky at his side, dressed to the nines. He'd never actually seen her in a dress. Or a skirt. He'd never even seen her legs; as she was always out with the dogs over fields and woodland, she wore jeans to protect them. She had the most fabulous hourglass figure though, a real buxom beauty with killer curves and her bottom *filled* those jeans.

Those same musings ran through his head as the guests arrived and he noticed that hardly any of the female guests had curves of any kind, and those that did had gained them with the help of an able surgeon. While hardly anyone had an ounce of spare fat on them, there was, he estimated, enough filler pumped into all the beautiful faces to fill a swimming pool. Becky, he was quite certain, would soon find laughter lines appearing around her eyes and mouth. He was equally certain that she wouldn't go the filler route. If he had his way, she would still be in his life—his *dogs'* life—long enough for him to find out personally.

As soon as this weekend was done, he would get straight onto the important task of convincing Becky to stay. His boys meant the world to him, and the peace of mind her care and attention for them gave was worth whatever it took to make her stay. She pretended not to care about money but everyone had a price. She must be holding out for something. Why throw in the towel on a job that paid well and had unlimited perks for a limited role in hospitality otherwise?

'Emiliano!' The shriek of his name pierced straight through him and, wincing, he turned to find Kylie, a spoilt English heiress, tottering over to him in heels so high they could be reclassified as stilts. A moment later and a pair of bony arms were thrown around his neck and his airways filled with a perfume so sweet and cloying he almost gagged.

'You are *so* naughty,' she pouted. 'You said you would call me.'

He grinned sheepishly and unlocked her wrists from around his neck. 'My apologies. Life has been hectic.'

Kylie had been at the polo competition when his dogs had briefly gone missing. She'd joined his team when they'd celebrated their semi-final win. He vaguely remembered promising to take her out for dinner once the competition was done with and then promptly forgot all about her.

Why was that? he puzzled. Kylie was exactly his type—beautiful, blonde and long-legged and with only a few brain cells rattling around in her head. Emiliano's one serious relationship a decade ago had been with a woman blessed with ferocious natural intelligence. It was his misfortune that she'd also been blessed with natural deviousness and criminality, something he'd discovered far too late and which had seen his world collapse around him.

As Kylie continued to chatter, his brother came into his eyeline.

What was going on with him? Something was up; he sensed it deep inside him. And what was he doing with a woman like Mia? The Brit Damián had brought with him to the party had joined the family for lunch the previous day and gone to the casino with them in the evening, and had immediately proved herself to be fun. The last woman Damián had introduced the family to had been as much fun as a Benedictine monk on a stag weekend. Emiliano sensed a dark undertone beneath his half-brother and his new lover's sociable smiles. It only increased the sense of doom that had been building since his arrival in Monte Cleure.

Something was going to happen. Something bad. He could feel it in his bones.

Becky was so deep in sleep that it took the dogs barking to rouse her to the banging on her front door.

Stumbling out of bed, she shrugged herself into her robe and padded out of the room, trying not to trip over the dogs.

'I'm coming!' she shouted at the unceasing banging, knowing perfectly well it was Emiliano, probably drunk and wanting to see the boys. He'd often turned up at the cottage he'd given her on his English estate after a night out just to see his dogs.

She unlocked the door and yanked it open but her prepared stern words died on her tongue when she saw his haggard face.

'What's wrong?' she asked, stepping aside to let him in.

He staggered to her small living room without answering or putting the light on, and slumped onto the sofa. He barely lifted a hand to pat his beloved dogs' heads.

'Emiliano?'

Haunted eyes met hers but he didn't speak.

Crouching next to him, she took his hand in hers. It was icy cold. She patted his arm. His dinner jacket was damp. She caught a whiff of chlorine. Had he been swimming in his clothes? And then she noticed the red marks blazing over his knuckles. Had Emiliano been *fighting*?

Her chest tightened unbearably. Something was wrong. Dreadfully wrong.

'Use the shower,' she urged. 'You need to get warm.'

He closed his eyes and rested his head back. His chest rose sharply, his features so tight she feared they could snap.

She patted his icy hand again and wished she could put it to her mouth and blow warmth onto it as her mother had done on winter days when Becky had been a little girl and her mother had been a real mother to her. 'I'll make you a hot drink.'

In the kitchen she put the kettle on and dug out the hot chocolate she'd spotted earlier in a cupboard. The rotors of a helicopter sounded above the lodging. Not even midnight and guests were leaving? What the heck had happened?

The living room was empty when she returned with his drink but, before she could worry, she heard the shower going. Then it occurred to her—he had nothing to change into. And she had nothing that would fit him.

Inspiration struck and she shrugged her towelling robe off. She knocked on the bathroom door and shouted that she was leaving it by the door for him.

She tried to keep the dogs calm while she waited for Emiliano to finish in the bathroom. Rufus and Barney had picked up on their master's mood and seemed unable to settle. She didn't have to wait long. Her heart tore to see his long, lean frame clad in her blue cotton robe. On Becky, it came to mid-calf. On Emiliano, it came to mid-thigh. On anyone else it would look ridiculous. It only made him sexier and she had to drag her eyes away from the deeply tanned, ridiculously muscular legs and snatch a deep inhalation to counter the rapid beat of her heart.

He hovered in the doorway. 'Can I sleep here tonight?'

The drawling voice that normally vibrated with life was monotone.

If she hadn't already guessed something bad had happened, this would have clinched it. Even the night he'd taken his polo team out to celebrate another cup win and knocked on her door at two in the morning more than a little inebriated, he hadn't asked to stay or even hinted at it. He'd accepted a black coffee then staggered back to his mansion with the dogs at his heels.

'Sure… I'll make the spare bed up.'

'I just need to get my head down for a few hours.'

'Stay as long as you like. I'll find some bedding for you. Your drink's on the table.'

He met her stare briefly and nodded.

The staff lodge she'd been given had two bedrooms but only one of the beds had been prepared. She found spare sheets in the airing cupboard. It wasn't much, just a couple of cotton blankets, but the summer evening was warm. Unable to find a pillow, she took one from her own bed and carried the bundle to the spare room. She made the bed then returned to the living room, where she found him looking out of the window, his drink in hand.

'The spare bed's made for you,' she said softly. 'I'm going back to bed. Are you going to be okay?'

He turned to look at her and blinked as if waking from sleep, then raised his mug in a half-hearted salute.

Her heart ached at his wretchedness. Her arms ached to wrap around him and give comfort. Her brain ached at all the possibilities of what could have caused such devastation. 'Get some sleep,' she whispered.

She felt his eyes follow her as she left the living room and headed back to bed.

Lying there in the darkness, she wondered how she could have slept through the noise of the helicopters considering the racket they continued to make. She hoped they weren't too noisy to stop Emiliano from sleeping.

When she finally fell asleep, thoughts of Emiliano were the last thoughts in her head. Just as they'd been every night since the day she'd met him.

She slept deeply until loud, haunted shouts woke her in an instant.

# CHAPTER THREE

A HAND TOUCHED his head. 'Emiliano, wake up.'

Emiliano opened his eyes with a start. His body was racked with tremors, flesh riddled with goose bumps, his insides feeling as if they'd turned into a mass block of ice. Perched tentatively on the edge of the bed, a hazy shadow in the darkness of the small room, was Becky.

He grabbed at his hair and tried to catch a breath.

He hadn't had a nightmare like that since he was a small child. He was living a nightmare. The wicked witch of childhood stories. His own mother. A killer.

She covered his hand and flinched. 'You're still freezing.'

He swallowed hard. The enveloping coldness had made his throat close.

'I'll get my duvet,' she whispered. Rising to her feet, she slipped out of the room, leaving him alone in the still darkness. He tightened the sheets around him but couldn't stop shivering. Didn't dare close his eyes. He didn't think he could endure the dreams that came with sleep. He was so damn cold his teeth chattered.

Becky returned in moments and draped the duvet over him before gently telling him to move over. The single bed hardly dipped as she slipped under the bedding and wrapped her arms around him.

She held him tightly, tenderly, rubbing her warm hands over his back and arms, her face pressed against his chest, the warmth of her breath gently heating his skin. He rested his cheek into the top of her head and held her just as tightly. The soft scent of her shampoo and silkiness of her hair played into his senses, soothing him.

Slowly, under Becky's tender embrace, his frozen body defrosted. The fog that had stupefied his brain began to clear.

He remembered trying hard to get in the party spirit, even throwing himself fully dressed in the swimming pool and horsing around. He remembered climbing the stairs, intending to change his sodden clothing but finding his brother outside his quarters. He remembered the damning evidence Damián had shown him against their mother, remembered the piercing agony when Damián had asked about his own involvement in the heinous act, the throbbing in his knuckles from when he'd punched a wall a reminder of how close they'd come to physical blows. And he remembered them pulling together as brothers for the first time in their lives to confront their evil, Machiavellian mother.

He remembered needing to escape the villa. Along with his brother, he'd detonated a bomb in the middle of the party but by then had been too numb to care about the wreckage.

But he barely remembered walking to the lodge. His aimless escape had taken him to Becky.

Her warming hands had reached the base of his spine when they suddenly jerked away. 'Are you naked?'

'Sorry,' he muttered, cursing himself. Until that moment, his nakedness hadn't even registered in his own head. He hadn't been aware, either, that his body had roused itself to the beautiful woman he'd curled into.

'It's okay…' Becky, who'd shifted sharply at the shock of heat that had torn through her at the realisation of his nudity, tried to breathe. Everything inside her had tautened like stretched nerves.

The foolhardiness of getting under the covers with this hunk of a man hadn't entered her head. A deep-rooted need to warm his freezing body and soothe him from the nightmare that had tormented him had overridden everything. Now she found herself sharing a single bed with a naked man but, instead of freezing in fear, she found her hands aching to touch the muscular smoothness again and repeatedly having to swallow back moisture and breathe through her nose because the musky scent of his skin was setting off crazy things inside her. The greater her awareness of the crazy reactions, the more she became aware of others, of the tight heat bubbling low inside her, the new, strange excitement thickening and building, the strange sensitivity of her skin, the tingling sensation of her breasts pressed against his chest…

'Sorry,' he repeated, speaking into the top of her head before rolling onto his back.

Still trying to breathe, she rolled onto her back too and shuffled up so her head was on the pillow…but that brought no succour as the bed was so small the sides of their bodies remained pressed together. Their heads were so close the strands of his hair brushed against her forehead.

If it wasn't obvious that something terrible had happened to him, she would go back to her own bed, use towels and anything else she could find as bedding. But she didn't want to leave him, not in this state. She could still hear the shouts of his nightmare in her ears.

By unspoken agreement they moved in unison and turned their backs to each other. Becky pulled the duvet over her shoulders and closed her eyes. Their bodies no longer touched but there could only be millimetres between them and her skin quivered with awareness. Her heart thrashed with such intensity the beats resounded in her head. How long they lay there, unmoving, barely a breath escaping their mouths, she didn't know. If the tension crackling between them had a colour it would be scorching red.

She fought her body, forcing it to lie like a statue, terrified to risk their skin brushing, terrified of unleashing the burn building inside her.

As deeply attracted to him as she was, Becky didn't want to be one of Emiliano's bedpost notches. No sane woman would. She didn't want to be another faceless woman on a list so long it should be called a scroll. The danger of her response to him had been apparent from the start and she'd imposed a friendly distance between them and sensed he'd imposed one too, an invisible line neither of them breached.

That line had been severed.

She couldn't breathe. Her quivering skin felt as if it had come to life. Never had she had such awareness of the mechanics of her body: her heart pumping so violently, the weight of her tingling breasts, the melting of her pelvis...

Emiliano tried to sleep. He'd turned his back to Becky and closed his eyes. The nightmare that had called her to him had dissolved, not even fragments remaining. Everything that had happened that night had been driven out, his senses attuned only to the woman lying so close to him.

Grimly, he told himself to stay exactly where he was and not move.

How the hell had he found himself in bed naked with Becky?

He did not involve himself with employees. He didn't

care how sexy they were or how heavily they flirted with him and batted their lashes, he kept his hands off. Becky had been the biggest test of that resolve since he'd made it ten years ago, and she'd never given him so much as a suggestive smile. Seeing her every day in those tight jeans that caressed her fabulous curves would test even the holiest man's resolve, especially when she bent over to scoop a ball up, and then there was the way her breasts bounced when she threw the ball… *Dios*, it was enough to make a man salivate.

And now he was naked in bed with her and the desire he'd kept under the tightest of leashes was pulling madly for release. Every inch of his body throbbed with awareness, heart beating weightily against his ribs, loins burning. A lock of her long hair lay against his back, the strands feeling like tickling silk against his skin.

*Dios*, this was torture.

He had to leave. Right now. Put his damp clothes back on and take his boys to the villa. They could run riot over the polished floors to their hearts' content.

Gritting his teeth, he sat up and threw the duvet off him. 'I have to go.'

A needle tip of panic pressed into Becky's chest and, before she knew what she was doing, she had pushed herself upright.

Though it was dark, her eyes were adjusted enough to see the rigidity of Emiliano's muscular back, and she clutched tightly to the duvet to stop her hand placing itself flat on it.

*Let him go. Lie back down and go to sleep.*

But the burn spreading like a wave from deep in her pelvis told her sleep was impossibly far away. For the first time in her life she was caught in desire's claw, the fight she'd been waging with herself liquefying.

Over the thudding of her heart, she heard him take a deep inhalation. Then another.

She inched closer to him without any thought. 'Emiliano?'

Slowly, his head turned.

The thudding of her heart became a thunderous canter.

Never had she seen his features so tight, the nostrils flare so rapidly. Or the expression in his eyes, which held hers so starkly.

The taut stillness stretched for an age before something that looked like pain contorted his face and in the whisper of a moment his body twisted and he lunged, hands cupping her face tightly as he crushed his mouth to hers.

Taken off-guard, Becky had no time to mount a defence. Heat ignited inside her like a furnace and she leaned into the kiss with a moan of relief. Her lips parted and then they were moving ferociously in time with his, her senses engulfed with the taste of something so hot and intoxicating that any defence she could have mounted would have melted instantly.

In what could only have been seconds, she was flat on her back below Emiliano's lean, muscular body. There was a moment of stillness as she gazed into his pulsing eyes before their mouths fused back together in a kiss so hard and deep it erased any coherent thought.

For the first time in her life she didn't want to think. She wanted to feel. She wanted to feel…everything.

Her suddenly greedy hands ran through Emiliano's hair and over his neck, fingers touching and exploring every part she could reach, his hands sweeping over her sides with the same urgency. Her cotton T-shirt was pulled over her head and then her naked breasts were pressed against his hard chest, right until he dived a hand between them and spread his fingers over the sensitised flesh, making her gasp at the pleasure this induced and Emiliano groan and mutter something unintelligible. His groan deepened when he slipped his hand into her shorts and touched her where no man had touched before.

The furnace in her grew with every kiss and touch, melting every part until she was nothing but molten liquid. There was a deep ache low inside her, the pulsations she'd often experienced at unbidden times when her fantasises about this man had pushed their way into her mind before she could stop them magnified. Every time his erection brushed against her thigh the pulsations turned into a strong spasm of need and she pressed herself even closer, her body taking the lead over a mind that had become lost in a drugged, sensitised fog called Emiliano.

Together, they pulled her cotton shorts off and then she was as naked as he and too drunk on the wonderful sensations rippling through her to care. Nothing mattered, only *this*, this hunger, this unquenchable fire.

Her legs parted instinctively as their tongues entwined in a heady dance of their own making, and then he was right where she craved him to be until, with one long thrust, he was buried deep inside her and she cried out the last of the air she had left in her lungs. If there was pain, she didn't notice. Emiliano was inside her, filling her, and it felt incredible. From the strangled groan that fell from his mouth into hers, the pleasure was shared.

Legs wrapped tightly around him, hands gripped together, Becky closed her eyes and submitted herself entirely to the intensity of his lovemaking.

In and out he thrust, his groin grinding against hers, driving the fever in her blood to boiling point. She responded by instinct, letting her body guide her, the pulsations inside her growing and growing, reaching, searching for *something*…

*Something* shattered inside her. Something that set off a riptide of unimaginable pleasure pulsing like a runaway train through her blood, her bones, her flesh, so powerful her back arched and a feral moan ripped from her throat.

The mutters in her ear from Emiliano's tongue had become a distant echo as she clung tightly to him while she rode the waves, but there was a dim awareness of his changing of tempo. His thrusts became harder and more urgent, and then her name flew from his mouth before he cried out and thrust so hard into her and for so long that their bodies fused together to become one.

The first thing that really penetrated Emiliano's brain was the strength of his heart. He'd never known it beat so hard or so fast. The second awareness was the strength of Becky's heartbeat crashing through their conjoined skin in time with his own and the raggedness of her breaths perfectly matching his. The third was that he was still burrowed deep inside her.

The earthy scent of their lovemaking filled his senses. His loins still twitched at the strength of his climax…

And that was when sanity came crashing down and he pulled away from her so quickly he created a draught.

Swinging his legs over the side of the bed, he grabbed at his hair, curses flying from his tongue in all the languages he knew.

'That was not supposed to happen,' he said between gulps of air.

The woman he'd just made love to didn't answer.

*Dios*, he couldn't bring himself to look at her. What the hell had he just done? Of all the stupid, idiotic, *foolish* things…

He should have left while he'd had the chance.

What the hell had compelled him to come to her in

the first place? Had he been subconsciously seeking his boys? But that only then begged the question of why he hadn't collected them and gone back to the villa. It wasn't as if he was going to see his mother; she'd escaped on a friend's helicopter.

Self-recriminating rage and nausea roiled violently in his stomach. What the hell had he *done*?

'Tell me you're on the pill?' he demanded as he scraped his fingers over his skull.

Her continued silence gave him the answer and sent his roiling stomach dropping to his feet.

Never in his life had he failed to use contraception.

Never had he lost control as he'd just done with Becky.

And never had he hated himself as much as he did right then.

Damn it all to *hell*.

'Where are you in your cycle?' He knew his tone was too rough, that he was behaving deplorably, but he was helpless to stop. He'd stepped into quicksand and was fighting to stop himself being swallowed up.

He sensed her flinch as she sat up.

'I think you need to leave.' Becky's words were delivered with a curtness he'd never thought to hear from lips that were even softer to the touch than he'd imagined. Sweet and plump like a marshmallow. A temptation too far, even for him.

'Don't worry, I'm going. Just tell me how worried we need to be first.'

Becky stared at the muscular back, as rigid as it had been before his whole demeanour had changed and passion had overtaken them both, and wanted to curl into a ball and sob her eyes out.

In the space of minutes she'd gone from feeling as if she'd learned to fly to feeling as if she'd been dropped in the gutter. What had been the most incredible experience of her life had been ruined. Emiliano's cruel belligerence made her want to scrub her skin clean.

If she'd ever thought about how it would be to face him straight after she would have expected bawdy humour before a subtle extraction from her bed, no promises but no recriminations either. Possibly a fleeting kiss and a wink before he said a nonchalant goodbye.

But she hadn't faced him yet. The coward was still to look at her.

'*You* have nothing to worry about,' she said, snatching up her discarded T-shirt.

'Don't play games,' he snarled. 'If my failure to use a condom results in a baby then it *is* my problem. How worried do I need to be?'

Becky would have laughed if she didn't feel so much like weeping. Her menstrual cycle had always been as regular as clockwork. She was exactly mid-cycle, the time of the month when signs of her fertility made themselves known. Tender breasts, a slight rise of body temperature…

Maybe that was why she'd been so receptive to Emiliano, she thought with only a minuscule amount of hope. It hadn't been *him* so much, more a primal part of her acting as nature had designed.

'Very.' Shrugging the T-shirt over her head, she pushed the duvet off, jumped out of bed and headed for the door. 'I'm going to take a shower. See yourself out.'

His head turned. There was one moment of eye contact, moment enough to make her heart leap into her throat, before she left the room, only to find his damp clothes in a heap on the bathroom floor. Holding her breath, she scooped them into her arms and flung them into the corridor, then locked the door.

Shaking, she stripped her T-shirt off but avoided looking at the mirror. She couldn't bear to see her reflection.

Emiliano felt as if he'd been punched by a heavyweight with guilt. All he wanted was to crawl into his bed and sleep for a year. When he woke, he wanted this whole day to have been a nightmare he could shake off and forget about.

Becky must have turned the hallway light on for he suddenly became aware of illumination pooling into the room.

Unsteadily, he got to his feet. It suddenly seemed imperative that he be gone before she finished in the shower. He vaguely remembered leaving his clothes in the bathroom. If necessary, he would walk back to the villa wrapped in the bedsheets.

About to leave the room, he abruptly stopped and cast his gaze around it one last time…

What was that on the bedsheet?

Rubbing his hand over his mouth, he approached it cautiously, as if it were something that could leap off and sink its venomous teeth into his neck.

When he saw what it was, comprehension of what it meant hit him and the world began to spin.

He wished it *had* been something venomous.

On the bedsheet was a smear of blood.

# CHAPTER FOUR

BECKY WAS ON her third coffee, her bags packed for the return journey to England, when a sharp rap on the front door announced Emiliano's arrival.

She'd packed those bags debating whether to just run. Leave. Find someone to whisk her to the airport and never look back. Anything but face him in the cold light of day.

But to run would be too much like what her father had done when the divorce had been finalised a year ago. The way she felt towards both her parents meant she would never do anything from either of their playbooks. More than that, she couldn't leave without saying goodbye to Rufus and Barney or leave Emiliano without care for them.

She needed to front this out. Only for another four weeks…no, three and a half weeks.

Heart lurching painfully, she pinched the bridge of her nose and took a deep breath before rising from the sofa to open it.

He stood at the doorway, stubble covering his jawline, eyes puffy, hair damp, casually dressed in black jeans and a white T-shirt that perfectly accentuated his gorgeous frame.

How she kept her features from crumpling she didn't know. Memories of that lean frame naked and entwined with hers flew through her, not in pictures—it had been too dark for her to see him in anything but shadows—but as sensation.

Damn her heart for beating so madly to see him.

Damn her pulses for surging to meet his eye.

And damn him for still making her senses swirl despite looking as if he hadn't slept a wink since leaving her bed six hours ago. Becky hadn't slept either and knew it showed on her face too.

The awkwardness of their first contact was eased by Rufus and Barney bounding straight inside, tails wagging happily, the pair oblivious to the tension between their two favourite humans.

Wordlessly, she stepped aside to let him in.

'Leaving already, are we?' she asked dully.

'No.' He rammed his hands in his pockets. 'We need to stay a few more days. Maybe a week.'

She shrugged. She wouldn't ask why.

He nodded at the coffee pot. 'May I?'

She shrugged again. 'Help yourself.'

Picking up her own coffee cup from the counter, she opened the French windows and stepped into the empty staff garden. It was easier to breathe in the fresh air, safe from Emiliano's freshly showered scent.

He followed a minute later, joining her at the outdoor table, the dogs racing outside with him. It was only nine a.m. and already the sky was a brilliant blue, the warmth of the sun falling gently onto them. In a few hours it would be hot enough to burn.

'About last night…' he began.

She cut him off. 'I don't want to talk about it. It happened. It won't happen again.'

If she could, she would pretend it had never happened. But that wouldn't happen until her skin stopped tingling. She could still feel the marks where his fingers had caressed her. She was having to fight her eyes from meeting his, terrified of the feelings that ruptured through her whenever she got caught in his gaze, terrified of the feelings erupting inside her at his closeness.

Jaw tight, he inclined his head. 'We might have made a life.'

Her stomach dived. This was the one thing she'd refused to think about since he'd gone but his words opened the floodgates she'd suppressed and almost made her double over with fear.

Nature wouldn't be so cruel, would it? She remembered a boy from school solemnly informing all the girls in their form that you couldn't get pregnant if you did 'it' standing up or if it was your first time. She'd asked her mum, who'd still been a loving mum back then, who'd smiled widely and shaken her head. 'Honey,' she'd said, 'don't believe anything a man tells you when it comes to contraception. Take charge of it for yourself.'

To remember that tenderness from the woman who'd so recently cut her out of her life was like prodding an open wound, but Becky had taken those nearly ten-years-old words of wisdom to heart. She'd believed that when she met the man she could build a relationship with they would take things slowly. She'd thought her first time would come after careful consideration and planning. She'd believed she would have time to protect herself.

And now she had to hope and pray that, despite everything she'd spent years learning about the human body, the boy from her form had been right. She needed all the divine intervention she could get.

Swallowing back the metallic taste in her throat, she said, 'If you're a man who believes in prayers, I suggest you put your hands together.'

He muttered something she didn't need to be a linguist to understand was a curse.

Time stretched in silence before he said, 'I'm sorry, *bomboncita*.'

She gritted her teeth against the surge of warmth that filled her. She'd always secretly liked it when he called her that. But that was before. Now, in the after, being called the name he must have called hundreds of women before her was just another reminder of Emiliano's womanising ways and her own utter stupidity.

'Don't call me that. And I don't want your apologies. We were both there.'

'The way I spoke to you after…' He breathed in heavily. 'I was out of order.'

Oh, God, she was going to cry. 'Agreed.'

'*Bom*… Becky, what happened…'

'I don't want to talk about it.' She blinked rapidly, doing her darnedest to stop the tears from spilling. 'It's history. I've already put it from my mind so I suggest you forget it too. If a baby's been made then we'll deal with it but, until that happens, I would thank you to never speak of it again.'

'Were you a virgin?'

Mortification thrashed through her and she shoved her chair back violently and got to her feet. 'I *said* I don't want to talk about it.'

His face only became grimmer. 'Answer my question first.'

'What difference does it make? None at all.'

He banged his fist on the table, features twisting with anger. 'Of course it makes a difference!'

'Why?' She threw her arms in the air and tried her hardest to keep a lid on the emotions crashing through her, so many of them: fear, anger, humiliation, despair and, worse than all that, awareness. For him. An awareness so strong that, should he touch her, she feared she would melt into him before she had the sense to smack him away. She'd guessed that making love changed a person but not like *this*. Whatever happened with the baby situation, Becky knew their night together had changed something in her, but for Emiliano…

She didn't doubt that within weeks of her leaving his employ he'd struggle to remember her name.

'Are you going to fake some chivalry?' she demanded, her voice rising to match the rising anguish and panic. 'Why should me being a virgin make any difference when it's never made a difference to your treatment of women before? You love 'em and leave 'em regardless.'

His anger finally reaching tipping point, Emiliano jumped to his feet. Since leaving Becky's bed he hadn't slept a jot, the memories of their explosive lovemaking so strong that they vied with the despair his mother's actions had evoked. But it was the evidence of Becky's virginity casting the darkest cloud.

Had he hurt her? The mere thought sliced his heart. It hadn't crossed his mind for a second that she could be a virgin. She was twenty-five years old! She should have had many lovers by now. If he could turn back time and stop himself from knocking on her door, he would do it in a heartbeat.

And if he could turn off the awareness still thrumming wildly in his blood and loins for her…

*Dios*, every inch of him ached to taste those plump lips again, then taste all the parts he hadn't tasted in the explosion of passion that had taken them in its grip.

'I might not be a saint but I've never treated women in the way you've just implied.'

'You *liar*. You have no respect for women. We're just a

commodity to you, something to use when you're in the mood and then discarded the next day.'

Something sharp stabbed his chest at this exquisitely delivered observation but he pushed it to one side. His past lovers had always known the score. He'd never lied to them. The only woman he'd slept with in the past decade without making the score clear beforehand was the woman who stood before him now, as many emotions blazing from her green eyes as he had curdling in his guts.

'If that was true then tell me what the hell I'm doing here right now.'

'Scared that your recklessness might have made a baby!'

'*My* recklessness?'

'You started it!'

'And you, *bomboncita*, were a *very* willing participant…' so willing his loins tightened to remember her breathless moans and the passion of her kisses '…so don't try and twist this mess onto me. It was a mistake that you've already admitted we were both party to, so stop with the blame game and take some responsibility for your own actions.'

'If I'm pregnant then it's a responsibility I'll bear for the rest of my life.'

'And my life too.'

'Oh, are you going to carry it and give birth to it and give up all your dreams for it?' Her laughter had a strong tinge of hysteria. 'The most you'll have to do is chuck some money at it and then carry on sleeping your way around the world as if nothing's changed.'

'We don't even know if you've conceived and already you've decided what my future actions will be? Your opinion of me is worse than I believed.'

'If you didn't want a reputation as a playboy you should have been choosier about who you shared a bed with!'

'I didn't hear any complaints last night,' he said pointedly, stepping closer to her as if her body had a magnetic charge his responded to.

'There wasn't time,' she retorted, the heat in her voice matched by the heat flushing over her cheeks.

'Is that the voice of experience talking?' he taunted. 'How about a repeat performance so you can judge accordingly?'

Green eyes pulsed as her chin jutted defiantly. 'If your first performance is the standard then I'll pass.'

'And you call *me* a liar?' Snaking an arm around her waist, he pulled her flush to him and fused his mouth to hers. Her response was as immediate as it had been the night before, arms looping tightly around his neck, kissing him back with the same rabid hunger that controlled him.

*Dios*, she tasted so damn headily sweet, even more than he remembered, and when he gripped her delicious bottom to press her even more tightly against him, and she felt his excitement through the denim jeans they both wore, her moan only made him harder.

Pressing her against the table for support, he slipped a hand up her T-shirt and groaned into her mouth, feeling the silky softness of her skin, his groan deepening when he reached the underside of her breasts, frustratingly enclosed by a lacy bra.

There had been no time for him to even look at her naked when they'd made love. The need to be inside her had been too strong, too consuming, a need he'd never felt before. Virgin or not, Becky's response had been every bit as fevered. She'd wanted it as much as he and, for all her taunts, her response right then was proof that fever still lived in her blood as much as it lived in his. Her thighs parted and a hand dived inside the collar of his T-shirt, nails scratching against his feverish skin.

Later, he would wonder how far they would have taken

it in the staff garden if Rufus hadn't decided that whatever the humans were doing looked like something fun he needed to join in with, and leapt at them.

In an instant, they pulled apart.

Becky scrambled to straighten her T-shirt but her hands were shaking so hard it took several attempts to get hold of the fabric then sink onto a chair, her boneless limbs struggling to support her weight.

Too mortified to look at him, she covered her face and fought to get air into her lungs. She wished the ground would swallow her up. Bad enough she'd melted into a puddle for him in the dark of night but to do the same in broad daylight when any of the live-in villa staff could be watching them…? Had she lost all her good sense and modesty along with her virginity?

She heard Emiliano sit heavily on the seat beside her. 'Becky…'

'Just go,' she whispered from behind her trembling hands. 'And please, find a replacement for me. Do it now. I'll stay until you find someone or until my notice has been worked, and I'll care for the boys as I always do but any communication about them can be done by phone. I don't want to see you or speak to you unless it's absolutely necessary.'

She heard his sharp intake of breath. It felt like forever passed before the sound of his heavy footsteps broke through the drumming of blood in her head.

She didn't drop her hands until she heard the French windows close. When she opened her eyes she found Barney and Rufus sitting beside her, both gazing at her with mournful expressions.

Emiliano, slumped on his late father's sofa, raised bleary eyes when his brother got unsteadily to his feet. They'd been holed up in their father's study for six hours, drinking to his memory.

'We need food,' Damián slurred.

Emiliano hiccupped. 'Eating's cheating.'

'What?'

'That's what the Brits say.'

'Oh.' Damián flopped back down, took another swig out of the bottle of Scotch then passed it over.

It suddenly occurred to him that he hadn't seen anything of Damián's lady friend since the party five days ago. 'Where's your Brit gone?'

'Gone.'

'Gone where?'

'Home.'

'Which home?'

'Give me the bottle.'

He pressed the bottle against his chest. 'Not until you tell me which home. One of yours or hers?'

'Hers. Now give me the bottle.'

He passed it over. 'Why her home?'

'She doesn't live with me.'

'How long have you two been together?'

'We're not together.'

'You looked like you were together.' He snatched the bottle out of Damián's hand.

'I paid her.'

'What?' Emiliano missed his mouth and spilled amber liquid over his chin. 'I thought she was an actress?'

'She is an actress. I paid her to pretend to be in love with me.'

'Why?'

'I needed help finding Father's will. I thought you'd hidden it somewhere.'

On that score, Emiliano had been right. He didn't

blame Damián for thinking that. 'I guessed Celeste had taken it.'

'Did you?'

'You were hardly likely to have hidden it, were you?'

Damián shrugged. 'I can't believe she burned it.'

'I can.' Now Emiliano shrugged. 'You're single-minded when you want something. She knew you'd find it if she didn't destroy it.'

Five days had passed since they'd discovered the extent of their mother's wickedness. She'd disappeared after they'd confronted her with the evidence on the night of the party, escaping on her friend's helicopter. But there would be a day of reckoning for her. On this, as on so many other things now, the Delgado brothers were united. Together, they'd handed all their evidence to the Monte Cleure police and an arrest warrant had been duly issued. They didn't expect her to be charged, not just because the evidence was all circumstantial, but because Celeste knew too many secrets about Monte Cleure's ruling class and wouldn't hesitate to remind those in power of it. The woman who'd taught her sons to always think like chess players, to anticipate and mitigate all eventualities, was the greatest strategist of all.

But should she step foot on Monte Cleure soil again, which she would eventually have to do as the villa was the only home in her name, all the other assets being held in their father's name, she would have the indignity of being arrested. Emiliano fervently hoped the world's press were there to witness it and report that the great Celeste Delgado was suspected of murdering her own husband.

'Do you know what else I can't believe?' Damián slurred.

'What?'

'That I'm sitting here and getting drunk with my brother.'

'Strange, huh?' Emiliano passed the bottle back. 'We should do this more often.' In the drunken fog of his mind, a part of him ached at all the wasted years spent loathing his brother. He didn't want to rewrite history by dissecting the past. Things had been said that could never be unsaid. The guilt in his guts was something he would have to learn to live with but, for the first time, he wanted the brotherly relationship he'd always denied them.

Despite all the alcohol he'd drunk, he felt cold. Snatching the bottle, he took another long swig and tried not to let his mind slip back to the night his body had been chilled to the bone and the woman who'd warmed him.

Other than to pass his boys between them, he'd seen nothing of Becky since she'd ordered him out of her staff lodge. With so many things of a business and personal nature to sort out with his brother, not thinking of her had been easy by day. Only drinking stopped him thinking of her by night too. He didn't want the time or space to think—not about Becky, not about Celeste, not about his adoptive father and all the things he would never get to say to him for good or ill.

But Becky refused to stay hidden. For the little he'd seen of her, she managed to be everywhere. He knew it was his mind playing tricks on him but he would see a figure in the distance and his heart would lunge.

And, just as Celeste would soon face her day of reckoning, for the sake of his liver and the hundreds of staff he employed, he must soon sober up and face the new reality of his life. His mother was a killer and there was the real possibility he'd got one of his employees pregnant.

# CHAPTER FIVE

THE TOOT OF the car horn made Becky's stomach clench tightly. Calling the dogs, she pulled her handbag over her shoulder and opened the front door. The dogs went tearing to the car, where Emiliano's driver was putting the suitcase she'd left out front in the boot.

She managed a tight smile when she got into the back and found Emiliano there. She'd hoped he would travel up front.

His smile was equally taut. 'You have everything?'

She nodded and looked away, but not before she'd taken a proper look at his face and found herself shocked at how dishevelled and crumpled his appearance was. She'd hardly seen anything of him since the party six days ago, opening her front door at designated times to either let the dogs out to him or receive them back, rather as she suspected warring parents did for small children. She'd hoped their lack of contact would make being with him again easier to endure but the painful drum of her heart proved that assumption a fallacy. He looked as if he hadn't slept at all since the party. She doubted he'd shaved.

Mercifully, the dogs chose to plonk themselves between the two humans so keeping a good distance from him was made easier.

'There's been a change of plan,' he informed her once

the car had set off, his gaze fixed ahead. 'We're going straight to Buenos Aires.'

'Erm… The rest of my stuff's in England.'

'You can collect it when you go back.'

'When will that be?'

'When you've worked your notice. I'll buy whatever you need until then.'

'Have you looked for a replacement for me?'

'I've been busy,' he said shortly.

She stifled a frustrated sigh. 'My notice is up in less than three weeks.'

'I know how a calendar works.'

'I was just…'

'Reminding me.' Clear brown eyes suddenly locked onto hers. 'Reminding me that you're counting down the days until you leave me.'

Taken aback at the way he made it sound as if she were ending a relationship rather than leaving a job that had only been temporary, and stung at his tone, Becky rested her hand on Barney's head for comfort and looked out of the tinted window in silence until they arrived at the airport.

It was less easy to ignore him on the eighteen-hour flight. The flying time would have been shorter but they made a couple of stops so the dogs could stretch their legs. How Emiliano was able to arrange such things was beyond her, and something she'd stopped being in awe of within days of working for him. Being the possessor of a great fortune, she'd quickly learned, meant the world bent itself to your will rather than the other way round.

It was dark when they landed in Argentina. An hour after leaving the airport and circumnavigating much of the main city itself, the twinkling lights of Luján, a province of Buenos Aires, greeted them from a distance. They reached Emiliano's home before the twinkling lights revealed any of their secrets.

The entire seven hundred hectares of land that made up his estate was fenced off from intruders. Security guards on patrol acknowledged their arrival. Soon they pulled up outside an illuminated sprawling ranch-style mansion. Of the many mansions Emiliano owned, this was the one he considered home.

The stillness of the night was incredible. With the vast black skies covering them and the scent of eucalyptus filling the air, Becky was struck by a sense of wonder that such peace and such space still existed in the world. If she closed her eyes, all she'd hear was nocturnal wildlife, but there was no time for such indulgence as a woman in her mid-thirties stepped out of the front door. Emiliano introduced her as his housekeeper before having a brief conversation in his native language while his driver removed their luggage from the car.

'I'm going to walk the boys to the stables,' Emiliano then informed Becky in a much stiffer tone than he'd addressed his housekeeper. 'Paula's prepared a meal for you. She'll show you to your quarters.' Then he tapped his thigh and strode off, the dogs bounding after him.

Becky exchanged an awkward smile with the housekeeper before following her inside.

Internally, the ranch was even bigger than she'd expected. Treading over terracotta flooring past a vast split-level living space, she was surprised when Paula went up a flight of stairs, beckoning her to follow. Who had their dining room on a different floor to their kitchen?

That question was answered shortly, when Paula opened a door to reveal a large, beautifully appointed bedroom. 'Your cases been brought up for you,' she said in English.

Pointing to a door, she added, 'You living area. Other door bathroom. You like dinner here or downstairs?'

'I think there might have been a mistake. I should be in the staff quarters.' She'd never been housed under the same roof as Emiliano before and knew he had plenty of staff accommodation here.

Paula smiled. 'No mistake.'

'Does Emiliano know?'

'They his orders.'

Exhaustion meant Becky didn't wake until mid-morning. The first thing she did was check her phone to make sure she had no missed calls from Emiliano. He'd messaged her before she'd gone to bed, telling her he'd keep the boys with him that day.

He hadn't tried to contact her while she slept.

Rolling onto her back, she closed her eyes. She'd dreamed of their baby. Only fragments of it remained and, as hard as she tried, she couldn't bring the rest of the dream back.

A rush of protectiveness crashed through her and she placed her hand on her belly, thinking again of the tense conversation she and Emiliano had had the morning after, and with it came the realisation that neither of them had mentioned the pill that could be taken to prevent conception if an accident happened.

Why had that been?

Her emotions had been so erratic back then that she couldn't say if she would have taken it, knew only that if she were to be offered a safe and effective pill now she would refuse it. For all that her hard-worked-for future could be ripped apart, there could be a life growing inside her, a precious, precious life. A baby to share her lonely life and shower all her love on…

Knowing it was dangerous to think like this when there was no way of knowing if she'd conceived, she threw the covers off and headed to the bathroom.

After showering and dressing in her uniform of jeans and shirt, adding an oversized cardigan to the mix as Argentina was currently much cooler than the baking temperatures of Monte Cleure, she headed downstairs in the hope of finding food.

This was the first time since working for Emiliano that she hadn't been given her own cooking facility. It felt strange to be reliant on someone else to be fed.

The ranch was so vast and she'd seen so little of it that, for a moment, she found herself disorientated and unsure in which direction to head. Paula came to her rescue, appearing suddenly to whisk her off to the kitchen.

'You like medialuna?' she asked as she poured Becky a coffee.

'What's that?'

'Breakfast pastries.'

'I love pastries, so yes please.'

Twenty minutes later, Becky was to conclude that she liked pastries a little too much and made a mental note to get the recipe before she returned to England. A cross between a croissant and brioche, the medialunas had a subtle hint of lemon and vanilla to them and she devoured three of them on the bounce and could easily have devoured three more.

She wished she were one of those women who lost their appetite when stressed or unhappy. Becky's appetite only increased, as was evidenced by the roundness of her hips. The past seven years had seen her go from a top-heavy skinny thing to someone with curves to match her breasts.

'What time you like eat lunch?' Paula asked when Becky had finished all the flaky crumbs on her plate.

'That's very kind but I don't want to put you out any more than you've already been. If you show me where everything is, I'll make myself something.'

'You guest. Guest no feed self.'

'I'm not a guest. I'm the dog-sitter.'

'Emiliano say you guest and dog-sitter.'

It was the first time his name had been mentioned between them and Becky's heart skipped a beat to hear it. 'That doesn't sound right,' she said doubtfully. 'Are you sure he meant it like that?'

'Am sure.'

'Very strange… I don't suppose you know where he is, do you?' She asked this as casually as she could.

'He gone see tenants.'

Becky remembered him telling her that he owned adjoining farmland to his estate that he rented out. But that had been in the time before things had become so awkward and tense between them. He seemed to be avoiding her as much as she avoided him, which only made his decision to house her under his roof the stranger. 'Am I okay to explore the estate?'

'Sure. What time lunch?'

'Actually… I don't suppose you have any of those medialunas left I could take with me, have you? Saves you having to bother with lunch for me and, if I'm being honest, I could bury my face in a plate of them and inhale the lot.'

Paula beamed with pride. 'I put in bag for you.'

Becky's long walk ended up being much shorter than anticipated when she found the stables, home to over a hundred and fifty of Emiliano's horses. There, she found many familiar faces from England, who'd recently flown in with the polo horses on specially adapted jets, and ended up sharing her precious medialunas with a couple of the grooms.

'Why aren't you in Greta's old rooms?' Louise asked. 'She used to share with us here.'

She shrugged. 'No idea. Are they still free?'

'We assumed you'd be taking them. You should speak to Emiliano about it. It'd be great to have you with us.'

The stable staff, as friendly and down-to-earth as they were, were such a tight-knit group that Becky flushed with pleasure at the inclusion. In fairness to them, they'd included her from the start but, awkward around new people, she'd initially found it hard to reciprocate. That she'd never had that initial awkwardness with Emiliano had been wholly down to their immediate bonding over his dogs. Besides, his good-humoured nature meant he could befriend the grumpiest hermit. She missed that Emiliano.

And she missed having friends. They used to come so easily to her, but then her happy world had been torn apart and she'd sought solace in her academic work, hardly noticing how insular she'd become. Until she'd started working for Emiliano, she hadn't made a single real friend since her school days. It saddened her to realise she hadn't even noticed.

Her lightening mood lifted some more when she spotted Bertie being walked out of his stable. A former polo horse who'd lost his speed after an injury, Bertie had been kept by Emiliano because Don Giovanni, the most intuitive of his polo horses, pined when separated from him.

Louise must have noticed her joy for she said, 'He needs riding if you fancy it?'

Becky had never ridden a horse prior to working for Emiliano. She'd been wary, frightened of entrusting her safety to such huge creatures, but the grooms had been so kind and supportive that she'd felt compelled to try. Bertie had been the first. He had such a gentle nature and was so intuitive that by the end of her first ride all her fears had disappeared and she'd come to love being on horseback and being at the stables. She'd ridden many of Emiliano's other horses since but Bertie remained her firm favourite.

In no time at all she was astride the stallion in borrowed riding boots and hat. Setting off at a pace as gentle as Bertie himself and with the sun warming her face, the angst that had turned her belly into a mass of knots loosened.

Deciding to explore, she soon found the equestrian circuit, where the dressage and eventers practised and which was used in competitions. A short trot from that were the famous polo fields, six in total, along with practice and schooling areas. Polo fields always looked massive with the players and horses hurtling around them but unoccupied, bar a groundsman on a ride-on mower, they seemed magnified. Vibrant green grass stretched almost as far as her eye could see. After exchanging hand greetings with the groundsman, she figured it was time to turn back.

The stables were as busy as they'd been when she'd set off but a tall figure amongst all the activity immediately caught her attention and her lighter mood plummeted.

Emiliano was back.

The closer she rode, the greater the beat of her heart. The closer she rode, the clearer his features. The clearer his features, the clearer the anger etched on them. She had the distinct impression that anger was directed at her.

Keeping a good distance so she could avoid him until she could be reasonably certain he wouldn't rip her head off, she rode straight to Louise and dismounted before finding the groom who'd loaned her the riding boots.

She was lacing her own boots when a shadow fell over her.

'Enjoyed your ride, did you?'

Taking a deep breath, she lifted her face to his. Somehow she managed to speak over the clatter of her heart. 'Is something wrong?'

Emiliano's fury was so visible she flinched. 'Do you have any idea how dangerous it is to ride a horse in your condition?'

She blinked. 'I beg your pardon?'

'You might have my child growing in you and you think it a good idea to ride a horse? Do you have no sense of self-preservation? Or are you thinking that if you have an accident, nature might take its course and the problem will be over?'

It took a few beats before she understood what he was implying and when comprehension sank in her own temper quickly punched through her.

Keeping her voice as low as she could manage, she snapped, 'We don't know if I'm pregnant or not and even if I am, horse riding is perfectly safe, especially on a gentle horse like Bertie, and how *dare* you imply that I would do *anything* to harm a life?'

Emiliano gazed at the beautiful angry face before him, heart throbbing, head pounding, and tried to get a grip on himself. Staff swarmed around them, a few curious eyes watching.

When Louise had blithely told him Becky had gone for a ride he'd had to stop himself from firing her on the spot. All he'd been able to see was Becky on the ground, helpless. If she hadn't appeared at that moment he would have set off in search of her.

'What if he'd bucked you off?'

'Bertie's softer than a marshmallow.'

But that only brought to mind the softness and taste of her kisses, something he'd fought hard to forget. 'What if he'd been bitten by something? Or trodden on something that lamed him?'

'What if I'd slipped going down the stairs and broken my neck?' she retorted. 'Do you want to ban me from using them on a "what-if?"'

'Don't be flippant. If you're pregnant then it is my job to protect you and our child and that means not allowing you to take any risks with your health.'

'Not *allowing* me?' Her face contorted into a host of incredulous expressions before she got to her feet and hissed, 'Don't you dare lay down the law to me. I'm not a child and I won't tolerate being treated as one. And, while we're on the subject, I understand Greta's old rooms are still available. I want to move into them.'

'Out of the question.'

'Why?'

Because there were no individual staff lodges or cottages here apart from his housekeeper's. Everyone else was housed in the huge staff complex. Because his staff played as hard as they worked. If Becky was carrying his child she needed to rest.

'Because I say so. In case you've forgotten, you are still in my employ until your notice period has been worked and what I say goes.'

Mutiny flared over the beautiful face, plump lips pulling in and out before she deftly sidestepped him and stalked off in the direction of the ranch.

The boys looked from Emiliano to Becky's retreating figure and decided to follow her.

Biting back an oath, Emiliano sucked a huge lungful of air in. When he turned at least a dozen figures suddenly jumped to attention and restarted what they'd been doing before he'd given them cause for diversion.

Damn her, he thought savagely. Damn her for her flagrant

lack of self-preservation and damn her for her obstinacy, and damn her for failing to show due deference in front of the other staff. That he'd never expected or wanted deference from staff before mattered not a jot.

'Saddle Nikita for me,' he ordered a passing groom, who started at his tone before hurrying off to comply.

Time for him to go on a long ride of his own.

# CHAPTER SIX

BECKY SPENT MUCH of the next week with the boys. She saw little of Emiliano. Their interactions were infrequent and always to the point and always about the dogs. When he'd curtly told her a couple of days ago that he was taking a short trip back to Monte Cleure, she'd breathed an inward sigh of relief.

She tried her hardest not to dwell on their short hate-filled exchange at the stables. But she carried the remnants of it inside her, alternating between hating him for his arrogant, high-handed manner and missing the man he'd been before they'd stupidly slept together. She wished that old Emiliano was still here. The prospect of being pregnant with the old Emiliano's child wasn't as worrying as it was with this closed-off stranger.

And yet, when she'd gone down for breakfast the day before, there had been a hollowness in her chest at his absence. That hollowness hadn't left her. He was due back that evening and every sound had her heart contracting that it could be him.

Feeling as if she would go mad if she rattled around the ranch with only her own thoughts for much longer, she was pleased to get out that evening for a staff party.

It was in full swing when she arrived with the dogs at her side. All the stable staff and other workers were out in force, apart from those doing the night shift—Emiliano did not take any chances when it came to his horses, and the grooms rotated the night shifts—taking full advantage of the chance to let their hair down after a long English polo season and the stressful journey with the horses back to Argentina. Music pumped, beer and wine flowed freely and some of the meat being cremated on the barbecue was actually edible.

Reluctantly, Becky stuck to lemonade. Alcohol was not something she could risk but she still hoped to enjoy herself. Thoughts of Emiliano made that impossible. She couldn't stop her gaze flitting around in dread—or was it hope?—that he'd retuned to the ranch and decided to join the party. Would he stride into the garden armed with kegs of beer and boxes of fine wine, that lopsided grin on his face, lifting the mood even higher with his mere presence as she'd seen him do before?

What was he doing now? Had he gone partying elsewhere? Gone on a date with one of the long-legged beauties who swarmed around him? The thought made her chest tighten painfully, just as it had during all his other absences that week. Strangely, in all the time she'd worked for him, she'd never seen him with a woman on his arm or witnessed a woman scurrying from his home in the early hours.

After a couple of hours of attempting to party, her cheeks hurt from faking smiles and fatigue crept in.

It was a ten-minute walk back but she barely noticed the stars twinkling above her in the dark sky, her thoughts too full of Emiliano and the horrible atmosphere that had developed and been sustained between them. She knew she was as much to blame for it as him. Neither of them had handled their night together and the possible consequences well.

As she approached the ranch she noticed the front porch

light was on, a dark figure in shadows. It wasn't until the dogs gave happy barks and bounded forwards, triggering the security lights, that she saw the figure was Emiliano, sitting on a swing chair, a bottle of beer in his hand.

But her heart had already known it was him. One glance at the shadowy figure had been enough for it to thump. For a moment, she was caught unawares enough to soak in his presence, every cavity in her body filling with a mixture of pleasure and pain.

Wearing black jeans and a T-shirt, he looked like the old Emiliano. The crumpled appearance he'd adopted since his mother's party had been smartened up, the dishevelment of his hair now by design rather than neglect. He'd even shaved.

For the first time in a week their eyes locked together. Becky's breath caught in her throat at his searing scrutiny.

He petted his boys then took a long drink from the bottle. 'How was the party?'

She had to untie her tongue to speak. 'Okay. Everyone looked like they were having fun.'

'But not you?'

'No.' She sank onto the wooden step to take the weight off her weary legs and rested her back against a pillar.

'Why not?'

'Because I'm a day late.'

She heard him suck an intake of breath. 'Is that normal for you?'

'No.' Panic and excitement swelled sharply in equal measure as they did every time she allowed herself to read the signs that were all there. Tender breasts. Fatigue. The ripple of nausea she'd experienced that morning when she'd passed Paula's husband outside and caught a whiff of his cigarette smoke. Excitement that she could have a child growing inside her. Panic at what this meant.

Scared she was going to cry, she scrambled back to her feet. 'Let's give it another couple of days. If I haven't come on by then, I'll take a test.'

She would have gone inside if Emiliano hadn't leaned forward and gently taken hold of her wrist. 'Sit with me.'

Opening her mouth to tell him she needed sleep, she stared into his eyes and found herself temporarily mute.

For the first time since they'd conceived—and in her heart she was now certain they *had* conceived—there was no antipathy in his stare, just a steadfastness that lightened the weight on her shoulders.

Gingerly, she sat beside him but there was no hope of keeping a distance for Emiliano put his beer bottle down and hooked an arm around her waist to draw her to him.

Much as she wanted to resist, she leaned into him and rested her cheek on his chest.

'Don't be afraid, *bomboncita*,' he murmured into the top of her head. 'We will get through this together.'

Nothing more was said for the longest time and for that she was grateful. Closing her eyes, she was able to take comfort from the strength of his heartbeat against her ear and his hands stroking her back and hair so tenderly. There was something so very solid and real about him, an energy always zipping beneath his skin even in moments of stillness.

He dragged a thumb over her cheek and then rested it under her chin to tilt her face to his. Then, slowly, his face lowered and his lips caught her in a kiss so tender the little of her not already melting to be held in his arms turned to fondue.

Feeling as if she'd slipped into a dream, Becky's mouth moved in time with his, a deepening caress that sang to her senses as she inhaled the scent of his breath and the muskiness of his skin. Her fingers tiptoed up his chest, then flattened against his neck. The pulse at the base thumped against the palm of her hand.

But, even as every crevice in her body thrilled, a part of her brain refused to switch off and it was with huge reluctance that she broke the kiss and gently pulled away from him.

'Not a good idea,' she said shakily as her body howled in protest.

Emiliano gave a look of such sensuality her pelvis pulsed. 'Why?'

Fearing he would reach for her again, she shifted to the other side of the swing chair and patted the space beside her for the dogs to jump up and act as a barrier between them. They failed to oblige. 'Aren't we in a big enough mess?'

Eyes not leaving her face, he picked up his beer and took a long drink. 'That depends on how you look at it. To me, the likelihood that you're pregnant makes things simple. I want you. You want me. Why fight it any more when we're going to be bound together?'

How she wished her heart didn't throb at his admission. And how she wished she could deny that she wanted him too. 'Because it was a one-night stand.'

'A one-night stand that has probably made a baby.'

She raised a helpless shoulder. 'We've hardly been on speaking terms since and the times we do speak we're barely civil to each other.'

Emiliano raised a heavy shoulder in acknowledgement. The past few weeks had been the longest and strangest of his life. The mess with his family would have been enough to screw with his head but the thing with Becky had swirled like a thick mist around him, tying him in a knot of self-recrimination that vied with kernels of excitement that he might be a father. But more potent than all of that was the hunger.

His desire had not kept its distance from her. It breathed in him, in his blood, in his pores, a weight so heavy it threatened to suffocate him.

'It's been a difficult few weeks for me,' he acknowledged. 'I have not behaved as I should. I want to put things right.'

Now that things with Damián were settled, he'd had time to think—something he'd had precious little time for in recent weeks, not in a clear sense. He'd found a clarity that had been missing.

She pressed a hand to her belly. 'Allowing things to become physical will not put things right. It will only muddy the waters more.'

'You mean making love again?' His loins, already tight from their kiss, throbbed at the memory.

'We hardly made love, did we?'

'What would you call it?'

'I don't know.' Her laugh was shaky. 'Whatever it was doesn't matter. If you hadn't been in such a state you would never have come to me and it never would have happened.' She twisted slightly to face him and hesitated before saying, 'What happened to you that night?'

His eyes narrowed. 'You don't know?'

She shook her head.

Sharpness pierced his chest. He'd wondered. Becky was not a woman to gossip. She didn't use social media and only rarely had he seen her use her phone for anything other than making calls. 'You must be the only person in the world who doesn't know,' he said wryly. 'I discovered Celeste killed my father.'

Her eyes widened. 'I thought he passed away in his sleep?'

'Clever, isn't she?' He downed the rest of his beer. So clever and cunning was the woman who'd given birth to him that he was surprised he'd felt any shock when he learnt what she'd done. If the afterlife existed, he doubted his father was up there scratching his head in puzzlement.

And people wondered why he preferred animals to humans!

Coldness had enveloped Becky's brain. She gazed at Emiliano, trying to read his face, desperately hoping he was jesting with her. But what kind of sick joke would that be? 'You really mean it? She killed him?'

He exhaled through his nose and inclined his head, then reached under the swing chair for another bottle and used the attachment on his pocket knife to open it.

She shook her head as nausea swirled violently inside her and her heart wrenched. She'd known something bad had happened that night but never in her wildest imaginings had she suspected anything like this. Who could imagine that?

'I'm so sorry.' What an inadequate platitude.

'So am I. Sorrier that she will never pay the price for it.'

'Why not?'

'All the evidence is circumstantial,' he answered with a shrug. 'Damián hacked the villa's old surveillance feed. He showed me the footage at the party. It shows Celeste carrying a drink from her quarters to my father—this is the woman who has never poured herself a glass of water in her life—and thirty minutes later he was dead. That same night, before his body was cold, she stole his will and a document giving my brother control of the family business. Those documents have been missing since. Presumably, she burned them. The police have seen the footage. They've issued an arrest warrant but unless she confesses there's not enough to charge her, let alone convict her.'

'But that sounds like strong circumstantial evidence.'

'Not strong enough.' He took a swig of his beer. 'My

father was cremated. He'd been ill for a long time so his death wasn't unexpected. There was no reason for them to take blood for toxicology. I think even if there was a smoking gun, as it were, she would still get away with it. She knows too many secrets of Monte Cleure's elite. They have to go through the motions of questioning her but she's too big a threat for them to risk charging her.'

She pulled her knees to her chest, trying hard to take everything in. 'Why did she do it?'

He raised his shoulders and rolled his neck. 'For control. She was running out of time to stop Damián taking over the business so took matters into her own hands. You see, she had great influence over Father but on this he was steadfast—he wanted Damián to have it. Damián's a control freak—any influence she had on the business would have been gone—so she killed our father and destroyed the documents with his legal wishes clearly stated because she knew the business would then fall to me.'

'Why?'

'Father had taken Monte Cleure citizenship. Under Monte Cleure law, if there's no will then the eldest legal son inherits everything. That's me. Celeste knew I wanted nothing to do with the business and that I would pass it to her to run.'

'Would you have?'

'If the truth hadn't come out, yes. And I would have taken great joy in publicly sacking my brother from the company he'd helped make such a great success.'

Her brow creased in disbelief. 'You would be that cruel?'

'Damián and I have hated each other all our lives.' He paused for a moment before correcting himself. 'I have hated *him* all his life. His loathing of me was always a reaction to my own cruel behaviour.'

'Why did you hate him?'

'Many reasons. Jealousy that he was Father's favourite and shared his blood, and then there was Celeste and the poison she dripped in my ear about him. I think she sensed from the moment he was born that he would take her place as Father's chief confidante and went out of her way to make his life as uncomfortable as she could.'

'And I thought my mother was bad,' she murmured but, before he could ask what she meant, she added, 'Do I take it from your tone that you two have made up?'

He nodded and breathed out slowly. 'We met again yesterday at the villa to finalise the legal documents. I've signed the business over to him.'

'The whole business?'

'I never wanted it. From as far back as I can remember I wanted to be outside with the horses, not stuck in an air-conditioned office.' He'd spent more time in the stables at his English boarding school than in the classroom. Even then, he'd preferred animals to humans. Animals were loyal and uncomplicated. Even now he had special distrust for anyone who disliked animals. 'I did work for the business once, a decade ago. I'd been struggling financially—truth is, I'd been living the playboy lifestyle but had no means to earn money for myself. In those days I played for another rich man's polo team and burned through my sponsorship money so quickly it hardly scorched my wallet. I could barely afford to feed the horses. Celeste convinced me to join the business and convinced my father to hire me. He put me in charge of one of the investment funds. I'd worked there six months before he, with Damián's backing, fired me.'

'Why did they do that?'

'It doesn't matter,' he said dismissively. That was something he would never discuss. To remember how his father and brother had treated him in that period was to fill his head with darkness and his guts with poison. He would never forgive them but the grief in his heart for the relationship he'd never had with his father was something he never wanted to experience with his brother. For the sake of his soul he needed to put the past behind him and move on.

'They set up a trust fund for me. Ten million a month for life to keep the hell away from the business. I look back now and see that was the turning point in my life. I was sick of everything. Sick of being financially dependent on them. Sick of being used as a pawn in Celeste's Machiavellian games… I wanted to earn my own living doing the things I love, so I took my hobby and turned it into an empire.' He looked at her. 'I used their first trust payment to get the ball rolling but haven't touched the rest of it. It all goes into a charitable fund for animal causes close to my heart.' He managed a half-hearted grin. 'And causes my father detested.'

'Did you always hate him?'

'Yes.'

She winced at his bluntness.

'He married Celeste because he needed an heir,' he explained. 'She had impeccable lineage, independent wealth and me: proof of her fertility. He adopted me but had no interest in me. Celeste bought me my first pony when I was four. He wouldn't come to the stable so I could show him off—just dismissed it. The only time he gave me attention was when I did wrong.' He grinned, although his heart wasn't in it. 'So I learned to do wrong.'

'That's really sad.'

He snorted. 'Hardly. I had a privileged upbringing. Homes around the world. A fleet of staff just for me. The best education money could buy. Father didn't beat me. He just ignored me. I was a spoilt brat.'

'Can I ask about your real father?'

'He was a polo player like me. He had the potential to be one of the best players in Argentine history but died in a freak horse accident. I was only a baby. I don't remember him.'

'Now that really *is* sad.'

'Sad for him. He never got to see the fantastic man his son would become.'

Amusement suddenly danced in her eyes. 'The fantastic, *modest* man you became.'

'Modesty is my greatest attribute. Apart from my skills as a horseman and a lover,' he added with a wink, and was rewarded with a bright stain of colour across Becky's cheeks before she darted her gaze from him.

*Dios,* she was irresistible. But he must resist for a short while longer. Until she took the test and the pregnancy was confirmed. Then both their futures would change. They would be bound together always.

She cleared her throat and resolutely said, 'You must get your horse skills from him.'

'Well, I didn't get them from Celeste,' he said drily. 'She only has to look at a horse for it to bolt.'

Her muffled snigger dived straight into loins already straining against the confines of his jeans.

Emiliano got to his feet. Time for bed before he threw the beautiful creature beside him over his shoulder, carried her to his bedroom and ravished her.

# CHAPTER SEVEN

EMILIANO SAT ON the armchair in Becky's bedroom and tried to distract himself by reading through the races he had horses running in that day. While he had limited first-hand involvement in the racing side of his business, he insisted on being kept fully abreast of all goings-on. When he retired from polo-playing he would take a greater hands-on role with the racing side. And the dressage side. He hoped that wouldn't be any time soon but, with his fortieth birthday only two years away, he knew it wouldn't be long until his body started protesting at all the punishment he put it through. He would not be like those polo team owners who let their teams carry them to glory. The moment he stopped pulling his own weight and leading from the front would be the day he hung up his stirrups.

He looked up when the bathroom door opened. Becky hovered at the threshold, face ashen, hugging herself tightly. She gave a tiny nod.

He dropped his face into his hands and breathed deeply to counteract the sudden rush of blood pounding in his brain. When he looked up, she was still at the threshold of the bathroom. She looked so much like little girl lost that a sharp stab of guilt plunged through him.

Forcing himself to get a grip, he straightened. This was not unexpected. He'd had plenty of time to prepare for this.

Arms still wrapped around her belly, she padded slowly to the other armchair and sank into it. 'What are we going to do?' she whispered.

'That is easy,' he said decisively. 'We get married.'

Her smile was weak. 'Hilarious.'

'No, *bomboncita*, I am serious. I've thought about it a lot and the best thing we can do is marry.'

He'd thought about his childhood. His parents. How he'd hated always being at a distance from them, physically and emotionally. How he wanted no child of his to go through the same. If he was going to be a father then he would be a real father, not some remote authoritarian figure.

And he'd thought about marriage to Becky, about sharing a bed with her every night. Before, when he'd assumed he would spend his life as the eternal bachelor, the mere thought of settling with one woman had made his skin go cold. Circumstance was forcing his hand in this but he did not deny the thought of sharing a bed with this sexy woman who turned him on with nothing more than a look made him feel anything but cold. In many respects, confirmation of the pregnancy was a relief. Becky would be his and in his bed. Why suppress the desire that bound them so tightly when fate had stepped in to bring them together permanently?

He hooked an ankle over his knee while he waited for her to show her relief. Because what was the alternative for her? For their baby?

She slumped back with a long sigh. Her green eyes held his for the longest time. 'I know you mean well but I'm not marrying you.'

He suppressed a smile at the game she'd just started. He knew his wealth made him a prize catch for any woman. But there was always a game to be played. Becky wouldn't want to look too eager to accept his proposal. 'Why not?'

'Because the idea is ludicrous. We hardly know each other.'

'We've known each other for months. We get along great...most of the time.'

She gave a faint smile. 'We don't know each other well at all and we certainly don't love each other.'

'So what? My parents didn't love each other—'

'And look how well that turned out.'

He winced at her well struck barb. 'But they were married for over thirty-five years before Celeste's megalomania got out of control. Some of those years were even happy.'

She arched a brow. '*Some* of them?'

'They were a great team. They both knew the score when they married for what each wanted. It worked very well. There's no reason a marriage between you and me shouldn't work well too.'

'There's lots of reasons.' She started counting off on her fingers. 'One, you're a self-admitted playboy. Two, my parents only married because Mum got pregnant with me—their marriage was never happy. Three, my life is in England and yours is wherever the polo season happens to be.'

Putting his own hands out, he counted off on his own fingers his rebuttals. 'One, if we marry I would do my best to be faithful...'

Her eyes flashed as she interrupted. 'Your best?'

'I will not make a promise I don't know I can keep but I can promise to try.' The way things were going, to feel an attraction for anyone else would be a relief. Since he'd met Becky there hadn't been so much as a kindling of desire for another woman. He didn't know if the two issues were related but, considering how even now, when both their entire futures were being decided, his body thrummed with awareness for her and he couldn't stop his greedy eyes taking in every detail of her beautiful face and fabulous body, he supposed it wasn't an unreasonable theory. 'Two, your parents' marriage is no indication of your own…'

'You used your parents as an example,' she interrupted again with an arch of her brow.

'I'm using the positive side of their marriage as an example,' he corrected.

'There weren't many positives in my parents' marriage, especially the ending of it.'

He fixed her with an exasperated stare at her continued negativity before continuing. 'Three, you would still spend the summer months in England.'

Her eyes narrowed in thought but stayed locked on his. 'Right, so you want me to marry you when you can't guarantee you'll be faithful, when you use our respective parents' disastrous marriages as a template and when I'd, presumably, have to give up my career to follow you around the world?'

'I use my parents' *longevity* as a template. They agreed the score from the beginning and stuck to it. We will do the same. I know the mistakes they made and have no wish to repeat them, and I'm sure you feel the same.'

'The biggest mistake my parents made was getting married in the first place,' she disputed flatly.

'Don't be so negative,' he chided. 'We will forge our own path for marriage.'

'A path that means I'd have to give up my career?' she pressed.

'Children need both parents. Mine were hardly ever in the same country as each other, let alone with me. I want to be involved in my child's life.'

'So you do want me to throw away my career?'

He smiled indulgently. 'When you marry me, *bomboncita*, you will never need to work again.' Under the weight of her darkening stare, he added, 'If you're bored when the baby's older, you can work for my charity—we host many events so your hospitality skills will not be wasted.'

Her green eyes stayed on his face, features tightening as the seconds ticked by. 'You still haven't read my résumé, have you?'

'I prefer to make my own judgements about people.' He'd employed Greta on the basis of her impeccable references and experience with dogs and look what a mess she'd made of things, neglecting the boys to flirt with Juan and any other members of his staff she took a fancy to. He had no issue with his staff bedding each other but only so long as it didn't detract from the job they were paid to do.

He ignored the sly voice in his head that pointed out he'd deliberately housed Becky under his roof here to keep her away from the lusty environment of the stables. That had been out of consideration for her, he told himself staunchly. Nothing to do with being unable to bear the thought of another man even looking at her inappropriately.

She shook her head slowly, grimly. 'This is what I meant about us not knowing each other, although really what I should have said is that you don't know *me*. I don't work in hospitality. I'm a microbiologist.'

Becky felt no satisfaction in seeing the smug smile freeze on Emiliano's face. She wished it didn't hurt that he still hadn't enough curiosity about her to read her résumé, not even after their conversation when she'd written her official resignation. To him, she was just one of many women, interchangeable, forgettable. The only difference between her and the rest of them was that she'd been stupid enough to get pregnant, and she had to push back the heated memories of how much pleasure she'd taken in that stupidity and keep her attention focused on their conversation before she was steamrollered into something she'd regret.

And yet, for the very real catastrophe this pregnancy represented, she could not bring herself to regret it; not the life growing inside her nor the moment of madness that had lit the fuse into its being. The joy that had filled her to see the stick showing positive had been so pure it had almost neutralised the fear. She wanted her baby and already she knew she would do whatever it took to protect and nourish and love it. But that did not mean marrying her baby's father, even if she did find herself weak with longing for him in unguarded moments. If anything, that was another reason not to marry him. With Emiliano, there was just too much danger of losing herself.

'No.' His eyes blinked back into focus. 'That is not possible.'

She shrugged lightly. 'I'm sorry you think that.'

'You were working in a hospitality tent when we met.'

'I was, yes, because I'd finished my doctorate and needed a break from years of brain work.'

He stared at her with the look of a man who'd been earnestly told the earth was flat. 'How the hell can you have a doctorate at your age?'

'By working my backside off. I went straight from my degree into it—I didn't need to do my Master's as I was blessed to get a place on a PhD research scheme. I completed it four months ago. When I go back to England I'll be joining a laboratory in Oxford, working to combat antimicrobial resistance.'

'Anti what?' he asked faintly.

'Antimicrobial resistance,' she repeated patiently. 'In layman's terms, it's what happens when antibiotics and other medicines used to kill infections stop working.'

Time ticked slowly as the handsome face tightened,

the clear brown eyes darkening, a pulse throbbing in his temple.

'All this time,' he said in a low voice, 'you've been lying to me.'

'You only had to read my résumé to know all this. Or, you know, ask.'

Emiliano's head had filled with white noise. He'd known Becky wasn't lacking brain cells. That in itself was obvious. But not in a hundred years would he have guessed she was a scientist. To have gained a doctorate at her age suggested an incredibly high IQ and tenacity. Two qualities she shared with his mother and the woman who'd come close to destroying him a decade ago, a thought that cut through the white noise and filled the space with acid. 'You let me believe you worked in hospitality.'

'No, I didn't.' Her tone remained steady. 'I'm proud of what I've achieved and proud of my work. I'll talk about it with anyone who asks. All your stable staff know—ask any of them. It's not my fault your world revolves around yourself and your animals.'

A stab of anger sliced him at this unfounded slur. 'Why work in a hospitality tent at a polo competition?'

She shrugged. 'I told you; I needed to give my brain a break. I was burnt out.'

'But why work there specifically?' At a polo competition, a sport known as the sport of rich men and royalty. Any woman on the search for a wealthy man would be certain to attend… 'How did you hear about the job?'

'This is starting to sound like an interrogation.'

'You're carrying my child. Naturally, I'm curious.' Curious to learn how badly duped he'd been by this woman.

Her eyes held his, the suspicion in his guts mirrored in their reflection. 'My dad used to run a catering company. I called around his old contacts to see who was hiring seasonal workers.'

'Why not go travelling like a normal person suffering burn-out?'

'Most normal people do not have the money to go travelling on a whim.' Her voice had an edge to it. 'I needed money. I'd done bar work to supplement my grant when I was doing my degree but earned nothing while doing my doctorate. I've been pretty much cloistered for the last three years so thought it would be good to mix with people who could hold a conversation about something other than microbes. I didn't figure on them all being drunk. When you offered me the job of dog-sitter I thought all my holidays had come at once.'

He managed a tight smile. 'I'm sure you did.'

'What does that mean?'

'Only that after all those years of hard brain work, being paid to live in a beautiful country estate and walk dogs must have sounded idyllic,' he lied smoothly.

She leaned forward and rested her elbows on her thighs. 'Why does it sound as if you're implying something?'

He raised his shoulders and pulled a nonchalant face. 'Maybe you have a guilty conscience about something.'

Her features were pinched together as she continued studying him. 'Out with it.'

'With what?'

'I can't be doing with insinuations. If you've something to say, say it.'

'I just find it curious that not once, in all the time I've known you, have you mentioned that you're a scientist.'

'You sound like a stuck record—not once did we have a conversation that led to it. There's something else, so go on, spit it out. What else is bugging you?'

'You're an intelligent woman. I'm sure you can work it out.'

'I'm not a mind-reader.'

'And neither am I, which means I have to take on trust that you forgot to tell me you weren't on the pill.'

Her eyes widened. 'You think I forgot deliberately?'

'I didn't say that.'

'Stop with the weasel words,' she hissed. 'We both got carried away in the heat of the moment, so stop blaming me for your own ignorance about my career. Do you know what I find curious? Your inability to deal with being proved wrong. You were angry after we slept together because it hadn't crossed your thick head that I might be a virgin, and here you are again, angry that your image of me as a simple country barmaid has been proved wrong too. Is it just me you don't trust or women in general?'

Her question was so astute that Emiliano found himself in the unedifying position of being wrong-footed. 'I don't trust anyone,' he snapped.

'Then you can doubly forget marriage if that's going to be added to the list of things I'd have to put up with.' Rising to her feet, she glared at him. 'I'm going to take the boys for a walk. Let me know when you're in a less cynical mood—we can discuss things properly then.'

She slammed the door behind her.

Emiliano rubbed Hildegarde's clever head before handing the reins to a groom. He was about to walk away when the groom asked about the night shift for the forthcoming party. He almost smacked his own forehead at the reminder.

With everything that had been going on in his life he'd completely forgotten about the party he was hosting in a couple of weeks for his polo team and all their respective staff. It had been the most successful English season they'd ever played in and it was only right he reward them for it, but a party was something he could do without right now. He needed to devote his energy to convincing Becky to marry him. And it wasn't just the party. The break he'd given his team came to an end in a few days and practice would resume; new ponies needed to be tested, the new player he'd signed needed to bed into the team and then there were the myriad issues that needed dealing with on the non-playing side of the business and the worry of a sickness that had infected a significant number of his horses in the Middle East.

How could he concentrate on any of this when the woman carrying his child was proving herself an enigma and refused to do the right thing and marry him?

As he thought this he suddenly spotted Becky walking past the stables, his boys obediently at her side. As if she sensed his stare, she turned her face to him and stopped. Across the distance their gazes locked and held.

His chest filled, cramping his lungs, forcing him to drag in a deep breath of air. All the anger that had been simmering in him since she'd stormed out of her bedroom three hours ago, anger that hadn't abated even after a long ride on Hildegard, left him.

He barely registered putting one foot in front of the other. One minute they'd been hundreds of yards from each other. The next, he was standing in front of her.

A strand of hair not tied back in her ponytail caught in the breeze. He locked his hands behind his back to stop his fingers reaching for it.

'That was a long walk,' he murmured.

She just stared at him. Her throat moved a couple of times before she said quietly, 'I needed thinking time.'

He knew that feeling.

'Hungry?' he asked.

The beginnings of a smile played on her lips. 'Starving.'

'Then let's get lunch.'

They walked in silence until they were out of earshot of the stables. After his long, vigorous ride, the cooling breeze was welcome. It couldn't cool the baser part of him though, he conceded ruefully, not when Becky was within touching distance.

'What did you think about on your long walk?'

Becky took her time before answering because there was no easy answer to give. She'd spent most of the walk fuming over his implication that she'd deliberately got pregnant and fuming over his reaction to finding out about her career. His arrogant assumption that she would be happy to commit herself to marriage with an unfaithful husband—a promise to 'try' was, in her view, an insult and, worse, a stab to a heart already filled with far too much emotion than was healthy for a playboy like Emiliano Delgado. And then she'd remembered all the family stuff he'd been dealing with and her anger had turned to an ache that made her want to cry for him.

How did he do that? How could he anger her to such a pitch that her head could explode with rage then tug at her heartstrings enough for her to weep? And how, stronger than her anger or empathy, was it that just to look at him was enough for her to fill with so much heat it felt as if her bones were melting?

'Everything and nothing,' she finally settled on.

'Evasion, *bomboncita*?'

Hating that her heart skipped a beat to hear that caress from his lips, she studiously kept her gaze fixed ahead and fought to keep her voice steady. 'Not deliberately.'

'Are you still angry with me?'

'No...' She couldn't resist turning her face to look at him for a brief moment. 'Well, a little.'

'That's encouraging.'

She couldn't help the laugh that escaped to hear the old playful tone in his voice.

But then the serious mood returned. 'You know, I have never thought before about how I react to surprises.'

'What do you mean?'

'What you said earlier, about my reaction to your virginity—don't think I didn't notice you confirmed that for me—and to your job. I reacted badly both times. I will try to do better.'

Her heart gave a little thump. 'Is that your way of apologising?'

'I wouldn't go that far but I can admit when I'm wrong.'

'Go on then.'

'Go on, what?'

'Admit you were wrong.'

'My reaction was wrong.'

'And your insinuation that I intentionally got pregnant?'

Emiliano's guts plunged. He reached out for her hand and, holding it firmly, stopped walking. He could only assume it had been wounded pride at her dismissal of his proposal that had made him lash out like he had. He wished he could still believe she'd been playing a game but he was not one to indulge in self-delusion. Becky had been a virgin. She hadn't deliberately set out to trap him.

And she didn't want to marry him.

But that didn't mean he had to accept it. People could change. Minds could be changed. He'd never backed away from a challenge in his life and wasn't about to start now.

'Wrong. For that, I do apologise.'

She stared at their clasped hands before slowly raising her eyes to his. 'I would never do that.'

'Many women would.'

'I'm not many women.'

'No,' he agreed. The breeze had caught that stray lock of hair again. This time he didn't resist, smoothing it off her face with the hand not holding hers. If he hadn't been studying her so closely he would have missed the little quiver his touch evoked. He stepped even closer to her. 'You are not like other women.'

'Not like the other women you normally sleep with, you mean,' she corrected, but with a hitch in her voice that gratified him as much as her quiver had done. It emboldened him, made clear the route he needed to take to extract the change of mind he wanted from her. That it was the most pleasurable route only made it the sweeter.

'That is possible.'

'I'd say it's definite.'

'You have been studying my previous lovers?'

'There's not enough hours in the day to do a comprehensive study.'

'There has been no one since you.' No one since she'd come into his life…

'Is that supposed to be a compliment?'

'Just a fact.' He slipped an arm around her waist and drew her flush against him. 'Just as it is a fact that I have never desired a woman more than I desire you.' He put his mouth to her ear. 'Tell me it's not the same for you.'

'I…' Becky unclasped her hand from his and pressed it against his chest, ready to push him away, but found her fingers grabbing hold of his polo shirt. The heat of his breath against her ear was doing crazy things to her, and when he took advantage of her loss of words to press feather-light kisses over her face, everywhere but her mouth, she was saturated with a desire so strong it was a struggle to even breathe.

Somehow she summoned the strength to let go of his shirt and step out of his reach. 'Please, we agreed...' God, she could hardly get her voice working.

'Agreed what?'

'Not to muddy the waters with...this.'

His eyes gleamed. 'I promised no such thing.'

'Then make that promise.'

'No.'

'Please, Emiliano, I don't want us to be at war, but...'

'I prefer to make love not war.'

She was saved from having to think of a response to words that made her abdomen clench by a huge pick-up truck stopping beside them. It was Emiliano's head groundsman, offering them a lift back to the ranch.

Snatching at this gift of respite, she practically flew into the passenger side. She could have screamed when Emiliano followed her in and she was forced to share the two-seat space with him and the dogs, who obediently sat themselves in the footwell. Space upfront was so tight and Emiliano so big that their bodies were tightly compacted together, thigh pressed against thigh, side against side. She folded her arms tightly across her chest but that did nothing to dull the wanton heat flushing through her.

God help her, she prayed. Help her before she self-combusted.

# CHAPTER EIGHT

THE RIDE BACK to the ranch took barely two minutes. For Becky it felt like hours, time suspended in a closed environment where her senses were filled with the heat of Emiliano's body pressed against her own and the earthy scent of his fresh sweat. It was torture.

When they pulled up outside the front door, Emiliano thanked Gabriel before jumping out. Murmuring her own thanks, Becky budged over to get out too but, before she knew what he was planning, Emiliano's strong hands were at her waist and he was lifting her out of the truck as if she weighed nothing at all.

He set her gently to the floor. Legs weakened, she had to fight not to sway into him. Hands lingering at her waist, his eyes gleamed as he leaned in to murmur into her ear, 'I'm going to take a shower before we eat.'

There was no relief when he released his hold on her waist and bounded into the ranch, not when every part of her ached and throbbed.

Inside, all was quiet. Or was it the steady beat of blood in her head deafening her?

She couldn't stop her gaze from following him up the wide staircase, the longing to follow him with more than her eyes more than she could bear. With a wrench, she turned on her heel and hurried to the kitchen for company that wasn't hunky Argentinian male. But the kitchen was empty of everything but the scent of cooking.

She poured herself a coffee from the prepared jug on the counter but her hands shook so much that when she tried to take a sip of it, it spilled over her shirt. She snatched at a tea towel and dabbed as much of it as she could, thankful that she liked her coffee half-filled with milk. Her skin already felt burned.

Needing to change her wet shirt, she approached the stairs with trepidation. To get to her room she had to pass Emiliano's, a fact she'd studiously tuned out every other time she'd walked past it.

This time it was impossible to tune out, especially when she found the door partially open. An invitation? The mere thought was enough for her knees to weaken all over again.

Why was she hovering there? And why was her hand reaching forward…?

'You can come in, you know,' a deep voice drawled from the other side of the door.

Immediately she pressed her shaking hand to the place where her heart would have been if it hadn't jumped to her throat.

The door opened fully. Emiliano, still dressed, lopsided smile on his face, eyes dark and knowing, swept an arm behind him in invitation.

'I was on a call with my English vet,' he explained casually, as if finding Becky hovering outside his door was an everyday occurrence.

She had no recollection of crossing the threshold or closing the door behind her.

Since their night together, Becky had kept a firm control of herself, aware of her susceptibility to him, aware that he'd left his mark on her in a deep-rooted way that had nothing to do with the pregnancy. She'd believed the awareness of her desire made it controllable.

She'd been a fool, she now realised hazily. The distance they'd both imposed had been the thing keeping it controlled. Now that Emiliano had breached that distance and turned those laser eyes and the full weight of his desire back on her, the walls she'd erected around herself had come crashing down. For the first time she could admit that she didn't want to build them back up and she didn't want to fight it any more.

Emiliano was right. They were going to be bound together for ever so why fight the inevitable? The longing in her blood made the inevitability clear to her.

And now she was in his room, trembling with nerves and excitement, her senses too overloaded with Emiliano to even give his inner sanctum a cursory glance. All she could see was him. All she could hear was her own heartbeat.

'Join me in the shower?' he said in that same casual tone before he pulled his polo shirt over his head.

Her mouth opened but nothing came out. She had no idea what she would have said even if speech had been possible.

Eyes back on her, he pinched the sides of his jodhpurs and without a modicum of shame pulled them down to his feet, stripping his underwear as he went.

Naked, barely feet away, he stared at her.

And all she could do was stare back, drinking in every part of his masculine perfection. She remembered so well the feel of him naked on her and in her, but to see him in the light took what little breath she had left away.

The lean yet muscular body she'd imagined vividly was so much more. Of everything. Harder. The shoulders broader, the biceps more muscular, the thighs more powerful. A smattering of dark hair whorled in the centre of his chest, narrowing to a thin line down his flat abdomen then thickening to where his erection jutted out as hard and as big as the rest of him.

Brown eyes darkening, he watched her soak him in.

'Your turn,' he rasped with a flare of his nostrils.

Her hands moved with no connection to her brain. Surprisingly steady, they opened the buttons of her shirt one by one before she shrugged the sleeves off. And then she moved to her jeans.

Emiliano's throat had run dry. Never in his life had he been as mesmerised as he was in that moment. He'd climbed the stairs to his room with Becky's dazed yet hungry eyes following him but no expectation that *she* would follow. He'd learned the hard way with Becky to expect the unexpected.

And now she was in his room, stripping off her clothes. Shyness had brought a blush to her cheeks but her beautiful green eyes, pulsing with unconcealed desire, did not waver. It was the most erotic sight he had ever seen.

He barely suppressed a groan when she stepped out of her jeans. The groan came unbidden when she unhooked her bra and released the breasts whose taste he remembered with crystal-clear clarity but whose image were shadowed.

And then she tugged her knickers down too.

He gritted his teeth and breathed deeply through his nose. *Dios*, a man could die and go to heaven in that curvy softness.

She was like a milkmaid of medieval times. Creamy weighty breasts were topped with perfect raspberry nipples, the hips wide and rounded, belly softly rounded, a cloud of soft dark hair in the arrow between legs much smoother and shapelier than he'd dreamed. *Everything* was more beautiful and perfect than he'd dreamed.

And he'd dreamed about her, waking and in sleep, so many times he'd lost count.

The dream was perfected when she pulled the hairband out and her chestnut waves came tumbling down.

Breathing deeply, he extended a hand.

Eyes not breaking contact with his, she reached out to take it. A spark of electricity pulsed through him at the first touch.

Becky let Emiliano lead her into the huge walk-in shower in his bathroom. The way she felt right then, she would have let him lead her anywhere. Any embarrassment at being naked in the light with a man for the first time had gone when she'd seen the effect it had on him. The heat in his eyes alone could power a station.

She let him position her under the wide shower head, facing him. He stretched an arm to press a button on the wall. An instant later, water at a perfect temperature rained down on them. She shivered at the effect it had on her highly sensitised skin then held her breath as she waited for what he would do next.

He turned slightly to fill his hands with gel from the dispenser on the wall and then, eyes on hers, lathered his magnificent body, cleaning every part he could reach. When he took hold of his manhood to clean that too, Becky experienced such a deep throb of longing that her lungs stopped functioning.

Eyes now hooded, he rasped, 'Turn around.'

Trembling with anticipation, she obeyed.

He gathered her hair and tucked it to one side over her shoulder before she heard him fill his hands with more gel. In slow, rhythmic movements, he washed every inch of her back, from the nape of her neck all the way to the base of her spine. When he gently massaged the gel into her buttocks she shot a hand out against the wall to keep herself upright.

Already lost in a bubble of desire, when he gripped her hips and pressed himself against her, his erection hard against her lower back, and growled seductively into the top of her head, she was helpless to stop the moan of need flying from her lips.

And then he gently turned her to face him.

Breathing heavily, he gazed into her eyes for the longest time before reaching again for the gel. He lathered his hands then placed them on her shoulders. His Adam's apple moved before he slowly lathered her arms, all the way to her fingers, then back up and around to the base of her throat before massaging her breasts.

The sensations his seductive caresses were firing through her were too strong to sustain. Her legs were shaking. But the caresses were relentless and when he'd finished massaging her belly and gently moved lower she would have fallen to the floor if he hadn't hooked an arm around her waist and carefully steered her to the deep tiled ledge running along the left of the vast space and helped her sit. The shower head must have moved by sensor for the spray followed them.

Dropping to his knees before her, Emiliano continued to lather her body. His strong hands massaged the gel into her thighs and calves then lifted each foot in turn and rubbed his thumbs into her soles and toes. All the while, the heavy sting of the shower drenched her skin, adding to the sensation filling her.

When every inch of her had been cleaned, he put a hand on each ankle then brushed all the way back up until he was gripping her hips and his eyes were staring into hers.

His breathing was as erratic as her own, she thought dimly, but it was the last coherent thought in her pleasure-saturated mind for he captured her lips in a kiss of such savage passion that she melted into him with abandon.

Her hand cradled the back of his head, fingers kneading as their tongues entwined in a fierce erotic dance that only fed the burning need inside her. When he hooked an arm around her waist to pull her flush against him and her breasts pressed against his hard torso, the burn in her pelvis turned into a throb that had her moaning for relief from the exquisite pain.

As if sensing her need, Emiliano broke the kiss to brush his lips over her cheeks and then down the side of her neck, sinking lower as his mouth moved over her aching breasts and captured the erect tips whole in turn. Oh, the *sensation…*

His mouth continued its erotic assault of her flesh. His appreciative groans stoked her responses, an instinctive knowledge that for every ounce of pleasure he was giving her, he received gratification too. By the time he reached the essence of her femininity she was so far gone in the thick haze of desire that when he pressed his mouth to it and inhaled deeply she grasped wildly for his hair to cling to, tilted her head back to rest against the wall and closed her eyes.

With one hand clasping her hip and the other roaming over her belly and breasts, his tongue stroked her with an incessant pressure that had her reaching a peak in moments.

Then, no sooner had the waves of rippling pleasure begun to ebb than Emiliano moved his mouth to kiss his way back up over her belly and breasts to her lips, his tongue plunging back into her mouth at the same moment he plunged deep inside her.

Emiliano groaned loudly and stilled. *Dios…*

How he held himself together he would never know.

Their first time together had been an explosion of passion with no time to savour or appreciate. This time, he wanted to savour the intensity of every perfect moment but it was hard when he was buried deep in Becky's tight heat and the weight of her perfect breasts pushed against his chest and the taste of her lingered so deliciously on his tongue. His senses were infused by so many intoxicating sensations that he had to grit his teeth tightly to stop the climax begging for release.

He kissed her, long and hard. And then he began to move.

Every thrust, every brush of her breast, every breathy moan that poured from her into his mouth, every knead of her fingers into his flesh fed the hunger in him. In and out he thrust, harder and harder, being pulled deeper and deeper into the abyss, clinging on by his teeth as Becky's movements became more frantic too and her moans deepened and then, just as he feared he could hold on no more, she pressed tightly against him with a cry that seemed to come from her very soul and shuddered wildly in his arms.

And then he was lost. His climax ripped through him, pleasure flooding him so thoroughly that, for the longest moment, the world around him turned into flickering white.

Slowly, the second wave of pulsations to have crashed through her settled and Becky drifted back to earth.

Her face was buried in Emiliano's neck and when she turned to breathe she was surprised to find the shower still spraying over their fused bodies.

When he shifted she held her only just regained breath as the aftermath of their first coupling suddenly played in her mind. When he moved the arm wrapped so tightly around her, fear swiftly clutched her heart.

She didn't think she could bear it if the beauty of what they'd just shared was tarnished with anger and recriminations. Not again.

Only when the shower stopped did she realise he'd moved so he could turn it off, but her relief lasted seconds for he pressed his lips to her forehead before pulling out of her and getting to his feet.

Cold at the abrupt loss of his heat and suddenly self-conscious of her nakedness, she pressed her thighs together and twisted away, afraid to look at him.

Becky heard him walk away and squeezed her eyes shut. She must not cry. Not until she was in the privacy of her own room with the door locked.

She kept them closed even when she heard his footsteps near her again, bracing herself.

A hand slid between her back and the tiled wall and gently pulled her forward, then the softest, warmest, fluffiest towel was wrapped around her. Strong arms held her securely before she was lifted up and carried effortlessly into the bedroom.

There, Emiliano sat her on the sofa and pressed another kiss to her forehead. 'Wait one second,' he murmured in a hoarse voice.

When he returned from the bathroom he'd wrapped a towel around his waist and carried another in his hands. He sat beside her and put the fresh towel against her hair. Working with infinite patience and without a single word being exchanged, he towel-dried it in sections until her chestnut locks no longer dripped everywhere.

Done, he stared at her before placing a finger under her chin and pressing a tender kiss to her mouth.

'I shall get food. Don't go anywhere,' he said in the same hoarse voice.

She nodded, still too choked with emotion to speak.

He disappeared into his dressing room, re-emerging wearing a pair of faded jeans and carrying a maroon towelling robe. He handed it to her with a smile before giving her another kiss and strolling out of the door.

Alone, Becky took a minute to gather herself before slipping into the giant robe. It trailed to her ankles and the sleeves needed rolling three times to stop them dangling past her hands, and yet there was something comforting and intimate in wearing something that was his. Gathering her towels into her arms, she carried them to the bathroom to hang on the towel-warmer, aware with every step of the tenderness between her noodly legs.

She looked in the mirror. The flushed face staring back at her had the dazed look of someone who'd been made love to.

# CHAPTER NINE

EMILIANO CARRIED THE tray piled high with food up the stairs, his heart beating more forcefully as he neared his bedroom. He only understood they'd been the beats of dread when he pushed the door open and relief washed through him to find Becky still there and curled up on the sofa. His heart bloomed when she lifted her head and smiled.

'I bring us a feast,' he announced as he placed the tray on the low table by the sofa.

Her eyes lit up. 'Medialunas.'

He grinned and sat beside her. Just in case she was inclined to move away from him, he grabbed her ankles and placed them on his lap, and was gratified when she didn't resist. 'Paula told me you have taken a liking to them.'

He'd also filled the tray with the fruits she liked and, after much head scratching, worked out how to make a fresh pot of coffee, which he'd balanced with the rest of the stuff. He could have called Paula or another member of his household staff to do it for him, but he'd had a strange compulsion to do it himself.

'I could scoff them all day.'

'I could scoff *you* all day,' he replied with a suggestive wink that made her blush.

After the way things had been between them the first time they'd made love, it loosened the knots in his guts to have things back on an even keel with her. Not that things had ever been *even* as such. Not with Becky. Right from the start there had always been that undercurrent of desire between them which they had both ignored with explosive results, leading to anger and recrimination but always, *always*, that desire burning brightly, waiting to be unleashed again.

To make her smile, to see her blush, to have her feet resting on his lap as if that was where they belonged…

Taking care not to hurt her feet, he leaned forward to pile a plate of pastries and fruit for her before sorting his own plate out and pouring the coffee.

As he devoured his first medialuna whilst observing Becky's more delicate approach, he had to concede this was the lightest he'd felt in a long time, certainly since the party that had seen his world fall apart, possibly even since his adoptive father had died.

'So, my little microbiologist,' he said teasingly. 'Tell me, were you a swot at school?'

Her pink tongue darted to the corner of her mouth and a tiny flake of pastry stuck there disappeared. 'I was the biggest swot going.'

'And were you always interested in germs?'

She raised her brows and pulled a bemused face. 'I wasn't a complete oddball.'

'So why specialise in them?'

'I'd actually intended to do a chemistry degree but I went to a university open day to get a feel for the place and got talking to a student doing a degree in microbiology. It just sounded really exciting so I applied and that was that.'

Now he was the one to pull a bemused face. 'Germs sounded exciting?'

'Bacteria, viruses, fungi and protozoa,' she corrected with a grin that made him want to kiss her until she ran out of air. 'And yes, it did sound *hugely* exciting to me—the course, I mean. And the career it could lead to.'

'And what will you be doing in your new job?' Privately, he hoped it would be something unimportant and inconsequential, a role she could turn her back on to spend her life with him. And their baby, of course, he quickly reminded himself.

She stretched her ankles and wiggled her pretty toes. 'I'll be joining a team working on inhibiting efflux pumps.'

'And they are…?' He did his best to sound interested but internally he was already partying in his head, celebrating that it did indeed sound unimportant and inconsequential.

'Think of them as naturally occurring minuscule pumps that sit on bacterial cells sucking out toxic substances. When you take antibiotics for infections, they're the blighters sucking *out* the antibiotics from inside the cells, essentially booting out the cure before it can get to work. If we can inhibit the efflux pumps then it will reduce the bacteria's ability to boot out the antibiotics and, hopefully, make the antibiotics effective again.'

The internal partying came to an abrupt halt. That did not sound either unimportant or inconsequential. Damn it.

'Think of the implications if we're successful,' she said quietly, her eyes holding his. 'It's not just humans that will benefit but the animal world too. Antibiotics are becoming less effective for all creatures. Horses too.'

And didn't he know it. Emiliano spent a small fortune vaccinating his horses and taking all the other preventative measures available to keep them free from disease but not everything could be prevented. In his world there was much awareness and fear of antibiotic resistance.

How the hell was he going to convince her to put work of such importance to one side and join him on the polo circuit with their child, to marry him, to be a family, without sounding like a selfish oaf?

The answer came to him. It would be done carefully. With stealth.

Taking her empty plate, he placed it on the table and exchanged it for her coffee. 'What's the maternity package at your company like?' he asked casually.

She took a sip of the coffee and wrinkled her nose. 'I don't know. It's in the company handbook but that's in England with the rest of my stuff. I'll read up on it when I go back next week.'

'You don't have to go back so soon.' He seized the open goal with gusto. 'Why not stay until your new job starts?' That would give him a few extra precious weeks to work his magic. For good measure he added, 'You can help me select your replacement.'

'I can't. I've got too much to organise.'

'Such as?'

'For a start, I need to buy furniture for my flat. And cooking utensils, crockery… You name it, I need to buy it.'

'I will get them for you.'

'No.'

'Yes,' he countered firmly. 'And when you say flat, do you mean something small and poky?'

'Compared to the homes you're used to then yes, but for a normal person it's fine.'

'How about for a normal person with child?'

'I'll manage.'

'No, *bomboncita*, you won't but we have plenty of time to sort that. The most pressing thing for now is to get your flat furnished. I will take you shopping tomorrow. You can choose whatever you want and I'll have it couriered to England and installed in the flat for when you return. Problem solved, see? You can stay here longer.'

Becky narrowed her eyes. His generosity didn't surprise her—Emiliano was unfailingly generous—but, even though her heart sang loudly to think of staying another three weeks with him, she had to be practical and not look at things with sex-sated eyes. Emiliano never did anything that wasn't to his own advantage. 'Don't bulldoze me,' she warned.

'It is not bulldozing,' he said with a disappointed tut. 'It is using my wealth to my own advantage to keep you in my bed for as long as I can.'

She almost laughed at this admittance so closely following her private thoughts. 'What do you mean by *in your bed*?'

'You're moving in here with me,' he told her cheerfully. 'And do not argue. If you won't move your stuff over, I'll do it myself.'

She finished her coffee, her brain racing. She got why he wanted her to stay longer but it hadn't occurred to her that he would actually want her to share his private space with him, even if only on a semi-permanent basis. From all the gossip she'd heard from the grooms, who got all their titbits from his various household staff across the globe, Emiliano had an aversion to women spending more than a night with him. It was a standing joke that come the morning, he would offer them breakfast and then a taxi. It was the standing joke that had made her determined never to act on her attraction to him.

'You want me to share your bedroom while I'm here?' she clarified, in case her thoughts had gone a little too wayward.

He held his hand out for her mug. 'What I want is for you to get it into your clever head that you and I are together.'

Her heart jumped so hard that if the mug she placed in his waiting hand had been full it would have spilt all over him.

'Together?' she echoed faintly.

'A couple.' He put the mug on the table then put his hands back on her ankles and pulled her flat. His eyes gleamed as he stared down at her. 'Change your social media settings to "In a Relationship".'

'I'm not on social media.'

He slipped a hand in the gaping front of his robe, still wrapped around her, and cupped a fabulously full breast. 'But you are in a relationship, so get used to it. You are my woman and I am your man and together we will find a solution to raise our child together.'

'Emiliano…' She sighed, torn between wanting to move his hand away so she could think properly and wanting him to carry on his wonderful caress. 'I said I didn't want to marry you.'

'Who said anything about marriage?' he asked with an innocent look that immediately made her think he was lying. 'I just think we owe it to our baby to try. Or do you disagree?'

Before she could answer, he dipped his head and took a nipple in his mouth.

Her sigh this time was one of pleasure, a sigh that turned into a moan when he pulled the robe apart completely to kiss and caress her other breast, hazily aware he was tugging his jeans down at the same time. She sank into the pleasure he was giving and groped for him, clutching at his hair, a deep ache between her legs which he gently parted as he kissed his way back up to her neck and nestled himself between.

His erection pressed at the top of her thigh as his face hovered over hers, brown eyes gleaming with lust. Those sensual lips would have fused against hers if she hadn't finally found the sense to turn her face.

'I don't want to be rushed into anything,' she managed

to say breathlessly, even though he'd slid a finger inside her and her pelvis had arched into his hand in automatic response. 'You're like a bulldozer when you want something.'

His thumb pressed against her nub, making her gasp. 'All I'm asking is for you to give us a chance.'

She turned her face back to gaze into his eyes and found her back arching so her breasts could press against his chest. 'Only if you promise to be faithful.'

'I will be faithful for as long as we're together,' he promised solemnly, slowly moving his hand away and pressing his erection to her. 'Now will you agree to move your stuff into my room?'

'Why do I feel like I'm being manipulated?'

He slid deep inside her with a long drawn out groan. 'Because, *bomboncita*, you're a very clever woman.'

'It is *what*?'

'A slow cooker,' Becky explained with a patience she was fast losing.

'How does it work?'

She shook her head, amusement suddenly replacing the exasperation. Every kitchen item she'd looked at in the Trapani Department Store Emiliano had brought her to had been met with questions. It was like going shopping with an overly curious toddler. Except Emiliano was a fully-grown man who'd never cooked a meal in his life. 'It cooks food slowly. It means I can chuck stuff in it before I go to work and then it will be all cooked and delicious when I get home.'

'I'll hire you a chef.'

'I don't need a chef. I need a slow cooker.' And she needed to find a way to at least contribute towards all the stuff he was buying for her.

If she'd realised he was taking her to a department store that only catered for the filthy rich she'd have insisted on going to one that catered for the opposite end of the financial spectrum. It wasn't until she'd sat on a sofa so comfortable she imagined it was used up in heaven and then looked at the price tag and almost had a heart attack that she'd understood just how astronomically expensive it all was here. She'd jumped off it and was on the hunt for a cheaper one—fat chance, she'd quickly learned—when Emiliano had appeared at her side and smugly told her it was hers. When she'd tried to get around his generosity by refusing to look at bedroom furniture, he'd fixed her with a look and said if she didn't choose stuff for herself, he would choose for her. When she'd then begged him to take her somewhere cheaper, he'd fixed her with that same look and said, 'I will not have the mother of my child putting up with second-rate stuff when I can afford the best.'

'But I don't need Egyptian cotton sheets with a thousand threads,' she'd protested.

'You might not, but I do.' He'd then put his mouth to her ear and added, 'Believe me, *bomboncita*, I will be sharing the sheets with you whenever I can.'

She'd had to press her thighs together to counteract the throbbing warmth his seductive words had roused and hoped no one could see the flush of colour staining her cheeks. The plan for him to take her shopping had been delayed by two days as, other than taking the dogs for long walks together, they'd found it impossible to drag themselves out of bed.

They had been the most heavenly days of her life.

They moved on from the slow cooker—Emiliano patted it to let the poor sales assistant tasked with helping them know they wanted it—and, after selecting a coffee machine, Becky found the utensils. She laughed to find a fish slice here cost as much as a slow cooker would have done in a reasonably priced store.

'Why don't you already have these things?' Emiliano asked while Becky dithered over which knife set she wanted.

'I lived in student digs when I was doing my degree but the university I did my doctorate at was close enough to my mum's for me to commute, so I moved into her annexe. My parents built and furnished it for my grandmother. She lived in it until she became too fragile and had to move into a care home.'

'You can show me it when you introduce me to your parents.'

She grimaced. 'We'll see. Anyway, that's me done here. I've enough to get started in the flat. Can we get something to eat now?'

But a kernel of distrust had unfurled in Emiliano at the expression on Becky's face. 'You don't want me to meet them?'

He had yet to spend more than a night with a woman without her hinting about meeting the parents, despite him making it very clear that what they were sharing was sex and only sex. Adriana was the only woman whose parents he'd wanted to meet. Only when they were over had he discovered why she'd resisted this—to stop him learning the truth about her. By then it was too late. The titanic damage had been done.

'My dad's in Europe somewhere having a midlife crisis,' she said, her tone shorter than he was used to.

'And your mother?'

She shrugged. 'We don't speak any more.'

'Why not?'

'For reasons I'm not discussing in the middle of a department store. Can we get some lunch?'

'Only if you let me buy you an outfit for the party.'

'I don't like wearing dresses.'

'It doesn't have to be a dress,' he stressed. Again. She'd been happy enough about going to the celebration party he was throwing until he'd mentioned the dress code and she'd become mutinous. He would never understand her. 'Just something that isn't jeans.'

'I feel comfortable in jeans.'

'Yes, but you won't feel comfortable if you're the only one wearing them. Everyone's dressing up.'

Her eyes narrowed and her lips pursed. 'Just don't expect me to wear heels. Not going to happen.'

'Fine.'

'Good. Can we get food now?'

Lacing his fingers through hers, Emiliano led her out of the store. The sun had risen, spring warmth filling the busy Buenos Aires streets. A short walk later and they were shown to an outside table at a chic restaurant that sold a mean *submarino*, a milk drink served with a chunk of chocolate he just knew Becky would love, especially as she'd vowed to only have one coffee a day for the duration of the pregnancy. His instinct on this was correct and he watched her stir the chocolate into the hot milk with an enchanted smile at this small pleasure.

While they waited for their food to be brought to them, he set about quizzing her.

'What happened with your mother?'

The enchanted smile fell. 'Can't we just relax for half an hour?'

'It is not relaxing to talk about your mother?'

'No.'

'Why not?'

She scowled. 'Honestly, you really are a bulldozer when you want something.'

'I don't like evasion.'

Her eyes flashed. 'That had better not be a dig.'

'I just find it curious that you've never mentioned you're not on speaking terms with your mother.'

'Seriously?' She leaned forward. 'You know what *I* find curious? That this is a repeat of a conversation we've had before. I work for you for months and you never ask me any personal questions whatsoever, then when you discover new things about me you act all surprised and immediately assume I've been hiding things. You are so cynical!'

'And you're still hiding.'

'I am *not*. I don't like to talk about it because it still hurts.'

'Your mother?'

She nodded and had a sip of her *submarino*. The chocolate must have soothed her for she closed her eyes to savour it and her shoulders loosened. 'We fell out at Christmas.'

'What happened?'

'We had an argument about her new husband and she kicked me out.'

As Emiliano took a moment to digest this, their food was brought to them. He hadn't known her mother had remarried.

He took a bite of his steak baguette before saying, 'What was the argument about?'

She looked away from him with a shrug.

'You remember that night when we spoke about my mother on the porch?'

Her eyes flickered.

'I didn't hold anything back.'

'Yes, you did.'

'I did not.'

'Did too. You wouldn't tell me why you were sacked from the family business.'

'It wasn't relevant to the conversation.'

Her narrowing eyes told him she saw straight through this evasion.

He sighed. 'Look, it's a time in my life that still makes me angry to think of. I never speak about it.'

'Did it involve a woman?'

Now his eyes narrowed.

Shaking her head, she dug her spoon into the *provoleta* still bubbling in the skillet it had been served to her in, and blew on the gooey cheese she lifted out. He'd learned these past few days that Becky's savoury tooth was as big as her sweet tooth.

'You have big trust issues when it comes to women,' she observed, before popping the spoon into her mouth.

'So would you if you had a mother like mine.'

'Nice evasion.'

'I must have learned it from you.'

Their eyes clashed and then, in an instant, her taut features loosened at the same moment he felt the tightness in his chest loosen and they both started laughing.

Emiliano caught hold of her hand and brought it to his lips. 'Just wait until I get you home.'

'Ooh, what are you going to do to me?'

'I'm going to make love to you for so long you won't be able to walk for a week.'

'Promises, promises,' she teased with a gleam in her eyes. Her foot found his calf and gently rubbed against it.

Still smiling, she dipped her rustic bread into her *provoleta* and had a bite that was pure provocation.

'You, *bomboncita*, could drive a saint to madness.'

'Just as well you're not a saint then.'

# CHAPTER TEN

EMILIANO WAS AS good as his word. Within minutes of them returning to the ranch he'd locked his bedroom door, stripped her naked and made love to her for so long she doubted she'd be able to walk for a month. It was glorious.

Utterly sated, she dozed while he went off to exercise the dogs, only stirring when he returned to the room and slipped back into bed to make love to her all over again.

When she finally left the bed to shower, she couldn't help but giggle to feel the delicious lethargy in her limbs.

Back in the bedroom, wrapped in Emiliano's way too big robe, which she'd claimed for her own, she was thrilled to see he'd had dinner brought to them.

He grinned. 'I thought it saved us having to get dressed.'

'I like your thinking.'

After they'd eaten a great dish of *carbonada* each, an Argentinian beef stew that had a wonderful sweetness to it, Emiliano put the television on and stretched out on the sofa. Becky lay beside him, her back against his torso, bottom resting against his groin, and he wrapped his arms tightly around her.

Although a tactile person, he'd never been a man for cuddling. It was one of the many intimacies he'd chosen to avoid and he found it a little alarming how good it felt to lie like this, not speaking, not making love, simply holding each other. He decided it was best not to ponder on this.

When the documentary ended he kissed the top of her head. She sighed and stretched her back.

'I thought you'd fallen asleep,' he murmured.

'Just thinking.'

'About?'

'Us. The baby. My parents. How we can avoid the mistakes they made.'

'Ready to tell me about it?'

She sighed again and wriggled onto her back. 'It wasn't that I didn't want to tell you, just that I didn't want to do it in public. It's still pretty raw for me.'

He adjusted himself so he could look at her face more clearly while still keeping his body pressed against hers. 'Was their divorce recent?'

'The divorce itself was finalised a year ago but the separation happened when I left for university. Literally, I left on the Saturday and Mum kicked Dad out on the Sunday. She'd been waiting for me to "flee the nest", as she put it.'

'Did you say they married because she got pregnant with you?'

She nodded. 'They were very young. Mum was nineteen; Dad was twenty.'

'My mum was only twenty when she had me. But they were already married.'

She smiled and brushed a thumb against his mouth. 'Mine should have stayed single. They spent my entire childhood arguing. Not passionate arguments or anything like that, but constant cold sniping at each other.'

'How were they with you?'

'Great. Very loving and supportive in everything I did. They just hated each other. They were like children taking constant pot-shots at each other. Mum told me after that she'd known since I was a toddler that the minute I was old enough to cope and understand, she would end the marriage.'

'Was it a relief for you when it ended?'

'It would have been if they'd stayed the same people, but they both changed. The only thing that didn't change was the bickering—if anything, the separation made them worse. They fought about everything, right down to the koi carp in the garden pond. That's why the divorce took so long to go through. In the end, the courts decided how the marital assets were split and neither of them was happy about it so it must have been the right judgement. Mum got the house, half their savings and half Dad's pension. Dad got the business.'

'Catering, wasn't it?'

'Event catering. He built it from nothing and it became very successful, which was just as well as the pair of them spent a fortune on lawyers' fees. The divorce was rubber-stamped a year ago and Mum remarried pretty much immediately. Dad sold the business and bought himself a motorbike to travel around Europe. He says he's recapturing his lost youth. He video calls every month or so. You should see him; he's grown his hair and a beard and has loads of young women falling over him. Amazing what a powerful bike and a wallet stuffed with cash does to a man's sex appeal. He's now planning to travel America so I've no idea when I'll see him again.'

'That must be rough.'

'It is.' A flash of real pain rang from her eyes. 'I miss him.'

'What happened with your stepfather?'

Her features visibly tightened at the mention of him. 'Ruddy gold-digging con-artist.'

Emiliano propped himself on an elbow to study her face even more closely. His nightmare with Adriana had made gold-digging con-artists a specialist subject for him. 'Really?'

'He's a slimy twenty-seven-year-old personal trainer who usually dates hot young women. Mum hired him a couple of years ago. He moved in within weeks of them getting together and they married a month after the divorce was finalised.'

'Why do you think he's a gold-digger?' he asked carefully, thinking that until he'd met Becky his own type had been blonde, stick-thin models and socialites with bust sizes higher than their IQs. 'I understand why her marrying someone your age would make you feel uncomfortable but the age gap between them is less than the one between Celeste and my father—my adoptive father, I mean—and tastes change. Is it because your mother is the older party?'

'I'd already got used to her having lovers my age. She put me in the annexe rather than let me move back into the main house as she said I needed privacy, but really it was to keep me out of sight and stop me cramping her style when her current lover was around. Anthony was the first one she really fell for. If I thought he was genuine I wouldn't care, but I've seen first-hand what a sly, spoilt, manipulative narcissist he is. He's got her wrapped around his finger. He hasn't worked a day since they married, but she's bought him a sports car, a wardrobe of designer clothes and had a gym installed for him. All he has to do is look at something and he gets it, and then the bastard thought he could have me too.'

A trickle of ice ran down his spine. 'What happened?'

Her chin jutted and her lips tightened before she answered. 'I'd run out of coffee so popped into the house to borrow some. I didn't know Mum had gone food shopping for the Christmas party they were hosting. The creep pinned me to the kitchen wall and said he'd seen me looking at him…' her face contorted with distaste '…and knew that I wanted him. Then he stuck his tongue down my throat and groped me.'

The trickle of ice turned into a sea that spread through his veins. 'Did he hurt you?'

Green eyes flashed with rage. 'My reflexes worked too well for that. I kneed him right where it hurts the most.'

'Good,' he said grimly although he was already thinking ahead to ways he could exact proper retribution. 'And then what happened?'

'I locked myself in the annexe until Mum got back but I was so upset and angry that I could hardly speak to tell her. Anthony was as cool as a cucumber and denied everything. He said I was jealous and trying to split them up because I wanted him for myself. She believed him and kicked me out right there and then.'

For a moment Emiliano couldn't speak. It was as if a hand had plunged through his ribcage, grabbed hold of his heart and twisted it.

'I haven't spoken to her since. She won't answer my calls or messages. I'm dead to her.'

To his horror, two fat tears spilled from her eyes.

'Have you told her about the baby?' he asked gently. 'That might be the bridge you two need to rebuild things.'

'I've been too scared.' She squeezed her eyes shut and pinched her nose. 'What if she ignores it like she's ignored all the other messages? I've begged her over and over to talk and I get nothing back. I don't know how I'd cope if she were to reject our baby too.'

Not saying a word, Emiliano lay back down and pulled her to him, wrapping his arms tightly around her and stroking her hair as she cried into his chest.

For Becky, his silent comfort spoke more than any meaningless words could say. All this time, she'd believed she was coping but she saw now that she'd only buried the pain out of reach.

Within weeks of kicking Becky's father out her mum had hooked up with her first young lover. Becky remembered being homesick and deciding to visit, only to have her mum send her back as she had a weekend of partying planned. Hurt—*devastated*—and at a loss at how to handle it, Becky had thrown herself into her studies. She'd tried to understand her mum's newfound enthusiasm for younger men, tried to pretend the maternal love she'd always taken for granted wasn't being tainted by suspicion from a mother who'd stopped looking at her as a daughter and begun seeing her as a rival. And then that horrendous day had come; her mum shrieking at her like a harpy, accusing Becky of jealousy and spite while her new husband watched with that hateful smirk…

Estranged from her mother, her father thousands of miles away, she'd thrown herself into her studies with a vengeance, completing her doctorate in record time, working her brain harder than she'd ever done until she burnt herself out. But even then she hadn't paused long enough to think and certainly not long enough to feel. She'd thrown herself into the hospitality work and then the work for Emiliano, filling the months before starting her new job. Anything rather than face up to the reality that she was truly alone.

Who would have believed, she thought in wonder as the tears dried up, that selfish, arrogant Emiliano Delgado would be the one she would finally open up to and confide in? And who would have believed him capable of listening so well and giving such tender comfort?

There were a lot of things she would never have believed about him. The spoilt playboy was only one facet of the man and, she was coming to believe, only the shiny surface of him. Beneath it, he was a man capable of great kindness and empathy.

'Where did you go after you left?' he asked quietly once all the tears had been purged.

'I moved into Dad's mobile home. He bought it when Mum kicked him out. He'd already gone off on his bike trip by then.'

'Why didn't you go to another family member or a friend?'

'The rest of my family live by the coast a hundred miles away—my parents moved to the Midlands when they married. As for friends…' She shrugged and tried to sound nonchalant. 'I didn't really have anyone I was close enough with to ask.'

He was silent for a moment. 'What happens when the baby comes? Will you have anyone close by to help?'

'No,' she admitted with a sigh.

'So when you go back to England you're not going to have any emotional support?'

Becky closed her eyes and held back fresh tears at his accuracy. She'd done enough crying for one day. 'I'll cope.'

'If you marry me you won't have to cope. We can do it together.'

'Not this again?' She wriggled out of his hold and rolled onto her back.

'There is no reason our marriage would be like your parents'.'

'But we'd be doing it for the wrong reasons, the same as they did.'

'And what are the right reasons?'

'Love, fidelity and commitment,' she said in as strong a voice as she could manage. 'None of which you can offer me.'

He stared straight into her eyes. 'If we marry, you will have my commitment as a husband.'

'But no guarantee of fidelity.' She couldn't bring herself to mention love again, not when her heart had started thumping so erratically. 'I would have to give up the career I've dedicated my life to before I've even started while you get to continue yours as if nothing's changed, except you'd have a wife and baby tagging along.'

He breathed heavily through the tense silence that developed. 'You do realise I want to be a father to our child?'

'Yes, I do know that and I want it too.'

'Then tell me how it'll work if you're living with it on the other side of the world from me? I never knew my real father and the man who adopted me never wanted me. I don't want that for my child. My real father had no choice about raising me. God took that choice from him but I do have that choice and I'm going to take it. I want our child to know they're loved and wanted by both their parents.'

'You have a home in England. You could always base yourself there. It's only twenty miles from where I'll be working…' She let her words hang and held her breath.

'That's impossible,' he said shortly, shifting upright.

'Why?'

'You know why. I move from country to country with the polo seasons and on top of that I have my stables around the world and—'

'I know the extent of your empire,' she interrupted wearily. 'I know how busy your life is, and we can argue all night over whose job should take priority and maybe we'd even come to an agreement, but one thing we won't reach agreement on is marriage. You can be as involved in our child's upbringing as you want but I'm sorry, I'm not going to throw away my career so I can stand on the sidelines cheering you on like one of your fawning groupies and lose my career and independence for someone who can't be faithful. I've lost too much already.'

'You don't know that I won't be faithful.'

'And neither do you.'

'I know I would never do anything to hurt or humiliate you. While we are together I am yours alone.'

Tightening the robe around her waist, Becky sat up and cupped his clenched jaw in her hands and looked him in the eye. 'Then you can't blame me for refusing to marry you or uprooting my life for you. Marriage should be a lifetime commitment. When you tell me you'll be faithful only for as long as we're together, that proves to me that you don't trust yourself to sustain it for a lifetime.'

At the darkening of his features, she sighed and pressed a kiss to his taut lips. 'It's still early days for us. We're still getting to know each other. We both want to make it work as best we can. Let that be enough.'

The darkness firing from his clear brown eyes softened. 'Marriage is the only thing that will be enough for me, *bomboncita*. But you are right. It's still early days for us. I have plenty of time to change your mind.'

Then, before she could refute his impossible arrogance, he'd pulled her into a kiss of such seductive passion that any protest melted under its heat.

Becky sat well back from the action on the polo field. The dogs were gazing at her with begging eyes for titbits of the picnic food she'd brought along. The ground beneath her bottom shook as eight ponies and riders thundered past.

Today was the Delgado team's first practice of the Argentine season. From the noise, speed and aggression taking place on the field, the players were approaching it as if it were a competition game. As had been the case from the first game she'd watched, she only had eyes for Emiliano. He just looked so magnificent on the sleek Arabian horse—sorry, pony!—he was currently charging around on, and for a moment she visualised him as a warrior from bygone days leading the cavalry into war. If he'd been around in those bygone times, she had no doubt he would have been a natural warrior, leading from the front and commanding respect wherever he went.

She watched him now, riding furiously as he chased the comparatively tiny ball up the field, his mallet aimed and ready to strike, a member of the opposing team cantering alongside preparing to ride him off, but for the first time the tingles she usually experienced seeing his raw power in action were absent. For the first time, a nugget of fear had clutched at her heart and that fear was spreading.

The strictly enforced rules of polo were designed for the horses' safety. She remembered a wife from an opposing team telling her that so long as the riders were properly taught and maintained their discipline the dangers were minimal.

For the first time Becky truly comprehended that minimal didn't mean zero. Maybe it was the pregnancy working its hormonal magic on her but suddenly all she could see were the potential dangers of this chaotically exhilarating game.

Emiliano's birth father had been a polo player. He'd died in a freak horse accident.

There was a great roar from the other spectators—only a couple of dozen or so stable staff, but loud enough to be mistaken for a dozen rowdy stag parties—and when she opened her eyes she hadn't realised she'd closed she saw Emiliano had scored. There was little time to celebrate as one of the umpires signalled the end of the chukka and they all trooped off the field to change their ponies and Becky was able to refill lungs that had barely snatched a breath in seven minutes. When Emiliano rode past her, every female eye in the vicinity glued to him, and winked, she had to force her lips and cheeks to perform a smile but her heart was thundering as hard as the horses' hooves.

Terrified as to why she should feel so frightened, she pulled her phone out of her pocket, hoping to have received another work email to distract her. They'd been coming thick and fast in recent days, preparing her for when she started. Right then, any kind of email would be welcome but her inbox was empty.

This must be why normal people used social media. It was easier to hide away from your thoughts with visual distractions.

The skills she'd adopted to distract herself from unwelcome thoughts were dismantling. Her fears had grown too great, crowding a head too full to cope. And now she had another to add to them. Emiliano being hurt. More than a fear. A poker of ice freezing her insides.

Impulse had her pressing her mum's contact details and selecting the call button. It rang three times before going to voicemail.

Becky closed her eyes and listened to her mum's chirpy voice telling her to leave a message.

'Hi, Mum… It's me. Please call me. I miss you. I… I have something to tell you. It's important. Please. I don't want to tell you in a message. Call me back, *please…* I love you.'

When she disconnected the call, Rufus and Barney both had their heads on her lap and were gazing at her dolefully.

She rubbed both their heads and blinked back the threatening tears. 'At least you two love me,' she whispered, and wished Emiliano's face didn't immediately float through her mind at the mention of the word love.

# CHAPTER ELEVEN

BECKY CHECKED HER appearance for the hundredth time before leaving the room. Excitement laced her belly. She felt as if she could cha-cha down the wide corridors.

Emiliano had been so busy preparing for the forthcoming Argentine polo season that the only time they'd spent alone together in recent days had been in the bedroom. That morning, when he'd dragged himself out of bed after making love to her, he'd winked and told her he'd be taking her out for dinner that night.

She'd spent the day smiling at the irony that their first date should take place weeks after the conception of their child and refusing to think that the countdown to her return to England was speeding up. Only ten days left.

She'd deliberated for ages over what to wear. Their shopping trip for a dress for the party he was hosting—she couldn't believe that was happening in two days; time really was flying by—had seen her wardrobe mushroom by far more than a single dress. She'd returned from that shopping trip to find box upon box of beautiful clothing, all of which had fitted perfectly and all of which suited her, laid out in their bedroom.

The personal shopper who'd helped her find the party dress had obviously been much busier than she'd credited,

Emiliano every bit as sneaky and as wholeheartedly generous as she already knew he could be.

For their meal out, she'd eventually settled on a knee-length silver shift dress that sparkled under the movement of light and a pair of flat black ankle boots, and she hurried out of the room before she could change her mind again. She'd dithered so much about it, she wouldn't be surprised to find the sun had risen in the intervening period never mind set.

The look on Emiliano's face when she stepped into the living room made all the dillydallying worthwhile. He whistled, the gleam in his eyes making her blush.

'You look good enough to eat,' he murmured in an undertone when he reached her, setting off her second blush in as many seconds.

He could talk, she thought dizzily as she slipped her hand in his. The man could wear sackcloth and she'd still feel faint with longing. Seeing him dressed in navy trousers and a black shirt that stretched across his lean yet muscular body like a caress, his spicy cologne coiling into her airways, she could, quite frankly, eat him alive.

The dogs left in Paula's care for the evening, they left the ranch in the waiting car.

The driver dropped them off at a corner of a huge plaza in Luján province and a quick stroll later they were inside a large, dark restaurant with a vibe that lent itself to intimacy despite the open kitchen where chefs could be seen working as in a hive over wall-length griddles.

A flustered waitress who clearly recognised Emiliano led them to a small round table near the corner of the room, close to a small stage and an even smaller dance floor. Just off the side of the stage was a tiny round table with a glass of red wine in the centre.

'Does this place do entertainment?' Becky asked.

He winked. 'Wait and see.'

Their table was so small that there was no way to sit comfortably without their legs brushing, which was fine by Becky. Any excuse to touch Emiliano was fine by her, and she knew it was the same for him. How long this passion could be sustained was something she now refused to think about. She might have refused marriage but she'd committed herself to him. They had only ten days left until she returned to England and she didn't want to waste them worrying about things beyond her control.

The waitress returned with their drinks. 'Ready to order?' she asked breathlessly, making gooey eyes at Emiliano.

Smothering the urge to throw her mocktail in the waitress's face, Becky smiled brightly and got the waitress's attention. 'I would like the ham and cheese *empanadas* to start, then the two-hundred-and-fifty-gram sirloin with fries and salad and Portobello mushrooms on the side.'

She caught the amusement on Emiliano's face before he gave his own order.

Alone again, he leaned forward. 'Do I detect jealousy, *bomboncita*?'

'Not at all,' she lied airily. 'I just think it's mean to openly make eyes and flirt with someone who's clearly taken.'

He stroked her hand and murmured, 'So long as you know I only have eyes for you.'

'I know.' She smiled, and swallowed back the pang she always felt when she wondered how long that exclusivity would last.

He opened his mouth but whatever he'd been about to say was cut off by the buzzing of his phone.

'I'll turn it off,' he said apologetically, then his eyes

narrowed as he saw who'd messaged him. 'Sorry, let me read this. It's from Damián.'

He read quickly. A wide smile spread across his face.

'Good news?'

He nodded. 'Celeste's been arrested.' He put the phone back in his jacket pocket. 'I know she'll be released soon but at least the press were there to witness her humiliation. I can celebrate that.' He raised his glass, smiled again and took a large drink.

'You seem remarkably serene about your mother being a killer,' she remarked, thinking back to the night he'd turned up at her door in such torment.

Emiliano laughed. 'Not serene, *bomboncita*. Accepting. I admit it was a shock when I first learned what she'd done.' And Becky was the only person in the world who knew how deeply it had affected him. 'But after it sank in, it was no surprise. I've always known she's capable of anything.'

'But *murder*?'

'Celeste's world revolves around Celeste. She doesn't do anything that isn't for her own benefit. Take Damián's conception. When she agreed to marry Eduardo, she agreed to give him a blood heir. As soon as that agreement was fulfilled, she got herself sterilised.'

He laughed at the disbelieving expression on Becky's face. 'You can't be surprised that she has no maternal instincts. She upheld her side of the agreement and gave Eduardo a child, Damián, then washed her hands of the task of actually raising either of us. Being a hands-on mother was *not* part of their agreement.'

'You sound as if you admire her,' she said with a furrowed brow.

'There was an honesty to their marriage I always

admired,' he mused. 'They both knew where they stood. No lies.'

'That must be where you get your honesty from,' Becky said. That was one thing about Emiliano; he was always honest.

He grinned. 'As long as that's the only trait I inherited from her, I can live with that. But the more I think about her killing him, the more convinced I am that she felt my father had not upheld his end of their deal. She'd believed she would always have involvement in the Delgado Group. Giving control to Damián pushed her out of the sphere of influence and she refused to accept it. She is not a woman willing to accept no as an answer to anything.'

Another trait he'd inherited from her, Becky thought, but chose not to vocalise it.

'Do you still want her to be involved in your life?'

'No,' he said without hesitation. 'She's poison. Literally. If anything, knowing I have a legitimate reason to cut her from my life is a relief. I see now that I was only ever a pawn she used for her own ends. Even when she talked me into working for the Delgado Group, it was for her benefit, not mine—she assumed I would spy on Damián for her.'

'Did you?'

'No. I told her to do her own dirty work.'

The breathless waitress brought their first course to them and for a while they were both too busy eating to talk. Once the course had been cleared and fresh drinks given to them, Emiliano took her hand and pressed a kiss to her fingers. 'No more family talk tonight, okay? Let's just enjoy the evening and each other's company.'

'That sounds good to me,' she agreed softly. Becky always enjoyed his company, even during the times when she could throttle him.

She had another drink of her mocktail. The rush of feelings she had simply being with Emiliano meant she didn't miss drinking alcohol. Being with him felt very much like being drunk.

When their main courses were brought to them, she inhaled the wonderful scents and cut into her juicy steak. The knife sank through the meat as if it were softened butter. She popped her fork into her mouth and for the breath of a moment forgot everything as her mouth filled with heaven.

Emiliano cut into his ribeye with the same unabashed appreciation. When he looked at her after taking his first huge bite, something in her belly moved, like an intense tug, a fist clenching simultaneously in her chest.

Was this what her mother had experienced with Anthony? With all the others that had come before him? Were these the heady feelings that had seen her believe the worst of her only child and cut her from her life?

But they'd agreed no more family talk so she pushed thoughts of her mother aside and relaxed into a conversation about the dogs, the subject they'd first bonded over all that time ago.

Becky had just taken the last spoonful of her ice cream dessert when a group of musicians suddenly appeared in the darkly lit room and climbed the three steps onto the stage beside them. 'Is there going to be live music?'

He drained his glass of wine and smiled knowingly.

Pushing her empty bowl to one side, she shifted her chair next to Emiliano's for a better view and laced her fingers through his.

She nodded at a man with what looked like an accordion in his arms. 'Do you know what that is?'

'It's a bandoneon. A type of concertina.'

Beside the bandoneon player, three violinists, a cellist

and a guitarist were tuning their instruments. A flautist shuffled his chair to his preferred position.

Another round of drinks was brought to their table and then the restaurant's already dim lights faded further, the candles on the tables casting their fellow diners into silhouettes. The bandoneon player struck his first notes and the band began to play. The music was dark and sensuous, with sharp staccatos and dreamy sections pitched perfectly.

A spotlight appeared on the dance floor and a woman in a tight-fitting black dress with a slit all the way up to her hip appeared. She walked to the small round table on the side of the stage and, to the sound of the solo cellist, took a sip from the glass of wine.

A man wearing a shiny black suit and fedora approached her and put a hand to her shoulder. He spun her round to face him in one graceful movement.

Becky gasped and tightened her hold on Emiliano's fingers. He squeezed back, enjoying the way her eyes stayed glued on the sinuous dance unfolding before them. The hand not holding his absently strummed on the table in time to the music. His gaze roved between the dancers, whose bodies seemed to move as one while their legs flicked and clicked around each other in a blur, and the beautiful, incredibly sexy woman beside him.

She shifted in her seat and pressed closer to him. Her fragrant scent unleashed and dived into his senses. Heat, never far away when he was with Becky, released in a tidal wave to grab him by the throat and suddenly Emiliano found himself enveloped in a heavy cloud of desire but with a weight in his chest that made it impossible to breathe or move.

For all its sensuousness, the Argentine Tango, at its essence, was a lament to lost love. Watching the desperate passion unfold before him… For a moment Emiliano felt as if he was watching a prophecy.

He blinked the unsettling thought away and released his hold on Becky's hand so he could wrap his arm around her.

Eyes not leaving the dancers, she leaned into him, her hand automatically groping for his.

Fingers laced through hers, the unsettling melancholy crept back on him. Only another ten days until she flew back to England.

He tried to find his usual positive mind-set, reminding himself of the progress he'd made with her. They'd worked the dates out and they were in his favour. Becky would start her maternity leave at around the same time as the US polo season finished. He would fly straight back to the UK and she would move into his home there, which would give them around a month to create a nursery for their baby in one of the spare rooms before its birth. He'd finally got her agreement that when she moved into his UK home it would be permanent. In the meantime, she had agreed to fly out to Argentina to spend Christmas with him. He would fly over to England whenever practicable.

Many conversations with diaries and schedules and a good deal of willingness had seen them find common ground but the one issue he couldn't budge her on was marriage. It had reached the stage where if he brought the subject up she would walk out of the room rather than discuss it.

He knew what she was waiting for. What was stopping him from saying the words?

Was it the control he was as guilty as the rest of the Delgados for craving?

Fear?

He didn't know and right then he didn't care. Screw

stealth. He'd proven himself useless at it. There was only one way to get Becky's agreement to marry him.

'If you marry me, I promise to be faithful for the rest of our lives,' he murmured. 'I will make that promise to you.'

She stiffened and tilted her head to stare at him with wide eyes. 'Is it a promise you can keep?'

'If that's the promise I need to make for you to agree, then I will make it and I will keep it, however hard it may be. I will do that for you.' He stroked her cheek and rubbed his nose to hers. 'Don't answer me now. Think seriously about it. Give me your answer after the party. If the answer's no then I will never mention marriage again. I give you my word.'

A voice whispered in his head that if her answer was no, then he would perform a lament of his own…

Emiliano brought Diggity to a stop and watched the army of people coordinate perfectly to heave the marquee upright. Rows of large vans were parked close by, filled with tables and chairs, and in the distance catering vans approached. In a few hours, the vans would be gone and the marquee would be ready for the two hundred or so people coming to celebrate the end of a successful English polo season and the beginning of the Argentine one. He wondered if they'd be better behaved than they'd been at the last party he'd thrown, at the end of the US season at his home in Palm Springs. Very doubtful, he thought with a wry smile, before tapping his ankle into Diggity's flank and setting off again, this time back to the stables.

Spirits were high when he returned. The practice sessions the team had had for the new season were proving their worth. Nicky, the new player he'd poached from a rival team, was fitting in smoothly, his horses even more so. Emiliano's own horses had recovered well from the journey from England.

He should be raring for the new season to start but his spirits were flat. Becky hadn't mentioned his latest proposal but he knew she was considering it. She hadn't dismissed it out of hand. He wanted to take that as a good sign, but with Becky…

He sighed. He could never take her thoughts or actions for granted.

Feeling too out of sorts to mix with people, he rode back out of the stables to one of his vast open fields at a canter. Riding his beasts at speed was one of life's greatest joys. One of Emiliano's biggest regrets was being born a foot too tall to be a jockey. He would have loved racing; coaxing his horse past all the others, leaving rivals in his wake and smashing past the finish line. Truth was, he loved winning. On a horse, he was invincible. He had a natural affinity with the creatures, which had allowed him to dominate the polo scene for so many years. Before he retired he wanted a year when his team, with him at the helm, won every major cup competition in England, Argentina and the US. He'd won them all individually but never the clean sweep. This year he'd already won the most prestigious English one and it had been a bitter realisation that he couldn't send a cutting of himself holding the trophy aloft to his father.

He'd done that for the past decade. While he'd stopped caring what his adoptive father or anyone else thought of him, whatever success he'd had, he'd made sure Eduardo had known. His three Argentine Open cups had all been couriered to him.

But now Eduardo, the man who'd adopted him then thrown him aside as if he were dirt, was dead and, for the first time, Emiliano could acknowledge the hunger that had driven him to succeed for so long had dimmed.

When had that happened? Eduardo had been dead for months before the English season started, and he'd approached that with his usual gusto.

He didn't know what was wrong with him, only that something was. It was inside him. Something off-kilter. Something that felt very much like fear.

# CHAPTER TWELVE

BECKY CAME OUT of the woods with the dogs and found the sun beaming down. Emiliano would be happy. He'd been concerned about the weather changing for the evening's party but, for the moment, there was not a puff of cloud marring the vast blue skies above. She didn't want to think about the autumnal weather she'd be flying back to when she returned to England. She should be there already, settling into her rented flat and preparing for her new job which started in exactly eight days.

Emiliano's promise of fidelity if she married him played constantly in her mind. A huge part of her wanted to say yes. So long as he respected her career, they could make it work. Maintaining a long-distance marriage wouldn't be easy but they'd already reached agreement on so much. They could make it work.

So what was stopping her from saying yes?

She was mere paces away from the ranch when her phone vibrated. Snatching it out of her pocket, her heart leapt to see her mother had finally messaged her back.

Hands shaking, she walked up the steps and sat on the swing chair.

And then she read it and the hope that had clutched her heart turned to despair. A whole week she'd prayed for a response. Seven whole days. And this was what she received?

A burst of fury suddenly blazed through her veins and, fingers working of their own accord, she typed out a response and pressed send before she had time to think about it. Her response consisted of two words: *I'm pregnant*.

Another burst of fury crashed through her at her stupidity in sending the message and, in a fit of pique, she hurled the phone through the air as hard as she could.

Emiliano, who'd returned to the ranch for food, had seen Becky, head bowed over her phone, clearly too caught up in whatever she was dealing with to notice his approach.

Crouching down to pick up the offending phone, which had landed only a foot from him, he took another two steps closer before she finally noticed him. He swiftly put his hands in the air. 'Whatever it is, I didn't do it.'

Her taut red, angry face softened to see him. A tiny splutter of laughter fell from her lips.

'Sorry,' she muttered, 'I didn't see you there.'

'So I gathered. Unless you really did see me and just don't want to admit you have a lousy aim?'

'I have that too.'

He handed her phone back before sitting beside her and taking her hand. 'What's wrong?'

She shrugged.

'Becky?'

'Mum's messaged me.' She took a long breath then swiped at her phone. She brought the message up and handed it to him.

His heart thumped as he read.

I thought I'd made it clear that I will not listen to your lies. Anthony and I are very happy. The last thing we need is for you to inflict more of your jealous spite on us. Get your head out of your books and find yourself a man and STOP trying to steal mine.

'Well, that's me told,' she said with a brave shrug.

'You tried to make contact with her?'

She nodded. 'I left her a message during your first practice session.'

'You never mentioned it.'

She shrugged again. 'I was scared to build my hopes up. Guess I was right.'

'She really thinks you're trying to steal her husband?'

'Looks like it.' She laughed morosely. 'She used to tease me about my reluctance to date. I would bite my tongue to stop myself shouting that the only way I could cope with the loss of my family and with my parents being at war and my mum turning into a cougar overnight was by throwing myself into the books she's now so dismissive of. It would have been easier if they'd split when I was a toddler. I wouldn't have gone from being a loved daughter to a rival. She's infatuated with him.'

Emiliano ran his fingers through his hair. He didn't know if he'd felt worse the other week when she'd bawled her eyes out or now, seeing her so wan and so utterly defeated. At least when she'd cried he'd been able to hold her and comfort her. Now, he just felt useless.

But there was one thing he could do that might help.

'I understand why she chose him over you,' he admitted heavily, and felt her freeze beside him. 'But I need you to understand that, as personal as it feels, it is not about you. It's about her. And one day she will come to her senses.'

She turned her head slowly to him, eyes wide. She gave one large blink.

'The truth will come to her sooner or later. It always does.' Emiliano dragged his hand down his face then leaned forward to rest his elbows on his thighs. 'The reason my time at the Delgado Group ended so badly was because I fell in love with a gold-digging con-artist.'

Becky almost jumped at the unexpected admission. Emiliano had been in *love*…?

'Her name was Adriana. I hired her as my PA. I'd been given control of a major investment fund—I won't bore you with the details but collectively the funds in it were worth tens of billions. I was new to the game and needed assistance from someone already in the industry.

'Adriana had an impeccable résumé…' he looked at her with a faint smile '…one of the reasons I don't bother with them any more. It was love at first sight for both of us. She was beautiful and clever and she played me like a pro. I wanted to go public but she always resisted, which just added to her allure. I thought she wanted to keep it special between us but she was protecting herself because, while I was imagining our future, she was hacking into my work accounts and performing a heist of such nerve that I admit to having a grudging respect for it.'

'What did she do?' Becky breathed, half afraid to hear.

'She syphoned exactly four hundred and ninety-eight million dollars from the accounts I had control of. She did it so subtly that it took weeks for the theft to be discovered but by then it was too late—she'd gone too. We'd spent a weekend together and I swear I had no idea anything was up. She went home on the Sunday evening, kissed me goodbye as normal and that was the last I saw her. When she didn't turn up for work I was out of my mind with worry. I went to her apartment and it was empty. She'd disappeared overnight. It took weeks for me to learn she'd left with half a billion dollars, all neatly deposited into an offshore tax haven I couldn't touch.'

'Oh, my God,' she whispered.

'I learned much later that I wasn't her first victim. She'd spent a year in an English prison for defrauding two companies. I'm sure there're others.'

'So what happened? Was she arrested?'

His eyes locked back onto hers. 'You're the first person I've told this story to.'

She just stared at him.

'I hired some private detectives to find her but I didn't give them reasons. They tracked her to a private island in the Caribbean in a territory with no extradition treaties. It's a criminals' paradise. She's still there, living the high life on stolen money…albeit surrounded by criminals. And she knows that I know where she is. I made sure of that. I have people watching her. She will never leave. She's too frightened of the consequences.'

She was almost afraid to ask. 'What will they be?'

'I've a file as thick as my arm with the trail she left. There's enough evidence in it to have her sent down for twenty years.'

Swallowing back the nausea churning in her belly and blinking away the blurring in her eyes, Becky forced her thoughts away from Emiliano being in love. 'So you didn't tell your family about it?'

He sighed and rubbed the nape of his neck. 'When the losses were discovered, their first assumption was that I'd messed up. I was still trying to unravel the trail Adriana had left. I knew she'd had something to do with it but at that point I had no proof. I would have enlisted their help but all they did was shout and rail at me, assuming I was at fault. Celeste had convinced them to hire me—she'd damn well convinced me to work for them too—and for them this was confirmation that I should never have been given a chance. I was booted out and paid off to keep quiet. They couldn't afford for it to come out that half a billion of their clients' monies had disappeared.'

'They kept it a secret?' she asked in astonishment.

'As far as I know, they paid the funds back from their

private accounts. I would have felt guilty for that but, as far as I was concerned, they could go to hell.' His smile was so cold she shivered. 'It just proved they'd never trusted me and that they'd been waiting for me to mess up. So screw them. I'd worked my backside off in an environment I hated and I think part of me did it because deep down I craved their approval. I wanted them to accept me as one of them. My mistake for trusting them when I should have known better. Never trust anything that walks on two feet.'

She couldn't think of a single thing to say. It was too much. The figures he'd mentioned—half a billion dollars!—the way his family had automatically assumed the worst of him and the cold war that had erupted in the Delgado family because of it…

And still, with all that racing through her head, the most shocking admission was that Emiliano had once been in love.

'I tell you this to give you hope,' Emiliano said quietly, although there was a part of him that thought Becky's mother should join Adriana in hell for the way she'd treated her daughter. But Becky loved her. She was pregnant and needed her mother. 'Love makes fools of us. It blinds us. And then one day you open your eyes and you can see again. Your mother's eyes will open to the truth and when they do she will need you. Keep the door open for her and she will come back to you…but when she does, resist the temptation to say *I told you so*,' he added with a rueful smile. 'She will already know.'

Her lips pulled in and she took a long inhalation as she considered his words. 'I hope you're right.'

'I am.'

She gave a tiny snigger which lightened the weight compressing his chest at making an admission he, in his pride, had vowed to never share with anyone. Then her eyes met his and the brief flare of amusement in them dimmed. 'I'm sorry you had to go through that alone.'

He grimaced. 'It was the worst time of my life. I'd been made a fool of. My ego smashed. I still don't know if I felt worse over Adriana's theft or my family's reaction to it. Their reaction would have been the same if I'd told them the truth, that the money had been lost through theft and not negligence. They would have blamed me for not listening to their warnings about gold-diggers.' He blew out a long puff of air. 'I hated the lot of them.'

'And now?'

He considered this. 'My father is dead. Our differences will never be resolved. I could blame Celeste for stealing that opportunity from us but I would never have taken it. He never loved me and nothing I did or said could have changed that. But I still have my brother and, as much as the rage at his treatment still bites me, I know I have to take my share of the blame where he's concerned. Why give someone the benefit of the doubt when he's been consistently horrible to you your entire life?'

'Maybe you should tell him,' she suggested softly. 'Put the past to bed once and for all.'

He rubbed the nape of his neck more vigorously. It was one thing admitting his blind stupidity to Becky but to do the same with Damián? 'What good will it do to rehash the past?'

'To stop the same mistakes being made in the future. From what you've told me, the pair of you are trying to rebuild your relationship after a lifetime of mutual hatred that your mother instigated. I don't see how you can do that properly if the past still has a hold on you.'

'It doesn't.'

'Doesn't it?'

The scepticism in her voice rankled.

'No,' he stated firmly. 'It doesn't. I have reached that greatly revered state of acceptance. I accept my birth father died before I could talk. I accept my adoptive father hated me. I accept that my mother is a psychopath. And I accept that my issues with my brother, although fed by our mother, were all caused by my jealousy. I know the mistakes I made and I will not repeat them. I never do. I learn from them and then I move on.' He lifted his head and flashed his teeth. 'Just as I did learn something from my time at the Delgado Group other than to never trust anyone.'

'Oh?'

'I learned how to play the stock markets. The minute they kicked me out I put that new knowledge into action. That's what I meant when I told you I used the first ten million to get the business rolling. I invested it. In one month that ten million became fifty million. Everything grew from there.'

The buzzing in Becky's head started up again as she thought about the assets he had: the homes, the jets, the art galleries, the world-class stables across the world, the exorbitant costs of running a polo team that travelled *en masse* with the seasons, never mind his racing and dressage horses… Until that moment, it had never occurred to her that the lifestyle he led and the outrageously high overheads his businesses incurred could not be funded with the income from winning races and competitions and stud fees.

But his Midas touch for creating money wasn't the cause of the buzzing in her head. It was the reiteration of his unwillingness to trust people and, for one long moment, she felt a real stab of hatred for Adriana. Ten years ago she hadn't just stolen money from Emiliano. The knock-on effect had stolen his ability to love and trust.

And it was in that moment that the truth Becky had been denying to herself slapped her in the face.

She loved Emiliano. That was what stopped her from agreeing to marriage. She loved him.

All the protections she'd believed she'd placed around her heart to stop him from having the power to break it had been an illusion. She'd given him her heart the night he'd sought sanctuary from his demons with her.

'Becky?'

He was staring down at her, brow furrowed. She hadn't noticed him get to his feet.

'Sorry,' she murmured. 'I was miles away.'

Unconvinced, he put a hand on her forehead. 'Are you not feeling well?'

'I'm fine. Just a little tired.' She managed a smile. 'Probably hormones. I'll have a nap and then I'll be rested for the party.'

He studied her with the beautiful clear eyes she'd come to love. 'Shall I bring you something up? Food? Mint tea?'

His evident concern was enough to make her want to weep. 'I'll get something later. But thank you.'

And as she climbed the stairs, aware of his penetrating stare still upon her, her hatred for the faceless Adriana and the whole rotten Delgado family filled her throat with bile.

Between them, they hadn't just stolen Emiliano's money and his ability to love and trust. They'd stolen Becky's future. Because she saw no way she could have forever with him now.

Emiliano finished his lunch, answered some emails, checked that the caterers who'd set up near the marquee were on schedule, then headed up to check on Becky. He was worried about her. She'd been fine one minute, then her face had drained of colour, almost as if she'd had a shock. He supposed that was how pregnancy worked. It must take up a lot of a woman's energy.

The curtains were drawn, darkening the room to a sepia hue. Becky was curled up under the covers, fast asleep.

He sat on the bed and gently stroked her hair. How damn beautiful was this woman. Every time he looked at her he saw something new that made his heart clench. This time it was a tiny mole on her eyelid, and he resisted the urge to press a kiss to it.

When, he wondered, would his desire for her fade? Would he ever reach the stage where he could walk into a room and see her there and not be filled with the compulsion to devour her whole?

She stirred and mumbled something. He wished he could see her dreams. Read her thoughts. Wished he could use telepathy to input thoughts into her beautiful head that proved he would do his damned best to be a good father and a good husband. Make her take that leap of faith.

Her eyes opened. They locked onto his, an emotion he didn't recognise ringing from them, but one that pierced straight into his chest.

She unfurled a naked arm from under the sheets and hooked it round his neck with a sigh. Their lips met in a kiss so relaxed and soft it felt as if he were drugged. Slowly, the sweet warmth of her breath seeped into his airways, rousing the last of his senses not already awoken to her, and he gently tugged the bedding off her so he could lie beside her.

With the same unhurried energy, together they stripped his clothes off him, kissing and stroking each other with a tender desire that burned his heart as much as his loins.

Their eyes stayed locked together when he entered her, fingers tightly entwined, lips brushing.

He would never get over the sensation of making love

to Becky or be able to put into words how different it felt, a difference that couldn't be accounted for by the absence of a condom. Although his desire scorched him, making love to her was far more than about sexual release. It was fundamental, as necessary to him as breathing, the need to touch her and be touched by her.

When they were finally spent, Becky's head on his chest, her body pressed against him, Emiliano closed his eyes and took a deep breath to counter the rising trepidation that she still hadn't given him an answer to his latest proposal.

As alien as patience was to him, he must find some. He'd only told her to wait until after the party to answer him to prove he wasn't the bulldozer she kept accusing him of being. He hadn't actually expected her to make him wait that long. Every hour that passed without her answer felt longer than the last.

# CHAPTER THIRTEEN

THE THREE-ACRE PRIVATE back garden of Emiliano's ranch had been transformed into a spring wonderland. Music pumped from the huge marquee taking centre-stage, tables and chairs beneath the canvas and sprawled across the lawn. The scent of barbecuing meat filled the air. One thing Becky had learned during her time in Argentina was that every day was a potential barbecue day.

The back doors of the ranch had been left open too, Emiliano being a generous host who never stood on ceremony when it came to entertaining. For those with children—every employee was invited to bring their family—beds were available if naps or downtime was needed, and specially employed babysitters were on site so the parents could continue partying. Those who didn't live in the staff quarters, including his polo team and all their staff, were welcome to stay the night.

Within two hours of it all starting, Becky had decided this was the best party she'd ever been to. It wasn't just the copious amounts of food available or the even more copious amount of drink—she, of course, stuck to soft drinks—keeping everyone refreshed and in high spirits, but the atmosphere in general. She was determined not to let her aching heart spoil things for Emiliano or anyone. The Delgado team and all the supporting staff had earned this night.

Seeing people she normally only saw in jodhpurs or jeans strutting around in pretty dresses and tieless suits made her glad Emiliano had talked her into buying a proper party outfit. Being on the receiving end of many admiring looks, she felt herself blossom like the pink Chinese flowers imprinted on her white dress. She was glad too that he'd convinced her to buy a pair of dusky pink heels to complement it. Compared to some of the women tottering around on heels that should really be called stilts, hers were nothing, but the extra two inches made her feel more elegant than she'd ever felt in her life. Now all she had to do was learn to walk in them!

Even the weather was holding. There were some pretty ominous-looking clouds in the distance, but to her untrained eye they seemed far enough away that they wouldn't disrupt the party any time soon.

'Coming to dance?' Louise asked as she joined her, clutching a cocktail.

Becky laughed. 'I can't dance.'

'Nor can anyone else.' Sliding her arm through Becky's, Louise bore her off as if they were friends. Which, Becky thought with a little burst of happiness, perhaps they were.

About to enter the marquee, she caught sight of Emiliano impressing a group of small children with his juggling skills. It impressed Becky too. She couldn't juggle one ball never mind three.

He caught her eye, winked and magically produced a fourth ball to juggle with. The children clapped manically.

Emiliano's impromptu performance finished with, he bowed to his audience and followed Becky into the marquee, promising the children trailing after him that he would perform again after he'd had a break.

Helping himself to a beer from the bar inside the marquee, he propped himself on a stool and watched Becky dance while he drank and tried not to laugh at her enthusiastic if graceless movements. Tempting though it was to join her, he knew perfectly well that should he press his body close to hers he would feel compelled to drag her off to the bedroom for an hour. He thought it best to wait a while longer for that particular selfish delight.

Moments later, she kicked her shoes off with a shout of laughter and her movements became a little less robotic.

Shoes on or off, dance moves graceful or not, nothing could dim her beauty. Tonight she shone and, from the reactions that had followed her every move since the revellers had arrived, he was far from the only man to have noticed.

For only the second time since he'd met her, she'd abandoned her stock uniform of jeans and a shirt, in their place a beautiful white Bardot dress that exposed her slender shoulders and flared out at her waist to fall just above her knees. The beautiful chestnut hair had been set free from its usual ponytail to fall in tumbling waves over her shoulders and down her back. Subtle make-up and hooped silver earrings completed the feminine package. His heart throbbed every time he looked at her. Every part of him throbbed.

As if she could feel his gaze upon her, her eyes darted to meet his. There was a moment of stillness before the most beautiful smile lit her face. Spellbound, he continued to stare, the beats of his thumping heart the only sound he could hear, but then the spell was broken when Juan, his stable manager, swayed over to her, took hold of her hips and began to dance suggestively with her.

For the breath of a moment, the world seemed to go off-kilter. Thick heat filled his head while a nasty rancid taste filled his mouth.

Juan leaned forward to whisper in her ear. She smiled, shook her head and took a subtle step back, and Emiliano's world resettled…which was the moment when a pair of arms suddenly flew around his neck and a pair of pumped-up rouged lips parked an enormous kiss on his mouth.

'There you are,' Jacinda purred into his face. 'I've been looking everywhere for you.'

Concealing a groan, Emiliano disentangled her arms from his neck. Jacinda, a glamorously beautiful model, had married one of his team mates, Facundo, a year ago. At their wedding she'd trapped Emiliano in a corridor of the hotel the reception was being held in and come on to him like a rash. He'd firmly told her to sober up, to which she'd laughed and said she and Facundo had agreed to an open marriage. That hadn't particularly shocked him—he knew plenty of couples who enjoyed open marriages, but on her own wedding night? That just smacked of disrespect.

He'd done his best to give her a wide berth since then but she was like a fox hound, always sniffing him out, always trying to tempt him. Before, he'd always resisted out of loyalty to Facundo. Now, he found there was nothing to resist. Even if she hadn't been married to a man he considered a friend as well as an employee, he would have felt nothing apart from irritation that she was distracting him from watching Becky.

Fixing a smile to his face, he let her pull a stool against his and chatter away while trying to keep one eye on the dance floor. When she put her hand on his thigh he removed it without comment. When she did it a third time, his patience finally snapped.

'I think your husband's looking for you,' he said pointedly before getting off the stool and walking away.

He'd lost sight of Becky on the now crowded dance floor and had to crane his neck before he spotted a flash of chestnut hair.

To hell with it, he thought. There was no one else he wanted to spend time with. Why not dance with Becky? If they needed to slip off for a quick bout of lovemaking then so what? It was his party. They could do what they liked.

Before he could reach her, though, his polo team appeared with shot glasses. Together they drank to a successful season then drank again for luck to the new season, and then Nicky, his newest signing, waylaid him further by enthusiastically telling him about a young mare with exceptional potential he'd heard about that morning.

By the time Emiliano had extracted himself and reached the dance floor, Becky had gone.

Becky danced until her feet cried for mercy. And then she danced some more. She did not want to leave this dance floor. She didn't want to step outside and deal with the emotions she'd tried so hard to squash but were now threatening to erupt. This was a party. She needed to keep it together.

But it was getting harder to breathe. The air had become suffocating.

Not bothering to hunt for her shoes, last seen pilfered by a group of small children prancing around in them, she pushed her way through the heaving crowd and out onto the lawn.

She didn't know if she'd overheated from all the dancing but it felt even more stifling outside. She looked up and saw the thick clouds had finally reached them. The vast skies usually filled with twinkling stars had closed in on her too.

'Becky!'

Turning wildly, she found a handful of the grooms sitting on a wooden table drinking an enormous jug of cocktail through straws. She raised a hand in a wave then set off in the other direction, away from the crowds and noise. From the splashes and squeals echoing in the distance, a group of partygoers had decided now was the perfect time for a swim and, as she thought that, she remembered Emiliano saying he'd employed lifeguards for that very reason and increased her pace.

She didn't want to think of Emiliano. She didn't want to think of anything. All she wanted was a few minutes alone to breathe, pull herself together and then return to the party and carry on pretending that nothing was wrong.

She walked aimlessly, lost in thoughts she wished she could hide from until she found herself at the stables.

Usually a hub of activity by day, at night the stables were peaceful, allowing the horses to rest. She knew a couple of grooms had been unfortunate enough to draw the short straw to do the evening's night shift, just as she knew they would be given a substantial bonus by Emiliano for having to miss out on the fun.

She could scream. No matter where she went, there was always something that made her think of him.

Why hadn't she trusted her instincts and returned to England when she was supposed to? She could have spent the rest of her life in relatively happy denial.

Instead, she'd stayed and given her love for him air to breathe and now she was consigning herself to a life following in her mother's footsteps.

One day she was going to look at Emiliano and hate him, not as her mum had come to hate her dad for being the wrong husband but for breaking her heart. Because, marriage or not, Emiliano was going to break her heart.

And one day he would look at her and hate her too for forcing a promise of fidelity he would never have made if he hadn't wanted their child so badly.

A gentle neigh filled the air and Bertie poked his head out of the open part of his stable door. Walking to him, she stroked his kind head and was gratified when he nuzzled into her hand.

What wonderful creatures horses were. And how intuitive. But then she saw Bertie's stablemate, Don Giovanni, lying on the clean floor, barely bothering to conceal his disinterest at her presence, and stifled a laugh that could easily have turned into a wail if a large raindrop hadn't landed on her nose.

She looked up again at the dark, heavy clouds, and this time she did let out a wail.

More fat raindrops fell on her. Just as she was thinking she should take shelter in one of the empty stables, lights appeared in the distance. To her relief, they were headlights, and they were coming her way.

The pickup truck stopped feet away from her. She shielded her eyes from the glare of its lights and so couldn't see who was driving until it was too late and Emiliano jumped out.

'What the hell are you doing here?' he demanded as he strode towards her. 'I've been looking everywhere for you.'

She shrank away from the fury etched on his face and hugged herself.

'Everyone's looking for you!'

She wiped off another splatter of rain from her face. 'What for?'

Spitting out a curse, he pulled his phone out of his pocket, pressed the buttons quickly and put it to his ear. Eyes not leaving her face, he spoke rapidly into it.

'I've called the cavalry off,' he said tightly when he'd finished the call.

'I've only been gone twenty minutes,' she protested, bewildered at his anger.

'Lottie saw you walk off an hour ago!' he shouted.

An hour? How was that possible? But any words she could have said in response would have been drowned by the heavens above them finally opening. In seconds she was soaked to the skin.

'Get in the truck,' he ordered.

But the emotions she'd fought so desperately hard to restrain suddenly erupted from her with the same force as the lashing rain. Heart pounding, emotions careering violently inside her, she took a step back and shook her head. 'Go back to the party. I'll join you when I'm ready.'

'Get in the damn truck or I will throw you in it.'

'Please,' she begged. 'Just leave me alone.'

Features as dark as the storm thrashing down on them, he took three quick strides to her, folded his arms across his chest and leaned down to snarl in her face, 'In the truck. *Now.*'

Anger suddenly punched through all the other emotions battering her and she snarled right back at him, '*Fine,*' before sidestepping around him and marching furiously to the truck. What other choice did she have? Either she got in willingly or he'd carry out his threat.

Emiliano's legs being so much longer than hers, he reached the passenger door before she did and yanked it open for her. The moment her bottom touched the seat, he slammed the door shut then strode to the driver's side and climbed in beside her.

Without saying a word, he reached into the compartment behind the front seats and pulled out a towel, which he shoved onto her lap, then turned the vehicle's heating on.

An age passed where the only sound was the muffled deluge pelting the vehicle and their ragged, angry breaths.

Fury at being treated like a child overriding the despair that had brought her to the stables, Becky was loath to accept anything from him, but her wet skin was starting to feel chilled. Mutely, she rubbed the towel over her sopping hair then leaned forward to wrap it across her back and hold it tightly under her chin like a cloak.

'Ready to talk?' he asked roughly.

'I asked you to leave me alone,' she snapped. 'Why couldn't you respect that?'

'What, leave the mother of my child to catch pneumonia?'

And that was all he saw her as, she acknowledged with angry pain even though it was confirmation of what she already knew.

He thumped the steering wheel in the silence, making her jump. 'I want you to tell me why you thought it was a good idea to abandon the party to walk *barefoot* in the pitch-black in the middle of a storm.'

She'd forgotten about her bare feet. Now he mentioned them she could feel the sting, but it was only a distant, dull ache.

'It wasn't raining when I left.'

'Anything could have happened to you!'

'On your private estate? Hardly.'

'Do you think scorpions care about boundaries? Or snakes? Or spiders?' he snarled. 'This isn't England. Our wildlife is dangerous. Damn it, there was a report of a jaguar on land only twenty miles from here recently.'

'I'm sorry if I caused anyone to worry,' she said stiffly.

'Why did you go?' he demanded. 'I assume it's to do with me from the way you just behaved. What made you do something so reckless and stupid?'

And, like a balloon deflating in one long puff, her anger drained out of her. Emiliano had every right to be angry. If he'd disappeared into the dead of night she would have been frantic.

'I really am sorry,' she said in a softer tone. 'I only meant to clear my head. I didn't realise I'd been gone for so long.'

Knowing he needed to get a handle on his temper, Emiliano pinched the bridge of his nose. He couldn't remember ever being so gripped by fear. He'd been worried when Becky had gone off for a ride on gentle Bertie but that had been nothing to the icy terror in discovering she'd disappeared into the black void.

'Just tell me why you left.'

'I saw you with that woman. At the bar.'

Gobsmacked, Emiliano stared at her, so many thoughts and emotions racing through him that it took a moment to separate them. 'You're talking about Jacinda?'

'I don't know her name. I'm talking about the woman who was all over you like a rash.'

'Then you are talking about Jacinda. She's married to Facundo.'

'She's married?' She covered her face. 'Does Facundo know his wife fancies you?'

'I have no idea.' But he had an idea of what Becky was implying. 'But let me assure you, when she couldn't keep her hands to herself I extracted myself from the situation.'

Just as he'd seen Becky neatly sidestep away from an amorous Juan on the dance floor. Had he assumed the worst? he thought angrily. No, he had not. Sure, there had been a tiny hint of something that could be construed as jealousy but at no point had that been directed at Becky herself.

He hadn't assumed the worst about Becky because he trusted her. It was a revelation that sucker-punched him.

'I know.' Her voice was devoid of emotion. 'I was watching.'

'If you know I gave her no encouragement, why run away?'

A fresh wave of pain-filled heat washed through her. The first time it had struck, Becky had been on the dance floor. She'd felt someone watching her and that someone had been Emiliano. The expression she'd seen on his face had cut through the noise of the music. There had been so much more than desire in that look. There had been tenderness too, enough to fill her heart with sudden hope. In that one tiny moment of time she'd thought she'd seen her own feelings mirrored back at her.

Which was why the pain of seeing her future had hit her so hard.

'Because I saw the day when you would *want* to give encouragement.' Jacinda had thrown herself at him and the smidgeon of foolish hope in Becky's heart had died.

'You think I would have an affair with a friend's wife?' he asked through tightly gritted teeth.

'No, I don't believe you'd do that but everywhere you go women throw themselves at you. Temptation travels with you.'

'Right, so you think I'm going to hook up with any woman who bats her lashes as me so long as she isn't a friend's wife? How many times have I told you? For as long as we're together, I will be faithful. Marry me and I will give you fidelity for life. What more do you want? For me to etch it in blood?'

'But that's just it.' She struggled to keep her tone even, every word feeling as if it was being dragged across a jagged blade. 'And that's why I can't marry you, even with that promise.'

His eyes snapped onto hers.

She tried to keep her words on an even keel but they fell from her lips like a runaway train. 'Sooner or later, all that's new and fresh and exciting between us will become stale and ordinary, but those women will still be new and exciting, and there are thousands of them scattered across the world, ready to bat their lashes and drop their knickers for you, and you will find yourself bound by a promise you never wanted to make. You said yourself you know it'll be a hard promise to keep! You'll want to act but your honour won't let you and then we'll be stuck in a marriage that's the worst of what our parents had—you'll be compelled to keep our deal just as your parents always stuck to theirs, but you'll come to resent me for tying you down and clipping your wings, just as my mother resented my father, and then that resentment will turn to hate and all that's good between us will be gone and our child will be the one to suffer for it.'

There was a long moment of stillness before he thumped the steering wheel again. '*Dios bendito*, you really do think the worst of me. You see a woman approach me and suddenly you're Nostradamus? You can predict my future thoughts and feelings?' His glare made her quail. 'You have a habit of doing that and it's never in my favour. Do you have any idea what that feels like? All my life, my father assumed the worst of me, my brother too, and now I learn that you...*you*, of all people...that your opinion *still* is no better than theirs. I have bent over backwards for you. I have treated you with respect and done my damnedest to compromise when others in my position would have used their wealth and power to ensure their child was in their care and under their protection, whatever the mother's opinion on it. I offer to marry you and when you run out of excuses you invent a future as an excuse.'

'I've agreed to move in with you when you return to England.' Her head was spinning again at the way the conversation had suddenly turned to be all about her. 'That hasn't changed.'

'Yes, it damn well has. You think I'm prepared to settle for crumbs? Live as a family for a few months each year but only when I'm in your country? Everything has to be on your terms. You'll have me begging like a dog to see my own child because your precious career comes before everything.'

'That's not fair!' she protested, her own fury regaining a foothold. 'I would never do that and how you can say that with a straight face when you refuse to consider retiring from a career where you've already achieved so much beggars belief. It's not as if you need to work any more—you have more money than a small country—but I've barely started and you want me to throw away all those years of work and dedication for someone who will never love or trust me because he's too stuck in the past to let it go.'

'You say *I'm* stuck in the past when you've just spouted all that prophecy rubbish?'

'None of which you denied! How can we have a real marriage without love? We *can't*, and without it we're doomed to repeat the mistakes our parents made. If you were ever capable of love and trust, Adriana stamped on it and the rest of your rotten family killed it. You're so damn cynical about *everything*. You don't want to marry me. You just want convenient access to our child.'

For the longest time they said nothing more, the only

sound in the truck's cabin their laboured breaths. The fury blazing from Emiliano's brown eyes would have scorched her if her own fury hadn't acted as a foil.

And then he whipped his gaze from her and, jaw clenched, turned the engine on. 'Put your seat belt on.'

# CHAPTER FOURTEEN

REALISING EMILIANO WAS about to start driving, Becky hurried to obey. The moment her seat belt clicked into place, he did a sweeping reverse and set off, windscreen wipers on the fastest setting to fight against the deluge still pouring down.

In caustic silence, they returned to the ranch. He screeched the truck to a stop and got out, slamming his door behind him.

For the first time since she'd met him, he didn't do the chivalrous thing of opening her door.

Covering her head with the towel for protection from the rain, she hurried up the steps behind him. They both came to an abrupt halt at the noise that greeted them when he opened the door.

Much of the party had moved indoors, out of the rain. People were *everywhere*.

His eyes briefly found hers. He raised them, indicating they should go upstairs.

Ignoring the people trying to catch his attention, Emiliano climbed the stairs two at a time. Barney and Rufus spotted them and came bounding up to say hello before dashing back off to scavenge more dropped food.

Previous experience had taught him to lock his bedroom when he threw a party and it was something of a relief to get inside and close out the noise of revelry.

Becky hovered by the door, her beautiful green eyes wary. The soaking her dress had suffered had turned it transparent. Through it, her strapless white bra and matching knickers were visible. He wished he'd noticed before and warned her to wrap the towel around herself when they'd cut through the house. She'd be embarrassed if she knew.

Raising his gaze to the ceiling, he took a huge breath. 'Why don't you have a shower? You're soaked.'

She bit into her bottom lip before nodding and disappearing into the bathroom. He closed his eyes hearing the door lock behind her.

Alone, he stripped his own wet clothes off and changed into a pair of jeans and a T-shirt. The adrenaline that had pumped so ferociously through his veins while he'd been searching for her, which had ratcheted up while they'd been shouting at each other in the truck, had gone. Feeling weary to his bones, he sank into the armchair and covered his face. His guts had tightened into a knot.

When she emerged from the bathroom with a towel wrapped around her, he averted his gaze while she slipped into the dressing room.

His heart squeezed when she joined him, dressed in her usual jeans and a check shirt but still as ravishing as when she'd been dressed so beautifully. She was limping.

'Are you hurt?' he asked.

She gave a rueful smile and perched on the sofa. 'My feet. Going for a walk in the dark barefoot was not my brightest idea. I've cleaned them and put antiseptic on the cuts.'

'Good.' He nodded his head and fought to keep all the thoughts that had raced through it while she'd showered in one place. 'I will arrange a flight back to England for you tomorrow.'

Her shocked gaze shot straight back to him. '*Tomorrow?*'

'It is for the best,' he said heavily.

'Why?'

'Because you're right. We'll end up hating each other.' He ruthlessly pushed aside the memory of the cold sweat he'd come out in, imagining Becky alone and injured on his estate. 'If we don't end it now, it won't take years. We'll hate each other before the baby's born.'

'But...'

'Don't say another word,' he warned, getting to his feet, averting his gaze so as not to see how quickly the colour had drained from her face. 'We've both made very clear what we think of each other. There is nothing left to say. We're going to be bound together for the rest of our lives. I would prefer to do that without thinking poison of my child's mother.'

He didn't want to hate her. That night he'd come damn close.

She'd accused him of being stuck in the past. Maybe he was. Maybe they both were. But he'd opened himself to her as he'd never opened himself to anyone and she still rejected him and assumed the worst of him. She'd seen all of him and she didn't want it. If he wasn't so determined not to hate her, he would hate her for staying these extra weeks when she must have known all along her mind was set.

It was time to let her go, and let go of the stupid dreams he'd had for them. A man had his pride. He wasn't going to beg. It wasn't as if he loved her and her return to England would break his heart.

That he'd realised he trusted her... That was a good thing, he told himself grimly. A man should be able to trust the mother of his child. Even if she lived on a different continent to him.

And that she sat there now, mute, not denying his own prophecy for them…

Fighting back the nausea bubbling like a cauldron in his stomach, he rammed his hands in his pockets. 'I'm going back to the party. I'll find somewhere else to get my head down tonight.'

'Okay.' Her voice sounded very faint and small to his ears.

'I'll be in touch soon.'

This time she didn't even open her mouth to acknowledge him, just gave a faint nod.

It wasn't until the bedroom door clicked shut that Becky gulped for air. She couldn't breathe. Oh, God, she couldn't breathe.

Stumbling to her feet, she staggered to the nearest window and fumbled with the latch to open it.

The rain had stopped. There was a fresh breeze. It kissed her face as she breathed it as hard as she could into her frozen lungs.

Emiliano didn't want her any more.

She'd pushed him away. She'd thought the worst of him one too many times and he'd turned from her as he'd turned from his father and brother for doing the exact same thing. He was already on the brink of hating her.

She didn't want him to hate her. Never that. Not the man who'd made love to her as if she were a precious gem to be cherished, the man who'd become more precious than any gem in her eyes. He'd become her friend as well as her lover. She'd shared things with him she'd never shared with anyone. And he'd done the same with her.

They'd shared something special and that was what she needed to cherish now. The memories. Because he was right, she knew it in her breaking heart. They'd reached the end of the road. Her love had no currency with a man who eschewed love. And her love wouldn't protect her when the inevitable happened and he grew bored of her.

But God, please help her—the *pain*.

Not bothering to strip off her clothes, she crawled into bed and tried not to think of the dreamy lovemaking they'd shared in it only hours ago.

'He still wants you,' she whispered to the tiny life inside her as she hugged her belly. 'Don't worry, your daddy will love you and protect you always.' Of that she had no doubt. He would support Becky too. If she needed help, he would give it.

The only thing he wouldn't give her was the one thing she so desperately wanted. His heart.

When the car pulled up outside the ranch the next day, Becky, who'd been hovering by the front door waiting, sank to her knees and cuddled the dogs goodbye. 'You two be good,' she said as she kissed their heads. 'I'll miss you.'

They nuzzled into her dolefully. If she was to anthropomorphise, she'd say they were sad about her leaving. In truth, they'd been up all night vacuuming any titbit of food they could get their greedy mouths on and having a marvellous time being petted by everyone. When she'd come down that morning, stepping over sleeping bodies strewn here, there and everywhere, she'd found the dogs curled together in the kitchen, too zonked out to do more than open an eye in greeting.

She kissed them again, then froze when a pair of huge feet in thick-soled tan boots appeared in front of her.

A wave of dizziness hit her and she sucked in a long breath before saying a prayer for strength and carefully straightening.

She hadn't seen him all day. While the great clean-up had been going on, the cleaning team sweeping and polishing around snoozing bodies, Emiliano had been nowhere to be found. But he'd arranged her flight home from wherever he'd holed himself up and asked Paula to pass on the details to her. The two women had already said their goodbyes.

She dragged in another breath to see his bloodshot eyes and stubbly face. He'd obviously slept in his clothes. Possibly in a bush. His hair had foliage of a sort in it. He must have really enjoyed his return to the party.

They stared at each other for the longest time before he rammed his hands into his jeans' pockets. 'Have a safe journey,' he said hoarsely.

She nodded and tried to smile. It was as impossible as speech.

'Let me know when you get home?'

Still unable to speak, she nodded again and opened the door. The sun shone so brightly it blinded her…or was that the flickering of her eyes from a body so choked that every single part of her felt paralysed?

Somehow she managed to drag her feet to the car.

'Becky.'

She stopped in her tracks, heart suddenly leaping.

He paused a few feet from her, jaw rigid and throbbing at the sides, muscular arms folded across his chest.

She was going to be sick. She could feel it building inside her…

'I want you to listen to me,' he said quietly. 'You have to stop using your studies and your work as a shield to hide behind. Make new friends. Enjoy your life. Everything will change very soon, so enjoy your freedom while you have it. Okay?'

She sniffed back the tears, managed a jerky nod and then, concentrating harder than perhaps she'd ever done, managed to find a smile for him to remember her by.

The next time they met she would be noticeably pregnant, her features subtly altered. Let him remember her as she was now. '*Hasta luego*, Emiliano.'

And then she got into the car and drove out of his life.

On the flight back, Becky was inconsolable. The tears would not stop falling. She kept her privacy pod up the entire journey and sobbed until she wore herself out and slept, only to wake and sob herself to sleep all over again. Fourteen and a half hours later, voice hoarse and eyes sore from all the crying, tear ducts pleading for a rest, she landed in the UK.

Emiliano had arranged for a chauffeur to collect her from the airport so the hour-long journey to her new Oxford home went without any hassle.

Then she stepped inside and it hit her all over again.

The furniture he'd ordered for her on that shopping trip that now felt so long ago had been delivered. She'd known it was being delivered here—she'd given Emiliano the address and her landlord's details—but it hadn't occurred to her that it would all be unpacked and set out for her. Or that the flat would have been freshly decorated and have a new carpet.

Emiliano had arranged this. If she closed her eyes she could see him on the phone, barking out his orders in that way he had that was both no-nonsense but with a tone that made people *want* to go out of their way to please him.

She traced her fingers over the sofa she'd fallen in love with before she'd seen the price and baulked. In her bedroom, filling it so that she doubted she'd be able to open the wardrobe doors fully, was the sleigh bed she'd thought she'd cooed over without him noticing. She'd actually enthused about a different, much, much cheaper bed. But he'd noticed.

He'd noticed everything, she thought in wonder when

she drifted into the small kitchen and found the slow cooker, and a food processor she'd run her fingers over before moving on to something else as she'd considered it an extravagance she didn't need.

But it was when she pulled the freshly laundered bedsheets back that her tear ducts were pulled back into service after their hard-earned break.

The pillow on the left-hand side of the bed, the side she'd slept when she'd slept with Emiliano, had a bespoke pillowcase on it. A picture of Emiliano's gorgeous face was imprinted into the silk.

Crying and laughing simultaneously, she cuddled his face to her belly.

She could picture him perfectly, his face alight with glee as he went to the trouble of ordering it and imagining her reaction when she discovered it.

When, much later, she was in that semi-conscious twilight state between sleep and wakefulness, her last coherent thought was that he must have forgotten about the pillow. Because it was the playful jest of a gift from a lover who expected or at least hoped for a future.

Not from someone who was preparing to let his lover go.

Emiliano stared at the screen before him. His finger hovered on the call icon in the laptop's corner.

This was something he would have preferred to do in the flesh but the person he needed to speak to was on a different continent to him. Europe. England, to be precise. Had flown there with no intention of returning to Argentina.

He clicked the icon before he could talk himself out of it again.

Moments later, his brother's face filled the screen. 'Emiliano! Great to see you!'

He had enough feeling left in him to acknowledge the small kindling of happiness that the man he'd tormented for most of his life should greet him with such enthusiasm and strove to inject the same enthusiasm into his own voice. 'Great to see you too. How's England? I bet it's raining.'

But his attempt at cheerfulness didn't fool Damián. His brows knotted. 'What's wrong?'

Before he could answer, Mia appeared in the background. She was the reason for Damián's uprooting of his life. The actress he'd paid to play the part of his lover… he'd fallen in love with her. And she'd fallen in love with him. This video call Emiliano had made had no doubt interrupted their wedding planning.

Mia waved at him with a beaming smile. He managed to raise his hand to wave back.

Damián turned from the camera to speak to her in a low voice. She looked briefly back at the screen before leaning down to kiss him, waved again at Emiliano and then walked out of the camera's range.

He heard a door close before Damián's face reappeared before him. 'What's wrong?' he asked again.

It took a few moments for Emiliano to gather his prepared thoughts back in order. Something about the way Damián and Mia interacted had knocked his thoughts off course, set off a tightening in his chest…

'Emiliano!'

With a snap back to attention he stared into his brother's concerned eyes and realised he was making this call for *her*. To swallow his pride and put the past behind him once and for all. Just as she'd told him to.

'There's something I need to tell you.'

'Oh?'

'About what happened during my time at the Delgado

Group. With the money.' And then he took a deep breath and for only the second time revealed how he'd been played for a fool by a gold-digging con-artist.

Later that night, alone in his bed, Emiliano stared at the ceiling. The cliché of weights being lifted from shoulders was, he'd discovered, a cliché that was true.

He'd confessed everything. And then he'd apologised. For everything, including treating his younger brother like dirt for almost his entire life.

And Damián had apologised too for his own part in everything. They'd talked for hours. By the time they'd ended the video call, both of them had sunk half a dozen bottles of beer.

The weight of guilt he'd carried all these years had gone. The past was, finally, in the past and it would stay there.

So why did he still feel so heavy and lethargic?

# CHAPTER FIFTEEN

AFTER THE NOISE and exuberance of Argentina, Becky had thought she would find it soothing to be back in such a quietly serious environment as a laboratory, a return to normality that she would easily settle into. And maybe she would have done if she didn't return home to her lonely flat every evening.

Last night, though, she'd gone for a meal with her new colleagues. She'd been touched that they were ready to include her in their social gatherings so soon and, remembering Emiliano's words about making new friends, had readily accepted. She'd enjoyed a good meal and even managed not to think about him for a few seconds.

And now here she was, alone in the huge bed he'd bought her with two whole days of nothing ahead and only the pillow with his image for company. The flat felt so small, not because it was tiny compared to the ranch but because Emiliano magnified everything with his presence alone.

She'd been back in England for thirteen days. It felt like thirteen months.

She wondered if he was awake yet. The first polo competition of the Argentine season would be taking place later that day. She imagined him supervising the loading of his horses into the transporters that would drive them to the venue. She imagined the bustle and noise involved with transporting the minimum of ten horses he would personally ride that day, all the equipment needed, the grooms and other staff rushing around making sure they hadn't forgotten anything, and felt an enormous pang of regret that she wouldn't be there to share the day with them and that she wouldn't be there with the boys at her heels, cheering the Delgado team on until her voice grew hoarse.

The morning drifted away from her. Just as she was contemplating fixing herself something to eat, her doorbell rang.

How exciting. Her first visitor. Except she was expecting a book delivery, so the first person to arrive at her door would be the delivery driver.

But it wasn't a delivery driver standing on the doorstep.

It was her mother.

Emiliano watched the shadows on the bedroom walls. They'd been changing with the rising sun. Thinning.

He felt as if he was thinning too. Losing substance.

He'd thought putting the past to bed with his brother would snap him out of his bad mood but he only felt worse.

Becky had been gone for thirteen days.

His alarm went off. Rufus and Barney woke and jumped on the bed, slobbering over him.

They missed her.

He remembered Adriana, how frantic he'd been when she'd disappeared. He'd believed himself in love with her but he'd never felt that every breath taken was for her. Within days of her disappearance he'd shocked himself with how little he actually missed her. He'd thought about her constantly but only because of the question of where the hell she was.

He knew exactly where Becky was, but she was in his

head every waking moment. She flooded his dreams—dreams that turned into living nightmares when he woke to find her side of the bed empty and he had to go through the grief process all over again, day after day.

To say he missed her would be like saying the sun was nothing but a yellow ball in the sky. There was a gaping hole in his chest filled with a pain so acute that it hurt to breathe and finally the truth penetrated his thick, stubborn head.

He loved her.

If he'd paid any attention to his feelings, he would have known the truth a long time ago. He'd fallen in love with Becky the moment he'd looked up from the trembling coward on the floor who'd dared kick his dog to see her holding Rufus so protectively in her arms. There had been no one for him since.

All these years spent actively avoiding commitment, going through women too quickly for them to feel the slightest hint of cosiness with him, cynically determined never to be fooled again by anyone, man or woman, driven by the sole ambition to prove that he was the best and that the whole world—his father and brother especially—should know about it, living his life with his own pleasures and needs at the centre of everything…

He was glad to now have his brother in his life *as* a brother, but nothing else mattered a damn.

He would give it all up for her. For Becky. The woman who'd stolen his heart, who made his world better with a simple smile. The woman with the tenderest heart. A woman he would trust with his life.

But a woman damaged. The years she should have spent drinking too much and having fun, having sex with her peers, had been lost as she'd wrestled with her parents' bitter divorce, which had culminated in her father's desertion and her mother's rejection, burying herself so deeply in her studies that she used it as a shield to protect herself from more hurt.

In his heart, he knew there would never be anyone else. If he couldn't have Becky then he would have no one.

He had to try. He knew that now. Maybe it was too late for them but he would try. He would get this competition done with and then he would fly to England, swallow his pride, get on his knees and beg for another chance. Because he'd been the one to end things. She'd refused to marry him but at no point had she said she wanted to end their relationship.

Trust had to be earned. When had he ever given her the chance to trust his vow of fidelity? He'd been so damn intent on keeping control of himself and control of his feelings that he'd made it sound as if he was giving that promise as a sop to her, like some stupid benevolent gift, when the truth was he didn't want anyone else because there couldn't *be* anyone else. He was Becky's, heart, body and soul.

And if it was too late then at least he would always have a part of her. Their baby. He would stay in England and, living together or apart, they would raise him or her together and lavish them with so much love that they would thrive and grow up healthy and secure and with the ability to love and be loved.

He would have to be satisfied with that.

But he could do nothing about any of it right now.

With a kiss for his boys first, he climbed out of bed and dragged himself into the shower. He had to pull himself out of this funk. In an hour he'd be travelling with his horses and his team to the first cup competition of the season. He needed to be sharp. He needed his wits about him. Polo was too dangerous a sport not to be on form.

* * *

Five hours later and the doorbell rang for the second time. This time, it was a delivery of Chinese food for Becky and her mother to share.

The shock and disbelief she'd experienced when she'd first opened the door had slowly seeped away as the awkwardness dissolved and they began to talk.

Anthony, her sex pest stepfather, was history. Her mother had woken a few days ago after a dream about her unborn grandchild. It had been her epiphany. Her only child was pregnant and she didn't even know who the father was or when the baby was due. When she'd idly mentioned this to her new husband, along with her intention to arrange a meeting with her estranged daughter, his reaction had been so over the top and incredulous that suddenly the veil had slipped from her eyes.

It was as Emiliano had predicted. Having taken his advice to keep the door to her mother open, Becky had messaged her new address the day she'd arrived back in England. Never had she believed her mother would turn up on her doorstep within two weeks of her sending it.

'Have you told your dad about the baby?' her mum asked after swallowing a huge forkful of *chow mein*.

Becky pulled a face. 'Not yet. He messaged last Wednesday. He was about to catch a flight to Chile to start his tour of South America. I'll tell him when we next speak.'

'Doesn't Chile border Argentina?'

She shrugged. She'd told her mum only that the baby's father was an Argentine polo player. It was too soon to start exchanging real confidences. Things couldn't return to how they'd been. Not yet.

'I bet your dad comes home for the birth,' she predicted.

Becky raised a brow in surprise at a comment about her father that was remarkably free of malice.

Her mum smiled ruefully and stabbed at a piece of sweet and sour chicken. 'I can't stand the man but he loves you. He was always a great father. He's dreamed of travelling the world since he was a kid. He put all his dreams on hold because he loves you and you needed him. He waited until you didn't need him any more.'

'I never knew that.'

'Well, now you do.'

'He never said goodbye when he left.'

'That's because he's selfish and immature.'

'I thought you just said he was a great father.'

'He was. And now he's a terrible one. Just as I've been a terrible mother in recent years.'

'I've hardly been the best daughter,' Becky admitted wretchedly. 'I'm a woman in my twenties expecting my parents to still put me first. If anyone's been selfish and immature, it's me.'

Emiliano had put her needs first, in all ways. Those weeks when they'd been lovers, he'd given her passion but also a security she'd never known.

'Becky?'

She blinked. 'Sorry, did you say something?'

'You looked lost in thought.'

The urge to spill all bloomed inside her. To confide how desperately she'd fallen in love and how it had been her own distrust and lack of confidence in herself that had destroyed them.

All those things she wished she could have said to him. Things she *should* have said. Like how wonderful he was. How he made her laugh harder than anyone in the world. How he infuriated her more than anyone in the world. How he was also the best person she knew and how glad she was that he was the father of her child. Their child could have no better protector and guide.

'Becky!'

She jumped at the sharpness in her mother's tone.

Eyes that were a mirror of her own softened. 'Talk to me, honey. Please. I might be able to help.'

Tears filled her eyes. The urge to confide had grown big enough to choke her but, before she could open her mouth, her phone rang. She would have ignored it if the name of the caller hadn't flashed on the screen. Louise. Who should be busy tending the horses during the ongoing cup competition, not taking time out to make a call.

Fear immediately clutched her heart and it was with a hand that had turned to ice that she answered it.

'What's happened?' she whispered.

'Becks…' A large intake of breath. 'I'm really sorry to call like this but I thought you'd want to know. There's been an accident. It's Emiliano… He's had a bad fall on Don Giovanni. They crashed into…'

'How bad?' she interrupted.

'He's been rushed to hospital. He's not conscious. They think there's bleeding in his brain.' Her voice dropped. 'Becks…it's really bad.'

By the time Becky landed in Buenos Aires, thirty-six hours had passed since Louise's call. Her mum had already been on her feet, putting her handbag over her shoulder, when the call had finished.

'Where do you need to go?' she'd asked.

'Argentina.'

'Get your passport.'

Four minutes after the call to Louise ended, her mum's car was screeching out of the parking space and pelting to the airport. Once there, she'd taken full charge. She'd bought Becky the first available ticket to Buenos Aires then, because the flight was twelve hours away, checked them into an airport hotel. For hours they'd lain on a lumpy bed watching rubbish on the television. In all that time Becky had hardly spoken. She was simply too numb to form a sentence, too numb to think coherently and too terrified to close her eyes to sleep. The hand not clutching her phone for news that didn't come had kept a tight grip on her mother's.

The long night had passed with agonising slowness. The wait to board the plane had been excruciatingly slow. The flight itself was purgatory. She couldn't even check her phone for news of his condition.

And then the plane landed and adrenaline kicked in. First to disembark, she was first at passport control too. With no luggage to collect, she ran straight to the exit, eyes glued to her phone as she waited for the messages she knew would have been sent from Louise and Paula during the long flight to ping through…

But disaster struck. Her phone died in her hand. She'd run out of battery and in the panic to get out of her flat and get to him she'd forgotten to bring a charger.

Stuffing her fist into her mouth, she screamed. She screamed for so long that when she finally pulled her hand out the sections of her fingers beneath the knuckles were bleeding from where her teeth had cut into them.

Not caring about the pain, she jumped into a cab and asked for the hospital. But she couldn't tell the driver which one. She didn't know! She knew the polo competition had been held in Buenos Aires itself so it had to be in the city. In desperation, she cried, 'Emiliano Delgado!'

To her horror, the driver immediately made the sign of the cross and put the car into gear.

Her brain turned to ice. Every part of her body began to shake.

She was still shaking when they arrived at the hospital, and when she saw the crowds of press outside her fear turned to terror.

Somehow she managed to fight her way through them but her battle was just beginning because no one—no one—would help her or tell her anything about his condition. They wouldn't even confirm if he was there!

But she knew he was. Why else would the press be camped outside? Emiliano had something akin to rock star status in Argentina.

Resolve filled her and she determined to find him herself. She didn't have to search long. At the far end of a long, wide corridor on the hospital's ground floor stood two security guards in front of a double door.

She ran to them. 'Emiliano Delgado?'

In unison, they folded their arms across their meaty chests and snapped at her in Spanish.

'English,' she beseeched, pointing at herself.

The taller one leaned down to speak in her face. 'Go 'way.'

'Please,' she cried. 'Just tell me if he's here and if he's alive. *Please.*'

'Go 'way.'

'No!' Too distraught to be intimidated, she shook her head vigorously. 'I no go.'

The smaller one scowled and spoke into a walkie-talkie. He'd hardly finished speaking when another security guard appeared and strode straight to her.

'You have to leave, miss.'

Turning her back to the door, she clasped her hands together and placed them to her chest. 'Just tell me how he is,' she begged.

Although he kept his tone pleasant, there was an edge of exasperation to it. 'I am not allowed to say. We have our orders.'

‘*Please?*’

‘You must leave or we will have to make you leave.’

Finally reaching the end of her tether, she clenched her hands into fists and shouted, ‘I’m not going anywhere until someone tells me how he is!’

‘Miss…’

‘Just tell me if he’s alive! You can do that! *Please!*’

‘I cannot, just as I could not tell any of the others. Now…’

‘Damn you, I’m not one of his *groupies*! I’m having his baby! Now, either you tell me if the man I love is alive or I’m going to…’

‘Becky?’

Spinning round, she came to a stumbling stop. The double doors had opened and between them, sitting in a wheelchair in a pair of shorts and a T-shirt, was Emiliano.

## CHAPTER SIXTEEN

EMILIANO BLINKED A number of times to make sure his concussion hadn't caused him to hallucinate.

But no. It really was Becky making all that racket outside his private hospital suite. It really was Becky who'd just shouted in the face of a man twice her size. It really was Becky who'd just screamed that she loved him…

Her eyes locked onto his and widened into orbs. Her trembling hands flew to her mouth and then reached out as she moved like a ghost towards him.

Silent tears streaming down her face, she tentatively placed her shaking fingers to his cheeks.

A burn stabbed the back of his eyes and he swallowed hard to ease his constricted throat.

While she explored his face with her shell-shocked eyes and gentle touch, Emiliano soaked her in too. His heart clenched and released over and over as he took in the exhaustion on her beautiful face, her crumpled clothing and hair that looked as if it had never seen a brush.

'*Is* it you?' He raised a hand to touch *her* face, still unsure whether she really was there or if he *was* hallucinating. Had he fallen back into one of the dreams that had plagued him in recent weeks, ready to turn into a nightmare any moment when he awoke?

Tremulous plump lips tugged at the sides as she gave

a jerky nod but then her face crumpled beneath his touch and the tears turned into sobs that sounded as if they were wrenched from her very soul.

The emotion in his heart exploded. Hooking an arm around her waist, he pulled her onto his lap and held her tightly, burying his face in her hair and praying as hard as he'd ever prayed before that this was real.

Tears soaking his T-shirt, she curled up into him and held him as tightly as he held her.

'It's okay,' he whispered into her hair. 'It's okay, *bomboncita*. I'm here.'

Slowly she disentangled her arms and adjusted her weight so she could cup his face and stare deep into his eyes.

He smoothed a lock of her hair and stared back in wonder. 'I can't believe *you're* here. How did you know?'

'Louise called. I got here as fast as I could.' Her voice broke. 'I've been so scared. I thought…' Her breaths shortened, chest hitching under the weight.

'Thought what?' he asked gently.

'That you were…' Becky squeezed her eyes shut, afraid to even whisper what her deepest fear had been.

'That I was dead?'

Every cell in her body spasmed in agony to hear it vocalised.

'Becky, look at me,' he commanded quietly. His warm hands caressed her face in tender motions.

She gulped some air in and forced her eyes to open but before he could say what was on his mind, a doctor appeared. She stared at them with incredulity then spoke rapidly, clearly telling them off.

Suddenly, Becky realised she was curled up on Emiliano's lap. While she'd been overwhelmed with relief that he was alive and conscious, it had totally bypassed her that he must be seriously injured to be in a wheelchair. Horrified, she tried to stand but his hold around her tightened.

'You're not going anywhere,' he murmured into her ear before addressing the doctor in their native language.

The doctor's lips tightened but she nodded and indicated to one of the security guards who'd been watching the whole thing in stunned amazement. The guard pushed the wheelchair back through the doors and wheeled them to Emiliano's private bedroom.

Alone, they stared at each other again, faces so close the tips of their noses brushed.

'How badly hurt are you?' she whispered.

'Kiss me and I'll tell you.'

'Emiliano…'

'You cannot fly across the world to my deathbed without kissing me.'

She shuddered.

'I'm not dying. Not even close.' He gathered her hair together in a fist and tilted his head. 'Now kiss me.'

Heart hammering, she inched her face closer, closed her eyes and pressed her lips to his.

Neither of them moved. Lips joined, they breathed each other in. The scent of Emiliano's skin and feel of his firm, sensual mouth against hers gradually seeped into her senses, creeping through her veins and slowly filled her with such joy and such relief that she cracked, and suddenly they were kissing with the desperation of two drowning sailors who'd found a last pocket of air.

She knew the dazed look in Emiliano's eyes when they finally came up for air was mirrored in hers.

Hands sweeping through her hair, he smiled and pressed his lips to hers again. 'Help me onto the bed?'

Smiling back, she wriggled off his lap and held a hand out to him.

His movements were heavy and awkward as he heaved himself from the wheelchair and twisted to rest his bottom on the bed.

When he was finally sitting on it with his legs stretched out, he patted the space beside him. Already missing the feel of being pressed so tightly against him, she climbed up and cuddled into him.

'Why do you need the wheelchair?' she asked softly as their fingers laced together.

'Bruised spine.' He grunted a laugh. 'Bruised everything.'

'Louise said you had a bleed on your brain.'

'Suspected bleed,' he corrected. 'I was given full body scans. Nothing broken. Just a nasty concussion and bruising.'

'How's Don Giovanni? Was he hurt?' She knew he'd be more concerned about his horse than anything else.

'Not a scratch on him.'

'Good… What happened?'

'I don't remember. I was knocked unconscious. The first I knew I'd been in an accident was when I woke up in this bed.'

She shuddered again.

'But I know what caused it.'

She tilted her face to his. 'Oh?'

'And I know it will never happen again.'

'How?'

'I'm retiring. As of now. I'll find a player to replace me and I'll still finance the team but I won't play any more.'

'But *why*? You love playing.'

'Not as much as I love you and our baby. It's you I need to be with and that's what I'm going to do… If you'll have me and let me share your life.' His eyes shone with an emotion that burned. 'Since you've been gone my concentration has been shot. I've lost my focus and, as my accident proved, polo is too dangerous a game to play without one hundred per cent focus, not just for me but for the other players and my horses. If Don Giovanni had been hurt I would never have forgiven myself.'

She didn't hear anything after his first few words. Raising herself, she gazed down at his face, almost afraid to hope. 'You *love* me?'

He palmed her neck and expelled a deep breath. 'I've loved you since the day I met you, and if these last weeks have proven anything it's that I can't live without you. I can't. The morning of my accident I made a vow to myself that I would fly to you and beg for another chance. If not for the accident, I would have come to you. There has been no one else for me since the day I met you and there never will be. I need to be with you. Nothing else matters. Only you, and if I have to spend the rest of my life gaining your trust then I'll take that, so long as you love me… and you do love me…don't you?'

His sudden vulnerability made her heart full to bursting. 'More than anything. You're my whole world.'

'I know you don't want to marry me, but will you…'

'I *do* want to marry you,' she interrupted gently, placing a finger to his lips. 'I'm yours, body and soul.'

He closed his eyes and took a few deep breaths. When his eyes opened again, they were filled with such wonder it made the emotion in her bursting heart spill over.

'I cannot tell you how badly I have wished for this,' he said hoarsely. 'I swear I will never give you reason to doubt me. I will do everything in my power to be a good husband to you and a good father to our baby.'

'I know you will,' she said, replacing her finger with her lips. 'And Emiliano, I've never doubted you. It's myself I doubted. I didn't trust that your feelings for me could sustain a lifetime because I'm an insecure fool.'

'But I didn't help.' His eyes blazed with self-recrimination. 'If I hadn't been burying my head in the sand and denying my feelings for you, I would have made the promise to be faithful without making it sound like I was doing you a favour. I buried my head in the sand rather than face the truth, and the truth is there has been no one else for me since the day I met you and there will be no one else but you for as long as I draw breath.'

'Even if you'd made the promise to be faithful without it sounding like a favour I wouldn't have believed it,' she said softly. 'I was too raw inside. I *did* shield myself in my studies and I didn't even realise, and I didn't realise I was running away from my hurt. You…' She sighed. 'Oh, you wonderful man, you've brought me to life and now my life is yours. I love you.'

And as she gazed into the clear brown eyes she loved so much she saw his love for her reflecting back at her and when their lips fused together she felt a rush of blood, knowing her heart would always beat for this man and that the blood in his veins would always flow for her.

Ten minutes later, the doctor opened the patient's door, having psyched herself to go in there and kick the visitor out. Really, this was not on. She didn't care how rich or powerful the patient was, he had a severe concussion and bruising and needed to rest, not be cavorting with women.

But then she saw the two fully dressed figures entwined on the bed and she stopped. The visitor's head rested against the patient's chest, the patient leaning into her, holding her protectively. Both were fast asleep.

There was something so symbiotic about the way they held each other that her breath caught and she sighed at the love she could feel enveloping them.

Hardly daring to breathe in case she woke them, she backed out of the room and softly closed the door.

# EPILOGUE

'REPEAT AFTER ME. I, Emiliano Alejandro Delgado, take you, Rebecca Jane Aldridge, to be my lawful wedded wife.'

'I, Emiliano Alejandro Delgado, take you, Rebecca…' Emiliano suddenly paused and mouthed, *Rebecca?* to the woman he was in the process of marrying.

She nodded, her face turning bright red with suppressed laughter.

'Take you, Rebecca Jane Aldridge, to be my lawful wedded wife.'

'To have and to hold…'

Once they'd exchanged their vows and their rings—there had been one heart-stopping moment when Damián, his best man, had patted in the wrong pocket for them—and been pronounced husband and wife, they followed the priest with their two witnesses, Damián and *Rebecca*'s mother, to a private part of the church to sign the official document.

'Rebecca?' he whispered in her ear as he squeezed her bottom.

It was the only part of her he could currently squeeze as she was eight months pregnant. Their honeymoon would be spent on their English estate. Once they judged the baby to be old enough to travel, they would be moving back to Argentina, the place they both agreed felt more like home than anywhere else. Rebecca had a job lined up at an English-speaking research company close to the ranch, doing something similar to her current job with much reduced hours.

'You never did read my résumé, did you?' She sniggered.

And it was with the pair of them in fits of laughter that they signed the document that tied them together for the rest of their lives.

* * * * *

# BREAKING THE PLAYBOY'S RULES

MELANIE MILBURNE

To all the dedicated frontline medical workers
soldiering on during the COVID-19 Pandemic.
You are all amazing to put your own lives on the
line to help others. You sacrifice time with your own
families, you work punishingly long hours
and you support those who work alongside you.
You are the true heroes of this era.

Love,

Melanie Milburne

# CHAPTER ONE

It was the first time in her life Millie had asked a man to meet her for a drink and now she was going to be late. Seriously, embarrassingly, late. But this was no ordinary date. This meeting with hotshot celebrity divorce lawyer Hunter Addison was not for herself but for her mother.

Her mother collected ex-husbands like some people collected coins. And, sadly, it was going to take an eye-watering amount of coins to get rid of husband number four—money that Millie could ill afford to lend her mum right now. Hunter Addison wasn't the cheapest divorce lawyer in London, but he was reputed to be the best.

And, for her mum, Millie wanted the best.

Millie walked as quickly as she could towards the wine bar where she'd asked Hunter to meet her after work. She hadn't spoken to him in person, only via text message. The thought of talking to him on the phone after their disastrous blind date two months ago was too confronting. So too was the prospect of meeting him again in person but this wasn't about her—it was about her mother's welfare. She could not bear to see her mother screwed over by yet another self-serving, narcissist ex.

Millie pushed open the front door of the wine bar and stepped inside, quickly scanning the room for any sign of Hunter. Couples and small groups were sitting at the various tables in the front section but there was no sign of a man sitting by himself. Of course, it would be incredibly rare for a man as good-looking, wealthy and sophisticated as Hunter ever to sit in a bar by himself. He had a reputation for being a fast-living playboy. Hardly a week went past when he wasn't snapped by the paparazzi with yet another gorgeous supermodel-type woman draped on his arm.

Interestingly, in the couple of months since their blind date, there had been nothing in the press about his sexual antics. Maybe Millie's immunity to his attractiveness that night had bruised his overblown ego. Not flipping likely. Men like Hunter Addison had industrial-strength egos. Trying to put a dent in his ego would be like trying to crack a brazil nut with a feather boa. Not going to work.

'You're late.' A deep and crisp male voice rich with censure spoke from behind her.

Millie spun round and, even though she was wearing vertiginous heels, she had to crane her neck up, up, up to meet Hunter Addison's whisky-brown eyes. It was hard not to feel a little flustered coming face-to-face with such arrant masculinity. Such heart-stopping male perfection. Broad-shouldered and tall, with a lean and athletic build, he exuded strength and potency. At a virile thirty-four, he was in the prime of his life and it showed.

And every female cell in her body sat up and took notice. 'Yes, I know. I'm sorry but—'

'Something wrong with your phone?' The smile

that wasn't really a smile matched the cynical gleam in his eyes.

Millie mentally counted to ten, trying to control her desire to snap out a biting retort. What was it about this man that made her feel so prickly, on edge and so…so combative? Her experience around men was limited. She had only ever had one lover and, since her childhood sweetheart Julian had died three years ago after a long battle with brain cancer, she hadn't dated again.

Well, apart from the wretched blind date with Hunter, which had been an unmitigated disaster from start to finish. But then, she had *wanted* to sabotage it. She had done everything in her power to give him the cold shoulder and hot tongue routine. She was *not* going to be set up by friends to 'move on'. She was not going to be flirted with and charmed by a man who hadn't heard the word 'no' from a woman his entire life.

But now she needed Hunter's help and she had no choice but to swallow the choking lump of her pride. And boy, oh, boy did it taste sour.

Millie straightened her shoulders and forced herself to hold his gaze. 'There was, actually. I forgot to charge it overnight and it ran out of battery just after I left work. Then there was some sort of security incident involving the police on my way here and I had to take a six-block detour.'

*In flipping sky-high heels and a tight-fitting pencil skirt*, she wanted to add, but managed to restrain herself.

It was hard to tell if he believed her or not. His expression was now largely inscrutable and yet there was something about the way his eyes drifted to her mouth for the briefest of moments that made the backs of her knees tingle.

'Come this way. I have a table in the back where it's more private.' His tone had a commanding edge that made her want to insist on a table out front instead. He probably thought she regretted giving him the brush-off. He probably thought she wanted a rerun of their date.

But no. *No.*

This was not a cosy little *tête-à-tête*. This was not a date in any shape or form. This was a meeting to convince him to act for her mother. But she found herself—meekly, for her—following him to the table in the quieter back section of the wine bar.

Hunter waited until she was seated before he took the chair opposite. She was conscious of his long legs so close to hers under the small table and kept her knees tightly together and angled to the right to avoid any accidental touching. Millie was also conscious of the way her heart was beating—deep pounding beats that echoed in her ears as if her blood was sending out a sonar warning. *Danger.*

Hunter picked up the drinks menu and handed it to her across the table. 'What would you like to drink?'

Millie took the menu and gave it a cursory glance before handing it back. 'Just mineral water, thank you.'

He made a soft sound of amusement and a sharper glint appeared in his eyes. 'Don't tell me you've gone teetotaller on me?'

Millie could feel a hot blush stealing over her cheeks. She had drunk three glasses of wine during their date, as well as a lethally strong cocktail, in an effort to get through the ordeal. The day of their disastrous date had been the anniversary of Julian's death, and each year she struggled to get through it—which was why her friends had organised the blind date with Hunter, hoping it would distract her and help her to move on. It had distracted her all right. Everything about Hunter Addison was distracting, back then and now. Especially now.

But it wasn't grief that had made that day so hard for her.

It was another G-word. Guilt.

Millie aimed her gaze to a point above his left shoulder rather than meet his probing gaze. 'No. I just don't feel like alcohol right now.'

Hunter signalled the waiter and ordered Millie's mineral water and a gin and tonic for himself. Once the waiter had gone to fetch the drinks, Hunter leaned back in his chair with a casual ease she privately envied. He was dressed in a smart grey suit and snowy-white business shirt, the top button undone above his loosened, finely checked grey-and-white tie, giving him a chilled out, laid back air. He was devilishly handsome with short black hair, a straight nose and a sculptured mouth—the lower lip fuller than the top one. His late-in-the-day stubble shadowed his chiselled jaw and around his mouth, and he had a well-defined philtrum between his nose and top lip.

*A sensual mouth...*

Millie sat up straighter in her chair, shocked at her errant thought. She wasn't interested in his mouth. She was interested in his professional expertise. And the sooner she engaged it, the better. But right now it was almost impossible to get her brain into gear, to be logical and rational and stay on task. Every time he looked at her, flutters and tingles erupted in her flesh, as if he had closed the distance between them and touched her with one of his broad-span hands.

One thing she knew for sure—she must *not* let him touch her. That would take her pretence of immunity way out of her skill set.

'So, here we are. Again.' Hunter's gaze went on a lazy perusal of her face, and something in her stomach turned over. And the way his voice leaned ever so slightly on the word 'again' made the roots of her hair tingle, as if tiny footsteps were tiptoeing over her scalp.

Millie licked her suddenly too-dry lips. She smoothed her skirt over her knees with her hands and tried to ignore the way her pulse was leaping. 'I feel I should apologise for how I behaved the last time we met.'

She chanced a glance at him and found him looking at her with studied concentration. Was that his lawyer face? The steady and watchful legal eagle quietly assessing his client. Reading between the lines of what his client said and what they did. But she wasn't his client. Although, she wasn't exactly a friend asking a favour either, was she? They had disliked each other on sight…or at least she had made up her mind she would dislike him.

She swallowed and continued. 'I wasn't in the best mood that night and I fear I might have taken it out on you.'

'You fear?' The edge of sarcasm in his voice was unmistakable.

Her chin came up and her gaze collided with his. 'Well, you were hardly Mr Dream Date yourself.'

Something shifted at the back of his gaze, as if he

was mentally recalling that night and didn't like what he saw. A dull flush slashed high across his cheekbones and his lips twisted in a self-deprecating smile. 'Point taken. My charm button was on pause that night.'

As apologies went, it wasn't the most gracious, but then, she had been the one who had acted with the most appalling manners that night. He had been a little broody and distant, but she had been downright rude. She'd been annoyed at the matchmaking attempt of her friends, who had been at her for over a year to get out more. Beth and Dan were well-meaning, but they didn't know the real reason she found the prospect of dating again so difficult.

Julian had been sick for six years before he'd finally succumbed to his illness, diagnosed just before he'd turned eighteen. The treatment had been gruelling, the first operation changing his personality from loving and kind to grumpy and short-tempered. But Millie had hung in there, hoping month after month, year after year, that things would get better. They hadn't. The thought of breaking up with him had not only crossed her mind, it had taken up residence and patiently waited for a good opportunity for her to raise it with him. It had never come. Julian had always been too sick, too depressed or in one of those rare but wonderful phases when the cancer seemed to be in remission.

How could she have destroyed him by saying she wanted out?

Millie was pulled out of her reverie when the waiter appeared with their drinks and it was a moment or two before she and Hunter were alone again. Millie picked up her glass for something to do with her hands. She took a sip and covertly studied him. There should be a law against men looking so hot without even trying. He exuded male potency and she wondered what it would be like to be in bed with him, those gym-toned legs entwined with hers. Her mind ran wild with X-rated images of his naked body in full arousal.

Sex with her late fiancé had been difficult due to the ravages of his illness and his limited stamina. She had cared for Julian rather than loved him and had allowed him to find quick pleasure in her body without insisting on her own. It had made her annoyed with herself rather than him, knowing he couldn't help being so ill. Since his death, she'd had fleeting thoughts about sex, but had never gone any further than occasional self-pleasure. Somehow, over the years with Julian and since his death, she had begun to associate all things sexual with disappointment, dissatisfaction and faint tinges of despair.

But now, sitting opposite Hunter, all she could think about was how it would feel to have his body thrusting within hers. She was pretty sure he would never leave a partner dissatisfied or disappointed. His sexual competence was an aura that surrounded him. Every time he locked gazes with her, she felt a jolt of electricity shoot to her core. She wriggled in her seat, her lower body restless, agitated, hungry, her cheeks feeling as hot as fire.

A slight frown settled between his ink-black eyebrows and, though he picked up his drink, he didn't take even a token sip. 'One wonders, if you had such a miserable time on our blind date, why on earth would you want to repeat it?' Hunter said, holding her gaze with his steely one.

Millie pressed her lips together. 'I don't. I wanted us to meet to discuss something…else.'

One of his eyebrows rose in a perfect arc. 'Go on.' His eyes never left hers—steady, strong, searching, sharply intelligent.

She ran the tip of her tongue over her parchment-dry lips, trying to ignore the way his gaze drifted downwards, as if he found the shape of her mouth fascinating. She drew in a breath and it shuddered through her chest like air in a damaged set of bellows. 'I want to engage your professional services.'

His eyes flicked to her left hand, where Julian's engagement ring still sat. Truth be told, Millie didn't especially like the ring, but she continued to wear it out of guilt. She knew Beth and Dan had told Hunter about Julian's death for he had mentioned it on their blind date. She had refused to discuss it with him and had abruptly changed the subject. 'You're not married. I'm a divorce lawyer. Not sure how I can help, unless there's something you're not telling me?'

There was a whole lot Millie wasn't telling him, or anyone else for that matter. She had a reputation among her friends as being a sniffer dog for other people's secrets. The thing was, she wasn't all that good at keeping them, unless they were her own secrets. She knew the tells of someone trying to keep something hidden, because for years *she* had being keeping things hidden. And doing a stellar job of it too.

She had not been in love with Julian. And, worse, she had actually felt something akin to relief when he had died three days before their wedding. She played the role of tragic heroine so well. Heart-sore and unable to love again after the tragic loss of her childhood sweetheart. Still wearing his modest little engagement ring after all this time. Still grieving her one and only love. Her soul mate.

But she was a big, fat fraud.

An imposter. Because, while she definitely grieved for the loss of a dear friend, Julian had not been the love of her life.

Millie leaned forward to pick up her mineral water, sat back again and looked at the ice cubes rattling against the glass for a moment. 'No, I'm not, but my mother is.' She brought her gaze to meet his and continued, 'Will you do it?'

Hunter held her gaze for so long without speaking, she had to moisten her dry lips again. His eyes followed the movement and something behind her heart fluttered like a trapped insect. 'Why me?' His tone was curt, business-like, but his darkening brown eyes belonged in the bedroom. The flutter in her chest travelled to her stomach—soft little wings beating against the walls of her belly, sending an electric tingle down the backs of her legs.

Millie leaned forward in her chair to put her glass of mineral water back on the table. She was going for cool and calm and collected, but inside she was trembling with strange, unfamiliar sensations. Smouldering heat coursed through her body. Her heartbeat accelerated, her skin prickling and tingling behind the shield of her clothes. But pride wouldn't allow her to tell him the truth about her mother's situation.

That was another of her well-kept secrets. Diamond heiress Eleanora Donnelly-Clarke was practically penniless after multiple divorces. Millie's mother had been blessed with stunning beauty but had severe dyslexia. Each of her exes had taken advantage of her literacy and numeracy issues, and ex number four was about to do the same. If it wasn't for the trust fund Millie's grandfather had set up for Millie, both she and her mother would have gone under by now. But Millie had her own jewellery business to run and couldn't afford to carry her mother too much longer, especially in the event of another costly divorce—hence her appeal to Hunter.

Millie met Hunter's gaze. 'Because I've heard you're the best.'

One side of his mouth came up in a half-smile, as if he found her comment mildly amusing but of zero importance to his own estimation of his competence. One of his muscled arms was draped casually over the back of his chair, one ankle propped over his strong thigh, just above the knee. Unlike her, he had cool and calm and collected down to a science. 'And here I was thinking you were after a one-night stand with me.' His voice was deep and smoky, his smouldering eyes doing a slow appraisal of her face and figure.

Millie gave a stiff smile, showing no teeth. 'Sadly, no.'

A single eyebrow rose again, his eyes glinting. 'Sadly?'

Millie's heart rate shot up as if she were drinking rocket fuel instead of mineral water. She sat straighter in her chair. She had to do everything she could to keep her body from betraying her in the presence of his sensual charm. *Everything*, including keeping her wayward gaze away from his sinfully sculptured mouth. 'In spite of what Dan and Beth think, you're not my type.'

Hunter gave a slow smile that did serious damage to her determination to resist him. 'Nor you mine, but they seemed to think we'd be a match made in heaven. I wonder why?' His question was idly playful, rhetorical, even slightly mocking. Strike that—*definitely* mocking, drat the arrogant man.

'They're under the misguided impression that a fling with you will somehow help me move on from the loss of my fiancé,' Millie said in a tone so starchy and prim, she could have been lecturing young Victorian ladies on etiquette. 'But I'm afraid they have seriously over-estimated the extent of your charm.'

He gave a wry laugh, but then his expression gradually lost its teasing playfulness, his eyes becoming dark and more serious. 'I guess you'll move on when you're ready to.'

Millie lifted her chin and held his gaze. 'I'm not ready.' Would she ever be ready? When she'd been young and first fancied herself in love with Julian, getting married and setting up a home together was all she had wanted. But, when the hammer blow of his diagnosis had come, everything had changed. Her dream relationship had become a nightmare in reality.

Hunter's eyes moved between each of hers in a pulsing moment that ratcheted up her heart rate. Time stood still—so still she could hear the roaring echo of her heartbeat in her ears. He was a top-notch lawyer. He spent hours listening to clients, making sense of the things they told him, both true and false and all the shady spaces in between.

Could he see the truth behind her lie?

His eyes went to her mouth, lingering there for a

heart-stopping moment, before coming back to her gaze. 'So, about your mother's divorce.' The subject change nudged her out of her thoughts. 'I should warn you, I don't come cheap.'

Millie tried to ignore the little niggle of panic about her bank balance. She was a moderately successful jewellery designer in an increasingly competitive market, but exorbitant legal fees were going to put a considerable dent in her savings. 'I can afford you.' She injected her tone with pride, her chin elevated.

Their gazes were locked in a power struggle for a beat or two but then he suddenly frowned. 'Why would you be the one paying your mother's legal fees?'

Millie lowered her shoulders in a despondent sigh. 'Because my mother's soon-to-be-ex spent a lot of her money in a get-rich-quick scheme that fell flat. Plus, she just found out he has a mistress on the side. Mum will pay me back once she gets back on her feet.' *If* she got back on her feet.

He studied her for another long moment that felt like an aeon. 'I'll do a deal with you. I'll give you a discount if you have dinner with me tomorrow night.'

Millie's mouth fell open. 'Dinner?'

One side of his mouth tilted upwards. 'You do eat occasionally, don't you?'

'Yes, but I thought, given what a disaster our last dinner was—'

'Maybe I want another chance to stun you with my charm.' A teasing glint appeared in his gaze.

'You said it yourself—you're not my type.'

'That doesn't mean we can't have a pleasant dinner together and clear the air after the last time.'

Millie wondered what motive was behind his invitation. Had her previous immunity to him presented him with a challenge he couldn't resist? She'd often wondered since that night, if they had met up on any other date other than the anniversary of Julian's passing, if she would have been quite so immune to him. In spite of her unfriendly behaviour that night, she *had* noticed his traffic-stopping good looks and superbly toned body. She had desperately tried not to notice but a woman would have to be brain dead and without a pulse not to be impressed by how gorgeous he was in the flesh.

*In the flesh...*

Her mind swam with images of him naked and her pulse shot up again. She schooled her features into a mask of cool indifference, as if his invitation was nothing to get excited about. No point feeding his morbidly obese ego. 'I'll have to check my diary.'

'So, check it.' He nodded his head towards her bag where her phone was housed, his tawny eyes containing a challenge. *Resist me if you can.*

Millie sent him a sideways look, picked up her bag and took out her phone. She gave her phone diary a cursory glance, knowing full well there was nothing scheduled for the following night.

Her mind was going up and down on a seesaw. Should she or shouldn't she meet him for dinner? He said he would give her a discount on her mother's legal fees. Was this his bargaining chip? The more time she spent with him, the more intrigued by him she was. She had never met a more confident and self-assured man. A man who set goals and went after them with a single-minded purpose. Exactly the sort of man she needed to help her mother get out of this latest financial hole. She put her phone back in her bag and clicked the fastening closed with a definitive snap. 'I'm free, as it turns out.'

'Good. Where do you live? I'll pick you up at seven.'

'Erm, that's not necessary. I can meet you, like I did the last time.'

An implacable light appeared in his unwavering gaze. 'Let's not do anything like we did it the last time. I'll pick you up and take you home.'

Millie decided against making an issue of it and gave him her address, then added, 'How soon can you meet with my mother? I know you're awfully busy and—'

'I'll clear a space first thing tomorrow morning. Eight a.m.'

Millie let out an audible breath of relief. 'That soon? I don't know how to thank you. But would you mind if I came with her for...support?'

'That's fine. Bring any necessary documentation with you—financial records of joint assets or debts, bank statements, tax returns, that sort of thing—plus a list of any questions you'd like to ask, and any relevant information about the other party. It will help speed up the process. How long has she been separated from her husband?'

'Only a couple of months.'

'How long have they been married?'

'Four years.' Millie waited a beat and added, 'She's been married three times before. They've all ended in divorce.'

Hunter didn't seem at all shocked, but then, she figured he dealt with this sort of thing day in and day out. People who had once passionately loved each other fighting it out as bitter enemies in court over the division of assets. He had taken her account of her mother's soon-to-be-ex's reprehensible behaviour with such implacable calm, as if he heard similar stories every day of the working week. She wondered if that was why he was such a freedom-loving playboy. Maybe he found the notion of long-term love nothing more than a Hollywood fantasy. Dealing with warring divorce parties would be enough to turn anyone into a romance cynic.

'Which of her ex-husbands was your father?' he asked.

'None of them.' Millie looked at the loosened knot of his tie rather than meet his gaze. 'He died a couple of months before I was born. I think it's why she's been so unlucky in love since. She tried to replace him but could never find someone good enough to fill his shoes. It's why she's always kept his name. It's the one thing she didn't get talked out of relinquishing by any of her subsequent husbands.'

Hunter uncrossed his ankle from where it was resting on his bent knee and leaned forward to pick up his drink. 'Life can be tough on some people.' He took a small sip of his drink and put it down again.

'Yes, it can…' Millie looked at her left hand where Julian's ring sat. Barely a day went past when she didn't think of him. Not because she still loved him, but because of how unfair life had been to his mother and him. Julian's life had stopped at his diagnosis—the life he had planned, that was. So too had his mother's, all her hopes and dreams for her only child shattered by that devastating diagnosis. The gruelling treatment and multiple surgeries had taken away Julian's potential, reducing him to a frailty that had angered and frustrated him in equal measure.

And Millie had been chained to his side through all of it, trapped by a sense of duty that, to this day, she couldn't free herself from feeling. Because she hadn't been honest about her feelings for Julian—platonic feelings, not romantic love.

Hunter's phone rang and he grimaced as he checked the screen. 'I'll have to get this. Sorry.' He rose from his chair and added, 'I'll be back in a minute.' And then he wove his way through the other tables, presumably to go outside to take the call in private.

Millie couldn't see the street from this section of the wine bar, so sat finishing her drink, wondering if she had done the right thing in asking him to help her mother. He was the best man for the job, but it would mean regular contact with him for her, as her mother's supporter. Some divorces were simple and clear cut, but none of her mother's divorces had been, and Millie had no expectation this one would be any different. Hunter was a disturbingly attractive man and she wasn't half as immune to him as she'd thought.

*He's not your type.* The words so helpfully supplied by her conscience were not as reassuring as they ought to be. Right now, she didn't care if he wasn't her type. She couldn't stop imagining what it would feel like to have that sensually sculptured mouth pressed to her own. She suppressed a little shudder and put down her empty glass.

*Don't even think about it.*

# CHAPTER TWO

HUNTER'S HEART PRACTICALLY came to a stop every time he got a call from one of his sister's carers. He went outside to take the call away from the background noise of the wine bar. And away from anyone—most particularly Millie—listening in.

'Rupinder? Is everything okay?' He cupped one hand over his other ear to tone down the sounds of the busy street. His heart rate would never return to normal until he was assured everything was all right with his sister who had a rare genetic disorder. Emma required round-the-clock care and he had set her up in a nice townhouse close to her medical specialists, and organised and funded a team of full-time carers for her.

'Yes, everything's fine to do with Emma, but I just wanted to let you know I'm going to have to take a couple of weeks off due to my mother suddenly taking ill. She needs surgery, so hopefully I won't be too long off work, just till she gets back on her feet. Judy is going to fill in for me—is that okay with you?'

Hunter let out a sigh of relief that the emergency at hand had nothing to do with his sister this time. 'Of course. Take all the time you need.'

Too many phone calls over the years had brought news of Emma having yet another *grand mal* seizure or some sort of serious infection. Meningitis, bronchitis, pneumonia, sepsis…the list went on. The worry was a constant background humming in his brain. One of the worst seizures Emma had had was on the day of his blind date with Millie. He had come straight from visiting his sister in the hospital, where the specialists and medical students had gathered around her bedside, gravely talking amongst themselves about her rare condition and what remaining options there were. Hunter had never felt less like going on a date, and certainly not one organised by his friends.

He was the last person who needed help in the dating department. He had no trouble attracting beautiful women to his side—his biggest problem was getting rid of them. He wasn't interested in settling down with a nice girl someday. Who would take him on with Emma as part of the package deal? Hunter was her guardian and he held power of attorney now their mother was dead. Their father had washed his hands of them long ago and now had a new family. A *perfect* family.

Hunter had seen a photo of Millie Donnelly-Clarke at a society ball in the press a few months ago and had been intrigued by her. She had an untouchable air about her, regal and aristocratic, and he'd found himself agreeing to his friends' suggestion of a blind date with her.

But then Emma…

A lot of his life was dictated by his sister's problems. Ever since he'd been twelve years old when his parents had divorced, and Emma only seven, he'd had to step up and take on heavy responsibilities to do with the welfare, care and support of his sister—not to mention support his devastated mother, who hadn't coped with being deserted by Hunter's father. Abandoned and ripped off in the divorce by the man who had once claimed to love her, Hunter's mother had been left to raise two children, one of whom required constant care and numerous expensive therapies.

Hunter hadn't been in the best of moods when he'd met Millie for dinner and, given how prickly and unfriendly she had been, he hadn't bothered to dazzle her with his usual charm offensive.

But strangely, ever since, he hadn't been able to get her out of his mind.

Was it because she'd been the first woman to give him the brush-off since he'd been a gangly, awkward teenager? Because she was the only one that had got away and now he wanted another chance? He wasn't the sort of guy who couldn't handle a bit of rejection now and again. He wasn't exactly short of female attention. He only had to click his fingers and a beautiful woman would be his for the asking.

But something about Millie's immunity to him had got his attention. And kept it.

Hunter ended the call with his sister's carer, pocketed his phone and walked back into the wine bar. Millie was sitting bent over her phone and it gave him a chance to look at her before he joined her back at the table.

Her silvery blonde hair was long and lustrous, exactly like a skein of silk. Her figure was petite and slim and yet utterly feminine. The first thing he had noticed about her was her grey-blue eyes—they seemed to change colour with her mood. One minute they were a smoky grey, the other an ice-blue. Her complexion was the classic peaches and cream, with high aristocratic cheekbones, a ski-slope nose and an upturned mouth that had been the stuff of his night-time fantasises for the last couple of months, since their ill-fated blind date. He hadn't so much as laid a finger on her, not even to shake her hand in greeting, much less kiss her cheek. And yet, every male hormone in his body throbbed with the desire to do so.

When he'd received the text from her about meeting up for a drink, he had thought she'd changed her mind about him. It had put a spring in his step the whole way to the wine bar, wondering why she had changed her mind when he hadn't exactly been Prince Charming that night. But she hadn't contacted him for a rerun of their blind date. She wanted to engage his services as a lawyer for her mother, yet she had agreed to another shot at dinner. Tick. That was a win for him. He was looking forward to making up for the disaster of their last date. Never let it be said a woman walked away from a date with him without a smile on her face.

Hunter walked back to the table and she glanced up from her phone. One of her neat eyebrows rose and her smile had a cynical tilt. 'One of your many lovers checking if you're free this evening?'

Hunter rarely spoke to anyone about his sister's circumstances and was certainly not going to do so now.

'Not this time.' Hunter sat opposite Millie and picked up his drink. That was all the explanation he was prepared to give. He didn't need her sympathy. He didn't need endless questions about Emma's condition and treatment options. It was pointless talking about something that could never be fixed. Emma was a part of his life that was sectioned off, mostly out of the desire to protect her from intrusive attention, and not just from the press.

Emma had a loving and trusting nature, and quickly formed attachments to people, but when they left she was completely and utterly devastated, just as she had been when their father had abandoned them. In his early twenties Hunter had made the mistake of introducing her to a girlfriend who had made a big fuss of her, but then, when she'd broken up with him, Emma had been dropped too. Since then, he had never introduced his sister to any other lover. They were too temporary, and he didn't want them using Emma to 'impress' him.

'Would you like another?' He gestured to Millie's now-empty glass.

She shook her head, her lips twitching, as if she was trying not to smile. 'No, thank you. I like to keep a clear head when I'm talking to a lawyer.'

He laughed at her dry wit. 'Good for you.'

There was a strange little silence.

Hunter couldn't stop looking at the shape of her mouth—ripely curved, evenly full lips with tilted up corners, as if smiling was their preferred position. He wondered if her lips were as soft and pliable as they looked. Wondered why he was even tempted when she was exactly the sort of woman he usually avoided. She wasn't the type for a quick hook-up or short-term fling, even if her gaze kept drifting to his mouth as if she couldn't help it. She was still in love with her dead fiancé, for God's sake. Her fiancé's ring was still on her finger. But there was something about her that captivated him in a way he had never been captivated before.

'Why are you looking at me like that?' Her voice jolted him out of his study of her face.

He gave a slow blink and brought his gaze back to meet hers. 'You know exactly why I'm looking at you like that. You've been looking at me exactly the same way.'

Two small circles of colour bloomed in her cheeks. 'Don't be ridiculous.'

Hunter gave another soft laugh and rose to his feet. 'I'll see you tomorrow in my office at eight a.m.' He handed her a business card with his contact details on it. 'This is just the initial consultation to get the ball rolling. I usually meet with my clients several times, depending on how things go, and how cooperative the other party.'

'Thank you.' Her index and middle fingers ever so lightly brushed against his palm as she took the business card from him, and lust slammed him in the groin. As first touches went, it was tiny, and yet it packed a knockout punch to his senses. His body tingled from head to foot and he could only imagine what would happen if he kissed her. That she had felt something too was obvious in the way she'd pulled her hand away, as if it had received an electric shock.

She slipped the card into her bag and rose from her chair. Her teeth sank into her lower lip and she added, 'Erm, would you mind if you didn't mention anything about us having dinner tomorrow evening, when my mother comes to your office in the morning?'

Hunter wondered why the need for secrecy. Most

women he took out to dinner couldn't wait to broadcast who they were seeing to all and sundry. It was a refreshing change, and an intriguing one that his 'date' with Millie be considered something to be kept private. 'No problem. It can be our little secret.'

Millie stood with her mother outside Hunter's office building the following morning with her heart doing funny little trots, hops and skips. 'Right. Here we go.'

'Are you sure he's the right person to act for me?' her mother asked, casting her a worried glance. 'I've heard he's terribly expensive.'

Millie linked her arm through her mother's. 'Don't worry about the expense. Think of the outcome. He's the one to get the job done. "Get him and get justice" is his tagline.'

Eleanora chewed her lip. 'You haven't told him about my—?'

'No, Mum. I haven't.' Millie was well used to covering up her mother's literacy issues. She had been reading and interpreting letters and documents for her mum since childhood. Her mother could sign her name and read basic sentences, but legal documents could be hard for anyone, let alone someone with severe dyslexia. Millie knew her mother felt great shame about her problem, but every time Eleanora had taken a remedial class she had given up after only one or two sessions. She relied on her current partners or Millie to do things for her. At times, she even relied on her household staff—some of whom had also taken advantage of her.

They took the lift to the top floor of the building where Hunter's suite of offices was housed. The shiny brass plaque read: *Addison and Associates, Legal Services*, and the swish reception looked like the foyer of a top-notch hotel. Plush ankle-deep carpet, a finely crafted timber credenza and priceless works of art on the walls spoke of a legal eagle who was at the top of his game. The beautifully dressed, coiffed and made-up young female receptionist behind the polished credenza gave a welcoming smile that was blindingly white. 'Good morning.'

'Good morning,' Millie said, with an answering smile. 'We're here to see Hunter Addison. Millie and Eleanora Donnelly-Clarke.'

'I'll tell him you're here.' The receptionist leaned towards an intercom on her desk, which was connected to her headset and microphone, and informed Hunter of their arrival. Millie didn't hear his reply, but the receptionist pressed the 'off' switch and pushed back her chair. 'I'll take you to his office right now. Come this way.'

Millie and her mother followed the receptionist down a wide corridor with more beautiful works of art, a mixture of modern and classical, that somehow didn't clash at all but worked in perfect harmony. The receptionist opened the corner-office door—of course he had the corner office—and indicated for Millie and her mother to go in.

Millie stepped over the threshold and her eyes went straight to Hunter seated behind his polished mahogany and leather-topped desk. Behind him was the most spectacular view over London, and if he hadn't been so heart-stoppingly handsome she would have been tempted to stare at the view rather than at him. But no view could ever rival his superb male form. He was wearing a crisp white business shirt with a blue tie with silver stripes, the charcoal-grey jacket of his suit hanging off the back of his chair. He rose from his chair with a welcoming smile and her breath caught somewhere between her lungs and her throat.

'Good morning.' He came from behind the desk and offered his hand to Eleanora first. 'Eleanora, nice to meet you.'

'And you too,' Eleanora said, blinking rapidly and blushing as if she had just been introduced to a rock star.

Hunter then offered Millie his hand. She disguised a quick swallow and slipped her hand into his. The gentle but firm pressure of his long, strong, tanned fingers closing around hers sent a shock wave throughout her entire body. Flickers, darts and tingles passed from his hand to hers in a current of electricity that made the fine hairs at the back of her neck stand up. His fingers were warm and dry, and she couldn't stop thinking of how they would feel gliding over other parts of her body…her breasts, her thighs… His eyes meshed with hers and her heart did a somersault in her chest, the sensual heat of his palm and fingers travelling through her body to stir warm liquid longing in the secret heart of her female flesh.

'I hope our eight a.m. meeting wasn't too early for you to get out of bed?'

His deep voice and the smouldering glint in his whisky-brown eyes sent another wave of heat through her. She was aware of her body's quiet but chaotic response to him. The fluttering of her pulse, the molten heat of arousal between her legs, the near-desperate urge of her body to get closer to him. It was like the powerful pull of a magnetic force drawing her to him, one she had to do something—anything—to counteract.

Millie slipped her hand out of his, but it continued to tingle, as if his touch had permanently disrupted the network of her nerves, like a powerful lightning strike on a computer. 'No, not at all. I'm an early riser.'

The glint in his gaze brightened. 'So am I.'

Millie could only imagine what part of himself to which he was referring as an early riser. Her mind was suddenly filled with images of him in a tangle of sheets, his gloriously naked body in full arousal. She could feel her cheeks glowing and her mouth went completely dry. She took a step backward to put more distance between them, and somehow almost lost her footing, but his hand shot out just in time and steadied her.

'Careful.' His fingers were a steel bracelet on her wrist and a shiver travelled the length of her spine as she thought about where else those fingers could touch her. Where else she *wanted* them to touch her. She was shocked at her body's betrayal. It had been years since she had even thought of her sexual needs and urges. Her sensuality had been put in a coma by her experience of taking care of Julian's needs. But now, with just a touch of Hunter Addison's hand, a wave of sexual awareness swept through her body, awakening her sleeping senses, stirring them into a feeding frenzy.

The hunger in her body was out of control. Could he sense it? Could he see the impact his touch had on her? She prided herself on being good at hiding what she was really feeling but she wondered if Hunter would all too easily see through her mask of indifference to the burning, yearning hunger buried deep inside her.

'Thank you.' Millie gave him what she hoped was an impersonal smile and his hand fell away from her wrist.

'Take a seat and let's get started,' Hunter said.

'Here's the paperwork you asked for,' Eleanora said, pushing a folder of documents across his desk. Millie could see her mother's nervousness but hoped Hunter would assume it was only because of the stress of going through yet another divorce. Millie had attended many meetings with her mother in the past—lawyers, accountants, doctors and even her own parent-teacher interviews as a child and teenager—all in an attempt to protect her mother from the shame of exposure of her severe learning disability.

'Great, thanks,' Hunter said. 'The less research I have to do on your behalf, the less money you have to pay me. But I'll try and keep expenses down as much as possible.' He picked up a pair of rectangular horn-rimmed glasses from his desk and put them on, pushing them further up the bridge of his nose with his index finger. Millie couldn't have taken her eyes off him even if she'd tried. The glasses only made him look more attractive. Dangerously attractive.

After a couple of minutes, Hunter glanced up from the documents to address Eleanora. 'The property in Surrey—that was in your name originally?'

Millie jumped in to help her mother out. 'It was left to Mum by her father-in-law, my paternal grandfather, but it was put in both Mum's and Derek's names soon after their marriage.'

Hunter gave a slow nod, his expression mostly unreadable, but Millie could almost see the working of his clever brain behind the screen of his brown eyes. Processing, calculating, assessing, analysing. 'And these shares that were sold in January…' he again aimed his comment directly at Eleanora '…which account did the money go into after the sale? Or was it used to pay off debt?'

Eleanora looked at him blankly for a moment but, when Millie opened her mouth to speak on her behalf, Hunter put his hand up in a silencing gesture and she clamped her lips together. 'Eleanora?' he prompted.

Eleanora flicked a worried *Help me* glance at Millie before turning back to face him. 'I—I don't really know. I always let my husband see to that side of things. He's got more of a head for business than I do.'

He quietly assessed Eleanora for a nanosecond before responding, 'That's okay. Lots of married couples manage things that way.'

He leafed through a few more of the documents and Millie held her breath until she thought her lungs would explode. She hadn't been happy about Riversdale being changed into Derek's name, but it had happened before she could do anything to stop it. Riversdale was where her father had grown up and it pained her to think it might have to be sold to cover legal costs. It was her only link to the father she had lost before she'd been born.

But it might not just be Riversdale on the line. She'd barely had time to cast her own eyes over the papers before the appointment with Hunter but she'd seen enough discrepancies to raise her alarm. Large sums of money had been taken out of her mother's accounts.

Why hadn't she stepped in earlier to protect her mother? Why had she let it come to this? It was financial abuse and it had happened—*again*—on Millie's watch.

After another few minutes that felt like an era, Hunter took off his glasses and placed them on top of the sheaf of documents on his desk, a small frown pulling at his brow. 'Okay, here's what I think we need to do. I have a friend who is a forensic accountant—one of the best, if not the best. Matteo Vitale. He's based in Italy, but he travels back and forth to London for work. If you're agreeable, I'll get him to run his eyes over your accounts and track all the activity during your marriage. Hopefully, it won't take too long, then we'll be in a better position to choose our approach going forward.'

'Thank you so much,' Eleanora said, looking vastly relieved.

Millie echoed her mother's thanks and added, 'It's very good of you to see us at such short notice.'

Hunter's gaze met hers and something warm and treacly slithered down her spine. 'The pleasure has been all mine.'

Millie rose from her chair with more breathless haste than grace and dragged her mother up with her. 'We should let you get on with your busy day. Come on, Mum.'

Hunter rose from behind his desk and came round to shake her mother's hand. 'Eleanora, would you be so kind as to give me a couple of minutes alone with Millie? We have some other business to discuss. My receptionist will get you a coffee or tea.'

'Of course,' Eleanora said, beaming and clasping his hand with both of hers, as if she was going to crush it with gratitude. 'I don't mind at all. Take all the time you need.' She finally released his hand, turned and left his office before Millie could do or say anything to stop her.

Hunter turned his gaze back to Millie. Dark, penetrating, intuitive. 'How well do you know your mother's husband?'

'Well enough to know I don't like him.'

'Did you ever like him?'

'Not really. He was charming at first, but I didn't like the way he spoke to mum once he got a ring on her finger. Or how he convinced her to put his name on the Riversdale deed without telling me.'

Hunter let out a short, harsh breath that sounded as if it might be code for *What a lowlife bastard and I can't wait to nail him for it.* 'I'll try to sort this out for her as quickly and efficiently as possible.'

'Thank you.' Millie's heart began to thump as if she'd run up the fifty floors instead of using the lift. How would she pay for a long-drawn-out battle in court for her mother? She couldn't expect Hunter to reduce his fees. He hadn't become one of the richest lawyers in London by doing pro bono work, especially for someone like her—a woman who had been insultingly rude the first time they'd met. 'I really don't want to take up any more of your time, so…' She began to turn away but for the third time in the space of minutes one of his hands came down on her wrist.

'Wait. Stop trying to run away.'

She stared at his tanned fingers against the cream of her silk sleeve and something in her stomach swooped. She couldn't stop thinking of those long, tanned fingers on other parts of her body. Parts of her body that were already tingling as the warmth from his touch seeped into her skin irrespective of the silk barrier of her top. She slowly brought her gaze back up to his. 'Please, let me go.' Her voice came out as a hoarse whisper, but she was worried her eyes were saying the opposite. *Please, hold me.*

He drew in a breath and released her wrist, and then expelled his breath on a heavy sigh. 'I probably don't need to tell you I'm worried about your mother's situation. It looks to me like her current partner is siphoning off funds into hidden accounts but that's only a hunch at this stage. But, let me assure you, I will get to the bottom of it.'

'Thank you.'

He gave a brief smile that melted her resolve to keep her distance like a blowtorch on butter. She could actually feel her stiff and guarded posture relaxing and wondered how on earth she was going to resist him if he didn't stop being so much of a helpful hero to the rescue.

'Try not to worry too much.' His tone was gently reassuring and melted another layer of her emotional armour.

'Lately, all I seem to do is worry about my mother. For years, actually,' Millie found herself confessing. 'She has appalling taste in men. She falls for good looks instead of good character. And they fall for her because she's beautiful and compliant, like most men seem to want their women to be.'

'Not all men,' Hunter said, holding her gaze with gleaming intensity. 'Personally, I like a bit of spirit and push-back.'

Millie swallowed and glanced at his mouth, her stomach bottoming out. She moistened her lips and hitched in a ragged breath. Was he flirting with her? Yes, he was, and, even more worrying, she was enjoying it. Way too much. 'Erm, what other business did you want to discuss with me?'

He stepped close enough to touch her. Close enough to set her heart rate stampeding again. Close enough for her to see the tiny dark-chocolate flecks in his mid-brown eyes and the impossibly thick and long lashes that fringed them. Close enough for her to smell the light citrusy tang of his aftershave, redolent of sun-warmed lemons with a woodsy understory. He had shaved that morning, but tiny pinpricks of regrowth were already evident, suggesting he hadn't been standing back and holding the door for everyone else when the testosterone had been handed out.

Millie hadn't been this close to such a virile man in years. Possibly ever. His sensual energy brushed against her in soundless waves, sending shivers, darts and flickers of awareness across her skin.

Hunter picked up a section of her long silver-blonde hair and lightly trailed it across his fingers like someone inspecting a skein of priceless silk. His expression was inscrutable, all except for the dark intensity of his eyes. 'Why are you frightened of me?' His voice was low and deep with an edge of huskiness that made her skin lift in a delicate shiver.

'I—I'm not.' It would have sounded a whole lot more convincing if her voice hadn't come out as a scratchy whisper. And if her heart wasn't beating as if it was going to work its way out of her chest and her legs threatening to fold underneath her.

'Liar.' He gave a lazy smile and tucked her hair behind her ear, then lowered his hand back by his side. But he stayed close to her, so close all she had to do was move forward half a step and her breasts would be in contact with his chest and her pelvis in contact with his. Her breasts began to tingle behind the lace cage of her bra, hot little tingles that made her aware of her female form in a way she had never been before. A pulse beat between her legs—a delicate contraction of intimate muscles waking from a long hibernation.

Millie licked her carpet-dry lips. 'You're too close to me. I can barely breathe.'

'So, step back. I'm not stopping you.'

She lifted her chin, her eyes warring with his in a battle of wills. He liked a bit of push-back, did he? She could give as good as she got. 'Why don't *you* step back?'

His eyes smouldered. 'I like seeing the effect I have on you.'

Millie steeled her spine, iced her gaze and stood her ground. 'You have zero effect on me.'

The air beat with tension—sexual tension that disturbed the atmosphere like a galaxy of hyperactive dust motes.

His gaze snared hers and there was nothing she could do to break the deadlock. 'I look forward to making you eat those words one day in the not-too-distant future.' The deep rumble of his tone sent a runaway firework fizzing and whizzing down every knob of her spine.

Millie gave a tight-lipped smile when what she really wanted to do was slap his face for his arrogance. 'Don't hold your breath.'

He gave a soft chuckle of laughter and stepped away from her and strode idly over to the door of his office, effectively bringing their private meeting to a close. 'I'll see you tonight. I'll pick you up at seven.'

Millie wanted to tell him where to stick his dinner date, but she needed him on side for the best result for her mother's divorce. She needed him as an ally, not an enemy.

And most of all she needed her head examined for looking forward to seeing him again.

Hunter closed the door once Millie left and walked back to his desk with a smile. Hot damn, but he was excited about their dinner tonight. Excited in a way he hadn't been in years. He had never had to talk someone into having dinner with him before. Usually, he asked, and they said yes. But he'd had to *convince* Millie.

Who knew how attractive a woman playing hard to get could be? He liked her spirit, the light of stubbornness in her grey-blue eyes. His office still carried a trace of her perfume, teasing his nostrils with the beguiling scent of sweet peas and sultry summer nights.

It had been all he could do to keep his hands off her. Drawn to her with such fierce attraction, he had been tempted to kiss her to see what happened. But he wasn't the type of man to force himself on a woman. He would only kiss her when he was certain it was what she wanted—or, even better, if she made the first move. Unless he had read her completely wrong, she was fighting her attraction to him. Stubbornly resisting the sexual energy that erupted between them.

Was it because of her late fiancé? Beth and Dan had

told him it had been three years since Millie's fiancé's death. At twenty-six, she was way too young to give up on dating. Not that he would be offering her anything but a temporary fling. He wasn't interested in tying himself down to one person. He wasn't interested in falling in love, the way his mother had fallen in love with his father and then had that love rejected, destroyed, poisoned by a brutally cold abandonment.

Not that Hunter could ever see himself sink to the lows of his father. It took a special type of lowlife to walk out on a child with a disability and never see her again. A child who loved her father devotedly and who, to this day, still couldn't understand what she had done wrong for him to abandon her.

Hunter sat back at his desk and looked back over the documents Millie's mother had provided. Alarm bells had rung as soon as Eleanora had walked into his office. He could definitely see where Millie got her stunning looks from but, unlike Millie, Eleanora had a submissive and compliant nature, like so many of his clients who got done over in a divorce—his own mother being a case in point. Financial abuse was a scourge—all forms of domestic abuse were—but he was not going to rest until he brought to light the dark dealings of yet another partner who thought they could get away with it.

But he had a gut feeling there was more to Eleanora's situation than either she or Millie were letting on. He had been a lawyer long enough to be able to read between the lines of what people said or didn't say, the inner emotions they desperately tried to conceal. It was his job to make sense of the grey areas, the black spots, the shadows, the secrets and lies.

He picked up the gold pen his sister Emma had bought for him for his last birthday, when she'd been out with one of her carers, and flicked it back and forth between his fingers, his mind replaying every moment of his meeting with Millie and her mother. Millie had answered for her mother as though she'd been the adult and Eleanora the child. He did it himself with his sister, because Emma had limited understanding of how the world worked and in many ways would always remain a child in an adult's body. He clicked the pen on and off, his mind still ticking over like the cogs of a machine. He dropped the pen back on his desk and pushed a hand through his hair.

This was exactly the sort of case he liked working on—bringing justice to those who needed it most. But, in order to do his job to the best of his ability, he needed to know the truth about his clients. The whole truth and nothing but the truth. And it was his job, his responsibility, to get it out of them, no matter what.

# CHAPTER THREE

MILLIE RUSHED HOME from work later that day to get ready for her dinner with Hunter. Ivy Kennedy—one of her two flatmates—was in the process of moving out in preparation for her wedding in a few weeks' time. She looked up from where she was kneeling on the floor, packing a box of her kitchen utensils, when Millie came in.

'How did your meeting with Hunter Addison go? Is he going to act for your mum?'

Millie slipped her tote bag off her shoulder and hung it over the back of one of the kitchen chairs. 'Yep. It went well. He's organising a forensic accountant to go over all of mum's accounts to see if there are any irregularities. She was so relieved, I thought she was going to hug him.'

Ivy got up from the floor and pushed her auburn hair out of her face. 'I'm so glad you were able to put your prejudices aside and contact him again.' She smiled and added playfully, 'You obviously didn't completely burn your boats with him. He wouldn't have offered to do it if he couldn't stand a bar of you. Ha-ha, no pun intended.'

Millie was conscious of her cheeks heating and

turned away on the pretence of taking her phone out of her tote bag. 'It's just another case for him. Nothing else.'

Ivy frowned and came a little closer. 'Is something wrong? You seem a little distracted. I thought you said the meeting went well?'

'It did, but this fourth divorce has made me realise how truly vulnerable Mum is, and how I can't really protect her the way I want to. I feel like I've let her down yet again. But I have my own business to run and I don't want to fail at it. I don't know how I can continue to be a good daughter and a good businesswoman at the same time.'

'Why do you always feel so responsible for your mum?' Ivy asked. 'She's an adult—and, yes, like my mum she's been terribly unlucky in her relationships—but that's not your fault. Anyway, you have your own life to live. You gave so much of it up for Jules, helping him through his treatment and so on. You can't keep putting your own needs on hold indefinitely.'

Millie wished she could share the burden of her mother's problems but for years she had kept silent out of respect for her mother's feelings. She trusted her friends, Ivy and Zoey, would be nothing but supportive and understanding if she told them, but she had kept it a secret for so long, she didn't know how to put it into words. Would they feel hurt she hadn't told them earlier? And, if she revealed *that* secret, how soon before she revealed her own more shameful one?

She hadn't been, and wasn't still, in love with Julian.

Millie looked at her friend and grimaced ruefully. 'I only hope she doesn't fall for another guy who only wants her for her beauty and her money, or at least what's left of her money.'

Ivy gave her a warm hug. 'You're a wonderful daughter and a wonderful support to everyone who knows and loves you.' She leaned back, smiled and added, 'And you'll make a wonderful bridesmaid. Will you do it? I want you and Zoey to be my bridesmaids. Zoey has already said yes, and it would be just divine if you did too.'

Millie smiled back, thrilled to be asked. 'Oh, wow, yes, of course! I've never been a bridesmaid before.'

Ivy glanced at the ring on Millie's left hand, a small frown of concern etched on her features. 'You won't find it…triggering, given you didn't get to have your own wedding?'

Millie shook her head, painting a smile on her mouth. 'I'll be fine. I'm just so happy you and Louis found each other.'

'I hope you find someone as special as Louis,' Ivy said, glowing with happiness at her upcoming wedding to the man of her dreams. 'Hey, maybe you and Hunter Addison will hit it off. Opposites attract and all that!'

'Don't be ridiculous.' Millie screwed up her nose, as if being with Hunter was the worst thing she could ever imagine.

Ivy's eyes began to twinkle. 'Never say never, my girl. Look what happened to me.'

Millie gave her a quelling look. 'You actually liked Louis and were already friends with him before you fell in love with each other. Hunter Addison and I can't spend an evening together without getting into a fight. Which is a problem because, in about an hour, I'm going to be spending the evening with him.'

Ivy gasped. 'On another date, you mean? Seriously?'

Millie shifted her lips from side to side. 'It's just dinner. I think he's only asked me because he's arrogant enough to assume I won't give him the brush-off a second time.'

'And will you?' Ivy asked, eyebrows raised. 'Give him the brush-off?'

Millie affected a laugh. 'But of course. He's not my type.'

And he damn well better stay that way, otherwise she was going to be in seriously big trouble.

Hunter arrived right on the dot of seven and Millie answered the door to his brisk knock with a cool smile on her face. 'Hi.' She tried not to notice how gorgeous he looked in a butter-soft black leather jacket and dark trousers teamed with a white open-necked shirt. Tried but failed. Her pulse kicked up its pace and her senses swooned at the crisp citrus notes of his aftershave and the dark glitter in his gaze.

'Hello there.' His deep voice did strange things to her heart rate, so too did the way his eyes ran over her baby-blue knee-length dress and cream pashmina wrap. 'You look very beautiful. That colour brings out the blue in your eyes.'

'Thank you.' A flutter of nerves erupted in her belly and she took a steadying breath, releasing it in a stuttered stream.

Hunter quirked a dark brow at her. 'Nervous?'

Millie lifted her chin and speared his gaze. 'Should I be?'

He lifted a hand to her face and trailed his fingertip from the top of her cheekbone to the base of her chin, his touch so light it barely grazed her, and yet her skin tingled as if touched by fire. 'Not with me.' His voice had gone down another semitone—deep, gravelly, sensual.

Millie rolled her lips together and looked at the open neck of his shirt where she could see a sprinkling of his dark chest hair—a heady reminder of the male hormones powering through his body. 'It's been a while since I went out to dinner with a guy.' She gave him a rueful smile and added, 'Well, apart from with you that last time, I mean.'

He gave a lopsided smile in return. 'Let's not talk about that night, hmm?' He placed his hand on her elbow. 'Shall we go? My car is just down the street a bit.'

Millie was conscious of the gentle warmth of his hand at her elbow, guiding her to where his car was parked a few doors down from her flat. His touch sent little aftershocks through her body. At six foot four, he towered over her, even though she was wearing heels. She had rarely worn heels going out with Julian, as he had only been a couple of inches taller, and somehow she had got into the habit of wearing flats so as not to make him feel inadequate.

Hunter helped her into the car, and she thought of all the times the role had been reversed in her relationship with Julian. Not that Julian had been able to help it, of course, but Millie had been the one to help *him* into the car, pulling down his seatbelt and making sure he was comfortable at all times and in all places. She had morphed into his carer rather than his partner and she'd had to suppress her resentment at how the tables had turned. Julian hadn't been to blame—it was his illness. If anyone had been to blame, it was her for not being honest with him from the get-go.

They spoke about inconsequential things on the way to the restaurant—the weather, the news, the state of the economy—and all the while Millie was aware of him sitting close enough for her to reach out and touch him. He drove with competence and care, no risks or tricky manoeuvres, but with patience and consideration for the other road users. Her gaze kept going to his left thigh, and she wondered what it would feel like to run her hand up and down those powerful muscles. To feel them bunch under the gentle pressure of her fingers, to explore his body in intimate detail.

Millie turned her gaze to the front of the car and sat up straighter in her seat, annoyed with the way her mind kept wandering into such dangerous territory. Why was she so darn attracted to him? She hadn't thought herself the shallow looks-are-everything type. She hadn't thought herself all that impressed by a man's wealth or status. She hadn't thought she could ever be tempted to sleep with a man again.

That part of her life was over…wasn't it?

A few minutes later, Hunter led her into a fine-dining restaurant in Mayfair. They were taken to their table by a courteous waiter who addressed Hunter by name. Within a short time, they were seated with drinks in front of them. Hunter had declined alcohol, and she was secretly impressed he had made that choice, given he was driving. She had opted for mineral water again, keen to keep her head in his disturbingly attractive company.

Hunter raised his glass of Indian tonic water, his

mouth tilted in a crooked smile. 'So, here's to second chances.'

With just a moment's hesitation, Millie lifted her glass to his. 'To second chances.'

The chink of their glasses sounded loud in the silence, their eyes locking over the table. A second chance at what—seduction? A one-night stand? A fling? The possibilities seemed to hover in the space between them. Sensual possibilities she hadn't allowed herself to think about until now. What would it be like sleeping with a man like Hunter? A man who had sexual experience on a scale she hadn't encountered before. She and Julian had been each other's one and only lover. Childhood sweethearts who had drifted into an intimate relationship that hadn't had a chance to grow and mature as it should, due to the impact of his illness. Over time, Julian hadn't had stamina or patience for her needs, and she had settled for a peaceful rather than passionate life.

But now her frozen passions were thawing, creating molten heat in her body she could no longer ignore, especially in the presence of Hunter. He triggered a fiery response in her with every glance, every touch. Who knew what would happen if he kissed her?

Could she risk such a conflagration of the senses?

Millie finally managed to drag her eyes away from his mesmerising gaze and took a tentative sip of her mineral water, wishing now she had asked for something stronger.

'Tell me about your fiancé.' The request was bluntly delivered, a command rather than a question, and it jolted her as if he had slammed his hand down on the table.

She drew in a quick breath and put her glass down, not quite meeting Hunter's gaze. 'I'd rather not, if you don't mind.' She wasn't going to spill all to him of all people. She hadn't even told her best friends the truth about her relationship with her late fiancé. Even her own mother knew nothing of Millie's tortured emotions over Julian.

'You find it painful?' His tone was disarmingly gentle.

*Yes, but not for the reasons you think.*

How could she tell him the truth about her relationship with Julian? How could she tell anyone? Millie chanced a glance at him to find his expression etched in lines of concern. 'Have you ever lost someone you loved?' she asked.

A shadow passed through his whisky-brown gaze. 'Yes. My mother. She died ten years ago. Cancer. We were close.' His tone was matter-of-fact, delivering a set of details dispassionately, and yet his eyes told another story. A story of loss and sadness that hadn't yet been resolved.

'I'm so sorry,' Millie said. 'Do you still have your father?'

He gave a snort that sounded more like a suppressed cynical laugh. 'The truth is, I never *had* my father. I just thought I did.' His hand curled into a fist where it was resting on the table. 'He left us when I was twelve. Completely walked out of our lives and didn't once look back.' His fingers uncurled and he picked up his glass again. 'He has a new family now. A wife, two perfect kids.' He used the same dispassionate tone but underneath she could hear the steely thread of anger.

Millie could see the same anger written on his features. It was in every tense muscle of his face. She could only imagine how devastated he must have felt as a young boy on the threshold of manhood to be left by his father in such a brutally callous way. No contact over the tough years of adolescence, no mentoring through young adulthood, no relationship at all.

How had Hunter coped with such heartless rejection? It gave her an inkling of why he was such a driven and goal-oriented man. Didn't they say that rejection from a parent in childhood could make someone strive to over-achieve all their life in an effort to make up for the abandonment? But it was a never-ending quest—it could not be resolved unless harmony was restored with the absent parent and yet in Hunter's case it sounded as if the chance of that sort of reunion was next to impossible. 'That must have been so terribly hurtful for you, especially at that age. Actually, at any age.'

'More so for my mother and sister.'

'You have a sister?'

Something flickered over his features and a shutter came down in his gaze. 'Emma is five years younger. Our father's desertion hit her much harder than me. She worshipped the ground he walked on.' The hard and bitter note in his voice was gone, and in its place was a sad resignation about things that had happened and couldn't be changed.

Millie found herself leaning closer to him, desperate to offer some sort of comfort, some measure of understanding. 'I'm so sorry to hear that. Little girls often idealise their fathers. He's usually the first man they fall in love with. You must be very angry with him even now for what he did.'

Hunter's expression was back to its hard lines of bitterness, his gaze glittering. 'He's the reason I do what I do. He ripped my mother off during the divorce. He hid money in offshore accounts just so he didn't have to provide for us. She had nothing, not even a house to live in or a car to drive. It was despicable, and I swore from the moment their divorce was finalised that I would never allow someone to do that to another person if I could help it.'

Millie felt a new respect for his work ethic. She had to readjust her image of him as a powerhouse lawyer intent on acquiring ridiculous amounts of wealth out of other people's misery to that of a man who sought justice for each and every client who walked in the door. He was driven, focussed, indomitable. The perfect ally in a battle. 'I think it's amazing that you've chosen to work in divorce law because of what happened to your mother and sister and you. Is your sister a lawyer too?'

A screen came down over his eyes and he adjusted the position of his water glass on the table with exaggerated precision. 'No. She's not in employment at the moment.' His voice gave no clue to his feelings regarding his sister's lack of employment but there was a muscle in the lower quadrant of his jaw that tap-tap-tippity-tapped like a miniature hammer being held by someone with a not-quite-steady hand.

Millie wasn't known by her friends as a sniffer dog for secrets for nothing. Hunter was better than most at keeping his cards close, but she could sense there was more to his sister's situation than he was letting on. Did Emma have mental health issues? Drug or alcohol problems? An eating disorder? Had her father's desertion so young in her life caused her to struggle during school and thus have difficulty finding gainful employment as an adult? Not everyone got a happy childhood, and those that had the more difficult ones often struggled throughout their lives. Millie wanted to press him for more details, but the waiter came with their entrees and the moment was lost.

Instead, she commented on the gorgeous entrees set down before them—she had caramelised scallops with strawberry salsa, Hunter had crispy duck-breast with cherry port sauce. 'Oh, my goodness, look at the sheer artistry of this food. Can you believe how incredibly creative chefs are? It never ceases to amaze me. Every mouthful is like a work of art.'

'They certainly do a good job here,' Hunter said, picking up his fork. 'Have you been to this restaurant before?'

Millie speared a scallop with her fork. 'No, never, but I've heard heaps about it.'

'You said earlier you haven't been out to dinner with a guy for ages,' Hunter said. 'I guess you didn't eat out much with your fiancé before he passed away.'

In spite of the delicious flavours exploding in her mouth, Millie could feel her appetite slipping away and put her fork back down. 'Well, certainly not at places as fancy as this, but sometimes we'd pick up a fast-food meal if Julian was feeling up to it.'

She paused for a beat and went on, 'Chemo kind of ruins one's appetite and even the flavour of food at times. And once Julian lost his hair he was really self-conscious and hated being seen in public without a cap or beanie on.' A tiny sigh escaped her lips before she could stop it. She picked up her fork and speared another scallop. 'It was hard watching him suffer…'

Hunter reached across the table and laid his broad hand over the top of hers, the gentle pressure soothing, comforting. 'It must have been heart-breaking for you. You were childhood sweethearts, right?'

Millie kept her eyes on their joined hands, conscious of the warmth spreading through her skin from his. Conscious of the lies she was feeding him about her relationship with Julian. 'Yes, we met in school. He only lived a couple of streets from my house, so we hung out a lot together as kids. We started officially dating when we were sixteen. He was diagnosed with a brain tumour just before his eighteenth birthday.'

'How tragic.' Hunter's voice was gentle and full of compassion.

'Yes, it was…' Millie flicked a glance his way and, pulling her hand from underneath his, continued, 'He fought it as bravely as he could for six years. Round after round of chemo, so many specialist appointments, long hours on the chemo ward while he had treatment. In and out of hospital when things got bad. I supported him and his mother. I still see her most weeks. She was understandably devastated when he died. He was an only child.'

'His father?'

Millie gave him a speaking look. 'Another one of those deadbeat dads who walked out on his family. He left when Julian was a toddler. Julian had no memory of him at all, which was probably a good thing in the end.'

But because Julian's mother Lena hadn't had a partner to share the emotional load, Millie had had no choice but to continue to offer support and comfort even though it had made her feel terribly conflicted. Julian was an only child and Lena had relied heavily on Millie when things had got tough. They'd become a tag team to help Julian get through the ordeal of his illness. They'd supported each other. They'd cheered the other on when the other one's hopes had faded. They'd stepped up when the other had had to step back. In some ways, Lena had become more of a mother figure to her than her own mother. Millie knew if she'd broken up with Julian, she'd have been breaking up with his mother as well. It had been easier in the end to continue her relationship with Julian, even though for the last couple of years it had felt like an emotional prison from which she might never escape.

Not that she wanted to reveal any of that to Hunter. She had already shared more than she usually did with someone she barely knew.

'Do you see yourself settling down with someone else one day?' Hunter asked after a short silence.

Millie arched her eyebrow in a pointed manner. 'No. Do you see yourself settling down any time soon?'

He gave a crooked smile that didn't make the full distance to his eyes. 'No. The marriage and happy-ever-after thing isn't for me. I see the other side of love and commitment every day at work. It's enough to turn anyone into a hardened cynic.'

'Yes, well, I've seen enough with my mother trying

to get away from difficult husbands who say they love her until they hate her,' Millie said with a sigh. 'She found true love once and lost it.'

'A bit like you, then.' His comment startled her, not because it was true but because it was false. His gaze was unwavering, penetrating, making her feel raw and exposed.

Millie looked back at the barely touched food on her plate, her heart thumping, her skin prickling. *You are a fraud. A liar.* The mental accusation was loud and clanging inside her head, making her increasingly uneasy under the piercing scrutiny of Hunter Addison. Could he read her 'tells'? The micro-expressions or tonal qualities she couldn't always control? She forced herself to meet his gaze, schooling her features into a mask. 'What about you? Have you ever been in love?'

His slanted smile was cynical. 'You're very good at deflection, aren't you?'

Millie held his challenging look. 'A simple yes or no will do.'

'No.' His tone couldn't have been more decisive.

'Let me guess—I bet lots of women have fallen in love with you.' Millie held up her fingers in a tallying motion. 'One—you're good-looking. Two—you're rich and successful. Three…' She decided against mentioning anything about his undoubted sexual prowess but could feel herself blushing regardless.

'Three?' he prompted with an arch of a single ink-black eyebrow, the sardonic smile still in place.

Millie disguised a tight swallow. 'I'm assuming you're a good lover.' Her cheeks were now hot enough to flambé food, her voice betrayingly husky.

His glinting tawny gaze held hers captive. 'I guess there's only one way you'll know for sure.'

The words hung in the silence like a lure, a temptation, a dare.

Millie's heart missed a beat, then another one. She called on every bit of acting ability she had perfected over the last few years to sit coolly composed in her chair. 'In your dreams, Addison.'

# CHAPTER FOUR

THE THING WAS, sleeping with Millie *was* exactly what most preoccupied Hunter's mind just lately. He couldn't stop his imagination playing with the idea of kissing the ripe curve of her mouth, trailing his lips over every delectable inch of her body, being *inside* her, feeling her pleasure spasm around him.

Was he so turned on because he hadn't had a lover in the last couple of months? Such a space between hook-ups was a little unusual for him. He had a healthy, some might even say robust, sexual appetite. He enjoyed the human contact; the physical touch and reciprocal pleasure was something he looked forward to on a regular basis.

But, since he had met Millie on that blind date from hell, he had lost interest in anyone other than her. Which was frankly kind of weird, because she wasn't his type. His type played the hook-up game by the rules. Short, satisfying flings that got the job done without anyone's feelings getting hurt. No strings, no promises, no expectations other than a good time—it could have been his personal tagline.

But something about Millie Donnelly-Clarke with

her feisty spirit and constant push-back excited him in a way he had never been excited before. He understood the word no when he heard it. He wasn't so egotistical that he couldn't accept when a woman wasn't interested in him.

But the question of why Millie kept staring at his mouth and blushing begged an answer. An answer he was determined to get one way or the other.

'What? You can't see yourself having a fling with me?' Hunter asked with a teasing smile.

Her cheeks were a rosy pink, her blue-grey gaze flashing with defiance. 'No. I cannot.' Her tone had a hint of starchy schoolmistress about it, but her gaze drifted to his mouth once more, as if pulled by a force outside of her control, and her throat rose and fell over a tiny swallow.

'Because you're not ready to move on from your fiancé?'

Her chin came up another imperious notch. 'Isn't it a little tricky for you, getting involved with a client?'

Hunter held her gaze. 'Ah, but you're not my client. Your mother is.'

Millie's expression faltered for a nanosecond and her small white teeth sank into the plump pillow of her lower lip. But then her gaze inched up to his again, her gaze clear and direct. 'I wouldn't want anything to distract you from doing a good job of sorting out my mother's divorce.'

'I never let my personal life get in the way of my professional one.' Except when it came to Emma. Hunter had lost count of the number of times Emma's issues had impacted on his professional life. He made up for it by working extra hard for his clients when Emma didn't need him so much, but it was there in the background of his mind all the time—the responsibility of making sure all her needs were met, that she was safe and cared for at all times and in all places. That the people taking care of her were trustworthy and dedicated. That no one could hurt her, upset her, frighten her or exploit her.

It was his commitment to his sister.

The only full-time, long-term commitment he had made so far and was ever likely to make to anyone.

As to being distracted… Well, Millie was the biggest distraction he'd encountered in a very long time, possibly ever.

'So, you're a true workaholic,' Millie said, giving him another uppity glance. 'Work first, play later—if at all.'

Hunter gave an indolent smile. 'Oh, I know how to play, sweetheart.'

Her cheeks darkened to a deep shade of rose. 'One supposes there aren't too many women who ever say no to you.'

'Not many.'

She ran the point of her tongue over her lips and glanced briefly at his mouth before meeting his gaze. 'Will you excuse me? I…erm…need to use the bathroom.' She slipped out of the chair and disappeared through the exit to the conveniences.

Hunter leaned back in his chair and smiled to himself. *You've got this.*

Millie stared at herself in the mirror over the wash basin. Her eyes were overly bright, her cheeks bright-pink, her lips parted as if she had just received a smoking-hot kiss from Hunter's sexy mouth. If she wasn't careful, she would be the next woman who couldn't say no to him.

She slammed her lips together so firmly, they turned white. Why couldn't she handle men like Hunter Addison? Or maybe it was more that she didn't know how to handle herself—the unfamiliar urges and desires triggered by his attention. How was she going to navigate her way through this? She needed him professionally, but her body decided it needed him personally. *Intimately.*

She drew in a ragged breath and finger-combed her hair, the tiny glint of her engagement ring catching the light from above. She lowered her hand and curled it into a fist, her right hand coming over the top of her left to cover the ring, as if that small diamond was acting as her conscience's critical eye on her behaviour. She slowly removed her right hand from her left and gripped the edge of the basin instead.

*You have to resist him. You have to.*

Millie straightened her shoulders, tossed back her hair and put her game face back on. When she got back to the table, Hunter was wearing his reading glasses and checking something on his phone. He looked up and gave a self-deprecating smile, put his phone down. 'I know. Bad habit. Phones and restaurants don't mix.'

Millie slid back into her seat and flicked her napkin across her lap. 'It's hard, though, isn't it? I'm always on mine.'

'That reminds me…' He picked up his phone again. 'You didn't give me your mother's mobile number or email address. I'll need to give it to Matteo Vitale, the forensic accountant, as he'll want to deal directly with her at some stage.' His fingers were poised over the keys ready to add her mother's details to his contacts.

Details that didn't exist.

Millie swallowed, her heart suddenly racing. 'Erm… she doesn't have one at the moment.'

His eyebrows came together in a frown. 'Then when will she have one, do you think?' There was something a little too lawyer-ish in his tone, bordering on interrogation.

'I'm…not sure. She's not a fan of them.'

'Okay, so how about an email address? She has one of those, I presume?'

She shook her head, her gaze not quite meeting his. 'No email address. You can send any official stuff to my email address or call her on her landline.'

His frown was now so deep it carved a trench between his eyes. 'No email address? You're kidding me, right?'

She briefly met his incredulous gaze before lowering her eyes once more. 'I'm not kidding.'

The silence was so thick she could almost feel it pressing against her chest like a giant hand.

Hunter put his phone back on the table next to his plate with a soft little thud. 'Okay.' He took his glasses off and slipped them into his top pocket. 'So, do you want to tell me what you should have told me before we had the meeting this morning? Or shall I tell you what I think is the problem?'

Millie slowly brought her gaze back to his. 'You've guessed?'

'Your mother has literacy issues.'

Hearing him say it, knowing he had discovered it himself, gave Millie the freedom to nod her head. 'My mother has serious dyslexia. She is functionally illiterate and innumerate.'

'Right, well, it seems my concerns over her finances were well-founded.' He released a long breath and added, 'Look—I wish you'd given me the heads up on it. How does she feel about it? Is she comfortable talking about it?'

Millie gave him a wry look. 'If she was comfortable about it, I would have told you.' She bit her lip and went on, 'I've never told anyone about this before. She's deeply ashamed and embarrassed, and I do everything I can to help her so she doesn't have to feel bad about something she can't help.'

'That must have been tough on you growing up.' His tone was disarmingly gentle, his expression full of empathy.

Millie shrugged one shoulder. 'I managed.'

'Do you have any half-siblings?'

'No, there's just me.'

'Hey. Look at me.' His voice had a commanding edge, but it was tempered by a low, husky note that dismantled another piece of her emotional armour. She had told him the truth about her mother's problem. Why not tell him how it impacted *her*? What had she got to lose?

Millie inched her gaze back up to his. 'I don't expect you to understand. Most people have no idea what it's like to have such a disability. They think she's dumb, but she's not. She's got so much potential, but she can't access it. The modern world isn't set up for people with literacy and numeracy problems. It's incredibly isolating for Mum and it's largely why she's in the financial mess she's in. Everyone rips her off. She gets exploited by husbands, and even her housekeepers at times. I do everything I can to help her, but it's not enough, not now my own business needs more and more of my time.'

By saying it out loud for the first time to another adult, she suddenly realised how much of a burden she'd been carrying—alone. The weight of it was oppressive. It impacted every part of her life. She loved her mum. Would do anything for her mum. But her mum couldn't always be a mum to her. Their places had switched a long time ago—Millie was the adult and her mother the child.

'I know you probably think I can't possibly understand but, believe me, I do,' Hunter said. 'I'll do everything in my power to help your mother. People like her are particularly vulnerable to financial abuse.'

'Thank you.' Millie could barely get her voice to work.

He reached across the table for her hand and, with only a moment's hesitation, she slipped hers into the warm, strong cage of his. His eyes held hers in a lock that made something in her belly wobble. He gave her hand a gentle squeeze. 'It's been a long day. Let's get you home.'

They didn't speak much on the way back to Millie's flat. She got the feeling he was mulling over what she had revealed to him. Every time she glanced at him, he was frowning in concentration. Perhaps he was planning his course of action for her mother's divorce now he had this new information. Millie wished now that she had told him from the outset, but then what if he hadn't offered to help her mother? She'd been walking a fine line with him anyway, given their blighted first date. She wasn't used to being so open with someone. Even her two closest friends knew nothing about her mother's problems. Why had she spilled all to Hunter Addison, of all people?

*You didn't spill all. He worked it out for himself.*

That was all well and good, but what if his perpetual frown was because he was changing his mind about acting for her mother? Maybe he thought it was too difficult, given her mother's disability. Too complicated and messy. Millie was already risking a lot financially—the divorce process could string out for months and months. How on earth could she ever afford to pay her mother's legal bills?

Hunter pulled up in a space in front of her flat and turned off the engine. He swivelled in his seat to look at Millie. 'Given what you've told me tonight, I think—'

'Don't say it,' Millie interjected, casting a cynical look in his direction before turning to face the front. 'I get it, I really do.'

'What did you think I was going to say?' She could hear the frown in his voice.

Millie glanced at him. 'You think I should get another lawyer to act for my mother.'

Hunter placed a gentle hand beneath her chin and turned her head to face him. He held her gaze for a pulsing moment. 'And why would I want you to do that?' The streetlight outside the car was reflected in his eyes, making them even more heart-stoppingly attractive.

She ran the point of her tongue over her dry lips, her eyes drifting to his mouth. 'Because...because...her situation is too difficult. And it's going to cost a bomb to fix it—if it can be fixed, that is.'

He bumped up her chin with one finger, meshing his gaze with hers. Something tumbled off a high shelf in her stomach and a whole flock of insects fluttered around her heart. 'Something you need to know about me, sweetheart. I thrive on a challenge. The more difficult, the better.' His voice contained a thread of steel, his gaze a glint of delight, his mouth a tempting curve. But somehow, right then, she didn't think he was just talking about her mother's situation.

Millie couldn't stop looking at his mouth, her gaze drawn to it with a magnetic force so powerful, it overruled her resolve to keep her distance. His evening shadow had thickened even in the couple of hours they had spent together.

*Spent together.* The words were faintly shocking. She had spent the evening with a man she had only met a couple of times. A man she was fiercely attracted to in ways she had never been attracted to in anyone else before. Erotic, primal ways that pulsated in her body whenever she was with him.

Hunter leaned closer, his head coming down as if in slow motion, his mouth so close to hers she could feel the soft waft of his breath against her lips. 'I want to kiss you, but I'm not sure it's worth the risk.' His voice was both smooth and rough honey poured over gravel.

'W-what do you think will happen?' Millie was shocked at the sound of her own voice—whisper-soft, breathless with anticipatory excitement. Breathless with lust.

He nudged one side of her mouth with his lips, just a

gentle bump of flesh on flesh, and yet it created a storm of sensation. Tingles, fizzes, darts of need that travelled straight to her core. His lemony aftershave intoxicated her senses. She felt tipsy—no, flat-out drunk and out of control. 'Well, let's see… One: you might slap my face.'

'I abhor violence of any type.' Who was this person sitting in the car with him, almost kissing him? Acting coy and coquettish, as if she had written the handbook on flirting?

'Two: you might kiss me back.'

Millie double-blinked. 'And th-that would be a problem?'

He smiled against the side of her mouth and a wave of incendiary heat coursed through her body. The slight rasp of his stubble made every female hormone in her body throb with pleasure and she wondered what it would feel like against her more intimate flesh. 'For me, yes.'

'W-why?' Her voice wobbled again, her senses reeling at his closeness, at his smell and touch and overwhelming maleness.

His mouth hovered above hers once more, his warm breath mingling with hers. 'I might not want to stop kissing you.' He trailed his lips over her face to the highest point of her cheekbone, just below her left eye, her skin erupting in tingles of pleasure.

'I—I'm sure you have much better self-control than that…' Millie was surprised she could still get her voice to work, let alone string a reasonably cogent sentence together.

He brushed his lips against her eyebrow and a shower of sensations shimmied down her spine. 'It's not my self-control I'm worried about.' His tone was lightly teasing, so too the gleaming light in his eyes.

Millie raised her eyebrows as though she were auditioning for a role as an affronted spinster in a period drama. It was high time his monumental ego got a slap down. 'What? You think I can't resist you?'

His lazy smile tilted even further. 'There's only one way to find out.'

She hoisted her chin. 'Is that a dare?'

His eyes held hers, then dipped to her mouth. 'Damn right it is.'

Millie stared at his mouth with her heart thudding so loudly she was sure he would hear it. The desire to kiss him was so strong, so tempting, it overrode every reason why she shouldn't feed his ego by proving him right.

But then, what if she proved him wrong? What if she kissed him and didn't respond at all? She could take her mind elsewhere, as she used to do sometimes with Julian.

She met Hunter's gaze with fortitude. 'All right. One kiss, and I start it and I finish it. Okay?'

Was that a glint of victory in his eyes or something else? Something much more dangerous to her self-control—raw, male desire. 'Done deal.'

Millie leaned closer, determined that only her lips would be in contact with his and no other part of his body. She placed her lips on his in a feather-soft touch before lifting off again. His drier lips clung to hers as she pulled away, as if calling her back, and she curled her hands into fists to stop herself pulling his head down to kiss him the way she really wanted to. The way her body was demanding she kiss him.

'Is that the best you can do?' He placed a fingertip on her lower lip, idly stroking it back and forth, back and forth, until every nerve was tingling. His tone was teasing, his look challenging, and her pulse went haywire.

'We agreed on one kiss.'

One of his hands slid up under her hair and cupped the back of her head, making her scalp prickle with delight. 'That wasn't a kiss according to my standards.'

Millie could only imagine his standards. Sensual, scorching-hot, sexy. She knew she was drifting into dangerous territory by not pulling out of his hold but she couldn't seem to get her self-control back on duty. The sensation of his large hand cupping the back of her head sent waves of pleasure through her body.

'I'm not sure I'm ready for this…' It was a coward's way out, but she used it anyway. She was frightened of the passion he stirred in her. Passion she hadn't experienced in her life before. Passion she wasn't sure she could control if she allowed it off the leash even momentarily.

Hunter picked up her left hand, his thumb slowly rolling over the diamond on her ring finger. 'Because of your late fiancé?'

Millie swallowed and looked down at their joined hands. 'I've never kissed anyone but Julian…'

He let go of her hand and inched up her chin, locking his gaze on hers. 'You wouldn't be betraying him, Millie. You have the right to move on with your life.'

Millie half-lowered her lashes over her eyes, worried he would see the truth she was trying to hide. 'Thank you for a nice evening. I'd better go in now.' She made a move for the door, but he put a hand on her arm and turned her back to face him.

'I want to see you again.' It was a command rather than a request.

'I guess you'll see me at the next meeting in your office with my mother.' Millie kept her tone cool and composed but inside she was trembling with excitement. Forbidden excitement she *must* and *would* control.

He traced a fingertip around her mouth in a slow-motion movement that sent a shower of sparks through her tender flesh. 'I didn't tell you my number three.'

Millie frowned in confusion. 'Number three?'

He gave a slanted smile. 'My third risk-assessment reason for deciding whether or not to kiss you.'

She glanced at his mouth before she could stop herself. 'What is it?'

He lightly tapped the end of her nose with his finger. 'I'll tell you when we next have dinner. I'll pick you up on Friday night, same time.'

'But what if I don't want to have dinner with you?' The truth was, she did want to have dinner with him again. He was the most intriguing and yet infuriating man she had ever met. Infuriatingly attractive.

He cocked one sardonic eyebrow. 'Then you'll never know my third reason.'

Millie gave him a quelling look. 'You're very smooth, aren't you? Do you ever not get your way?'

'Occasionally.' He flashed her another smile and opened his door to get out of the car and walk her to the door, adding, 'But it sure is fun when I meet a little resistance. Makes me all the more ruthlessly determined.'

# CHAPTER FIVE

ZOEY, MILLIE'S OTHER FLATMATE, was curled up on the sofa watching a movie when Millie came in after Hunter had walked her to the door. He didn't ask to come in, nor did she invite him, but she was seriously tempted. The only thing stopping her was seeing the light on, signalling her flatmate was home. Zoey clicked the pause button and got off the sofa. 'How was your date with Hunter Addison? I hope it was an improvement on the last time.'

Millie rolled her eyes. 'It wasn't a date. It was just dinner to discuss my mother's divorce.'

'Was your mother there too?'

'No.'

Zoey folded her arms and angled her right hip in an 'I'm older and wiser than you' pose. 'Then it was a date. Did he kiss you?'

Millie could feel her cheeks heating and turned away to the small kitchen to get a glass of water. 'What makes you think that?' She reached up for a glass and then took it to the sink to fill it from the tap.

Zoey padded across the floor to join her. 'Hello? You're gorgeous and single, and he's gorgeous and single, and you spent the evening together. And I took a peek out of the window and saw you practically sitting on his lap in his car.'

Millie turned off the tap and faced her friend. 'I was not!'

Zoey's eyes danced. 'Look at you, getting all defensive. Did he kiss you? Go on, tell me.'

Millie let out a long breath. 'Actually, I kissed him. But only a little peck on the lips, nothing else.'

Zoey's eyes widened. 'No way. Really? You made the first move? Good on you.'

Millie took a sip of water and then put the glass down on the counter with a little thud. 'He dared me to.'

Zoey's expression was a picture of intrigue. 'Oh, really? Gosh, this is way better than that movie I was watching. Tell me everything.'

Millie frowned and speared one of her hands through her hair and let out another sigh. 'He's the most infuriating men I've ever met. I can't believe he got me to agree to another dinner date with him.'

Zoey gave a tinkle of laughter. 'You do look in the mirror occasionally, don't you? No man worth his testosterone could resist asking you out. But I have to say, Hunter must be pretty damn good at the dating game if he got you to agree. Heaps of guys have been asking you for close on three years and you've always said no.'

Millie bit down on her lower lip and picked at a chipped edge on the counter-top with one finger. 'I'm not sure Hunter is the sort of man I should encourage.'

'Why?'

Her hand fell away from the counter-top. 'He's very...experienced.'

'So? You don't want to be in bed with someone who doesn't know his way around a woman's body. He might be just the thing you need to kick-start your dating life once more.'

'But I never really had a dating life in the first place,' Millie said, perching on one of the kitchen stools. 'Jules and I kind of drifted together rather than dated. We were friends for years and then became lovers and, well, you know the rest.'

Zoey came closer and touched Millie on the shoulder. 'Hey, I know Jules getting sick like that really sucked. It was so unfair when you had your future together all planned. But he died while still loving you. You were by his bedside and holding his hand when he left this earth. It's tragic but somehow special that he died feeling totally secure in your love.'

But Millie hadn't been in love with him. She had silently dreaded it as each day had drawn closer and closer to their wedding date. She had felt so trapped, so imprisoned by her inability to let Julian know she loved him as a friend, not as a life partner.

And she was still imprisoned by her web of lies, unable to move on with her life, still trapped and feeling horribly claustrophobic.

Millie couldn't meet her friend's gaze. 'I know...'

Zoey sighed and reached for a mug off a shelf above the counter. 'At least most of your memories are good ones, I mean, before Jules got sick, that is. What do I have after Rupert did the dirty on me?'

She put the mug down on the counter-top like she was slamming it down on her ex's head, her expression so sour it could have curdled milk. Long-life milk.

'What he did tainted every memory of our time together. I can't even look at photos of us now without wondering how many other women he slept with behind my back. And, worse, how did I not know until I finally stumbled upon his latest squeeze in *our* bed? *Urgh.*'

Millie grimaced in sympathy. 'I can only imagine how devastated you must have felt. But not all men are like that. Maybe you'll find someone who is loyal and fall madly in love with—'

'Oh, no.' Zoey waved her hands in front of her body in a criss-cross motion, in a *no way is that ever going to happen* gesture. 'I am never going to fall in love again. It's not worth the pain. From now on, I'm going to be head girl of the "single and loving it" club.'

'And are you loving it? Being single, I mean?'

Zoey gave her a hooded look and reached for a tea bag from a canister on the counter. 'I'm working on it.'

Hunter drove home from Millie's flat with a smile on his face. What was it about her that made him so energised? So turned on? If it had been one of his usual dates, he would have been in bed with her now. But nothing about Millie was run-of-the-mill. She was captivating, intriguing and so damn gorgeous, he wanted to break his three-date rule.

But hey, he *was* breaking his three-date rule.

Normally, he didn't stay with a lover more than a night or two. He didn't want or need the complications of a longer term relationship. His responsibilities for his sister precluded him from investing in anything other than short-term hook-ups. He knew from experience that most women didn't like taking second place. And any lover of his would have to take second or even third place, when it came to Emma and his career.

But Millie fascinated him, and he couldn't wait to see her again. He wanted to feel her lips on his again—not in that light-as-air way but with full-on passion. He knew she was more than capable of it. He saw it in her eyes, felt it like an electric energy charging the air. She wanted him but was resisting him out of some sense of loyalty to her dead fiancé.

Was it love that held her back or something else?

But there was another reason he wanted to see Millie again. He was determined to get justice for her mother Eleanora, who reminded him so much of his own mother. It churned his gut to see how badly she had been treated, exploited by every husband, this latest one by far the worst. It could take months to uncover the fraudulent behaviour of her husband and that would come at a cost. A cost Millie was paying on behalf of her mother. Hunter wasn't going to see Millie go under financially. He had plenty of money. He didn't need her to go bankrupt to pay him. He regularly did pro bono work. Of course, he didn't broadcast it too widely, in case everyone expected it. But now and again a case would come along, it would light a fire in his belly and he would give it his all.

And this case had created an inferno.

Millie was trying not to count the days until her next 'date' with Hunter. She was in her studio working on some new designs on Thursday afternoon when her assistant Harriet came in from the shop front. 'Someone here to see you, Millie.'

'Who is it?'

'That hotshot lawyer guy—Hunter Addison,' she said, and then added in a stage whisper whilst pretending to fan her face, 'Oh, my goodness, he's gorgeous!'

Millie put down her flat-nosed pliers and rose from her chair. 'Send him in.' She could only imagine what her assistant would make of Hunter coming to visit her. Harriet, just like everyone else in her life, was keen for her to go out more. But was going out with Hunter going to do more harm than good?

Hunter came into her studio, having to lower his head to get through the doorway. 'Hard at work?' he asked with a smile.

'Always.'

He placed a hand on his chest. 'Ah, a girl after my own heart.'

Millie gave him a quelling look. 'I don't think so.'

He came further into the room and the space shrunk as if it had turned into a shoebox. A child's shoebox. He looked down at the piece she was working on—a bespoke diamond engagement-and-wedding ring ensemble for a client. 'Nice. I had no idea you were so talented.'

'Thank you. I guess you'll know where to come now if you ever find yourself in the market for an engagement or wedding ring.'

He gave a deep chuckle of wry laughter. 'Unless I undergo some sort of personality bypass, that is not going to happen.'

Millie lifted her chin a fraction, her gaze steady on his. 'Never say never.'

Hunter's eyes darkened and her heart skipped a beat. 'Right back at you, sweetheart.'

She frowned. 'What's that supposed to mean?'

He took another step closer, so close she could see every black pinpoint of the stubble peppering his jawline, and every fine line and crease on his sensual lips. Lips she had ever so briefly touched with her own and ever since had wished she had not lifted them off so quickly.

'What are you doing tonight?' he asked.

If Millie lifted her chin any higher she was going to fall over backwards. What was it about his arrogant confidence that infuriated her so much? 'Why?'

'I want to see you.' His gaze flicked to her mouth. 'I have something I want to discuss with you. I decided I couldn't wait until tomorrow.'

'Don't you know that patience is a virtue?'

He gave a devilish grin that made him look even more dangerously attractive. 'I'm afraid I don't have too many virtues, only vices.'

'I can only imagine what they might be.' Her tone was straight out of a nineteenth-century Sunday School room. But nothing in her body felt as prim as her tone. Molten heat was pouring into all her secret places, flames of heat licking at her flesh, ignited by the glint in his gaze.

Hunter sent an idle finger down the curve of her hot cheek. 'I have this irresistible urge to kiss you.' His voice dropped to a deep burr of sound that made the base of her spine fizz.

'I'm not sure that's such a great idea right now...' Millie's heart was beating so hard and so fast, it felt as though she was having some sort of medical crisis. Hunter kissing her might not be a great idea, but it was what she desperately wanted. But admitting it to him would come at the cost of her pride. 'I—I'm at work and my assistant could come in and—'

'So, we'll lock the door.' He took the couple of strides back to the door and clicked the lock into place, the sound in the silence like a gunshot. 'See? Problem solved.'

Millie had a feeling her problems were only just beginning. 'I kissed you the other day and—'

'That wasn't a kiss.' He took her by the upper arms in a passionate hold straight out of a nineteen-fifties Hollywood movie. 'This is a kiss.' And then his mouth came down on hers.

Millie was not prepared for the inferno of lust that slammed into her body as soon as his mouth connected with hers. Her lips moulded to his as if fashioned specifically for him. His lips were firm, hard and insistent, and yet gently persuasive too. He angled his head to deepen the kiss, a low, deep groan coming from the back of his throat. She opened her mouth on a breathless gasp to the commanding stroke of his tongue, her senses whirling as potent heat shot through her entire body.

He crushed her against him, his arms winding around her so there was nothing between them but their clothes. And even through their clothes she could feel the urgent rise of his body against hers. Her own body was responding with primal instinct, melting, liquefying, yielding. His mouth continued its sensual exploration of hers, fuelling her desire to a level she had never experienced before. Hot, urgent, pounding desire that raced through her body with an ache that was part pleasure, part pain. Both extreme tantalisation and exquisite torture.

Hunter loosened his hold and brought his hands up to cradle her face, his mouth still clamped to hers as if he couldn't bear to be away from it. Millie returned his kiss with equal passion, hungry for the taste and texture of his mouth, greedy for the heightening of her senses that drove every thought out of her head other than how much she wanted him. He changed position again, releasing another guttural groan as his tongue mated with hers in a dance as old as time. Desire travelled in a lightning-fast streak up and down her spine, smouldering in a pool of liquid fire between her legs.

She had never been so aroused.

Never been so turned on by a kiss.

Never wanted someone so much it felt like a pain she would do anything to assuage.

Hunter fisted one of his hands in her hair, his mouth moving with hers in an explosively hot exchange of need. Need she could feel pounding in his body where it pressed so shockingly, intimately against hers. The same need she could feel in her own body, the low, dragging ache, the tension of inner muscles, the dewy heat of lust.

He finally dragged his mouth off hers, his breathing as erratic as her own, his eyes glazed with desire. 'So, that clears up that, then.'

Millie tried to disguise the way he had completely ambushed her senses by retreating into a cool mask of indifference. 'Clears what up?'

He smiled and traced around her mouth with a lazy finger. 'You want me so bad.'

She batted his hand away as if it were an annoying insect, frowning for good measure. 'It was just a kiss, Addison. Nothing else.'

'Ah, yes, but what a kiss.'

Millie folded her arms across her body—her traitorous body, her still aching with lust—and cast him another look cold enough to mess with the air-conditioning thermostat on the wall. 'I know what you're trying to do.'

'What am I trying to do?'

'You see me as a challenge.'

'You're definitely that but a delightfully entertaining one.'

Millie turned away before she was tempted to fling herself back into his arms. She went back behind her work bench, using it as a barricade. 'You said you had something to discuss with me. Is it to do with Mum's situation?'

He straightened one of the cuffs of his business shirt. 'I have a proposition to put to you.'

Millie held his smouldering gaze with her frosty one. 'I hope it's not an indecent one?' Seriously, she could have been transported from a Victorian ladies' college.

The atmosphere began to throb with tension. Erotic tension that made her skin tighten all over and her heart rate spike.

Hunter smiled an enigmatic smile and picked up her jeweller's saw from the work bench and ran his fingertips slowly over the row of teeth. After a brief moment, he put the tool down again and met her gaze with his inscrutable one. 'I've decided to do your mother's divorce pro bono.'

Millie rapid-blinked and her heart missed a beat. 'Why on earth would you do that?' Suspicion was ripe in her tone.

He gave a rueful smile. 'Not for the reasons you're thinking.'

Her chin came up a fraction. 'How do you know what I'm thinking?' She was thinking how wonderful it would be if she didn't have to pay thousands of pounds in legal fees. Pounds she could ill afford.

But she was also thinking, *What does Hunter want in return?*

And, worse, how was she ever going to find the willpower to say no to him?

Hunter's eyes moved back and forth between each of hers in an unnervingly assessing manner. 'You have very expressive eyes and they're not always in agreement with what you say.'

Millie looked away, worried he was seeing far more than she wanted him to. 'It's a very generous offer but I'm afraid I can't accept it. It would...complicate things.'

'How?'

She brought her gaze back to his. 'You know how.'

He arched one eyebrow, one side of his mouth lifting in a lopsided smile. 'You really do have an appalling opinion of my character, don't you?'

'I speak as I find.'

'Let me assure you, I don't need to resort to blackmail to get a woman to sleep with me.'

Millie couldn't drag her eyes away from the shape of his mouth. She could still taste him on her lips—the salty tang that was as addictive as a drug. 'I—I don't understand why you'd make such an offer to go pro bono if you didn't want something in return.'

'Suffice it to say, I feel sorry for your mother.' He scraped a hand through his hair and gave a rough-edged sigh. 'She reminds me of my mother. Gentle, sweet, trusting, naïve. I hate seeing people like that get done over. It's highly likely it will take quite some time to uncover all the funds that have been siphoned off, and that is extremely costly.'

Millie searched his gaze for a long moment. 'But what about the forensic accountant you mentioned? We'll have to pay him, won't we?'

'I've already spoken to Matteo about it. He's happy to go pro bono too.'

Millie chewed at her lip, torn between wanting to howl with relief and throwing her arms around Hunter to thank him. 'I don't know what to say…'

He came round her side of the work bench and placed his hands on the tops of her shoulders. 'Hey, you're not going to go all weepy on me, are you?'

She gave a tremulous smile. 'I might…' She brushed the back of her hand across her right cheek. 'But I should warn you, I'm a messy crier.'

He brushed the pad of his thumb beneath her left eye where a couple of tears had leaked out despite her best efforts, his gaze warm. 'I'm used to it. My sister is the highly emotional type. Cries at commercials featuring puppies or kittens or babies. Drives me nuts. Not to mention costing me a fortune in tissues.'

'She sounds like a really nice person.'

*And so do you...* Millie wanted to add, but stopped herself just in time. She couldn't allow herself to *like* him…could she?

Hunter's hands came away from her shoulders and a mask dropped down over his features, as if he regretted talking about his sister. It intrigued her as to why. He sounded as if he really cared about Emma. And why was he the one paying for her tissues? Why would he not want to talk about her? What was going on in Emma's life that made it difficult for him to be open about her?

'What time are you wrapping up here?' Hunter waved a hand towards her workbench, his business-like tone so different from only moments ago.

Millie glanced at the clock on the wall. 'Gosh, is that the time? Harriet was meant to leave half an hour ago.'

Hunter moved across to unlock the door. He undid the lock and asked over his shoulder, 'Dinner tonight? I'll pick you up at the same time.'

'Why don't you let me cook you dinner? I mean, as a thank you.' The invitation was out before Millie could monitor her tongue. What was she thinking, asking him back to her flat when it was likely Zoey would be home? Not only that, her flat was hardly penthouse material, and she was pretty sure Hunter Addison was the penthouse-residing type. Besides, he was used to fine dining in fancy restaurants. How gauche and unsophisticated of her to offer him a home-cooked meal.

'How about we both cook dinner? At my place.'

'That would be…fun, thank you.'

*Fun? Don't you mean flipping dangerous?* At least if they had gone to her flat she would have had safety in numbers with Zoey there. Not that she could always rely on Zoey being there, as she was often away on advertising business with her father.

But maybe it was better to see Hunter out of the public eye. He attracted a fair bit of press attention and was often photographed with his latest lover. How would

Julian's mother feel to see Millie gallivanting around town with an out-and-out playboy?

'I'll organise mains—you do dessert,' he said. 'How does that sound?'

'Sounds like a plan.'

He opened the door and Harriet almost tumbled in, as if she'd been listening at the door, her face going beetroot-red. 'Oops, sorry. I just wanted to see if it's okay to go home now?'

Millie nodded. 'Yep. Sorry to hold you up. We had…erm…some business to discuss.'

Hunter winked at Millie. 'Until tonight.' And then, with a flash of a charming smile to the star-struck Harriet, he was gone.

# CHAPTER SIX

MILLIE BARELY HAD time to get home and shower and change before Hunter was due to pick her up. She had rushed home via the supermarket and bought fresh raspberries and cream and some hand-made chocolates, her anticipation of the evening ahead rising as every minute passed.

But, just as she was putting the last touches to her make-up, her phone buzzed with a text message. She picked up her phone and read the text from Hunter.

Slight change of plans. Will send a car for you. I have to see someone for half an hour. Sam will take you to my house and let you in. Make yourself at home. Hunter.

Millie quickly texted back.

Do you want to take a rain check?

The three little dots showed he was typing back and within a couple of seconds his reply came through.

Definitely not. :)

She clicked off her phone and finished her make-up, wondering who he was seeing. Her stomach nose-dived. Surely not another woman? A quick little hook-up in case she didn't put out? She bit down on her lip until it hurt. She didn't like to think he was the sort of man to do something like that. The more she got to know him, the more she saw the commendable traits in his character. Yes, he was charming, teasing and playful, but underneath that she could sense he was a deeply loyal and principled man. Why else would he be doing her mother's divorce pro bono?

Hunter checked in on Emma on his way home because Judy, the carer, had phoned him to say Emma was being a little obstreperous. He suspected Emma was probably having trouble adjusting to Rupinder's absence, as she was her favourite carer, and Emma had become rather attached to her. He organised for his handyman-cum-gardener, Sam, to pick up Millie in case visiting Emma took longer than expected, but he didn't tell her he was visiting his sister. He had already told her far more than he would tell anyone. Millie was exactly the sort of person Emma would be drawn to—warm, sweet, compassionate. Emma would fall for her in a heartbeat and then what would he do? The last thing he needed was any more complications in his life.

But his attraction to Millie was already one big complication. He had never felt so drawn to someone before. Not just physically, although that was off the charts, but more a sense that she might be a little difficult to walk away from the way he did so effortlessly with other lovers. Would she agree to a short-term fling?

That was also part of the attraction—she resisted him, and it turned him on all the more. Not in a creepy 'I'm going to wear her down' way, but because he was sure, underneath that prim and proper exterior, she was a deeply passionate woman who had locked herself away.

Unfortunately, when Hunter arrived Emma was in the middle of one of her temper tantrums over some perceived slight by Judy.

'Whoa there, poppet, what's got you all worked up?' he said, crouching down beside her on the floor where she was thrashing about like she was three years old. But in a way, she *was* still three years old. The anguish over that fact never failed to grab him by the guts in a cruel fist. He often wondered who and what Emma could have been if it hadn't been for the genetic mix-up that had happened in utero. And he also wondered in his darkest moments why it had got her and not him. He had dodged a genetic bullet, and a large dose of survivor guilt was the payoff.

Emma lifted her red and tear-stained face off the carpet and pouted. 'Judy won't let me have what I want for supper.'

Hunter stroked her tangled hair back off her face. 'And what do you want for supper, poppet?'

She sniffed and pulled herself up into a sitting position and began to wipe her nose on her sleeve, but Hunter whipped out a tissue just in time—years of practice made him faster than lightning at such tasks. 'Here. Use this.'

Emma took the tissue and blew her nose and hiccoughed a couple of times, and then scrunched up the tissue into a ball in her hand. 'I want chocolate,' she said with a mulish look.

'Em, you can't eat chocolate at every meal.' He'd lost count of the number of times they'd had this conversation. 'Remember what Dr Nazeem said? You have to eat a balanced diet otherwise you'll—'

'But I *want* it!' She howled like a banshee and began to drum her heels on the floor, throwing the used tissue away like a missile.

Hunter took her hands in his and drew her into his chest, holding her securely, rocking her gently to soothe her. 'It's okay, poppet. Let's go for a compromise, okay? You have a little bit of proper supper and then you can have some chocolate for dessert. How does that sound? Fair?'

''Kay…' Emma came out of her hyped-up state as if a magic wand had been waved but Hunter knew it wouldn't last. There would be another day, another time when she would lose it again. It was a knife-edge existence for her carers, as it had been for him and his mother over the years. He sometimes wondered if the stress of caring for Emma was why his mother had not been able to survive her blood cancer. She hadn't had the strength or endurance to cope with the chemo—all her strength and endurance had been used up, worn away by the stress and arduous task of caring for her disabled child. And it made Hunter feel all the more guilty that he hadn't been able to do more to help his mother.

Once Emma was settled with her supper on her lap in front of her favourite children's television show, Hunter took Judy aside. 'Are you okay?'

She gave him a weary smile. 'I'm paid to be okay. And very generously, thanks to you. But how are you?'

How was he? What a question. It was times like this that he wondered how he had managed to build the career he had with the burdens he'd carried over the years. Not that he considered Emma a burden. She was his little sister and he loved her. Besides, he didn't know how long he would have her. The doctors hadn't expected her to live this long with her complex condition. He dreaded the day he would lose her. His life had revolved around taking care of her for so long, he didn't know any other way of living.

Hunter forced his lips into a smile. 'I'm fine, as always.'

*I have to be.*

Millie was driven to a three-storey Georgian house in Bloomsbury by a pleasant older gentleman called Sam, who told her he often drove Hunter to and from district courts when the need arose. He also did odd jobs around Hunter's house and garden and his wife, Ada, did the housekeeping. Sam showed her into the house and assured her Hunter wouldn't be too much longer, and informed her Ada had dropped off some things for dinner earlier and had set the table in the dining room.

Once Sam had left, Millie took the things she had bought through to the kitchen, quietly marvelling at how well appointed it was—no less than a chef's dream of a place in which to work. She put the raspberries and cream in the smart fridge and left the chocolates on the acre of island bench.

It was strange to be in a person's house without them

being there, especially the first time. She couldn't stop herself from having a little snoop around, looking for clues to the man behind the enigmatic smile. Judging from the contents of his fridge, he was a health-conscious eater. And the clean, streamlined décor hinted at a neat and ordered mind…or maybe a very efficient housekeeper. Or both.

Millie continued her tour to the sitting room, complete with shiny black fireplace and a French carriage clock on the mantelpiece above softly ticking in the background. The sofas were deeply cushioned, and she could imagine curling up there with a good book, a glass of wine and Hunter's arm around her…

She jerked back from her wayward thoughts, shocked at the picture they had constructed in her brain. A domestically cosy picture that had no chance of ever becoming a reality.

Because she didn't want it to…*did she*? And, more to the point, nor did he. He wasn't the sitting-by-the-fireplace-with-the-love-of-his-life type. He was a freedom-loving playboy who was adamant he would never be tied down by matrimony. She could hardly blame him, given his line of work.

But there had been times just lately when Millie wasn't sure what she wanted any more. Being around Hunter, being kissed by him, had shifted her out of a long period of stasis. A guilt-ridden lockdown of her wants and needs. Needs she had pretended for so long didn't exist. But he had stirred something in her, something that had been asleep for a long time. It was like waking from a coma realising nothing was the same as it had been before. How could it be? She could recall every moment of Hunter's explosively passionate kiss. She could recall the hard press of his aroused body against her. Her body was still agitated, restless, wanting more contact. Needing more contact, like an addict needed another fix.

But it wouldn't do to get addicted to Hunter Addison. He was heartbreaker material and the last thing she needed was her heart smashed to pieces. Launching into an intimate relationship again was definitely not on her agenda. She had done the commitment thing and look how it had turned out. She had been trapped, imprisoned by her own promises, and those chains were still around her to some degree.

But the thought of a fling was tempting…especially with Hunter. Dangerously tempting.

Millie moved to the bookshelves at the back of the room to see what sort of taste he had in literature. There were plenty of crime and thriller novels, many legal texts, and history books and biographies. There was even a row of children's picture books, some of the very same titles she had had as a child. So he was a little bit sentimental, was he? He hadn't thrown out his childhood books. How interesting.

She drew out one of her favourites, flicking through the pages, recalling how she had been the one to read them to her mother, not the other way round. She had even tried to teach her mother to recognise the simple words and sentences, with moderate success. But being able to stumble her way through a kindergarten-age picture book was the limit of her mother's ability. Her mum had missed out on early intervention due to the long denial of Millie's grandparents that anything was wrong. And, of course, her mother had developed numerous cover-up strategies to cope. Pretending she'd left glasses which she didn't possess at home, or had sprained a wrist so she couldn't write—the list went on and on.

Millie slid the book back into place with a sigh. So many things would have been different for her mother if she had been able to learn to read.

She glanced around the room for photos and spied a couple on a walnut table near the window overlooking the garden. There was one of what appeared to be his mother as a young woman, gorgeous, with dark hair and the same whisky-brown eyes as Hunter. There was another one of him at about age five, proudly cradling a new-born baby—his sister Emma, presumably. There was another one of him when his sister was a toddler—he had his arm around her, and she was looking up at him with adoration, and his smile was just as loving.

Millie traced her finger over Hunter's beaming smile and wondered why he wasn't interested in settling down and having children of his own. She put the photo back down but couldn't help noticing there were none of his father. There was, however, one a little separate from the other photos—Hunter as a young boy with his arm around a shaggy dog, smiling broadly, the dog looking up at him in rapt affection.

The sound of Hunter's firm footfall as he came into the room made her swing round with a gasp. She quickly put down the photo. 'Oh, I didn't hear you come in.' She smoothed her hands down the front of her dress. 'I was, erm, looking at the photos. You were a cute kid. Your sister too.'

He put a hand up to loosen his tie, his expression difficult to read. 'Sorry I kept you waiting. I got held up longer than I expected.'

'No problem.' Would he come over and greet her with a kiss? Why was he keeping his distance and acting so aloof? It made her feel uneasy, as if he was regretting asking her to his house. Or maybe his little meeting with whoever it was had put him off spending the evening with her.

'Would you like a drink before we start on dinner? I got my housekeeper to pick up some things.' His voice was polite but formal and it made her feel as if a chasm had opened up between them. He was on one side, she was on the other. After the scorching kiss they had shared in her studio, it seemed an odd way to behave. Was he regretting kissing her? She could never regret kissing him. She ached to do it again, to feel his mouth moving with such heat and passion against hers.

Millie forced her lips into a smile. 'Why not?'

He opened a cleverly concealed bar fridge and took out a bottle of champagne. 'Since you like a few bubbles in your glass, how about this?'

There were quite a few bubbles fizzing in her bloodstream right now from just being in the same room as him. 'I would love some. I guess this is kind of a celebration, isn't it? Well, for me anyway, given you're not charging any legal fees. I still don't know how to thank you. When I told Mum this afternoon, she burst into tears. She's so terribly grateful, as I am.'

He expertly removed the cork from the bottle with a soft little pop, an enigmatic smile curling the edges of his mouth. 'Everyone deserves a break now and again.'

He poured two glasses of champagne and carried them to where she was standing. He handed her one. 'To seeing justice done.'

Millie clinked her glass against his, her eyes unable to move away from the magnetic pull of his gaze. 'Thank you.'

His lips quirked in another fleeting smile, and he tipped his glass back and took a measured sip, but the uneasiness she'd sensed in him was still there. He hid it well, but she could sense it in the way he held himself aloof. He hadn't touched her other than to hand her the glass of champagne, and that seemed odd, given their kiss that afternoon. And he had a faraway look in his eyes that reminded her of the first time they had met. Preoccupied and distant. Brooding.

'Is everything all right?'

He blinked, as if he had forgotten she was there. 'Sorry. What?'

Millie touched him on the arm. 'You seem a little distracted. Are you okay?'

He placed his hand over the top of hers and gave a crooked smile. 'You're the second person to ask me that today. I'm fine.'

'I just thought…after what happened this afternoon in my studio…well, maybe you'd changed your mind about dinner. Or you have other more important things to do.'

He put his glass down and then took hers, setting it down on the table next to them. 'Let's do a replay. I'll come back in and greet you the way I should have the first time.'

Millie watched him stride back to the door of the sitting room, disappearing for a moment outside and then coming back in with a winning smile.

'Hi, honey, I'm home.' He swept her up into his arms and swung her in a full circle, then slid her down his body until she was back on her feet. 'Pleased to see me?'

Clearly *he* was pleased to see *her*. She could feel the proud bulge of his erection pressing against her belly. A shiver passed over her flesh and, on an impulse she couldn't stop in time, she linked her arms around his neck and smiled. 'That's much better.'

'But still needs improvement, right?' He gave her a mock-serious look, his eyes twinkling.

'Depends what you have in mind.' Who knew she could be so flirtatious? And have heaps of fun doing it? Her blood was singing through her veins, her heart hopscotching in her chest.

'Believe me, sweetheart, you do not want to know what's on my mind right now.' His tone was dry, his glinting gaze sending another shiver down her spine and a pool of liquid heat straight to her core.

'Try me and see.'

He pressed a light kiss to her lips and released her, leaving her aching, hungry for more. His gaze lost its playful spark and his expression became full of gravitas. 'There's something I need to make clear. I don't want you to sleep with me out of a sense of gratitude. If we sleep together, I want it to be because you want to have a fling with me as equals, okay?'

A fling. Millie rolled her lips together, suddenly lost for words. He was offering her a fling. A short-term relationship that would satisfy the needs he had awakened in her. Needs she had never felt so powerfully before. A fling was not a long-term commitment, so that would be fine, wouldn't it? Long-term commitment was not her thing any more. No more emotional prisons. No more entrapment. Hunter wanted what she wanted—a short-term fling to explore the passion that had fired up between them.

'I don't know what to say.' She couldn't hold his gaze and looked at the loosened knot of his tie instead. 'It's…tempting…'

'But?'

She brought her eyes back to his. 'I've only had one lover. I have so little experience compared to you. I'll probably disappoint you, or won't excite you enough, and—'

He placed his hands on her hips and drew her back against his hard frame. 'You can already feel how much you excite me.'

She gave a gulping swallow, her legs trembling with desire so hot and strong, it threatened to engulf her. 'I—I can't imagine why you'd be excited by someone like me.'

He smiled and brought his mouth down close to hers. 'Everything about you excites me. You're funny and cute and whip-smart. And I like how you stand up to me. It turns me on big time.'

Millie breathed in the scent of him, the male musk and expensive citrus notes that intoxicated her senses into a stupor. She was under some sort of magical spell, turning into a wanton woman with no other motivation other than to get her physical needs met. And sooner rather than later. She wanted to say yes. She ached to say yes. Every female hormone in her body was screaming, *say yes!*

But there were other things to consider, other people's feelings to take into account. Lena, for instance. How could Millie have a full-on and very public fling with Hunter Addison without hurting her? And there were her own feelings to consider. Hunter was a heart-stoppingly attractive man with so many wonderful qualities. What if she were to lose her heart to him? He wasn't interested in anything long-term. A fling was what he was offering. She had only ever been in a long-term and totally committed relationship—so committed she was still in it in a sense, because that was what others thought. She had encouraged them think it.

'Hunter…there's something I need to tell you…' She glanced down at the engagement ring on her hand.

He placed his hand over her left one, his expression sombre. 'I can only imagine how hard it must be to move on from the love of your life. But it's been three years. Do you think he would have waited as long as that?'

Millie sucked part of her lower lip into her mouth, her mind spooling back to the last words Julian had said to her. *I will love you for ever.*

She lifted her gaze back up to Hunter's. 'It's not what you think… *I'm* not what you think.' She took a ragged breath and continued, 'I fell out of love with Julian years before he died. I—I didn't have the heart to tell him. He was devastated enough over the prognosis. He had a really difficult to treat form of brain cancer. The first surgery changed him. When he woke from the induced coma they had him in for a few days post-op, he wasn't the person I used to love. I kept hoping the old Jules would come back but he never did. But he needed me, and I stayed.'

Hunter frowned darkly. 'Oh, you poor, sweet darling.' His arms came round her and held her close against his chest, one of his hands gently stroking the back of her head. 'I can't imagine how trapped you must have felt.'

Millie glanced up at him through misty eyes. 'It's why I never refer to him as Jules any more, always Julian. The old Jules had gone and nothing I could do could get him back.'

He cradled her face in his hands. 'What you did was brave and honourable and incredibly selfless. But don't you see, it's time to move on? You've made enough sacrifices for Julian. You don't have to beat yourself up over not loving him the way you used to.'

'I feel so ashamed…' She looked at the knob of his Adam's apple rather than meet his gaze. 'Everyone felt so sorry for me when Julian died three days before the wedding. But I was glad I didn't have to take the pretence that far. Glad. Don't you think that's dreadfully shameful of me? To actually be *glad* he died?'

Hunter raised her face so her gaze meshed with his. 'Is that why you still wear his engagement ring? As a form of self-flagellation?'

Millie bit her lip and nodded. 'I've spent the last three years playing the role of grieving fiancée. Looking back, I guess it was easy enough to act, because I genuinely cared about him as a friend—as indeed I care about lots of people close to me. The irony is, I'm usually hopeless at keeping secrets. I couldn't even keep my friend Ivy's surprise thirtieth birthday party from her, but I've lived this lie for so long, I don't know how to live my life any other way.'

'There is another way,' Hunter said, holding her by the shoulders in a firm but gentle hold. 'You move on. Live your life. Do the things you want to do, things Julian would want you to do. He wouldn't want you throwing your life away. Not the old Jules, anyway, right? The one you loved?'

Millie blinked back tears. How brilliantly he had put it. She was allowing the sick, changed version of Julian to hold her back from living an authentic life. The Jules she had loved would not have wanted her to throw her life away. How had she not realised that until now? 'You're right, but it's still going to be difficult. I might have to feel my way for a bit.'

He smiled and stroked her cheeks with his thumbs in a slow, spine-tingling caress. 'That's my girl.'

*His girl.* But for how long? She was a temporary diversion for him, just like all his other lovers. Nothing permanent. No commitment other than the duration of their fling. No sitting by the fireplace in each other's arms for the rest of their lives.

Just for now.

Perfect...wasn't it?

'Don't you mean your girl of the moment?' Millie injected her tone with light playfulness.

Something flickered over his features—a rapid blink, a muscle twitch near his mouth, a slight dimming of his smile. 'There's nothing wrong with living in the moment as long as it's an unforgettable one.' And his mouth came down and set fireworks off in hers.

# CHAPTER SEVEN

MILLIE GASPED AS his lips moved against hers with incendiary heat and purpose. Streaks of fire flashed through her body, her growing desire for him leaving her breathless and pliant in his arms. His tongue stroked the seam of her mouth and she opened to him, her lower body going to molten lava as his tongue mated with hers. The flickering movements, the bold thrusts and darts, heated her blood to boiling.

He crushed her to him, his hard body imprinting every soft curve of hers with his unmistakable erotic intent. An erotic intent she welcomed with every cell of her body. Her intimate female flesh tingled and tightened, her breasts aching for his touch. Her breasts suddenly felt too small for her bra—they were straining against the lace barrier, desperate to feel the caress of his hands.

He groaned against her lips, one of his hands sliding up to the nape of her neck, his touch electrifying. 'I want you so damn much. Do you have any idea what you do to me?'

Millie shivered as his mouth blazed a trail of heat from below her ear, over her neck and to the V of her top. 'I want you too.'

And what he did to *her* was a revelation. A spine-tingling, bliss-inducing revelation that shocked her to the core. She hadn't felt anything like this level of desire before. It was all-consuming, taking over mind and body in a storm of heightened sensuality. She was conscious of every movement of his lips against her skin, the cup of his hand at the back of her neck, the stroke of his tongue below her ear, the feather-light caress of his lips on her jawline as he moved down to her chin and back again.

His mouth came back to hers in a deep kiss that made the hairs on her head tingle at the roots and her heart rate escalate. His tongue played with hers in a teasing dance that sent shivers racing down her spine and heat to pool between her thighs. Lava-hot heat that made her limbs tremble like a new-born foal's. She would have fallen if he hadn't been holding her so firmly.

His mouth left hers to move back down her neck, one of his hands pushing aside her top so he could access her décolletage.

'You smell divine…' He breathed in deeply, as if he was taking in an intoxicating vapour. He let his breath out and added, 'I want to taste you all over.' His voice with its husky edge, and his lips with their silken caresses as they moved across her skin, set her flesh alight. She had never felt such powerful sensations moving through her body. He tugged her top out of her skirt and slid a warm hand up to cup a breast still caged in her bra, and she gave a little gasp as a shudder passed through her.

'Oh…oh…'

His hand stilled on her breast, his hooded gaze meeting hers. 'Tell me what you like.'

Millie pushed herself further into his hand, desperate to feel him skin-on-skin. 'I'm still discovering what I like. My erm, preferences weren't always a priority with Julian.'

'You didn't enjoy sex with him?'

She lowered her gaze, unable to meet his searching look. 'Not really… It became a chore, to be honest.'

He stroked his thumb over her tight nipple, the bra still in place, but even through the lace she could feel the tingling sensations in her flesh. 'I want you to enjoy everything we do together.' He tipped up her chin so her gaze meshed with his. 'Hey, don't be shy. It's important you communicate to me what works for you.' He gave a slow, sexy smile and added, 'And, if you don't know it yet, then we can discover it together.'

Millie reached up to stroke his lean jaw, her lower body flush against his, her senses reeling from the close contact. 'That sounds like fun.'

Hunter lowered his head and smiled against her lips. 'It will be.' The confident assurance in his tone sent another shiver coursing down her spine.

Millie opened to him again, her arms winding around his neck, her breasts crushed against his chest, need spiralling through her body. His hands cupped her bottom, holding her tightly against the ridge of his erection, a deep, guttural groan escaping from his lips as he deepened the kiss even further. His tongue teased hers in a cat-and-mouse game that made her pulse race and her heart pound.

After a few breathless moments, he lifted his mouth from hers. 'Let's go upstairs.'

Millie knew by following him upstairs to his bedroom that she would be stepping over a threshold. Over a threshold to a fling. A short-term affair that had no future. Some of her hesitancy must have shown on her face, for he took her hands in his, his expression etched with lines of concern. 'You're having second thoughts?' he asked gently.

Millie twisted her lips into an almost-smile. 'I want you. I didn't think it was possible to want someone so much…'

'I'm sensing a big "but" coming.'

She released a stuttering sigh. 'This is so…so normal for you. Having sex with someone who catches your eye and moving on when it's over. I don't know how to play this game. I've only been in one relationship. What do I know about having a fling? Nothing.'

Hunter placed his hands on her hips. 'Millie, listen to me. I'm not long-term relationship material. What I'm offering is a short-term fling. No strings, no promises of for ever—just a good time for both of us while it lasts. If you can't accept that, or feel it's too much of a compromise of your values, then we'll go no further.' He spoke as if he was reading out a legal contract. The terms. The points. The clauses.

Millie could feel the searing heat of his hands on her hips, his hold not quite possessive but not far off. Her body was drawn to him even as her mind kept raising little red flags. But he had awakened something inside her—something that ached and willed her to step across the threshold and explore the sensuality he promised in every kiss, every caress, even in every look of his tawny gaze. She looked at his mouth, her own mouth aching to feel the firm press of his once more. 'I've never felt so attracted to someone before.' Her gaze lifted to meet his. 'It's kind of scary, given how much I disliked you when we first met.'

Hunter stroked her left cheek with a lazy movement of his thumb, his expression wry. 'Was I that much of a crashing bore that night?'

Millie linked her arms back around his neck and raised herself up on tiptoe so her mouth was within a breath of his. 'If you had been, maybe I wouldn't be here now wondering if I'm completely out of my mind to accept your offer of a fling.'

His eyes darkened, his breath mingling intimately with hers. 'So, that's a yes?'

She brushed her lips against his in a butterfly-light caress. 'It's a yes.'

Within a few moments, they were upstairs in Hunter's luxuriously appointed bedroom. The king-sized bed would have dominated any other room, but this room had space to spare. Tastefully decorated in white with touches of navy-blue and grey, the room had a masculine feel without it being oppressively so. It made her small bedroom at her flat look like a broom cupboard.

Hunter drew her close to him, his arms going around her body, his look searching. 'Are you sure this is what you want?'

Millie pushed her doubts to the back of her mind, allowing her body to take charge. 'I want you to make love to me.'

His mouth came down to hers in a leisurely kiss, as if to show her he wasn't going to rush her, or perhaps to give her time to change her mind. Millie wasn't going to change her mind—she couldn't. Her need for him was so intense it consumed every part of her body, ripples of clamouring longing coursing through her flesh with increasing force and speed. His mouth moved to her décolletage, his hands gently unbuttoning her top, button by button, the brush of his fingers sending another wave of want through her body.

'You are so beautiful.' His voice was low and deep and rough around the edges, his gaze hungry, dark and glittering with lust.

Millie shivered as her top slipped from her shoulders like sloughed skin. But, instead of feeling embarrassed to be half-naked in front of him, she felt proud, especially when he sucked in a breath and brought one of his hands up to cup her breast. His other hand reached behind her to undo the fastening on her bra and it too slipped to the floor at her feet. He brought his mouth down to her left breast, his tongue circling her nipple, teasing it into an even tighter bud. He took her nipple in his mouth, sucking on her with the gentlest pressure, the sensations rioting through her flesh like tiny starbursts of pleasure.

Hunter moved to her other breast, the slight rasp of his stubble against her sensitive skin sending another wave of delight through her body. 'Everything about you is so damn beautiful.'

'You don't look too bad yourself, but I need to see more of you.'

He gave her a devilish grin and held his arms out wide as an invitation. 'Go for it.'

Millie set to work on his shirt, determined to get her hands on him, needing to feel the warmth of his skin against hers. She managed a couple of the buttons but he helped her with the rest, shrugging off the shirt and tossing it over his shoulder. She placed her mouth on his chest, tasting his salty skin with her lips and tongue, delighting in his swift intake of breath. She kissed her way up to his mouth, relishing the crushing pressure of his lips as he took masterful control. The rest of their clothes were removed in between passionate kisses and fervent caresses.

Millie was a little surprised at how comfortable she was, being completely naked in front of him. It felt the most natural thing in the world to stand before him with his eyes greedily drinking in her feminine form. She glided a hand down his chest to his rock-hard abdomen, her lower body melting with desire to see him so aroused and ready for her.

'Touch me.' It was one-part command, two parts plea, the edge of desperation in his voice thrilling her senses into overdrive.

Millie stroked her fingers over his proud length and he sucked in a breath, as if her touch delighted him as much as his did her. She grew bolder, taking him in her hand and massaging his swollen flesh. 'You're so…big…' Her voice came out as a breathless whisper.

He cupped her face in his hands and held her gaze with his smouldering one. 'We'll go at your pace, not mine. You are the one in charge, okay?'

'Okay…' Millie couldn't express how touched she

was by his assurance, but she tried to show it in how she caressed him. She explored his length with her fingers, circling the head of his erection with her thumb, relishing in his indrawn breaths and shuddering groans. She ached to be joined to him, her body on fire with longing. She removed her hand and pressed her hips against him, delighting in the thickness of his arousal against her belly. 'I want you.'

'Then you shall have me…but first things first.' His sexy drawl and glinting gaze sent a shiver of heat through her body.

He led her to the bed and laid her down, coming down beside her, his hand on her hip. Now it was time for Millie to suck in her breath. His mouth moved down her body, from her breasts to her belly button and then to her mound. She shivered as his lips played with her female flesh in soft little movements, his warm breath skating over her skin.

He parted her folds and tasted her, and she shuddered as tingles of pleasure shot through her body. He continued the sensual caress with increasing speed, ramping up her response to him until she was feverish with the need to let go, but unable to give herself permission. It was so new to her, foreign, and out of her bounds of experience to be so vulnerable in front of a lover.

Hunter lifted his head to look at her. 'Relax into it, don't fight it. Don't be scared of letting go.'

*Easy for you to say*, Millie thought. He'd probably had dozens of women going down on him. She was an oral-sex virgin. 'I—I don't think I can. I've never done this before…'

His brows came together. 'Never?'

Millie shook her head, a sigh escaping her lips. 'Julian was a bit prudish when it came to the female body.'

Hunter placed one hand on her belly, the other gently brushing the hair back from her forehead, his eyes holding hers in a lock that felt as tender as a caress. 'You're beautiful and taste gorgeous. Let me pleasure you. Don't think, just feel. Promise?'

Millie released a shaky breath. 'Promise.'

He brought his mouth back down to her folds, slowly caressing her with his lips and tongue, exploring her, tasting her, drawing from her a response she hadn't thought herself capable of—a powerful, earth-shattering response that sent shudders of pleasure throughout her body in cascading waves. She heard someone crying out and then realised with a little jolt it was her. She had never made such voluble sounds during sex before, but then, why would she have? She had never felt anything like the pleasure Hunter was evoking in her.

Millie flopped back on the pillows with a breathless sigh. 'Oh, my gosh… Did that really just happen?'

Hunter smiled and stroked the length of her thigh. 'It just did. And I'm going to make it happen again.' He angled himself away for her in order to get a condom out of the drawer beside the bed. He applied it to himself and came back to her, his eyes glittering with lust. 'But remember, you're still in control. If you want to stop at any point, then we can stop.'

Millie pulled him down to her. 'Please make love to me. I want to give you pleasure too.'

Hunter brought his mouth back to hers in a drugging kiss that made the hairs on her scalp tingle and her desire reignite. His tongue played with hers, calling it into an erotic dance that sent quivers of delight through her body. He positioned himself at her entrance, his muscled thighs entwined with hers, his powerful body poised to take intimate possession. She arched up her pelvis to encourage him, desperate for the connection, hungry for more of his potent passion.

He slid into her body with a deep groan, her body wrapping around him, her senses reeling at the contact. He began a slow rhythm, the friction of their joined bodies sending darting arrows of pleasure through her body. The tension in her intimate muscles grew and grew, the swollen heart of her aching for the release it craved.

Hunter brushed back the hair from her face, his body deep inside her, his eyes locked with hers. 'Am I going too fast?'

Millie pulled his head down so she could access his mouth. 'Not fast enough.'

'Let's see what I can do about that.' The playful edge to his tone was a new experience for her. There had been little playful about sex with her late fiancé. It had been more of a blink-and-you'll-miss-it session in which her needs and pleasure hadn't even been on the agenda.

But with Hunter it was all about her pleasure and needs.

Millie's senses were so heightened, she could feel the cool caress of the cotton sheets against her skin, the exquisite softness of the feather pillow beneath her head, the sensual stroke and glide of his hands on her body and the driving force of his erection sending her senses into a tailspin. He went deeper, harder, faster, his own breathing becoming ragged, his groans of delight thrilling her to the core of her being. Then he slipped a hand between their rocking bodies and caressed her intimately, his touch like magic on her flesh. She soared into another hemisphere, a place of intense physical pleasure that rippled through her in giant coursing waves, leaving no part of her body unaffected.

She was still in the throes of her release when he shattered around her, the shudders of his body sending another wave of pleasure through hers. She held him in her arms during the storm, breathing in the musky scent of their coupling. And then breathing in time with him during the quiet peaceful time afterwards.

Hunter lifted himself up on one elbow, his gaze holding hers in an intimate tether that made her heart kick against her breastbone. 'If I'd known it was going to be as good as that, I would have worked a little harder on that blind date to charm you into my bed then and there.' He gave a rueful grimace. 'What a missed opportunity.'

Millie smiled and traced the contour of his mouth with an idle fingertip. 'You didn't seem to even notice that I was a woman that night. You had a perpetual frown on your face the whole time.'

Something flickered over his features and his eyes dipped to her mouth. 'Yes, well, let's not talk about what a jerk I was that night.'

'Why were you so…so brooding and unfriendly? And don't say it was because I was an absolute cow from the moment we met, because I saw you frowning even before I got to the table.'

He captured her finger and kissed the end of it, his gaze locking with hers. 'You weren't any such thing. I was kicking myself for agreeing to a blind date in the first place, but Beth and Dan were pretty insistent, and caught me at a weak moment.' He gave her hand a tiny squeeze and continued, 'I probably should have cancelled rather than turn up in a foul mood. Forgive me?'

Millie pressed a kiss to his lips. 'Forgiven. But you still haven't told me why you were in such a foul mood. Was it a work thing? I mean, your job must be pretty stressful at times.'

He smiled with his mouth but not with his eyes. 'Something like that.' He dropped a light kiss to her lips. 'Is your work stressful?'

Again Millie idly stroked a finger across his collarbone. 'Now and again I'll get a couple in who can't agree on what they want. But mostly it's great. I love designing. I grew up around diamonds, as my grandfather—my father' father, that is—started the business as a young man. I started making my own jewellery in kindergarten. But pasta tubes and coloured beads are not as exciting as diamonds, I have to say.'

He laughed and picked up her left hand. 'And this?' He rubbed his thumb over her engagement ring. 'Is this one of your designs?'

Millie twisted her mouth and then sighed. 'No. Julian proposed to me a couple of weeks after he was diagnosed with cancer. It caught me completely off-guard. I mean, we were teenagers, and not even thinking about setting down just yet, and then suddenly he's asking me to marry him. I didn't know what to do.'

'So you said yes.' There was no judgement or criticism in his tone, just gentle understanding, and it totally disarmed her.

Millie glanced up to meet his eyes. 'I felt so trapped from the moment he put the ring on my finger. Don't get me wrong, I cared about him, but not enough to marry him. We were only eighteen years old. I found myself playing a role that became increasingly claustrophobic, especially when he changed. He wasn't the same person, but then nor was I.'

Hunter passed the pad of his thumb over the small diamond ring again. 'Why don't you take it off?'

She looked at his thumb moving over the ring and something in her chest tightened. 'I can't get it off now. I'd have to saw it off, and I can't quite bring myself to do it.'

He turned the ring on her finger and tested it against her knuckle but it refused to budge. 'That could be a problem if someone else wants to give you an engagement ring.' His expression was inscrutable, his tone mild.

Millie gave a light laugh. 'That's not going to happen. I'm not interested in settling down again. Been there, done that.'

Hunter tapped her playfully on the tip of her nose. 'See? I told you, you're a girl after my own heart.' He brought his mouth back down to hers in a lingering kiss, his hand stroking up and down the flank of her thigh. After a moment, he broke the kiss to look down at her. 'I never did tell you my number three reason for not kissing you that day in your studio.'

'Oh, yes, that's right. What is it?'

His eyes held hers in a glittering lock. 'Stay here with me tonight.'

Millie raised her brows. 'You mean all night? That's your number three?'

He swept a strand of hair back off her forehead, his

expression set in more serious lines. 'I generally don't do sleepovers.'

'But you're making an exception in my case? Why?'

He traced a line down the curve of her cheek, a shutter coming down in his gaze. 'You and I want the same thing—a fling without strings. We both understand what this is and know it can't go any further.'

Did she want the same thing, though? No strings. No promises of 'for ever'. No long-term commitment. Tiny doubts were assembling at the back of her mind, like extras on a theatre set waiting for a call to step on stage. Doubts that lingered in the shadows of her conscience, every now and again drifting into a thin shaft of light.

Millie brought her hand up to his face and trailed her fingers down his stubbled jaw. 'Can we keep our… fling private for now? I mean, I don't want Beth and Dan to get any funny ideas about us. Nor do I want to be painted as your latest squeeze in the press.'

Hunter captured her hand and pressed a kiss to her bent knuckles. 'Fine. But I have the perfect place to take you where we will be entirely alone.'

'Where?'

'I have a private yacht moored in Greece.'

Millie widened her eyes. 'You must have handled a lot of very expensive divorces in your time.'

He gave a crooked smile. 'I was lucky with some investments early in my career.' He released her hand and added, 'Was that your stomach or mine growling for food?'

Millie placed a hand on her empty stomach. 'I think it was mine.'

Hunter swung his legs over the edge of the bed

and then held out his hand for her with a wolfish grin. 'Come on. We need our energy levels boosted for what I have mind later.'

A shiver coursed down Millie's spine and she took his hand. 'That sounds…interesting.'

He gathered her close, naked skin to naked skin, and another shiver cascaded over her flesh. 'But first, a little entrée.' He brought his mouth down to hers in a scorching kiss that set her senses on fire.

Millie forgot all about food. All she could think about was the taste and texture of his mouth and the molten heat he evoked in her body. If this was what happened during a fling, then she wanted more of it.

Much more.

# CHAPTER EIGHT

ONCE DINNER WAS OVER, Hunter sat with Millie in front of the fireplace in his sitting room, their glasses of wine on the coffee table in front of them. His body was replete with food but hungry again for her. But he was conscious that she hadn't had sex in a long time and too much too soon could be uncomfortable for her.

Her response to him delighted him in ways he could barely describe. He had electric tingles from just having his arm draped across her slim shoulders. His senses were intoxicated by the fragrance of her skin and hair, his body still humming from their explosive love-making before dinner.

*You're having a sleepover with her?* The voice of his conscience prodded him, but he pointedly ignored it. They were on the same page about their fling. Neither of them wanted anything more than a short-term affair. Millie was still wearing her late fiancé's ring and she had no intention of replacing it with anyone else's.

And Hunter was certainly not going to put one on her finger. A commitment of that sort had been ruled out in his head long ago. It was a decision that was reinforced, confirmed as the right one, every day of his life.

He only had to think back to his mother to understand the heartache of lost love. He had no desire to experience it himself or cause someone else to experience it through his actions.

And then, of course, there was Emma.

If he were to marry and have a family of his own, Emma would no longer have full access to him. He would have other priorities, other responsibilities that would have to come first. She hadn't coped when their father had left. How would she cope if Hunter created a new family, even if he did his best to be there for her? Even the most accommodating partner would find the rollercoaster of caring for his sister tiresome.

No. He was fine living his life as he did. He knew how to get his physical needs met without compromising his own or another's interests. He never promised what he knew he couldn't deliver. Unlike his father, who had promised to love and protect his wife and family and then dumped them when things got a little tougher than he'd expected.

One of the things he had never been able to forgive his father for was the loss of his beloved dog Midge. When they had been forced to move into a tiny flat, Midge had had to be rehomed. He could still remember the look of confusion on Midge's face when they'd driven away after dropping her at the rescue shelter. Something had shut down inside him that day, a steel cage going around his heart. He had decided he would not love and lose ever again.

Hunter lifted a hand to Millie's head and threaded his fingers through the silk curtain of her hair. She glanced up at him and smiled, her grey-blue eyes clear and pure. Her beauty at odd moments like these stole his breath clean away. He wasn't so shallow that looks were high up on his list of preferences, but Millie had the whole package—intelligence, looks, a kind nature and the ability to fight from her corner. He found her spirited attitude towards him potently, powerfully attractive.

He placed his hand on the curve of her cheek and angled her head so he could plant a kiss on her soft mouth. Her lips clung to his, her arms winding around his body, her breathless sigh of encouragement sending a wave of red-hot heat through his pelvis.

He pressed her back down on the sofa, coming over her with his weight propped on one elbow, the other hand stroking the sweet curve of her breast. 'Whose idea was it again to get dressed before dinner?' His tone was lightly teasing.

Her smile made her eyes sparkle like diamonds. 'I'm not used to wandering around naked.' She lifted a hand to his face and traced the outline of his mouth, making his skin tingle and his desire for her to stampede in his blood. 'Maybe you should have a guest bathrobe on hand for your lovers when they sleep over.'

'I'll think about it.' He nibbled on the shell of her ear and she writhed in delight.

'How many have slept over?' There was nothing in her tone to suggest anything but mild interest, but the slight bracing tension in her body was a giveaway.

Hunter meshed his gaze with hers, his hand caressing her breast underneath her top. 'You're the first.' It was true. He hadn't taken this step before. His home was his sanctuary and he didn't want any lovers leaving toothbrushes or toiletries and thinking they had a chance of changing his mind about settling down any time soon.

Millie's brows shot up in surprise. 'Really? So why me?'

He dropped a light kiss to her mouth. 'Someone had to be the first. It might as well be you.'

She tugged at his hair in a playful manner. 'That's not a proper answer. Tell me exactly why you wanted me to stay over tonight.'

Hunter's gaze went to her mouth and another lightning bolt of lust slammed him in the groin. 'Fishing for compliments, Miss Donnelly-Clarke?' He used his court voice.

She arched her brows, her eyes twinkling. 'Evading the truth, Mr Addison?'

The truth was a little too confronting for him to examine it too closely. He pushed it to the back of his mind, unwilling to cast any light on its shadowy presence. He wasn't in any danger of falling for her. His rules were the rules for good reason.

Hunter set to work on unbuttoning her top. 'The truth is, I wanted to get you naked and keep you naked for hours. Any objections?' He uncovered her breast and cradled it in his hand.

Her cheeks flushed with pleasure and she shivered under his touch. 'No objections.'

Millie woke during the night to the sound of a telephone ringing downstairs in the sitting room. She glanced at Hunter, who was sound asleep beside her, one of his strongly muscled legs flung over hers. She knew it wasn't her phone, for she had turned it to silent, and it was in her bag on the floor next to the bed. She nudged him gently. 'Hunter? Is that your phone?'

He sat bolt-upright and lunged for the bedside lamp switch. 'Shoot. I forgot to bring it upstairs.' He swung his legs over the side of the bed, dragged a hand through his hair and stood. 'Go back to sleep. It's probably a prank call anyway. I sometimes get them from an aggrieved ex of a client.' He snatched up his bathrobe and shrugged it on, loosely tying the waist ties as he left the room.

Millie knew there was no way she would get back to sleep without knowing if there was some sort of threat coming Hunter's way. How awful it must be to be targeted by disgruntled people who didn't get their way in court proceedings. It didn't bear thinking about. She pushed back the covers and slipped on Hunter's shirt that he had left hanging over the back of a chair. It came to just above her knees but at least it offered a small measure of modesty. She padded downstairs to the sitting room, where Hunter was speaking to someone on his phone. His head was bent forward, he had a deep frown on his face and he was pinching the bridge of his nose.

'Okay, I'll be there as soon as I can.' He clicked off the phone and turned and saw her standing there. 'Sorry. I have to go out for a bit.' His expression became shuttered, like curtains being pulled down on a stage.

Millie frowned. 'What for? What's happened?'

'Nothing.' He began to move past her in quick strides.

She caught his arm on the way past. 'It can't be nothing if you have to go out in the middle of the night. Was it one of those calls?'

He looked at her blankly. 'What calls?' His tone was blunt to the point of rudeness.

'The threatening calls you told me about, just then upstairs.'

'No.' His eyes flicked away from hers. 'It's…something else.'

'What, though?'

A flash of anger backlit his tawny gaze. 'What part of "go back to sleep" are you having trouble understanding?'

Millie straightened her spine and met him glare for glare. 'What part of "I want to know what's going on" are you having trouble understanding?'

He held her feisty look for a pulsing moment. But then he expelled a heavy breath, the anger going out of him with a weary drop of his broad shoulders. 'Look—I don't mean to be rude, but this is something I'm best left to deal with alone.'

'I shared my body with you tonight, Hunter. That was a big deal for me. At least have the decency to share with me what's going on. How do I know you're not going out to a booty call or something?'

Hunter let out another ragged sigh. 'It's my sister. She's having a difficult moment. I have to go to her to help settle her down. Her carer is not coping.'

Millie rapid-blinked, her own anger at his intractability leaking out of her like air out of a punctured balloon. 'Her carer? Emma needs a carer?'

His expression was grim. 'Yes. Her favourite one is on leave at the moment and she's having trouble adjusting. I won't be long. Just go back to bed and I'll see you in the morning.' He turned to leave the room but Millie followed him.

'I'm coming with you.'

'No, Millie. Please. This is not your affair. It's mine.'

She wasn't taking no for an answer. How could she go back to sleep *in his bed* as if nothing was the matter? 'Hunter, I'm coming with you, even if I just sit in the car and wait for you. It's three in the morning. You might fall asleep at the wheel coming home and cause an accident.'

He was either too tired to stand up to her or something about her argument got through to the lawyer in him at last. 'Okay. But be quick. I haven't got time to waste.'

Millie was so quick getting dressed, she could have set a world record. She followed him out to the car, and they were soon on their way. It had rained during the night and the streetlights cast starbursts of glistening light on the road. It seemed to take for ever, but in reality it was only a short time later when Hunter pulled up in front of a lovely little townhouse nearby.

He opened his door and glanced at her, his features set in somewhat bitter lines of resignation. 'You'd better come in. I don't like the thought of you waiting out here alone in the car.'

'Okay.' Millie didn't give him time to come round and help her out—she was beside him on the footpath before he'd even got out himself.

Hunter used his own key to open the front door and led the way into the house. Millie got the sense that as soon as he crossed over the threshold he forgot she was even there—he was focussed intently on going straight to his sister. She hung back, caught between wanting to help but also not wanting to intrude. She could hear sobbing from one of the bedrooms and then the gentle soothing of Hunter's deep baritone.

'Hey, poppet, what's all this fuss about, hmm? Shh. I'm here now.'

There was the sound of sniffling. 'I had a bad dream that Rupinder decided not to come back. She's going to, isn't she? She promised me she would come back.'

'Of course she's coming back,' Hunter said. 'She's just looking after her mother for a bit. She'll be back in a couple of days.'

Millie couldn't stop herself from approaching the bedroom. She stood in the doorway and caught the eye of the carer who was standing to one side looking rather helpless. Hunter glanced over his shoulder as if he sensed Millie's presence. A mixture of emotions passed over his face in a lightning-fast moment—annoyance, frustration, despair. It was the despair that made her step further into the room, thus capturing Emma's attention.

'Hello,' Millie said with a smile. 'You're Emma?'

'Yes, who are you?'

Millie came closer to the bed. 'I'm Millie. I'm a… friend of your brother's.' A friend? A lover? It was hard to describe exactly what she was to him now. A fling partner?

Emma's gaze swung to Hunter, a smile lighting up her features. 'Are you going to marry her? She's very beautiful, like a princess.'

Millie could feel herself blushing to the roots of her

hair, but Hunter took his sister's question with implacable calm. 'I don't think she would have me, poppet.' His voice contained a distinct note of ruefulness, but Millie knew it was for show. The last thing he wanted to do was marry anyone, much less her.

Emma glanced at Millie's left hand and frowned. 'But she's wearing an engagement ring.'

'It's not mine.' Hunter said.

Emma swung her gaze back to Millie. 'Whose is it?'

'My…erm…fiancé's. He passed away three years ago.'

Emma's brow wrinkled as she processed the information. 'Passed away?'

'He died,' Millie said, realising Emma might not understand the euphemistic term. 'He had a brain tumour.'

'My mummy died ten years ago,' Emma informed her gravely. 'But she's in heaven now, watching over me, isn't she, Hunter?'

Hunter gave a tender smile that sent an arrow straight to Millie's heart. 'Yes, poppet, she is. Now, it's time you got back to sleep and let Judy finish her shift. I need to get Millie home.'

So, he didn't intend to take her back to his place for what was left of the night. Millie fought back her disappointment, knowing it was completely understandable, given the circumstances. But she desperately wanted to talk to him about Emma's situation. It was clear the young woman had some sort of disorder, giving her an almost childlike understanding of the world. Why hadn't he told her about his sister in more detail? Or did he think that would have been a breach of Emma's privacy? All the same, Millie had shared so much of her own background, it didn't seem fair he hadn't trusted her with his.

Judy came out to the sitting room with them once Emma had settled back down with her princess night-light on. 'I'm really sorry about tonight, Hunter. She got herself into a full-blown panic attack. I thought it best to call you.'

'You did the right thing,' Hunter said. 'She's still having trouble getting used to Rupinder being on leave. I'll clear my diary in the morning and take her out for brunch. I'll let the morning-shift carer know.'

They said their goodbyes and soon after Hunter led Millie back to his car. His expression was set in frowning lines and her heart ached for the burden he carried with regard to his sister. She waited until they were both seated in the car before she spoke.

'Hunter, I'm sorry if you thought I was intruding back there.'

He flicked her an unreadable glance as he tugged his seatbelt across his chest and clicked it into place. 'You *were* intruding. Emma doesn't cope with strangers all that well. You could have made a difficult situation so much worse.' His curt tone cut the air like a flick-knife.

Millie suppressed her desire to snipe back at him. 'I'm sorry. It must be so hard for you worrying about her all the time. You're an amazing big brother. She's so lucky to have you.'

He gripped the steering wheel even though he hadn't yet started the engine. His gaze was fixed straight ahead, his jaw locked tight, a pulse beating in his neck. 'Emma has a rare genetic disorder. So rare they haven't even got a name for it. She has complex medical issues that require twenty-four-seven care. So, forgive me for being a little over-protective.'

As apologies went, it certainly wasn't gold standard, and his tone was hardly what anyone could call friendly, but Millie didn't care about that. She cared that he had carried the burden of care for his sister for so long on his own. She placed her hand on his muscled thigh. 'You were being absolutely how you should be, given the stress you're under. I can't imagine how hard it must be to have the constant worry hanging over you. I thought my concerns over my mum were bad, but your situation with Emma is so heart-breaking.'

He released his grip on the steering wheel, his shoulders going down on a heavy sigh, his weary gaze meeting hers. He lifted a hand to her face and tucked a strand of hair back behind her ear, his mouth set in a rueful line. 'Thank you for being so nice to Emma. And so understanding.'

'I understand how hard it is to have someone you love limited by things outside of their control,' Millie said. 'My mother obviously isn't in the same category as Emma but it's certainly been a struggle at times.'

'You're a good daughter. I could see that the moment you came into my office that day. She's lucky to have you.'

There was a small silence.

Hunter let out a long breath, his eyes still on hers. 'I should get you home.'

Millie stroked her hand down his lean jaw, her gaze searching his. 'Is that what *you* want?'

His eyes lowered to her mouth and another serrated sigh escaped his lips. His hand went to the back of her head and inexorably drew her closer to his descending mouth. 'I think you know what I want.' His voice was a low, deep rumble that set her pulse racing and, before she could answer him, he covered her mouth with his.

His lips moved against hers almost angrily at first, as if the night's stress had found an outlet in blistering passion. But then his lips gradually softened into an exquisite tenderness that made her heart squeeze. He held her face in his hands and his tongue glided through her parted lips, playing with hers in a sexy tango that sent her heart rate soaring.

He finally eased back to look down at her, his hands still cradling her face. 'The night of our blind date? I'd come straight from the hospital. Emma had a *grand mal* seizure. She has milder ones occasionally but this one was serious.' His mouth twisted. 'That's why I wasn't in the best of moods.'

Millie threw her arms around him and hugged him tightly. 'Oh, I'm so sorry. And I was such a cow to you that night. What a shallow person you must have thought me. I'm so ashamed, now I know what you had to deal with. You must have been out of your head with worry.'

He put her from him to smile at her. 'Don't beat yourself up too much. It didn't stop me noticing other things about you.' His hooded gaze dipped to her mouth once more.

Millie brushed her finger over his bottom lip, her skin catching on the rich crop of stubble just below. 'It was the anniversary of Julian's passing… I always find that day hard, but not for the reason most people think. I don't even know why I agreed to go on the date with you, other than Beth and Dan kept at me to get out more. I guess I thought, if I went once and it was a complete and utter disaster, then they'd let it drop.'

Hunter stroked her cheeks with his thumbs in a slow caress, his eyes holding hers. 'Don't you think it's time to be honest with your friends about what you felt for Julian? Keeping up the pretence is hurting you, holding you back from living life to the full.'

Millie pulled away from his hold and sat back in her seat and fisted her hands in her lap. 'It's not just about me, Hunter. I have to consider Julian's mother.'

'Why?'

She flashed him an irritated glance. 'Why? Because he was her only child and she lost him. And if I tell her I didn't love him, and would never have promised to marry him if he hadn't got sick, what do you think that will do to her? It will destroy her.'

Hunter placed a hand on her shoulder, but she shrugged it off. 'Hey, aren't you second-guessing how his mother might react?'

Millie looked down at her tightly knotted hands, her engagement ring winking at her, as if to remind her of her impossible situation. 'I know Lena well. We've spent a lot of time together over the years. I've spent more time with her than my own mother. I don't want to do anything that will cause her further pain. Now, please, can we just get going? Judy will wonder why we're sitting out here for so long.'

Hunter started the car with a sigh, and put it into gear and eased out of the parking space. 'I think it's best if I run you home instead of coming back to mine. It's almost time to get up anyway.' There was nothing in his tone to suggest he was annoyed with her, but she sensed his frustration all the same.

'Fine.'

The evening hadn't gone as either of them had planned, and yet she understood far more about his situation now. It gave her an insight into his character, his love and concern for his sister more than obvious. His tenderness towards Emma had been so touching to witness. Millie could only imagine how his sister's health issues had impacted him over the years. And his mother's death, which must have been such a cruel blow on top of everything else.

There was a long silence broken only by the swishing of the car tyres on the rain-slicked roads.

Hunter pulled up outside Millie's flat in Islington and she turned to him. 'Thanks for dinner and…everything. And for letting me meet Emma. She's very sweet.'

Something flicked over his features like a zephyr rippling across sand. 'Yes, she is.' He turned off the engine and got out of the car, striding round to her side with an inscrutable expression on his face. The rain had slowed to a half-hearted drizzle and the sounds of the city waking up sounded in the distance—a far-off siren, the rumble of a delivery lorry, the distinctive sound of a London cab.

Millie stepped out and touched him on the forearm. 'I meant what I said earlier. You are an amazing brother to Emma.'

Some of the tension in his features relaxed and he gave a rueful half-smile and covered her hand with his. 'Sorry our first night together ended the way it did. Let's see if we can do it better tomorrow night, hmm?'

Millie licked her dry lips, her pulse already racing with anticipation. 'Don't you mean tonight?'

He gave a light laugh and pulled her up close. 'So I do.'

## CHAPTER NINE

HUNTER DROVE BACK home wondering if he'd been a fool to allow Millie to come with him on his middle-of-the-night mission to calm his sister. He had always been so careful to keep his lovers away from Emma. They were temporary, and had no long-term place in his life, and therefore none in his sister's. But Millie's response to Emma and her immediate, intuitive and compassionate understanding of the situation touched him deeply.

How could it not? He'd been carrying the weight alone for so long that sharing it with someone, even for a moment, was heartening. She got it. So many people didn't. The stress of never being able to relax in case there was another crisis just around the corner. The sense of always being on duty, the background noise of persistent worry overshadowing every other thing in his life.

The night had been a show-stopper in so many ways. He'd always suspected making love with Millie would be wonderful, but he hadn't been prepared for just how wonderful. Her passionate response to him was electrifying and he couldn't wait to make love to her again. His body craved her like a forbidden drug, but he knew he would have to be careful not to get too addicted to her. He had his fling rules written in stone in his head and nothing and no one—not even someone as delightfully entertaining and gorgeous as Millie Donnelly-Clarke—was going to change them.

Her openness about the situation with her late fiancé had been humbling. He was not the heart-on-the-sleeve type, but he could still understand how difficult it must have been for her to reveal the depths of her anguish over her past relationship. He understood the way guilt could grind you down, eat away at you until you could taste it in your mouth and feel it swirling in your gut. The fact that Millie had let him into her private world of pain had in some ways made it easier for him to let her into his. Was that why he hadn't insisted on her staying in the car? Why he had taken her with him instead of dropping her at her home first? He could have put his foot down.

He smiled to himself when he thought of her feisty reaction to when he commanded her to do something. But he liked that about her, right? Her push-back was a turn-on. She stood up to him, challenged him and dared him to do differently, which in the long run could be a problem. A big problem. Even the most closed off part of his brain sensed the dangerous territory he was drifting into. He had allowed her closer than he had allowed anyone in years, possibly ever.

But, hot damn, it felt good, and he would enjoy it while it lasted.

When Millie came out for breakfast the next morning, Zoey was sitting at the kitchen table with a tub of yoghurt in front of her and a teaspoon halfway up to her mouth. She put the spoon down and her mouth shaped into a teasing smile. 'I'm surprised you're up at this hour, given how late you came in. Dare I ask where you were and what you were doing until almost daybreak?'

Millie checked the water level in the kettle and then switched it on. 'It was certainly a night to remember.' She took out a mug from the cupboard and turned to look at her friend. 'I met Hunter Addison's sister, who has a disability. She's lovely.'

'He took you to meet his sister? Oh, and here I was thinking you had bed-wrecking sex with him all night and—'

'I did. Well, before I met Emma, that is.'

Zoey's eyebrows shot up. 'You actually slept with him?' Her gaze went to Millie's left hand for the briefest of moments. 'Wow. I wondered if you'd ever get back on the horse, so to speak.'

Millie turned back to the hissing kettle and, placing a tea bag in her mug, poured the boiling water in. 'Yes, well, I was wondering about that myself.' She jiggled the tea bag a few times and then took it out and popped it in the bin beside the counter. She came back and sat at the table opposite Zoey, cradling the mug in her hands.

'So, how was it?' Zoey was leaning forward, her face alive with intrigue.

Millie could feel her cheeks growing as hot as the mug in her hands. 'It was amazing.'

'Are you seeing him again or was that just a one-off thing?'

Millie put the mug down on the table between them. 'We're having a fling, but I want to keep it quiet for the sake of Julian's mother. It's only a fling. It's not going to go anywhere. But I don't want her to feel I'm cheapening Julian's memory by having it off with a notorious playboy.'

Zoey frowned. 'Do you really think Lena is going to mind if you finally move on with your life?'

Millie pushed a tiny crumb on the table a few millimetres away with her finger, her gaze lowered. 'She will find it difficult, of course. How could she not? If I were to one day marry someone else and have the children she thought I was going to have with her son, then how else do you think she'd feel?'

Zoey sat back in her chair with a thump. 'I think you're overthinking it, truly I do. She might be pleased for you. Yes, of course she will always be sad about losing Jules, but I don't think she would want you to lock yourself away for ever.'

'I can't risk it.'

Zoey made a snorting noise of disdain and leaned forward again, her violet gaze probing. 'But what you do *you* want? Do you want to spend the rest of your life wearing a dead man's ring, never knowing what it feels like to be a bride, a wife, a mother? All the things you wanted so badly with Jules?'

Millie placed her hands around the mug again and stared at the dark liquid inside. How long could she keep this dreadful pretence up? Especially with her friends? She had told Hunter. Maybe it was time to tell Zoey and Ivy too.

She slowly lifted her gaze back to Zoey's searching one. 'The thing is… I didn't want those things with Julian.'

The silence was so intense, the air seemed to ring with the echo of her words.

'You didn't?' Zoey's tone was beyond shocked, her mouth hanging open. 'But I thought—'

'I know what everyone thought,' Millie said, whooshing out a breath. 'And I encouraged them to think it. I wanted to end things with Julian even before he got sick. He didn't seem the same person to me, and he certainly wasn't once he'd had the first round of surgery. Thinking back now, it was probably the brain tumour growing that first changed him, and then the surgery made it worse.'

'Oh, Millie…' Zoey seemed completely lost for words, which was somewhat out of character for a girl with a razor-sharp intellect and rapid-fire tongue. She reached across the table and grasped Millie's hand. 'Why didn't you say something earlier?'

'I couldn't. I felt so guilty. How could I have told him it was over when he had just been diagnosed? Or just after surgery or when he was in and out of remission? It would have been cruel, not just to him but to his mother too.'

'And all this time you've carried this…' Zoey's eyes were suspiciously moist, and her throat rose and fell as if she was trying to gulp back a sob. She leaned back again and brushed at her eyes with an impatient hand and added, 'Gosh, now you've made me cry, and nothing *ever* makes me cry.'

Millie wondered if Zoey's self-confessed hard heart was quite as tough as she made out. Zoey was good at the tough-as-nails façade, just as Millie was good at being the heart-sore fiancée left all alone. Once you played a role long enough, it became an entrenched part of your persona, sort of like a typecast actor. 'I know, it kind of snowballed, you know? One decision turns into two decisions and then three and four and, before you know it, you're trapped in a web of your own making.'

'Would you have married him if he had lived a few more days?'

Millie lifted one shoulder in a shrug. 'I know this sounds weak and pathetic of me, but I probably would have. It's amazing what guilt will make you do.'

'I don't know why you should be feeling guilty. You didn't give him the cancer.'

'I know, but once he had it I gave him hope, and I couldn't bear to take it away from him when he needed it the most.'

Zoey pushed back her chair and came round and wrapped her arms around Millie's shoulders. Her friend wasn't normally a physically demonstrative person, so the hug meant a lot. 'Jules was lucky to have you by his side. You did what you thought was the best thing at the time but now you have to think about what you want.' She pulled back to look at Millie. 'And, if you want Hunter Addison, then go for it.'

'Even if it's only for a fling?'

Zoey shifted her mouth from side to side, deep in thought. 'Not ever having had a fling myself, I can't advise you on that. But, hey, if you're going to have one, maybe I will too.' She picked up her tub of yoghurt and the teaspoon. 'I just have to find someone as hot as Hunter Addison. Wish me luck?'

Millie smiled. 'Be careful what you wish for.' But she might as well have been saying it to herself.

* * *

The following day Hunter was relieved to hear that Rupinder was back on duty with Emma now that her mother was making a good recovery. After taking Emma out for brunch—and hearing her chatter incessantly about how nice Millie was, and asking when she could come for a visit again—he finally settled her back in at home. He was determined there would be no more visits from Millie. It wouldn't do to get Emma's hopes up when all he and Millie were doing was having a short-term fling.

A friendship between his sister and Millie was out of the question, even if a part of him acknowledged that Millie was exactly the sort of person who would be good for Emma. She was sweet, compassionate and understanding. She didn't gawk or stare or ask intrusive questions. She accepted Emma as she was and for that he was immensely grateful. But a cosy little friendship between his sister and Millie couldn't happen.

He handed Emma over to Rupinder with the confidence to know it would be unlikely he would be called in the middle of the night, for the time being. It gave him the freedom to slip away for the weekend with Millie—the next hurdle, of course, would be convincing Millie to come with him at such short notice.

He decided to call her at work between clients, wishing he had the time to go and see her in person. He knew he was acting like a hormone-mad schoolboy with a crush but he couldn't seem to help it. His mind was preoccupied with her, reliving every moment they spent together making love. His body was on fire for her, eager to experience again the mind-blowing passion they had created together. He was used to having good sex, he was a competent and sensitive lover, but he had never had such off-the-scale sex. Was it the novelty aspect? Millie wasn't exactly his standard fling partner. She hadn't even liked him the first time she'd met him but in a way that had added to the attraction. The challenge of winning her over had fired him up in a way he had never been before. But that fire would have to go out at some point, right?

He couldn't—*wouldn't*—allow their fling to morph into anything else.

Millie reached for the buzzing phone on her work desk. Her heart gave a skip when she saw Hunter's name pop up on the screen. 'Donnelly-Clarke Jewellery Design, Millie speaking.' She used her most professional tone in an attempt to keep a little distance. It wouldn't do to answer the phone to him in a breathlessly excited voice like a lovesick schoolgirl. She was a fully grown woman who was having a simple fling. Casual. No strings. How hard could it be?

'Hello, Millie speaking,' Hunter drawled.

She leaned back in her chair and tried not to notice the way her insides quivered at the sound of the deep, sexy burr of his voice. 'Hi. How was your brunch with Emma?'

'It was good. Rupinder is back, so Emma is happy.'

'Oh, that's nice,' Millie said. 'I'm so glad. You must be relieved.'

There was a small silence.

'Are you free this weekend?' Hunter asked.

Millie ran her tongue over her lips. 'Erm, I might be. What did you have in mind?'

'Champagne. No clothes. A plunge pool. Sex. On a private yacht in the Aegean Sea. Have I tempted you?'

'You had me at champagne.'

He laughed. 'What time can you be ready?'

'What time do you want me?'

'I want you now.'

Millie shivered from head to foot at the rough desperation in his tone. 'I want you too. Last night was… wonderful.'

'Apart from Emma interrupting things.' There was a rueful edge to his voice.

'I didn't mind. I enjoyed meeting her.'

'So, can you be free at six? I'll book flights. It'll be a late night, but worth it when we get there.'

'Sure.' Millie put down the phone a short time later, wondering why he had so swiftly changed the subject back to their travel arrangements when she'd said how much she had enjoyed meeting his sister. He hadn't even acknowledged her comment. Did that mean he didn't want her to visit Emma again? Was he somehow ashamed of his sister? But that didn't sit with her understanding of his love and care for Emma. He was devoted to her, going out of his way to make sure she was safe, secure and well looked-after.

Or was it because Millie was only a temporary phase in his life? She had no permanent footing and he didn't want Emma getting too attached to her. But surely Emma was entitled to have relationships independent of her brother?

* * *

Millie barely had time to get home from work and pack before Hunter's pick-up time. They got to the airport and checked in, and soon after boarded their flight. First class, of course. She sat back with a glass of champagne in her hand and smiled at him. 'Is this how you spend your free time? Flying off to Greece to sail off into the sunset?'

'I wish.' His mouth twisted. 'I haven't been on the yacht for months. I'll probably have to whack away the cobwebs as we board.'

She gave a tiny shudder. 'You're joking…right?'

He grinned at her, his whisky-brown eyes twinkling. 'I have staff who maintain the boat for me. I call them ahead of time and they prepare the food and so on.'

Millie toyed with the stem of her glass, her eyes following the movement of her fingers rather than hold his gaze. 'I guess you've done this a few times now? Taken a lover away for a sex-fest weekend?'

Hunter picked up a strand of her hair and curled it around his finger. 'I've taken groups of people—colleagues, friends, that sort of thing—but never a lover by herself.' There was a husky quality to his voice.

Millie turned her head to face him, wondering why she was the first woman he had chosen to spend the weekend alone with on his yacht. He was looking at her mouth with a hooded gaze, his fingers still playing with her hair, sending shivers dancing down her spine. 'Careful, Hunter. You're making me feel rather special.' She injected her tone with teasing playfulness. 'We're having a temporary fling. You don't have to make me fall in love with you.'

His hand fell away from her hair and every muscle on his face froze. 'It would be most inadvisable for you to do so.' His lawyerly tone was strangely jarring. Of course she wouldn't be so foolish. He didn't need to remind her of the terms of their liaison. She had drawn a line under falling in love with anyone ever again. She had once thought she loved Julian, but that had been a teenage love that all too soon had faded once tested. How could she be sure a future love for someone wouldn't do the same?

Millie gave another playful smile. 'Have you considered the possibility *you* could fall in love with *me*?'

Something moved at the back of his gaze with camera-shutter speed. 'No.' His answer was brutally blunt, his gaze now screened.

Millie gave him an arch look. 'No, as in you've not considered it, or no, as in you don't think it's a possibility?'

He held her gaze with a steely determination. 'It's a possibility I will strenuously avoid giving any traction whatsoever. But while we're on the subject—I don't want my sister to develop feelings for you either.'

Millie frowned. 'So, what does that mean? You don't want me to visit her with you?'

'It would be best if you didn't. She has a tendency to form strong attachments to some people and, when those people leave, she's devastated. I've learned the hard way to keep things simple where she's concerned.'

'But don't you think she's entitled to have friendships of her own? She needs social contact beyond her carers, surely?'

'She has a handful of friends at a nearby group home she visits now and again.'

'But surely she needs more than that?'

Hunter's mouth tightened. 'You don't understand how difficult it is for her. She has the mentality of a small child. She believes what people say, and then they go and do the opposite, and it almost destroys her.'

'Like when your father left? Is that what happened?'

'Yes.' There was a bitter light in his eyes.

Millie placed her hand on his tense forearm. 'And you were the one who was left to pick up the pieces.' She spoke softly, desperate to show she had some understanding of picking up the pieces after someone had their heart broken. Hadn't she done it for her mother time and time again?

He glanced down at her hand on his arm before meeting her gaze, his hand coming over the top of hers, holding it in place. 'She cried for weeks. My mother and I tried to console her, but it was impossible. She used to sit in the front window of the flat we were living in, waiting for him. It was heart-breaking to watch. She would sit for hours like that.'

'Oh, how sad,' Millie said, blinking back the sting of tears. 'Why do you think your father deserted Emma and you? I mean, he was divorcing your mother, not you and Emma.'

Hunter took her hand and held it between each of his, one of his thumbs massaging the back of it in an almost absent fashion. 'He was one of those fathers that never failed to tell us he loved us. He spoilt us, buying us lots of expensive presents at birthdays and Christmas. We lived in a nice house in a well-to-do suburb. But, once Emma's condition became a little more obvious and lot more difficult to manage, he got cold feet. He didn't want a damaged child. He wanted a perfect family so everyone could pat him on the back and say, well done.'

'That's so selfish.'

'Tell me about it.' His tone was wry. He rolled his thumb over the diamond on her ring in the same absent fashion. 'It turned out he'd been having affairs for years on his business trips away. The presents were his guilt offering, I suspect.'

'You haven't seen him since?'

'No. He didn't even come to Mum's funeral. Didn't even send a card or flowers.'

Millie gripped his hand. 'I can only imagine how hurtful that must have been. I've never known what it's like to have a father—mine died before I was born. And none of my stepfathers were great stand-ins, in that sense. But to have one you truly believed loved you and then be rejected by him is just soul-destroying.'

He gave a movement of his lips that wasn't even close to a smile. 'Yes, well, I got over it pretty quickly, but Emma still asks about him occasionally. She has the deep-love gene. I don't.'

Or had he suppressed it in order to avoid further hurt? 'If he came back and asked for forgiveness, would you give it to him?'

'No. There are some things you can never forgive.' His gaze met hers again and he added, 'The words "I'm sorry" are like the words "I love you". So easy to say, but whether people mean them or not is another thing.'

Millie wondered if there would ever be a time when Hunter would say those words—*I love you*—to some lucky woman. Or had he become so jaded and embittered by the hurt his father had caused that he would never risk it?

She raised her champagne glass to his in a toast. 'Here's to never falling in love.'

Hunter tapped his glass against hers, his gaze unwavering. 'Here's to sticking to the rules.'

But Millie had a strange feeling those rules were just begging to be broken.

# CHAPTER TEN

HUNTER HADN'T BEEN wrong about the late night, Millie decided when they finally arrived in the wee hours of the morning to collect his yacht, moored just outside of Athens. Luckily she had dozed on the plane, so she wasn't feeling quite as wrecked as she might have been. Hunter led her on board in the moonlight and she looked around in wonder at the magnificently appointed ocean-going craft. It was like a floating hotel, with a plunge pool on deck and a hot tub, and sun loungers set up to make the most of the view once at sea.

The streamlined elegance of the yacht only added to the air of supreme and decadent luxury. Inside was a deluxe kitchen and dining area, and a lounge area off that leading to a home theatre. The master bedroom was on the level below and had a bank of wide windows with a set of sliding doors that wrapped around two-thirds of the room, offering a spectacular view, even at night.

Millie knew she was giving a very good impression of a child let loose in a sweet shop, but she couldn't help it. She gazed around at everything, touching the butter-soft leather of the sofas and the velvet scatter cushions. 'Oh, my…it's just amazing, Hunter. How you ever tear yourself away to fly back home to work is a mystery to me. I'd want to stay here for ever.'

'I'm not sure what Emma would have to say about that if I never came home. Or my clients, for that matter.'

She turned from stroking her hand over a brass fitting on the wall to look at him. 'Have you brought her on board?'

'No. It's too complicated with her medical needs. She needs to be close to a hospital in case anything goes wrong.'

She came over to him and linked her arms around his neck, toyed with the ends of his dark hair above the collar of his shirt. 'The worry must eat away at you all the time. Can you ever relax?'

He smiled and drew her closer. 'Aren't I relaxed now?' His eyes glinted, his body hardening against hers.

'You feel quite tense to me,' Millie said with a smile. 'But maybe I could help you with that? How does that sound?'

'It sounds like heaven.' And his mouth came down and captured hers.

The sleepiness she had felt earlier completely disappeared, her body alive and wanting him with heated fervour. She opened to the thrust of his tongue, welcoming him into her mouth with a whimper of delight. His hands got working on her clothes and, as each piece was removed, her excitement grew. He pressed kisses to her neck, each of her breasts and down her sternum, kneeling in front of her to anoint her most intimate flesh with his tongue. She broke apart within seconds, shuddering under the magic of his touch, waves of ecstasy rippling through her entire body.

He straightened and, still holding her by the hips, drew her against him once more. ‘See what you do to me? I’m crazy for you.’

*Crazy enough to fall in love with me?*

The thought popped into her head and she couldn’t get it out. She didn’t want him to fall in love with her… did she? She certainly didn’t want to fall in love with him. They had agreed to keep their feelings out of this. To keep things casual. But what was casual about experiencing the most mind-blowing pleasure of your life with the man of your dreams? For Hunter was all that and more, she realised in that moment. He had qualities and values that aligned so well with hers. How could she stop herself from admiring him? How close was admiration to love? It was barely a footstep away and she had to be careful not to take it.

Millie slithered down his body and set to work on the zipper of his trousers. ‘Let’s see if I can make you a little crazier.’

He placed a hand over hers. ‘You don’t have to do that.’

She looked up at him. ‘But I want to.’

‘Are you sure?’ His eyes glittered with anticipation, his body tense as a coiled spring.

Millie stroked her hand over his turgid length through the light barrier of his underwear. ‘I wouldn’t offer if I wasn’t sure.’

Which was a new thing for her, she suddenly realised. With her fiancé, she had often done things she hadn’t wanted to do just to please him. But with Hunter she wanted to please herself as well. Touching him in this most intimate way was almost as pleasurable as when he did it to her. It was a mutual expression of intense desire, and one thing she was sure of when it came to Hunter Addison—she had intense desire for him.

She finally got his underwear and trousers out of the way and leaned closer to stroke her tongue down his steely length in a cat-like lick. He shuddered and his hands grasped her by the head, his legs almost buckling as she went back for more. She licked and stroked him, suckled and drew on him, until he was quaking with the need to let go.

But he wouldn't let her go that far. He dragged her up to her feet, his eyes dark, glazed and wild with lust. 'I want to be inside you. Now.' His tone was ruthlessly determined and within seconds she was lying on her back on the king-sized bed, her breathing hectic as he quickly sourced a condom.

And then bliss…

His thrusts were hard and fast, as if he had finally allowed himself the freedom to express the explosive desire that rocketed through his body. Millie was with him all the way, relishing the almost primal way of coupling—the mutual desperation to get to the highest point of human pleasure.

She went over the edge first with a high cry, her body shuddering as each crashing wave tossed and swirled and hurled her around in a tumultuous sea of sensation. Hunter followed with his own powerful release, his body finally sagging against hers in the aftermath, his breathing still heavy.

Millie ran her hands down the length of his strong back and shoulders, enjoying the muscled weight of him on top of her. Enjoying the quietude after such an earth-shattering experience. How had she not realised making love could be this amazing? She had been short-changed in her relationship with Julian, which was partly her own fault. She had settled for second best. Held on to a flagging relationship out of a sense of duty and despair rather than deep and abiding affection. The sort of affection that could withstand anything thrown at it, even illness, even terminal illness. She hadn't loved Julian like that. She had never loved him like that.

But she was worried she *could* love Hunter that way. Deeply worried.

Hunter eased himself up on one elbow to gaze into her eyes, one of his hands idly playing with a few strands of her hair, letting them slip through his fingers before capturing them again. 'I'd really like to stay here in bed with you like this, but I have to get this vessel out to sea.' He dropped a kiss to the end of her nose and added, 'I considered employing a skipper I use sometimes, but I didn't want anyone else on board in case I can't control myself around you.'

Millie stroked her finger down the length of his strong nose, a teasing smile lifting up the edges of her mouth. 'Don't tell me the notoriously iron-clad self-control of Mr Hunter Addison is getting a little shaky around the edges?'

His eyes darkened and his mouth came inexorably closer to hers. 'You'd better believe it.' And then his mouth swooped down and covered hers.

Millie woke to the dawn sunshine pouring in through the bank of full-length windows in the master suite. The streaks of pink and red with an indigo backdrop that were reflected in the ocean were beyond spectacular.

She left Hunter peacefully asleep beside her and got out of bed. She picked up the silk wrap she'd brought with her and slipped it on, loosely tied it around her waist and padded over to the window, staring out at the view in wonder.

It would be a photographer's dream to see such exquisite colour and light, the hues changing with each passing second, the intensity of the sun as it peeped its golden eye above the horizon promising a beautiful day ahead.

In the distance she could see a faint disturbance in the smoothness of the sea's surface, and then the distinctive shape of a dorsal fin, soon followed by the smooth silver back of a breaching dolphin. And then eight or more followed the first, and she gasped out loud as they breached in tandem, as if following some sort of ancient aquatic choreography. 'Oh, wow! Hunter, look—dolphins!'

The sheets rustled as Hunter threw them off and he came and joined her by the window, completely and utterly naked. He placed his arms around her waist, standing behind her, drawing her back against his body. Being so much taller than her, he had an uninterrupted view of the ocean and its pod of playful dolphins over her right shoulder. And she had the delight of feeling his hardened body pressing against her bottom.

'Nature at its finest,' he said, and began to nibble her right ear.

Millie shivered and turned in his arms, winding her arms around his neck, but not before a greedy glance at his morning erection. She gave him a sultry smile. 'That's for sure.'

He lowered his mouth to hers in a long, drugging kiss that made her forget all about the glorious sunrise and sea life. His proud length throbbed against her belly, a potent reminder of the pleasure she had experienced in his arms in the early hours.

'Where are we?' she asked against his lips.

'In heaven.' He nudged her lower lip with his mouth. 'Or at least, we soon will be.'

Millie laughed and kissed him back. 'I meant apart from sensual heaven. I must have fallen asleep after you got the boat moving last night.'

'I've taken us far enough away for us to have some privacy. A mate of mine has a private island a short distance from here. We can moor there, so we can have a picnic on the beach.'

'That sounds amazing. I think I'm going to remember this weekend for the rest of my life.'

He smiled a lazy smile. 'Never let it be said I don't know how to show a lady a good time.'

'You're definitely excellent at doing that.'

Hunter brought his mouth back to hers in a scorching kiss that made every hair on her head rise in a Mexican wave. Her blood began to pound in her core, swelling her most intimate tissues, making them throb with a delicate pulsing ache that only he could assuage. His tongue danced with hers in an erotic imitation of love-making and she all but melted into a pool of longing.

He broke the kiss to peel the silk wrap from her body and it slipped to the floor at their feet. His hands ran down from the tops of her shoulders to her hips and back again—slow, caressing, mesmerising strokes that made her pulse race with anticipation. His gaze was sheened with lust, glittering, primal lust of a man who wanted a woman so badly it was killing him to stay in control. It thrilled her to think she was able to stir him up so much, and only fair, given the sensual havoc he caused her. Her body trembled under his touch, aching with need, hungry to feel the hot, hard friction of his body within hers.

'Make love to me. Please.' She didn't care that she sounded as if she was begging. Damn it, she *was* begging.

'Don't you want breakfast first?' There was a teasing glint in his gaze.

'Later.' She bit gently on his lower lip and added, 'I'm hungry for you right now.'

Hunter lifted her as if she weighed nothing more than a feather pillow and laid her on the bed. He came down beside her, his hands stroking her body into a frenzy of want. He circled her belly button with a lazy finger, tiptoeing it lower, lower, lower until he got to her feminine folds. Her back lifted off the bed in heady anticipation, her breath catching in her throat. He separated her and gently began to caress her already sensitive flesh, his eyes watching her response as if spellbound.

Millie was the one who was spellbound. Spellbound, mesmerised, dazed by the sensations he was creating in her body. Spasms, contractions and flickers of pleasure darted through her flesh, tension building, the ache for release increasing in intensity. She was getting closer and closer to the edge, the build-up tightening every nerve to a centre of concentration. And then she flew up into outer space, the sensations ricocheting through her body with rocket-ship speed. Spinning her round and round until she was gasping with the sheer bliss of a planet-dislodging orgasm.

Hunter waited until she was coming back to earth before he applied a condom and moved over her, turning her so she was straddling him, his hands holding her by the hips. His eyes were dark and lustrous with desire, his erection full and thick inside her. She squeezed herself around him, rocking with him, watching the contorted expression of pleasure play out on his face. It excited her to see him as undone by her as she was by him just moments ago. His pace increased, her pace increased, his groans and gasps matching hers. And then they were both riding the wave together, spilling out the other end in a tangle of limbs, the sound of their ragged breathing the only sound other than the sea lapping at the hull of the boat.

Millie lay across him, her head buried in his neck, breathing in the scent of him, storing it in her memory for the time when she would no longer be with him. How long would it be? A week or two? A month? A couple of months? He hadn't specified the time frame, only that their fling would be temporary.

It occurred to her that one day in the not-too-distant future he would be photographed by the press with someone else. Someone who would occupy his bed for a short time and be completely satisfied with the arrangement.

The thing was, could *she* truly be satisfied with a fling?

*You're going to have to be. Those are the rules.*

Millie rolled over onto her back and untangled her legs from his, her thoughts still in turmoil. Was she making another prison for herself? Her prison with Julian had been the lack of true love. But her prison with Hunter would be an over-supply of it.

*If* she fell in love. If. Such a small word for a massive change of circumstances. Circumstances Hunter was at pains to avoid, no matter what. And so had she been, until now…

Commitment. Life-long love. Marriage and children. Those were the things she had denied herself, pretending she didn't want them any more. But the truth was, she hadn't wanted them with Julian.

Hunter reached for her and gathered her close, rolling onto his side, resting on one elbow. He brushed hair away from her face with his other hand, his mouth tilted in a wistful smile. 'This was a great idea, stealing you away for a weekend.' He interlaced his fingers with hers. 'I wish I could keep you with me longer.' His voice went down a semitone, low and deep with a trace of huskiness.

*Longer as in past the weekend, or longer as in for ever?* The unspoken words seemed to hover in the silence. Millie returned his smile and lowered her gaze, circling each of his hard, flat male nipples with a slow-moving finger. 'We both have our businesses to run. A long weekend is about the only holiday I get these days.'

'Are you breaking even? Making a profit?'

Millie gave a slight grimace. 'I was until I had to help Mum out.' She sighed and added, 'That's why it means so much to me that you waived your fees. It's the most generous thing anyone has ever done for me.'

He leaned forward and pressed a soft kiss to her mouth, pulling back to look at her with a hooded gaze.

'My career has never been about making heaps of money. I enjoy the financial reward, and I've had good results with investments and shares and so on, but it's not something that drives me.'

He gave a rueful twist of his mouth and continued, 'I wish there had been someone who could have helped my mother during the divorce. It still sits like a stone in my gut that she got so done over. She believed everything my father told her. He spun her lie after lie after lie. I know it killed her in the end—the stress of him leaving her practically destitute and with a disabled child to take care of. It tortures me that she might have survived her blood cancer if she'd been stronger, both physically and mentally. But she just seemed to get ground down and then stopped fighting.'

He took a deep breath and let it out in a ragged stream. 'It was the saddest day of my life when she passed away.'

'Oh, Hunter,' Millie said, reaching up to stroke his face with a tender hand, tears clogging the back of her throat. 'I'm sure she would be so proud of how you take care of Emma. And how you've set out to help other people with your work. You truly are the most wonderful man. I'm even more ashamed now that I didn't see it the first time I met you.'

One side of his mouth lifted in a smile and he brushed his thumb over her lower lip, sending tingles through her flesh. 'You're making me sound like a saint, and I'm hardly that.'

Millie stroked his jaw, delighting in the sexy rasp of his stubble against her fingers. 'I've been thinking about

Emma and how she's so reliant on you when Rupinder is away. Have you thought of getting her a therapy dog?'

Hunter frowned. 'A dog? Are you crazy? She can't take care of herself, let alone a dog.' His tone was dismissive, and a coldness came over his face that chilled her to the bone. He moved away from her and scooped up a pair of undershorts and stepped into them. 'Look—sorry to be blunt, but Emma is my problem, not yours.'

Millie sat up and pulled the sheet up to cover her body, suddenly feeling naked and exposed under his searing gaze. 'Have I upset you? I didn't mean to. I was just offering a suggestion that—'

'That is unwelcome, unworkable and unnecessary.' He turned his back on her to continue dressing, his movements jerky with barely suppressed anger.

Millie pushed away the covers, got off the bed and slipped on the bathrobe, tying the waist ties with equally jerky movements. 'I don't understand why a simple suggestion should trigger such a response in you. I was only trying to help.'

Hunter turned to face her, his expression dark and forbidding. 'I've been responsible for my sister for years. I know what works and what doesn't, and a dog would make things way more complicated than they already are. Dogs need to be walked and fed, and trained appropriately. Emma isn't capable of it.' He blew out a breath and added in a weighty tone, 'And dogs rarely outlive their owners. What would that do to Emma if the wretched thing dies?'

Millie bit her lip, understanding his logic, but also seeing the other side of the argument. 'No pet comes with a guarantee of a long, healthy life, but a therapy dog is trained to be a companion and helper to people with disabilities. They come fully trained for the person's needs. Perhaps you could ask the carers to help with the walking and feeding? And maybe Emma is capable of more than you give her credit for. She could groom it, at the very least. The dog would be with Emma all the time, night and day. It would provide continuity and comfort when Rupinder or whoever goes on leave. Dogs can be sensitive to mood and can be trained to detect when a seizure is about to happen. Surely there are more positives than negatives in getting one?'

His expression became one of grave reflection, as if he was mentally sorting through her arguments in a logical and sequential fashion. Then, after a long moment, he finger-combed his hair and let out another long, serrated breath. 'Look—I'll think about it, but I'm not making any promises.'

Millie smiled and approached him, placing her arms around his waist and looking up into his eyes. 'I seriously don't think you'll be disappointed. You've had a dog before—I saw the photo at your house. It looked like you were great mates.'

A shadow flickered through his gaze and he gathered her closer. 'I had a dog called Midge but she had to be given away when we moved into a tiny flat after my parents' divorce. That was the second-saddest day of my life.'

Millie tightened her arms around him, as if reaching back in time to comfort the young boy who had lost his faithful friend in such a heart-wrenching way. 'That's terrible, Hunter. So terribly sad. How did Emma cope with that?'

'She didn't.' Another deep, ragged sigh. 'In the end, I had to pretend it was no big deal to me so I didn't ramp up her distress.'

Millie leaned back to gaze into his shadowed eyes. 'I can see now why you got so triggered by my suggestion of a therapy dog…'

He gave a glimmer of a smile, his arms a strong, warm band around her. 'You have a habit of triggering me in lots of ways.'

'Good or bad triggers?'

He bent down to press a light-as-air kiss to her lips. 'I think you already know the answer to that.' And his mouth came down and covered hers in a spine-tingling kiss.

# CHAPTER ELEVEN

AN HOUR OR SO later, Hunter anchored the yacht a short distance from the private island and, using the Jet Ski that was housed in a special section of the craft, took Millie and a picnic breakfast to the secluded cove. She hopped off the Jet Ski into the shallow water and waded the rest of the way to the golden sand.

If she had been asked to imagine paradise, then this would have been it. The beach was accessible only by boat or Jet Ski, and vertiginous cliffs rose on either side of it, creating absolute privacy. The beach was about four hundred metres in width and the water the quintessential deep Aegean blue, and as you got closer to the shore, the more shallow water, with its sandy bottom, became a stunning turquoise and then a gorgeous cyan.

'This is just…amazing…' Millie could barely find the words to describe the exquisite beauty surrounding her.

'It is pretty special.' Hunter leaned down to put the picnic hamper and their towels on the sand. He straightened and smiled. 'Breakfast or swim first?'

Millie laughed and began to strip off her shorts and top, leaving just her bikini on. 'Definitely a swim.'

His eyes roved over her from head to foot, his pupils darkening with unbridled lust. 'You don't need your bikini.'

'Are you sure?'

His gaze smouldered. 'Absolutely.'

Millie untied the strings of her bikini top and tossed it to the towel he had laid down and spread out just moments before. Next, she untied the strings at her hips, letting the bottoms fall to her feet. Never in her wildest dreams had she ever thought to be standing naked in front of a gorgeous man on a jaw-droppingly beautiful beach. Nor had she ever thought said man would look at her as if she was even more stunning than their surroundings.

'Aren't you going to get undressed?' she asked.

'Sorry. I got distracted by the view.' He hauled his white T-shirt over his head and tossed it to the towel. Next came his shorts and underwear and Millie couldn't drag her eyes away from his gloriously male body.

Hunter held out a hand to her and she slipped hers into it, shivering at the scorching look in his brown eyes. 'Have you ever skinny-dipped before?'

'No. I seem to do lots of things with you that I've never done before.' *Like fall in love.*

Millie knew she had taken the fatal last footstep and was now madly, fiercely, desperately in love with him. How could she not be? It had been stupid of her to think she could keep her feelings out of their arrangement. Their arrangement was all about feelings. Feelings she had never felt before. Feelings that had sparked at their first meeting, flickered into a bright flame at their second and by their third she'd been all in. Engulfed by desire, which she had fooled herself was only a physical thing. A mutually driven lust that would burn out in time.

But it wasn't burning out, it was burning brighter, hotter, more intensely.

And, like a silly little moth, she was flying right into the heart of the blistering flame.

Hunter led Millie into the warm water, determined to refrain from making love to her until after they had a swim. But it was hard. Damn hard. She looked like a beautiful mermaid, slim with curves in all the right places, her hair a long silk curtain down her back. But making love in the water was tricky when it came to condoms and the one thing he wouldn't do was make love without a condom. The last thing he needed was another complication in his life, and an unexpected pregnancy would top the list.

He held her hand until they were waist-deep and then turned her into him, running his hands down the sides of her body, his own body thick, tight and hot with desire. 'We're supposed to be swimming,' he said, leaning down to nibble at her ear lobe, breathing in the scent of her until he was almost drunk with it.

'I'm not stopping you.' She nestled closer, sliding one of her hands down between their bodies to stroke him.

He pulled her hand away even though it almost killed him. 'Yes, you are, little minx.' He tapped her on the end of the nose and added, 'Hold that thought until after breakfast.' He gave her bottom a playful pat. 'Now, go and swim.'

Millie gave him a mock pout and then turned and

swam off with neat fluid strokes. He watched her, spellbound for a few seconds, before striking out after her. She was a lot harder to catch than he'd expected, and he had to up his kick-and stroke-rate to get to her.

He finally caught her around the waist and trod water with her, smiling down at her sparkling eyes and laughing mouth. 'Now I've got you.'

Her legs wound around his waist and her naked body tempted his to the point of pain. 'So you have. But not for long.' Water droplets clung to the end of her long eyelashes and her lips curved upwards in a smile that made something in his chest tighten like a vice.

*Not for long…* The words were a jarring reminder of the time frame on their fling. *His* timeframe. But that was the way he wanted it, wasn't it? He couldn't offer her anything other than this—a short-term fling that would burn out just like any other had in the past.

So why, then, wasn't it burning out?

There was no boredom on his part, no sense of claustrophobia or dissatisfaction. The sex was mind-blowing, her company and conversation were stimulating and he enjoyed every minute he spent with her. Yes, even when she offered unwelcome suggestions about getting a therapy dog for Emma. Millie had made him think about it, more deeply than she probably realised.

And she had got yet another secret about his childhood out of him. A painful episode that had left its mark on him to this day. Saying goodbye to Midge was the hardest thing he had ever done. Letting his beloved pet go had ripped his heart out. He had taught himself at that moment never to love anyone or anything so much that he was unable to say goodbye. He had always known he would one day lose his parents, as most children expected to do. And he had always known he would one day lose Emma because her condition precluded a long life.

And he would say goodbye to Millie at some point and be fine with it, just as he had been fine with it with everyone else.

Hunter brought his mouth down to hers in a blistering kiss that sent his blood hammering through his veins. Lust swept through him and he grasped her by the hips and held her against his pounding length, relishing the silky feel of her body so temptingly close to his. His tongue played with hers in a cat-and-mouse caper than sent his heart-rate up and his self-control teetering. He wanted, wanted, wanted to sink into her velvet wetness and take them both to paradise. He wanted, wanted, wanted her with a driving, drumming ache that was beyond anything he had ever felt before.

He set her down before him and lowered his mouth to her breasts, her nipples already tightly puckered. He tasted the salt water dotting her flesh, and the scent of her fresh-summer-flowers fragrance sent his senses haywire. He caressed her other breast with his lips and tongue, enjoying the sounds of her pleasure. Enjoying the sensual power he had over her. But, hey, didn't she have the same power over him? So much power it was driving him crazy, turning him into a man of such desperate need, it raised a red flag in his head.

How long would this continue? This driving need for her that wouldn't abate. It had to peter out eventually. It *had* to. Otherwise he was in deep water.

'I want you so badly it's becoming a problem.' He didn't realise he had spoken his thoughts out loud until Millie caressed his jaw with her soft little hand, her eyes shimmering with need.

'Why is that a problem?'

Hunter stroked his hands down from the top of her shoulders to grasp her by the wrists. 'I can't make love to you without a condom.'

'You brought some with you, though, didn't you?'

He nodded towards their towels and hamper. 'They're back with the towels.'

She tiptoed her fingers down his sternum to his belly button, hovering tantalisingly close to his jutting erection but without actually making contact. His blood thundered and roared, and he had never felt so turned on in his life. Her eyes were dancing, her lips curved upward in a smile that was as sultry as the sunshine beating down on his head and shoulders.

'Then maybe we'd better get back to the towels before you or I lose control.' Her voice had a breathless edge and there was a gleam of mischief in her eyes.

Hunter had a feeling he was the one in far more danger of losing control. Her hand drifted lower, her fingers going around him, and he let out a curse through tight lips. 'Your touch drives me to distraction.'

'That's only fair, since yours does the same to me.' She squeezed him tighter, an on-off squeeze that sent his pulse racing.

Hunter moved her hand away and scooped her up in his arms, walking back through the waist-deep water to the sandy beach. 'I think that's enough swimming for now.'

Millie laughed and linked her arms around his neck. 'Spoilsport.'

He laid her down on the towels and quickly rummaged for a condom and applied it. He came over her, pinning her with his body, wanting her so badly he had to count backward to slow himself down. He drank in the sight of her shining eyes and slightly parted mouth, her rosy-red lips eager for his kiss. Her legs opened for him and he surged into her wet warmth with an agonised groan of pleasure, his skin peppering in goosebumps as her inner muscles wrapped around him. He set a fast pace, but she was with him every step of the way, urging him on with gasps and groans and whimpers that thrilled him to the core of his being. She wanted him and he wanted her and that was enough for now.

It had to be.

Later that day, Millie and Hunter sat on the yacht after showering and changing and shared a glass of wine as the sun went down. Every inch of her body felt alive and tingling, and every time she caught Hunter's eye a frisson would pass over her flesh as she recalled their explosive love-making on the beach.

But then one of the thoughts she was fighting so hard to suppress crept up on her and began to taunt her. Would he one day bring someone else out here and make mad, passionate love to her? Would he wine and dine them and make them feel like a princess for the weekend? No doubt there would be numerous women after her—he was a playboy, after all. A man who wanted no ties, no long-term commitment.

Millie traced her finger round the rim of her wine

glass in a reflective manner. 'You know, you've set rather a high benchmark for any other lover I might have in the future.'

There was a silence broken only by the gentle lap of water against the hull of the yacht.

Millie chanced a glance at him to find him wearing a brooding frown, his fingers tightening around his wine glass. He appeared to give himself a mental shake and his frown disappeared from his forehead, but not his eyes. It lingered there in the background like a shadow.

'So, you think you'll be ready to move on with your life after…us?' The slight hesitation over the word 'us' could have meant nothing or everything, but how could she tell? His tone gave nothing away.

Would she be able to move on? If he was coming with her on the journey then, sure, it would be a cinch. But without Hunter by her side, the man she had fallen in love with so deeply… How would it be possible to move on without his love in return? Millie stretched out her legs and crossed her ankles, twirling her top foot this way and that. Her left hand was resting on her thigh. The lowering sun caught the top of her engagement ring and she pointedly looked away, not wanting to be reminded of the mistakes she had made in the past.

'I'm not sure…' She gave him a forced little smile and added in a lighter tone, 'So, who will be the next woman you bring out here to impress?'

His frown deepened and he put his glass down on the table between them on the deck. 'I didn't bring you out here to impress you, Millie.' His voice was low and had a deep note of gravity.

'Why did you bring me, then?'

His eyes held hers in a tight little lock that seemed to go on for endless seconds. She counted every one of them with the hammering beats of her heart. Boom. Boom. Boom.

'I brought you here because I wanted to be alone with you.' His tone dropped half a semitone to a deep burr.

'We were alone at your house in London.'

His mouth twisted. 'Until Emma needed me.'

Millie twirled the contents of her glass, looking down at the whirlpool she'd created, so similar to her swirling thoughts. 'Is Emma one of the reasons you don't want to settle down and have children of your own?' She raised her gaze back to his. 'Because you're worried you might have a child with a genetic disorder like hers?'

Hunter leaned forward to rest his forearms on his bent thighs, his broad hands flat against each other in the space between his knees. He let out a long breath, his expression hard to see at that angle, but she suspected he hadn't lost the frown.

'I saw what Emma's condition did to my parents. As soon as it became obvious Emma couldn't be cured, my father bolted. My mother never lost hope that one day Emma would be miraculously healed. It was painful to see her scrabbling the money together for numerous alternative-health therapies. She went without to get Emma yet another experimental cure. None, of course, worked. Emma is a child locked in an adult's body. Nothing is going to change that. She will never get married and have children. She will never enjoy the things most people take for granted. I just try and make her life as comfortable and happy and secure as I can.'

Millie moved closer so she could touch him on the forearm. 'I think what you do for Emma is wonderful. Which makes me think you'd make the most wonderful father yourself. It seems a shame to rule out the possibility. You couldn't possibly turn out like your father. It's not in your nature. And think of the joy you'd bring to Emma if she became an auntie. She would love her nieces and nephews to bits, I'm sure.'

Hunter straightened but something about his tight expression cautioned her that she'd stepped over a line. 'Careful, Millie, it sounds like you're dropping hints about making our fling into something it's not.' His tone had a chilled edge that made her spine stiffen.

Millie removed her hand from his arm as if it had been burned. 'I wasn't doing any such thing. I was simply suggesting—'

He stood so abruptly, she flinched. 'You're very good at suggesting but not so good at understanding the implications of those suggestions.' The derisive edge to his voice cut her to the quick, the flash of his brown eyes even more so. He turned his back and gripped the ledge on the side of the yacht, staring out at the dipping sun, and added, 'Let's not ruin a perfectly nice weekend arguing over things that aren't important.'

Millie rose from the seat and came over to him but didn't touch him. She stood beside him, glancing up at his brooding expression. 'What could be more important than your happiness?'

He turned his head to look down at her, his top lip curled. '*My* happiness? Don't you mean your happiness? That's what this conversation is all about, isn't it?'

'I'm not sure what you're suggesting but…'

He pushed himself away from the side of the yacht, sending a jerky hand through the thickness of his hair. 'You're suggesting we make our fling permanent. That I pop a ring on your finger and marry you and have a bunch of babies. That just about sums it up, doesn't it?' His biting tone and cold gaze lashed at her nerves, already on edge.

Millie opened and closed her mouth, not sure how to respond. Those were exactly the things she wanted him to do, but not out of duty or because of her expectations, but because he loved her and wanted to be with her for the rest of his life. What a time to realise how much she loved him—the same time he was bluntly making it clear he didn't love her back.

'I would never want to tie anyone to me, as I once tied myself to my fiancé, out of a sense of duty or expectation. I would only want someone to be with me because they loved me too much to be away from me.'

Hunter glanced at the ring on her left hand, his expression still set in tight lines. 'Then maybe it's time you took that ring off.'

'Maybe it is.'

'But don't expect me to put one in its place because that is not going to happen.' His words were delivered in an adamant tone, his gaze glittering with disdain.

Millie raised her chin, determined not to show him how crushed she was feeling. 'I never expected you to. You say you don't want the things other people want, just like I used to do. You're punishing yourself, denying yourself the most basic joys that life can offer, because you feel guilty about Emma. You are not to blame for her genetic disorder. You are not to blame for your father abandoning your family. You are not to blame for your mother's death. But you are to blame for not opening your heart to the possibility of love.'

Hunter stood with his hands low on his hips. 'Nice little speech, sweetheart.' His tone was cuttingly scathing. 'Let me guess what made you fancy yourself in love with me. Was it the house in London? The yacht? My private island?'

*His* island? Millie frowned in confusion. 'It's not your island. You said it belonged to a friend.'

He gave a grating laugh. 'Yes, well, that didn't seem to work with you, did it? You apparently saw through my little white lie and decided a man who owned a private Greek island was worth falling for.'

Millie's spine was so stiff, she swore she could feel every muscle bunching into knots. 'Are you calling me a gold-digger?'

'I'm calling you a romantic fool who got a little in over her head.' His expression was so cold, she wanted to shiver. 'I should have known this could never work. You're not the fling type. You were with the same man until he died, and you still wear his blasted ring.'

Millie automatically twisted the ring on her finger, testing to see if she could get it off, but it was still stuck. 'I explained my reasons for staying with Julian. I told you more than I've told anyone. I opened up to you, but you told me so little about yourself. I found out about Emma only by circumstance. I suspect if we hadn't been together that night at your home in London I would *still* know nothing about her.

'You're a closed book. You don't allow anyone close

because you don't like giving people the power to hurt you. But life isn't truly a life if we lock ourselves away from the possibility of hurt. Life is all about hurting, and dealing with and healing those hurts the best way we can, surrounded by those we love and trust to help us through the best and worst patches. That is what I want in a future relationship—knowing someone has my back in the same way I have theirs.'

Hunter was still frowning darkly, his mouth tightly compressed, a muscle beating in jaw. 'So, the question is, what do we do now?'

Millie knew exactly what she had to do but doing it was going to be the real kicker. But she had dawdled too long in the past and got trapped in a prison of her own making. She would not allow herself to do so again. She had learned her lesson and learned it well. Too well, for this time it really hurt. It hurt in a way she had never thought possible. Her heart physically ached inside her chest—ached like it was being compressed in a vice. 'Hunter, we have to end this. I have to end it. I can't see you again, or at least not in this context. Of course, I'll still attend meetings with my mother, unless you'd rather not—'

'Don't be ridiculous,' Hunter cut in. 'I will continue to act for your mother regardless of what's gone on between us. I can organise a support person for her if you'd rather not be there.' There was nothing in his tone to suggest any engagement of his feelings. He spoke clearly, politely, dispassionately, unemotionally. His expression also showed no sign of any disappointment, and his earlier anger had completely disappeared. It was as if he had stepped into another persona, a business-as-usual persona that had not been one bit affected by her decision to end their fling.

Millie searched his features for a long moment, clinging to the hope that there might be a tiny chink in his armour, but in the end she had to accept the inevitable. It was over. They were over. And she hadn't even told him she loved him, nor would she. He wouldn't want to hear it anyway. 'Thank you for…everything. I had a great time.'

His lips moved in a vestige of a smile, but it didn't reach his eyes. 'Glad to hear it.' He let out a short breath and swung away. 'I'd better get this yacht back to its moorings. We have a flight to catch in the morning.'

'Hunter?'

He glanced over his shoulder, his hand still on the railing. 'I'll sleep in the spare room tonight.'

She bit down on her lip, a little surprised and somewhat embarrassed he had read her mind. 'Fine. Thanks. I think that's best.'

On the painfully long journey back to London Hunter was determined that he would not reveal how disappointed he was with Millie's decision to end things between them. It was always going to happen, right? It just stung a little that she had ended it before he had. He was the one who usually walked away—that was something he had perfected over the years. Knowing when enough was enough, knowing how to read the signs that things were getting a little too serious. He was a master at avoiding messy break-ups. And he wasn't going to sink to the level of grovelling now, even if he could eke out a few more weeks of their fling. And it would only be a matter of weeks—he didn't ever let a relationship go much longer than that.

But somehow the short time with Millie had made him hungry for more. Ravenously hungry. Awakened a need in him he hadn't known he possessed. A need for a deeper connection with someone, a mutually satisfying relationship where the usual guards were down and inner vulnerability exposed. She hadn't told him straight out that she loved him, but he could read between the lines enough to know she wanted more. Much more. But he wasn't the person to give it to her, so the wisest and surprisingly hardest thing to do was let her go. Surprising, because walking away from a fling had never hurt in the past. It had never sat uncomfortably with him, annoyed him or agitated him in any way whatsoever.

But boarding the plane back to London, sitting beside her and acting with indifferent politeness, was one of the most excruciating experiences of his life.

They walked off the plane together but, when they got to the exit, Millie turned to him with a look of resignation on her face. 'If you don't mind, I'll make my own way home from here.'

'Don't be silly, I'll drive you.'

Her small, neat chin came up and her eyes glinted with determination, and something in his chest collapsed like a sail. 'No, I don't think that's a good idea.' She held out her hand. 'Goodbye, Hunter.'

He ignored her hand, not trusting himself not to haul her back into his arms and remind her of all the reasons they should continue their fling a little longer. Why was this hurting so much? It was crazy. He never allowed anyone to get under his skin. Never.

He stripped his face of all emotion, determined not to show his inner turmoil. Determined not even to acknowledge it to himself. Why should he care they were over? It was a fling, damn it. Flings were meant to end sooner or later. 'Goodbye, Millie. I guess I'll see you in court.'

'Let's hope it doesn't come to that.' Her stiff little smile didn't quite reach her eyes, but it reached his heart like a sharp little dart.

Then she turned on her heel, walked out through the exit and he stood watching her go without moving a muscle to go after her. But then, why would he? He wasn't in love with her. He wasn't a believer in the romantic fantasy of happy-ever-after. He was a realist, a cynic, a man who knew how to avoid messy emotional entanglements.

And, by letting Millie go, he knew in his bones he had avoided one of the most potentially messy of them all.

## CHAPTER TWELVE

Millie got home to her flat to find Zoey on her way out to visit her father.

'How did your weekend go?' Zoey asked, shrugging herself into a lightweight jacket and lifting her dark hair out of the collar.

'I'd rather not talk about it, actually.' Millie plonked her overnight bag on the floor with a despondent sigh.

Zoey frowned and walked over to her. 'It's over?'

Millie nodded. 'I ended it.'

'Why?'

Millie sank to the sofa and laid her head back against the cushioning. 'I don't want to make a fool of myself over him. I got out before I started gushing about how much I love him.'

Zoey's neat eyebrows lifted, her eyes wide as violet orbs. 'You *love* him?'

Millie pressed her lips together. 'Yes, well, it kind of happened before I could stop it.'

'Yeah, apparently it sometimes works that way.' Zoey sat down beside her. 'I'm sorry. How did he take it?'

Millie gave a gurgle of humourless laughter. 'Without a flicker of emotion. It kind of proves I did the right thing in ending it. If he cared a jot for me, you'd think he'd at least have said something, wouldn't you?'

Zoey shrugged one slim shoulder. 'I'm no expert on men, as you already well know. I have enough trouble understanding my own father without trying to understand men of our generation. But I do know one thing—you have to do what's right for you.'

'If it's right for me to end things with him, then why does it hurt so much?'

Zoey made an 'I'm sad for you' face. 'It really sucks to get your heart kicked around. But at least he wasn't unfaithful. And you ended it before it got really messy.'

Millie got off the sofa and began to pace the room. 'I need to do something to take my mind off this or I'll go crazy.'

'Come to dinner with Dad and I. You'll have a ball watching him get blackout-drunk and telling everyone in the restaurant how much he wished he'd had a son instead of a daughter.'

Now it was Millie's turn to do the sad face. 'I really don't know how you cope with him.'

'Yes, well, he's all I've got, so I have to suck it up.' Zoey got up and scooped her tote bag off the floor where she'd left it earlier. She hung it over her shoulder and added, 'I'm sorry it didn't work out the way you wanted it to. And if I wasn't such a cynic I'd say, hang in there. He might come to his senses and realise what he's given up.'

Millie's shoulders slumped on another sigh. 'I can't see that happening any time soon.' She dared not hope for such an outcome. It was in the realms of impossibility, knowing him the way she did.

* * *

Later that day, Millie unlocked the door to her studio and went to her workroom. She picked up one of her jewellery saws and passed it from one hand to the other, preparing herself for the thing she should have done long ago. A clean break was the best break. She began to saw through the gold band on her left hand, tiny sawing movements that finally released her from a promise she should never have made in the first place. 'I'm sorry, Jules. I hope you're at peace now. I'm going to give this to your mum. I hope you don't mind.' She carefully placed the cut ring into an envelope and sealed the top down, placing it in her tote bag to deliver to Lena.

Millie sat down at her desk and began some preliminary sketches of a charm bracelet for Hunter's sister. She didn't want to walk out of Emma's life without leaving something behind to tell her she would be thinking of her. Hunter might not approve but she was determined to do it anyway.

Hunter threw himself into work in order to distract himself from thoughts of Millie. As usual, plenty of work was coming through the door—kind of proving his view of romantic love being nothing but a fantasy. He spent extra time and effort on Millie's mother's divorce, but he was still waiting on further details from Matteo Vitale over some missing funds and some suspicious offshore accounts. Matteo suspected a serious case of fraud and didn't want to act until he had all the facts on the table, but it held up the process, and meant Hunter couldn't get the closure he wanted.

He needed the distance.

He needed to stop thinking about Millie, period, but acting for her mother meant Millie was almost constantly on his mind. He was too much of a professional to let his bitterness over their break-up interfere with how he processed Eleanora's divorce. And he was still perfectly happy to do the work pro bono. It gave him a good feeling, and what he needed right now was good feelings because he felt rubbish most of the time. He had no appetite for food, no interest in the punishing exercise routine he usually enjoyed and no ability to hold a sensible conversation with anyone without his mind going elsewhere—most particularly to his island in Greece and the image of Millie walking out of the sea like a goddess.

Hunter groaned and snatched up his car keys and phone from his desk. Why couldn't he let it go? He was acting demented, like some sort of love-sick fool who didn't know how to walk away from a fling. He knew exactly how to walk away. He'd been doing it for most of his adult life. Why was it killing him now?

*Because you miss her.*

The words dropped into his head like stones in a pond, the circles going outward in waves with follow-up thoughts.

*You miss her smile. You miss her touch. You miss her intelligence. You miss the love-making. You miss every damn thing about her.*

So? He could go on missing her. He had no business picturing a happy-ever-after with Millie Donnelly-Clarke. There was no such thing as happy ever after, or at least not for people like him. He had Emma to think of—poor little Emma who would never be a bride, never hold her own baby in her arms. But he would do what he could to make up for that, using Millie's suggestion. Yes, he had listened and taken on board the notion of a therapy dog. He had one lined up that very day.

Hunter had arranged to meet the dog trainer and handler at Emma's townhouse. He hadn't told Emma anything about it, wanting to surprise her, as well as gauge her reaction in case she didn't warm to the dog at all.

He shouldn't have worried on that score, for as soon as the handler, Kate, brought in Ruby, the chocolate-coloured labradoodle, Emma wrapped her arms around the dog's neck and cried for joy.

'Do you really mean it? She's mine? All mine, to stay with me all the time?' Emma asked, happy tears shining in her eyes and dripping down her face.

Hunter smiled, in spite of his own misery, and felt a suspicion of moisture in his own eyes. 'Yes, poppet. Ruby is yours.'

'I can't believe it,' Emma said, petting the dog lovingly. Ruby lapped it up with a doggy smile and melting brown eyes and a wagging plume of a tail. A bond was forming right before Hunter's eyes and it touched him deeply.

But then he caught sight of a bracelet on Emma's wrist. 'Hey, poppet, where did you get that bracelet? Did Rupinder give it to you?'

Emma shook her head. 'No. Millie came by the other day. She made it for me. Isn't it beautiful?' She held out her wrist and swung the little charms around, making them tinkle. 'She's so clever. She told me to hold this charm here if ever I feel scared and lonely. See, this one? It's got a smiley face. I love it. But I might not have to hold it now I've got Ruby, huh?' She wrapped her arms back around the dog and Ruby's tail swept the floor like a shaggy broom.

Hunter suddenly felt tight in the throat and chest. Millie had taken the time to make Emma a bracelet. She had delivered it to Emma and encouraged her to self-soothe, giving her a strategy with which to do so. Millie hadn't dumped his sister along with him. She had thought of Emma and taken it upon herself to make sure Emma was protected from any hurt resulting from their break-up.

What a pity Millie hadn't spared him the hurt in the first place. Maybe he needed a charm bracelet to rub every time he thought of her. He knew one thing for sure—he would have rubbed the metal to the thinness of paper in no time at all, so incessant was his thinking about her. He had a bad case of something, and he didn't want to admit it. The L word was hovering at the back of his brain, but he pushed it away. Love and hurt went hand in hand and he wasn't signing up for that any time soon.

But, oh, how dreadful it was to know he might never see Millie again. He would never hold her in his arms and kiss her or make passionate love to her. There was that wretched L word again. Sex used to be sex, but with Millie it was *always* making love.

Why had he been such a fool to let things go that far? Far enough to make him feel as if the bottom had dropped out of his world?

He had always determined never to love enough to feel the pain of losing, yet he had lost Millie. But had he ever had her other than in a physical sense? From the outset, he had closed off his heart, only giving her his body. How could that ever be enough for someone as caring and loving as Millie? She wanted the whole package because anything less would be an insult. He was insulting himself, let alone her, not to open his heart to her.

There was a strange feeling in his chest, a loosening of bolts around the cage in which his heart was locked. It was like allowing a beam of light into a darkened, closed-off room, light that showed all the secret longings hidden inside. He had ignored and denied those longings for most of his life. Like his sister, he had been desperately hurt by their father, and had sworn never to allow anyone close enough to hurt him again. But he was hurting himself by not loving fully, openly and wholeheartedly. He was living half a life—he wanted more. Needed more. He needed Millie. She had challenged him from the start, triggering something in him which was only becoming obvious now.

Hunter leaned down to stroke the dog's silky ears and was rewarded with a lavish lick.

'So, you'll keep her?' Kate asked from a short distance away.

'Yes, I'll keep her.' Hunter had never been more certain of anything in his life, but he wasn't talking about the dog. Why had it taken this long to realise it? He was madly in love with Millie. Madly, deeply in love, and he had been a fool not to recognise it earlier. No wonder he'd been fighting it from the first moment they'd met. No wonder he was so miserable and lost. He was lost without the hope she gave him, the love she taught him to feel. She had unlocked his frozen heart, released him from his emotional prison.

He. Loved. Her.

'She's not yours,' Emma said, possessively hugging the dog to her chest with a fierce little stare at her brother. 'She's mine.'

Hunter laughed and ruffled Emma's hair. 'I'm not talking about Ruby, poppet.' He turned to Kate. 'Will you excuse me? Rupinder will fill me in with any instructions later. I have to propose to the love of my life.'

'Sure,' Kate said with a beaming smile.

'You're going to marry Millie?' Emma asked, eyes wide, smile wider.

'If she'll have me,' Hunter said. He leaned down and kissed his sister on the top of the head. 'Look after Ruby. She's part of our family now.'

And he hoped Millie was going to be too.

Millie walked back to her flat after visiting Julian's mother. It had been a poignant meeting, with tears on both sides, but it had given Millie some much-needed closure to hand Lena the engagement ring. She had soldered it together and put it back in its original ring box.

She hadn't told Lena she hadn't ever loved her son in a romantic sense. She didn't think it necessary, and nor did she want to taint the treasured memories Lena had. Instead, she'd told Lena she was now ready to move on with her life and hoped that Lena would find some joy of her own in spite of her loss. And, much to Millie's surprise, Lena announced she was actually seeing someone—her first relationship since Julian's father had left all those years ago. Her new beau was a widower with three school-aged children and Lena was already enjoying helping to take care of them.

Millie crossed the street at her usual place, lost in her thoughts—mostly of Hunter and how much she missed him—when she happened to look up and see him standing at her door. For a moment she wondered if her mind was playing tricks on her. She blinked a couple of times to reset her vision, but he was still standing there. She climbed the steps with unsteady legs, her heart racing. Why was he here? What possible reason could he have for coming here after they had said all that needed to be said?

'Millie, can I have a word with you?'

'Sure.' Millie was surprised at how even her voice sounded, given how fast her heart was beating. She began to work the key in the lock, but her fingers wouldn't cooperate. 'Sorry about this, the lock is a bit—'

'Here, let me.' His large hand came over the top of hers and turned the key with her, and the lock turned as smoothly as anything.

Millie removed her hand from under his and stepped inside, trying to ignore the tingling on her skin where he had touched her. Would she never be immune to his touch? He closed the door behind him and stood looking at her for a moment.

'You, erm, wanted to talk to me about something?' she prompted in a cool tone.

He let out a shaky breath, his hands seeming restless by his sides, his fingers opening and closing as if he was trying to control the urge to touch her again. 'I got Emma a therapy dog.'

'Oh, that's lovely. What's its name?'

'Ruby. Emma adores her already.'

'I'm so glad.'

A silence fell between them. A silence so thick, Millie heard herself swallow and suspected he did too.

'So, can I get you a drink or…?'

He stepped forward and grasped her by the upper arms, his expression tortured. 'My darling girl, can you forgive me for being a blind fool and not realising how much I love you?'

Millie stared at him speechlessly for a moment. 'You…you love me?'

His hands tightened on her arms as if he was frightened she was going to pull away. 'Madly. Deeply. Desperately. I think I fell in love with you that day we met for a drink, when you asked me to act for your mother. I've resisted it all this time, not even recognising what I felt as love until today. I've been flat-out miserable without you. I can't believe I let you walk away. I was so blind to what I was really feeling. Losing you made me finally realise how I was short-changing myself in life. My life can't be what it's supposed to be without you in it. I can't imagine life without you by my side. Please come back to me and make me the happiest man alive.'

She wrapped her arms around his waist and hugged him. 'I didn't want to walk away. I love you so much. I can't believe how much.'

He looked down at her with love shining in his eyes.

'Will you marry me? Please? Nothing would give me more joy than to have you as my wife and partner in life.'

Millie smiled and hugged him again. 'Yes, yes, of course I will, you darling man. How could you think I would ever say no to you? That was my problem almost from the moment we met. I saw what a danger you were to my heart. I tried to keep my feelings under guard, but it was impossible to resist you.'

He framed her face in his hands, looking down at her with loving tenderness. 'I'm a package deal, you know. It won't always be easy with Emma. Her health is tricky to manage, and she can be quite possessive over people. She's already glued to that dog.'

'I adore Emma,' Millie said. 'I hope you didn't mind that I visited her?'

He smiled. 'I saw the gorgeous bracelet. She loves it, and I can't thank you enough for not walking away from her because of me.'

'Do you think she could be one of our bridesmaids? I would love that so much.'

Hunter blinked back tears. 'You truly are a one-in-a-million girl. What have I done to be so lucky to have you in my life?'

Millie stroked his face with her hand. 'I'm the lucky one. I never thought it was possible to love someone the way I love you. I love you with all my being.'

'Do you remember when I told you how the pretence over your situation with Julian was hurting you more than anyone else? What a hypocrite I was. I realised I was doing the same. Hurting myself by not acknowledging what I really felt for you.'

Millie had never thought she would hear such wonderful proclamations of love from him. All her dreams were coming true. Her heart had never felt so full, her love for him knowing no bounds. 'I just love hearing you say how much you love me. I don't think I'll ever tire of hearing it.'

'I'm going to keep saying it for the rest of our lives.' He pressed a lingering kiss to her lips, then continued, 'I got to thinking about what you said about having children. Emma can't be a mother, but she would certainly love being an auntie. I want a bit of time with you first, since we've rushed our relationship so far, but let's have a family together.'

Millie pressed another kiss to his mouth. 'I would love to have a baby or two with you. Nothing would please me more. I didn't realise how much I wanted to be a mother until I met you. You will be the most wonderful father. I just know it.'

'And you will be a beautiful mother.' He captured her left hand and stroked his thumb over the vacant space on her ring finger. 'You cut it off.'

'Yes, I was finally ready. I gave it to Lena. She might end up using it herself, as she's seeing a nice man who has a young family.'

Hunter smiled and leaned down to kiss her. 'I can't wait to tell Beth and Dan about us. They saw the potential for us before we even met. That's kind of spooky in a way.'

'Spooky but lovely,' Millie said, kissing him back.

'Now, about a ring.' His tone was mock-business-like.

'Well, I could design one for you, if you think you can afford me.'

He grinned. 'I was hoping you would say that. I want no expense spared. I only want the best for my beautiful bride. I love you, my darling.'

Millie linked her arms around his neck and smiled against his mouth. 'And I love you right back.'

* * * * *

# MILLS & BOON

## Coming next month

### THE GREEK'S CONVENIENT CINDERELLA
Lynne Graham

'Mr Alexandris,' Tansy pronounced rather stiffly.

'Come and sit down,' he invited lazily. 'Tea or coffee?'

'Coffee please,' Tansy said, following him round a sectional room divider into a rather more intimate space furnished with sumptuous sofas and sinking down into the comfortable depths of one, her tense spine rigorously protesting that amount of relaxation.

She was fighting to get a grip on her composure again but nothing about Jude Alexandris in the flesh matched the formal online images she had viewed. He wasn't wearing a sharply cut business suit, he was wearing faded, ripped and worn jeans that outlined long powerful thighs, narrow hips and accentuated the prowling natural grace of his every movement. An equally casual dark grey cotton top complemented the jeans. One sleeve was partially pushed up to reveal a strong brown forearm and a small tattoo that appeared to be printed letters of some sort. His garb reminded her that although he might be older than her he was still only in his late twenties and that unlike her, he had felt no need to dress to impress.

Her pride stung at the knowledge that she was little more than a commodity on Alexandris's terms. Either he would choose her, or he wouldn't. She had put herself on the market to be bought though, she thought with sudden self-loathing. How could she blame Jude Alexandris for her stepfather's use of virtual blackmail to get her agreement? Everything she was doing was for Posy, she reminded herself squarely and the end would justify the means...*wouldn't it?*

'So...' Tansy remarked in a stilted tone because she was determined not to sit there acting like the powerless person she knew herself to be in his presence. 'You require a fake wife...'

Jude shifted a broad shoulder in a very slight shrug. 'Only we would know it was fake. It would have to seem real to everyone else from the start to the very end,' he advanced calmly. 'Everything between us would have to remain confidential.'

'I'm not a gossip, Mr Alexandris.' In fact Tansy almost laughed at the idea of even having anyone close enough to confide in because she had left her friends behind at university and certainly none of them had seemed to understand her decision to make herself responsible for her baby sister rather than returning to the freedom of student life.

'I trust no one,' Jude countered without apology. 'You would be legally required to sign a non-disclosure agreement before I married you.'

'Understood. My stepfather explained that to me,' Tansy acknowledged, her attention reluctantly drawn to his careless sprawl on the sofa opposite, the long muscular line of a masculine thigh straining against well washed denim. Her head tipped back, her colour rising as she made herself look at his face instead, encountering glittering dark eyes that made the breath hitch in her throat.

'I find you attractive too,' Jude Alexandris murmured as though she had spoken.

'I don't know what you're talking about,' Tansy protested, the faint pink in her cheeks heating exponentially as her tummy flipped while she wondered if she truly could be read that easily by a man.

'For this to work, we would need that physical attraction. Nobody is likely to be fooled by two strangers pretending what they don't feel, least of all my family, some of whom are shrewd judges of character.'

Tansy had paled. 'Why would we need attraction? I assumed this was to be a marriage on paper, nothing more.'

'Then you assumed wrong,' Jude told her without skipping a beat.